M000215716

ELIZABETH BOWEN

Elizabeth Bowen was born in Dublin in 1899, the only child of an Irish lawyer and landowner. She travelled a great deal, dividing most of her time between London and Bowen's Court, the family house in County Cork which she inherited. Her first book, a collection of short stories, *Encounters*, was published in 1923. *The Hotel* (1927) was her first novel. She was awarded the CBE in 1948, and received honorary degrees from Trinity College, Dublin in 1949, and from the University of Oxford in 1956. The Royal Society of Literature made her a Companion of Literature in 1965. She died in 1973.

TESSA HADLEY

Tessa Hadley is the author of seven highly acclaimed novels, including *Clever Girl* and *The Past*, and three short-story collections, most recently *Bad Dreams*. Her stories appear regularly in *The New Yorker*. In 2016 she was awarded the Windham Campbell Prize and the Hawthornden Prize; in 2018 she was awarded the Edge Hill Short Story Prize.

ALSO BY ELIZABETH BOWEN

Novels

The Hotel (1927)
The Last September (1929)
Friends and Relations (1931)
To the North (1932)
The House in Paris (1935)
The Death of the Heart (1938)
The Heat of the Day (1949)
The Shelborne (1951)
A World of Love (1955)
A Time in Rome (1960)
The Little Girls (1964)
Eva Trout (1969)

Short Stories

Encounters (1923)
Ann Lee's (1926)
Joining Charles (1929)
The Cat Jumps (1934)
Look at All Those Roses (1941)
The Demon Lover (1945)
A Day in the Dark (1965)

Essays

Collected Impressions (1950)
Afterthought (1962)

ELIZABETH BOWEN

Selected Stories

SELECTED AND WITH AN INTRODUCTION BY
Tessa Hadley

VINTAGE

1 3 5 7 9 10 8 6 4 2

Vintage is part of the Penguin Random House group of companies
whose addresses can be found at global.penguinrandomhouse.com

Penguin
Random House
UK

Copyright © Elizabeth Bowen 1980

Introduction copyright © Tessa Hadley 2021
A version of Tessa Hadley's introduction first appeared in *London
Review of Books*, February 2020

This selection first published in Vintage Classics in 2021
Collected Stories first published in Vintage in 1999
Collected Stories first published in Great Britain in 1980 by
Jonathan Cape

penguin.co.uk/vintage

A CIP catalogue record for this book is available from the
British Library

ISBN 9781784877156

Printed and bound in Great Britain by Clays Ltd, Elcograf S.p.A.

The authorised representative in the EEA is Penguin Random House
Ireland, Morrison Chambers, 32 Nassau Street, Dublin DO2 YH68.

Penguin Random House is committed to a sustainable future for our
business, our readers and our planet. This book is made from Forest
Stewardship Council® certified paper.

MIX
Paper from
responsible sources
FSC® C018179

Contents

Introduction

My relationship with Elizabeth Bowen's books has a long history. At a certain point in my reading life, aged twelve or thirteen, I promoted myself to the adult section in my local library in Bristol, climbing up three wide steps covered in yellow linoleum. There, not knowing how to choose, I gravitated to Bowen – along with others, including Compton Mackenzie and Hugh Walpole, of whose writing I now can't recall even the faintest flavour. I'd never heard of any of them – I'd not heard of anybody much – but I liked the reassurance of bound sets of collected works, because in the children's section I'd been sustained by the endless-seeming supply of *Swallows and Amazons* and *Anne of Green Gables*. And I liked the woodcuts by Joan Hassall on the covers and in the frontispieces of each Bowen volume, which – although I still like them a lot – I can see now are quite a few shades more sentimental and simplifying than the words inside.

I read my way through quite a few of Bowen's books, and when I had finished I hardly knew what had happened in them. Her prose was sophisticated, her references depended upon all kinds of knowledge and insights I didn't have: this writing was not addressed to me, but over my head. Who were these people and what did they want, what did it all mean, why did they dress for dinner? What was it about Ireland, anyway? And yet I loved this writing, it excited me and made its mark on me. It seems strange that you can love what you can barely understand, but childhood consists of such foggy intimations and yearnings towards what's out of reach. I loved the furniture in Bowen, the thickness of her detail and its coloured, textured specificity. No doubt – inveterate fantasist and nostalgic in those days – I was drawn, too, to the posh pastness of her world – 'The Carbury's two little girls, Penny and Claudia, went upstairs again with their governess, Miss Rice, as soon as lunch was over', or, 'Mrs Nicholson, who was on her way out to dinner, paused in the act of looping a gauze scarf over her hair'. (Needless to say, this was nothing like my life.)

And there was something so sensually spiky in her sentences. The chunky solidity of her words, and her difficult word order, put up their resistance to any easy reading, or left one merely skimming along the top of apprehension. She made positions inside her words, for intelligence to use its leverage on what it saw; I felt the force of her ironies aesthetically, even if I couldn't altogether follow them. 'His mother seldom openly punished him, but often revenged herself on him in small ways. He could feel how just this was.' What was unobvious in her prose held out a promise, even as it frustrated my efforts at comprehension: that nothing was, after all, obvious – everything was interesting, because complicated. Hungrily, needing it to be true, I leaped at this. Now, the memory of that uncomprehending reading, all at sea in a bright scatter of words and things and half-grasped insights, seems to me the pattern of most initiations. Trust begins in the aesthetic: not in the argument, or in what's said or shown. Something feels right, smells right, in the colour and flavour of the work.

So Bowen was one of my writers, at the beginning of my adult education. And then I forgot her for a while: she wasn't in Leavis's Great Tradition, and wasn't on the Eng. Lit. curriculum in my university in the mid-nineteen-seventies (she died, although I wasn't aware of it, in 1973, aged 74). No one mentioned her name. The literary world was on the brink, in fact, of its great feminist re-appraisal of twentieth-century women writers – and Virago – but I was slow to notice. Bowen was probably one of my mistakes, I thought, like *Anne of Green Gables* or Compton Mackenzie.

It was only long after I'd left university behind that I became curious to seek out again what I'd once cared for, to see what it was worth; rereading Bowen in my thirties, when my reading horizons had widened in every direction and I was myself trying and failing to write, I renewed my love. Now, I've never not got something of hers open on my desk. As the years of reading and becoming pass, an inner family of writers assembles itself around your imaginative core. There's the wide outward connection with a whole constellation of books, all significant: and then there's this other, more intimate thing, more prejudiced and visceral. It feels like kinship – an elective kinship; there's almost a blurring between your own sensations and impressions and self, and these writers'. (Writers, incidentally, get no say in being elected to a reader's inner family. You can imagine the dismay of the great dead sometimes, if they ever could return, at finding themselves so adored, and by such adorers. But publishing is a relinquishment – you don't get to choose who reads you, or who feels with your words.)

Now literary history has been rewritten with Bowen on the Eng. Lit. curriculum, her significance in the Irish tradition of writing and perceiving is understood, and she's very much in print. And it's such a pure delight for me, to be choosing a new selection of her stories for Vintage Classics. Bowen is one of those rare writers who's equally good at novels and short stories; in fact, because her novels are short, densely written, formally deliberate, it's not easy to characterise any differences between these and the stories, apart from the merely obvious length and development. In the essence of her style and her way of seeing, she's a short writer: preferring less to more, concision to expansion. She herself makes best the distinction between her novels and stories, describing 'the steadier influence of the novel, with its calmer, stricter, more orthodox demands'. Into the novel, she writes, 'goes such taste as I have for rational behaviour and social portraiture. The short story, as I see it to be, allows for what is crazy about humanity: obstinacies, inordinate heroisms, "immortal longings"'.

The description is characteristic as well as insightful. On the one hand there's her forceful authority, the economy and decision in her summing up: on the other hand there's the romantic excess confessed to – 'immortal longings' set apart inside quotation marks because they're immortal and funny, both at once. The overreach of imagination and the containment of strong intelligence are inseparable inside Bowen's essential gesture. And no doubt those polarities derive somewhat from her class and her history – the dryness and smartness from an upper-class style, the excess out of a long tradition of Irish Protestant gothic, as well as from her own experience. She was an only child, born in Dublin where her father Henry worked as a lawyer for the Land Commission, but with Protestant Ascendancy roots in a big, plain, rectangular eighteenth-century house in County Cork, on land that was granted to Bowen ancestors in the Cromwellian settlement. She tells her ancestors' story with finely judged generosity and critique in a family history, *Bowen's Court*. Her father broke down when she was seven and suffered episodes of mania; doctors advised that her mother move with Elizabeth to England, where they lived in seaside towns in the south-east, and she gained the alienating vantage point of exile. Nothing could seem more exotic, she reflects, to a child brought up amid the symmetries of Georgian Ireland, than the rambling villas of Kent, with their inglenooks and ornate porches, their 'bow windows as protuberant as balloons'. 'What had to be bitten on was that two entities so opposed, so irreconcilable in climate, character and intention, as Folkestone and Dublin should exist simultaneously, and be operative, in the same lifetime, particularly my own'. Then, when Elizabeth was thirteen, her mother died of cancer. Boarding school with its regularities and impersonality was a refuge from grief and chaos.

Bowen published her first collection of stories, *Encounters*, in 1923, when she was twenty-four; in the same year she married Alan Cameron, who worked first in education and then in Schools' Broadcasting for the BBC. The marriage worked – Elizabeth liked making a home, and entertaining – and lasted as a fond childless companionship, although she had passionate love affairs, until Alan's death in 1952. They lived in Northampton and Oxford, then eventually in Clarence Terrace, one of the Nash terraces round Regent's Park, spending what time they could in Bowen's Court, where they invited friends to stay, literary and otherwise. After his death she realised eventually, with great regret, that she couldn't afford to keep up Bowen's Court, and sold it to a local farmer, who assured her he would move his family there, but then demolished it and cut down the timber. She spent her last years in Hythe.

From the very first stories, even when they are slight, the writing is ambitious. And behind whatever working-out of plot – to begin with mostly satirical, keeping the faintly ridiculous characters at amused arm's length – there's from the beginning this touchstone of *place* for Bowen's imagination, the place that's more-than-place, place as being, laden with history and implications. Her writerly passion seems to spring first from the desire to catch in words a particular moment, amid a particular weather and light – in a landscape outdoors, or, more often, surrounded by the right furniture, inside a particular house. These moments of conjured atmosphere often dwarf, in her first collection, the story's actual content and point: Bowen herself called her early stories 'a mixture of precocity and naivety'. In 'The Confidante', for instance, the twist of whose love-entanglement is neat and negligible as a card trick, 'the room was dark with rain, and they heard the drip and rustle of leaves in the drinking garden. Through the open window the warm, wet air blew in on them, and a shimmer of rain was visible against the trees beyond'. Bowen said she was trying 'to make words do the work of line and colour' and that she had 'the painter's sensitivity to light'.

The best story in *Encounters* is 'The Return', whose protagonist Lydia is a plain young lady companion. She's had the house to herself while her ghastly middle-aged employers, the Tottenhams, are away at a hydro; now they're back and she can't bear to give it up to them.

> The hall outside was cold and quiet. The sense of the afternoon's invasion had subsided from it like a storm. Through a strip of door the morning-room beckoned her with its associations of the last six weeks. She saw the tall uncurtained windows grey-white in the gloom.
>
> Her book lay open on a table: she shut it with a sense of desolation.

And Bowen doesn't close down, in the rest of the story, the dreaming possibilities opened in that moment's vision: neither in Lydia's thwarted sensibility, nor – generously, unexpectedly – in Mrs Tottenham's. Mrs Tottenham's old lover has written to her; she rubs lipstick hopefully into her cheeks, then looking in the mirror scrubs it off, and burns his photograph. Lydia opens her imagination to the older woman's long history for the first time, feels her own youth suddenly 'hard and priggish and immature'. The recognition alters everything, 'as though a child had been born in the house'.

In her second collection of stories, *Ann Lee's* (there were to be seven collections eventually), Bowen stakes out her distinctive terrain more boldly. The contained form and the mannered stylishness persist, and the author's all-seeing irony is set apart from her protagonists'; inside this frame the vision deepens and grows more strange, and more sympathetic. When Bowen began to write short stories she hadn't read many: no 'Hardy, Henry James, Maupassant, or Katherine Mansfield' says Victoria Glendinning in her 1977 biography; 'she was not following any genre theoretically familiar to her'. And for whatever reason, as she finds her way, it isn't along the lines of a Mansfield- and Woolf-inflected drift, avoiding closure or narrative certainty. Bowen's stories don't break the genre-frame, her vision rather swells it from inside and makes it strange: that's her modernism. And although the novels she's writing in those years are often about Ireland too, her short stories are still as yet all set in an England twisted round and made odd enough to be interesting. She plays up and down the range of the middle classes and into the gentry, though nobody is impossibly lofty or titled (unless the title's Italian). Sometimes when she strays down the social hierarchy – into the new housing estates, say – there are strong whiffs of condescension.

There's no condescension, though, in the title story, 'Ann Lee's', which is about a hat shop – though not just any hat shop. The milliner is a Diana-goddess in her feminine lair; society ladies Mrs Dick Logan and Miss Ames are humble votaries permitted to enter, consumed by desire for Ann Lee's hats' wonder-working. The only man venturing unwisely inside the shop – indifferent to hats, desperate for Ann herself – is horribly punished; he's not torn by his own hounds exactly, but passing the two ladies afterwards in the street he 'went by them blindly; his breath sobbed and panted … they knew how terrible it had been – terrible'. The frame of the story is comic: it's conventionally funny to invert the usual scale of importance and treat these silly women's belief in the hats' power to transform them (despite Mrs Logan's dread of her husband's wrath over bills on quarter day) as if it were religious belief and sacred ritual. And it *is* funny! ('These were the hats one dreamed about – no, even in a dream one had never directly beheld them; they glimmered rather on the margin of one's dreams.') But funny doesn't mean it isn't also sacred. Outside the frame of the story Dick Logan presides, with his disapproval and his control of the finances; inside its magic space, style is mystery and the women are initiates. This is Bowen's way of imagining how a terrain is gendered; what feels masculine in her authority – her tone, her control – enables in effect an upending of hierarchy, opens up a wild female space of the absurd, the inadmissible. Which isn't, however, sentimentalised: because of the tone, the control.

It's on those absurd female intimations – the crazy ones, obstinacies and 'immortal longings' – that the meanings of her stories begin to turn. In 'The Parrot', for instance, also from her second collection, a repressed young paid companion chases her mistress's wretched escaped parrot into a forbidden garden several houses along, where the arty Lennicotts entertain, to the outrage of their neighbours. The headlamps of the Lennicotts' visitors' cars lend 'an unseemly publicity to the comings and goings of everybody's cats'. Eleanor, in pursuit of the parrot, ends up on the roof, along with Mr Lennicott; the novels he writes are improper and he wears a dressing-gown embroidered with dragons, but turns out to be amiably game for parrot-chasing. 'A girl like you,' he encourages her, 'ought to be able to climb like a cat'.

> He gripped both her hands and hoisted. He was sitting astride the roof, and Eleanor sat side-saddle, tucking down her skirts around her legs. White clouds had come up and bowled past before the wind like puff-balls; the poplars swayed confidently towards one another, then swayed apart in mirth. One of the Philpot girls was mending a bicycle down in their garden, but she did not look up. Her bowed back looked narrow and virginal; Eleanor half-laughed elatedly…

In 'Joining Charles', from the third collection, Charles's disenchanted young wife stays with her husband's mother and sisters before setting off to meet him in their new home in France. She falls in love with the women's gentle domesticity, which is wholly subordinated to an idea of Charles, everything he actually isn't: 'generous, sensitive, gallant and shrewd'. (In a gothic touch, Polyphemus the cat knows better: Charles put out its eye.) The entanglement of desire with constraint is intractably knotty: if Mrs Charles were to break with the whole frame of his family's belief, and declare that she didn't love him – as surely eventually she must? – she would lose everything, couldn't be connected to them any longer. (And are Charles's women able to be so innocent *just because* he's so awful in the world on their behalf? Just as, after all, Dick Logan earns somewhere the money his wife spends on hats.)

Bowen's children are especially good, and naturally more at home than the adults are, with intimations of the inadmissible. Roger in 'The Visitor' is staying with two maiden ladies, waiting for news of his dying mother, whom nobody mentions. When the early morning sun washes over the garden, shadows in the strange bedroom make him feel, luxuriating in the sensation, 'as though he were a young calf being driven to market netted down in a cart'. In 'The Jungle', girls negotiate their friendships around the delicately cruel etiquette of a boarding school; in a beautiful culminating scene, Rachel and Elise escape into a patch of wild ground just beyond the school boundaries. Tramps have left scraps of rag in the bushes there, and Rachel's afraid of dead cats, but when Elise wants to lie in Rachel's lap, a realm of irresponsible pleasure becomes real. Bowen's literary world view is distinctive among English-language ironists in the mid-twentieth century, partly because in her imagination of the erotic (as in late Henry James, though not in Woolf or Mansfield) love's object may be worthy, and consummation isn't only for dreams. There's always irony, but there's always more-than-irony.

> '...I say, Rachel, I tell you a thing we might do...'
> Rachel wound herself up in her muffler by way of a protest. She had a funny feeling, a dancing-about of the thoughts; she would do anything, anything. ''Pends what', she said guardedly.
> 'You could turn round and round till you're really comfy, then I could turn round and put my head on your knee, then I could go to sleep again...'

As she chronicles the Home Front in World War II, the extreme distortions of wartime correspond to an extremity in Bowen's vision. Rising to the occasion, she makes vivid in her fiction 'the thinning of the membrane between the this and the that', and the invisible presence of the dead 'who continued to move in shoals through the city day, pervading everything to be seen or heard or felt with their torn-off senses'. In 'Mysterious Kôr', lovers under a bomber's moon search in vain for somewhere they can embrace unseen; in 'Ivy Gripped the Steps', a soldier revisits in wartime a privileged house on the south coast where he was betrayed as a child – it's shut up and overgrown now, behind barbed wire defences. Bowen was an air raid warden in London and stayed on in her Regent's Park house until it was bombed. When she went over to Ireland she sent back confidential reports on morale to the British Ministry of Information, although Roy Foster says she was only 'warmly defending neutrality' in them, 'as an Irishwoman'. Foster has made the case convincingly for Bowen's thoroughgoing Irishness. 'As long as I can remember', she wrote, 'I've been extremely conscious of being Irish'; her work, he says, is always shot through with characteristics of Irish literary tradition, its 'sensuous language, baroque humour ... uncanny ability to recreate childhood, and a sense of place experienced with a paranormal intensity'.

There's more of Ireland proportionately in the novels than in the short stories, and yet the Irish stories are among her very best, particularly the long 'Summer Night' of 1941, ripe with the disruptive magic of a midsummer night's dream. A young woman, Emma, is driving south in the west of Ireland as the sun sets – 'its light slowly melted the landscape, till everything was made of fire and glass' – away from her husband and children, to spend the night with her lover, Robinson, a factory-owner in a provincial town. When she stops at an hotel to make telephone calls, everyone's away at the dog races; it's wartime in England and the reverberating absence feels like the eerily suspended state of Ireland holding its breath, while according to newspaper headlines 'an awful battle' rages elsewhere, in the air. The story sprawls across distances (though in time it's tightly chronological), yet all its elements feel marvellously, mysteriously linked, making a psychic map of its moment: Emma's left-behind wild daughter Vivie bouncing on the bed and painting her nakedness with schoolroom chalks; Emma's husband's inhibited forbearance and the cramped malevolence of his old aunt; Robinson's friends who've unfortunately chosen this same evening to make their social call – the intelligentsia of the small town, Queenie, a beautiful deaf woman, and her clever troubled brother, who is in love with Robinson.

The enigmatic Robinson, 'big, fair, smiling, off-hand', seems to stand for new Irish possibilities, with his charisma, his pragmatism, his all-electric kitchen and his straightforward bluntness, desiring Emma. She, out of her Anglo-Irish heritage – her husband's a Major and listens to the war on the wireless, her cook works in a kitchen all 'blacklead and smoke and hooks' – wants agonised adulterous romance, a 'ruin, a lake'. Robinson's only impatient for her to 'come out of that flower bed' and inside his house; she's frightened of his 'stern, experienced delicacy on the subject of love'. 'But have I been wrong to come?' she asks, all sensibility. 'That's for you to say, my dear girl… You have got a nerve, but I love that. You're with me. Aren't you with me?'. Sexual love isn't a dream, it's for real beds not flower beds, and in truth Emma's had enough of her romantic Major, with his defeated decency. And yet, because this story spreads everywhere, its last word in fact goes to Queenie, dreaming of the ruin and the lake.

Bowen wrote fewer short stories in her last decades, while she was working on her strange, late novels. She had begun to seem old-fashioned, her stylishness belonging to another era, her perceptions no longer quite mapping onto contemporary experience. But now, fifty years after her death, when the sixties are past history too, we can do justice with clearer eyes to the scope of her achievement: it can seem as fresh to us, or fresher, than writing that was in its moment more fashionably *avant garde*. I think – but then I'm prejudiced – that she's as good as anyone: better than Woolf for instance, who's enshrined at the heart of the canon. Bowen is more confidently passionate, without Woolf's debilitating doubt; her apprehension is more acute, she's funnier, the flow of her words is more elegantly sure and more original.

I've ended my selection with one of her last short fictions: 'A Day in the Dark' from 1956, a brilliantly suggestive scrap of a story set in Ireland, which seems to look forward to Edna O'Brien or Claire Keegan. It's about the despoiling of a young girl's first love. Barbie is living one summer with her uncle, in a sensual dream of happiness, in love with him without knowing it. He sends her to pay a visit to his neighbour, a thwarted, fascinating, clever woman his own age, who also wants him; in a few cruel words she awakens Barbie from unknowing. Here, in its last leaping, throwaway sentences, so lightly managed, in such a perfect conjunction of form and meaning, freedom opens up exhilaratingly in the reader's imagination, just by seeing what there is to see – even as poor Barbie, disabused, steps back presumably inside the story of the rest of her life:

> At the same time, my uncle appeared in the porch. He tossed a cigarette away, put the hand in a pocket and stood there under the gold lettering. He was not a lord, only a landowner. Facing Moher, he was all carriage and colouring: he wore his life like he wore his coat – though, now he was finished with the hotel, a light hint of melancholy settled down on him. He was not looking for me until he saw me.

> We met at his car. He asked, 'How was she, the old terror?'

> 'I don't know.'

> 'She didn't eat you?'

> 'No,' I said, shaking my head.

> 'Or send me another magazine?'

> 'No, not this time.'

> 'Thank God.'

> He opened the car door and touched my elbow, reminding me to get in.

Tessa Hadley, 2020

The Return

Mr and Mrs Tottenham had come home.

The moist brown gravel of the drive and sweep bore impress of their fly wheels. Lydia Broadbent listened from the doorstep to the receding gritty rumble of the empty fly, and the click and rattle as the gate swung to. Behind her, in the dusky hall, Mr Tottenham shouted directions for the disposal of the luggage, flustered servants bumped against each other and recoiled, and Porloch the gardener shouldered the heavy trunks with gasps and lurches, clutching at the banisters until they creaked.

Lydia heard Mrs Tottenham burst open the drawing-room door and cross the threshold with her little customary pounce, as though she hoped to catch somebody unawares. She pictured her looking resentfully round her, and knew that presently she would hear her tweaking at the curtains. During her six weeks of solitude the house had grown very human to Lydia. She felt now as if it were drawing itself together into a nervous rigor, as a man draws himself together in suffering irritation at the entrance of a fussy wife.

'Were these all the letters, Lydia? I hope none were forwarded to Wickly? Porloch, do be careful of the paint! The fly was very stuffy, Lydia. I wish you'd ordered one of Bicklesfield's. His are always clean.'

Mrs Tottenham had darted out of the drawing-room, swept up her letters from the table, and stood hesitating at the bottom of the stairs.

'You might order tea immediately. Yes, the drawing-room for today.' A red shimmer of firelight invited them through the open door. 'Herbert, *Her*-bert!'

Mr Tottenham was clattering in the smoking-room. His face peered crossly at them round the door.

'I wondered if you had gone upstairs. Porloch has been very careless of the paint. You might have watched him, Lydia!' She vanished slowly into the gloom above.

Lydia went into the drawing-room and stood warming her hands before the fire. A servant with a lighted taper passed from gas-bracket to gas-bracket and the greenish lights sprang upwards in her wake. Outside the brown gloom deepened over the November garden. The young distorted trees loomed dark and sullen, the air was thick with moisture, heavy with decay.

Today there had been no time to think. Lydia was aware but dimly of a sense of desolation and of loss. Something was shattered that had built itself around her during these coherent weeks, something violated which had been sacred unawares. Every fibre of her quivered with hostility to these invaders who were the owners of the house. She was at odds with herself again, at odds with her surroundings. She stared at her gaunt reflection in the fireplace and knew that her best companion had drawn back again, forbidding her. She would be baffled once again by the hostility of Lydia Broadbent, her derision, her unsparing scorn. 'I was such friends with myself when they left us together; we were so harmonious and at ease with each other, me and myself and the house. Now we are afraid and angry with each other again.'

Mr and Mrs Tottenham were impossible. They were childless, humourless and dyspeptic. They were not even funny. There was nothing bizarre about them, or tragic or violent or farcical. They neither loved nor hated each other, there was nothing they did not know about each other; no mystery or fear between them. In the early days of their marriage they had been actively and articulately unhappy. She had had a lover; he had left her for months together and lived in some drab wickedness elsewhere. Then her lover had deserted her, he had been left more money; they had drifted together again, bought 'The Laurels', spun the shams and miseries around them like a web and lurked within them. They visited, were reputable and entertained; and kept a home for Mr Tottenham's nephew, their expectant heir.

'Lydia?'

The thin voice fluted over the banisters. Lydia hurried upstairs, flicked at a panel of Mrs Tottenham's door and entered, her footsteps muffled among the woolliness of many rugs. There was a blot of yellow light from a candle on the writing-table. Mrs Tottenham stood beside the bed, staring at two sheets of close-written paper and an envelope, which she held out fan-wise between rigid fingers, as one holding a hand at cards.

'Did – has my husband taken his mail yet? Did he overlook the letters?'

'I think Mr Tottenham's post is still lying on the hall table. Is there anything you want to show him?' They had all their correspondence in common; it was quite impersonal.

'No, no, Lydia, shut the door, please. Is tea up? It *is* draughty: I should have liked a fire. You might get the things out of my dressing-bag – there, it's over on the sofa.'

This constant attendance was to begin again. Lydia was well schooled to it; why had she forgotten?

She unpacked the combs and brushes, and Mrs Tottenham fidgeted before the glass.

'Light the gas, please. I hate this half-light!' There was resentment in her glance towards the window, where the last daylight leaked in faintly through draperies of parchment-coloured lace. Why was Mrs Tottenham so agitated, tugging her hat off and patting at her crimped and faded hair?

She bent to a level with the mirror; haggard-eyed and grinning with anxiety, she searched her bleached and baggy face to find what prettiness was there. Lydia watched her with apathetic curiosity from where, on her knees beside the sofa, she unwrapped the shoes and bottles from their little Holland bags.

'Have you seen the photo,' asked Mrs Tottenham suddenly, 'of me when I was twenty-five? On the chiffonier – the plush-framed one – you *must* know it!'

Lydia assented.

'It's a good one, isn't it? D'you think it's like me – now, I mean?'

'Quite a likeness, really, considering.'

'*Considering?*' (How sharp her voice was!)

'Oh, change of fashions makes a difference, doesn't it, and, well . . . time, of course.'

'Of course I know it wasn't taken yesterday, Lydia. *I* don't need telling. But I'm a lot younger than Mr Tottenham to look at. There was a gentleman at the Hydro took us for father and daughter, really he did!'

Her voice was by turns peremptory, confidential, almost appealing. It died out into silence.

The room was restive and disturbed. 'Oh, you unhappy house,' thought Lydia. 'They have broken into your silence and given you nothing in return.'

'Tea will be ready, I think,' she reminded. Mrs Tottenham turned sharply from the glass, and Lydia saw with amazement that she had reddened her lips. They shone with sticky brightness in her sallow face.

Mrs Tottenham was conscious of her glance. 'Shows rather, doesn't it?' she queried diffidently, and rubbed her mouth with the back of her hand till the red was smeared out over her cheeks.

'One looks so washy after a journey. Just a touch of colour – one wouldn't notice it, hardly, if it wasn't for the glare.' Her muttered extenuations were not addressed to Lydia.

They heard the tea-tray rattling through the hall. Lydia turned the light out, and they prepared to descend. Mrs Tottenham pawed her in the twilight. 'You needn't mention to Mr Tottenham I've opened any of my letters. I'll be showing him the rest. This one was rather particular – from a friend of mine, it was.' An appeal still quavered in her husky tones which her paid companion had never heard before.

From the drawing-room they saw Mr Tottenham scurrying across the grass, drawn teawards by the lighted window. There was something quick and furtive about him; Lydia had never been able to determine whether he dodged and darted as pursuer or pursued.

'Wretched evening, wretched.' He chattered his way across the crowded room. 'Been talking to Porloch – garden's in an awful way; shrubberies like a jungle. Did 'e sell the apples?'

He darted the inquiry at Lydia, turning his head sharply towards her, with his eyes averted as though he could not bear to look at her. At first she had imagined that her appearance repulsed him. She knew herself for a plain woman, but now she had learnt that he never looked at anybody if he could avoid it.

'Oh, he sold them well, I believe. I thought he wrote about them?'

'Oh yes, yes, sharp man, Porloch. Dickie been running round for his things?'

'Not often. He says he wants his letters forwarded to Elham till further notice.'

The reference to Elham tickled Dickie's uncle. He put his cup down, giggled, mopped at his mouth and darted a side glance at his wife.

Mrs Tottenham was not listening. She sat very stiff and upright, staring straight before her, crumbling at her cake.

'Hey, Mollie! Dickie's gone to Elham. Didgehear that? Pore old Dickie's gone to Elham again! Never wrote and told me, never told me anything. The young dog!'

The silence was once more outraged by his falsetto giggles.

He held his cup out for Lydia to refill, and she watched with fascination the convulsive movements his throat made while he drank.

'Hey, Mollie! Don't forget we're going to the Gunnings tomorrow. Write it down, my dear girl, write it down, and tell them about orderin' the cab.' He always referred to Lydia obliquely as 'they' or 'them'.

'Gunnin's a good fellow,' he informed the fireplace.

'This cake is uneatable, Lydia. Wherever did you buy it?' Her grumble lacked conviction; it was a perfunctory concession to her distrust of her companion's housekeeping.

'Birch's. I'm sorry, Mrs Tottenham. Aren't you ready for more tea? It's nice and hot for you, isn't it, after the journey?'

Lydia felt as though she had caught her own eye, and was embarrassed and discomfited. She listened with derision to her glib and sugary banalities of speech. 'The perfect companion!' taunted the hostile self. 'What about all those fine big truths and principles we reasoned out together? Yesterday we believed you were sincere. "*Nice and hot after the journey.*" Bah!'

The mirror in the overmantel now fascinated Mrs Tottenham. She finished her tea mechanically, laid her cup down and stood before the fireplace, patting and tweaking at her hair. Her husband looked at her contemptuously. 'Pretty little daughter I've got!' he mumbled, with his mouth full of cake. It was a bitter comment on the mistake made by the gentleman at the Hydro.

Mrs Tottenham put her hands before her face and hurried from the room.

Lydia began to gather up the tea things, and a servant darkened the windows with a musty clatter of Venetian blinds. Mr Tottenham's chair creaked as he stretched his legs out to the fire. The room was hot with the smell of tea and tea-cakes, and the smell of upholstery and wilting ferns was drawn out by the heat.

The hall outside was cold and quiet. The sense of the afternoon's invasion had subsided from it like a storm. Through a strip of door the morning-room beckoned her with its associations of the last six weeks. She saw the tall uncurtained windows grey-white in the gloom.

Her book lay open on a table: she shut it with a sense of desolation. It would never be finished now, it was too good a thing to read while *they* were in the house; to be punctuated by *her* petulant insistent chatter, *his* little shuffling, furtive steps. If only this room were all her own: inviolable. She could leave the rest of the house to them, to mar and bully, if she had only a few feet of silence of her own, to exclude the world from, to build up in something of herself.

If she did not go upstairs now Mrs Tottenham would call her, and that, in this room, would be more than she could bear. Vaguely she pictured headlines: '"Laurels" Murder Mystery. Bodies in a Cistern. Disappearance of Companion.' The darkness was all lurid with her visionary crime.

Mrs Tottenham had not been round the house. She did not say the rooms smelt mouldy, and she left the curtain-draperies alone.

Lydia wondered deeply.

'Did you know Sevenoaks?'

The question abashed her. What had Mrs Tottenham to do with Sevenoaks?

'N – no. Scarcely. I've been over there sometimes for the day, from Orpington.'

'A friend of mine lives there – a Mr Merton. He wrote to me today. He's come back from the Colonies and bought a place there. It's funny to hear from an old friend, suddenly. It makes me feel quite funny, really.'

She did not sound funny. Her voice was high-pitched with agitation. Lydia had been told all about Mrs Tottenham's friends, and seldom listened. But she did not remember Mr Merton.

'He wants to come and see us. I really hardly like, you know, to suggest the idea to Mr Tottenham.'

'I thought you'd all your friends in common. How well these night-dresses have washed! They must have laundered nicely at the Hydro.'

'Ah, but this is different, you see.' She laughed a little conscious laugh. 'Mr Merton was a particular *friend* of mine. I – Mr Tottenham didn't used to know him.'

'I see,' said Lydia vaguely. 'A friend of yours before your marriage.'

'Well, no. You see, I was very young when I was married. Quite an inexperienced young girl – a child, you might almost say.'

Lydia supposed that Mrs Tottenham *had* been young. She strained her imagination to the effort.

'I did very well for myself when I married Mr Tottenham,' the wife said sharply. 'I must say I never was a fool. My mother'd never brought me up to go about, but we did a good deal of entertaining at one time, Mr Tottenham's friends and my own, and we always had things very nice and showy. But it was a lonely life.'

Mrs Tottenham's confidences were intolerable. Better a hundred times that she should nag.

'So you liked the Hydro – found it really comfortable?'

'Oh yes, But it's the coming back – to this . . . Lydia, you're a good sort of girl. I wonder if I ought to tell you.'

'Don't tell me anything you would regret,' said Lydia defensively, jerking at the drawer-handles.

'You see, Mr Merton was a good deal to me at one time; then we tore it, and he went off to Canada and married there. I heard he'd been unhappy, and that there was the rumour of a split. Of course he didn't write or anything; we had ab-so-lutely *torn* it; but I couldn't help hearing things, and she seems to have been a really bad sort of woman – there were children, too. He's bringing the children back with him to Sevenoaks.

'He wants to come and see me. He's been thinking about me a great deal, he says, and wondering if I've changed, and wishing – He always was a straight sort of man; it was only circumstances drove him crooked. I dare say I was a good bit to blame. I've kept his photograph, though I know I didn't ought, but I liked having it by me to look at.'

She had unlocked a drawer and held a stiff-backed photograph up beneath the light, scrutinizing it. Lydia listened to a distant surge of movement in the house beneath her; steps across the oil-cloth, windows shutting, voices cut off by the swinging of a door.

She felt, revoltedly, as though Mrs Tottenham were stepping out of her clothes.

'He says he's hardly changed at all. Seventeen years – they go past you like a flash, he says, when you're working.'

'Seventeen years,' said Lydia deliberately, 'are bound to make a difference to a woman. Did you care for him?'

Mrs Tottenham made no answer; she was staring at the photograph. Her eyes dilated, and she licked her lips.

'I suppose you'll be glad to see him again?' suggested Lydia. She felt suddenly alert and interested, as though she were watching through the lens of a microscope some tortured insect twirling on a pin.

Mrs Tottenham sat down stiffly on the sofa, and laid the photo on her lap. Suddenly she clasped her hands and put them up before her eyes.

'I couldn't,' she gasped. 'Not after all these years I couldn't. Not like this. O Lord, I've got so ugly! I can't pretend – I haven't got the heart to risk it. It's been so real to me, I couldn't bear to lose him.

'It's all gone, it's all gone. I've been pretending. I used to be a fine figure of a woman. How can I have the heart to care when I couldn't keep him caring?'

'You broke it off. It was all over and done with, you told me so. It was wrong, besides. Why should either of you want to rake it up when it was all past and done with seventeen years ago?'

'Because it *was* wrong. It's this awful *rightness* that's killing me. My husband's been a bad man, too, but here we both are, smirking and grinning at each other, just to keep hold of something we neither of us want.'

Lydia was terrified by the dry, swift sobbing. She felt suddenly hard and priggish and immature. All her stresses, her fears and passions, were such twilight things.

Mrs Tottenham stood upright and held the photograph in the flame of the gas jet, watching the ends curl upwards. For all her frizzled hair and jingling ornaments and smudgy tentative cosmetics she was suddenly elemental and heroic.

It was over.

Lydia went quietly out of the room and shut the door behind her.

The place was vibrant with the humanity of Mrs Tottenham. It was as though a child had been born in the house.

Ann Lee's

Ann Lee's occupied a single frontage in one of the dimmer and more silent streets of south-west London. Grey-painted woodwork framed a window over which her legend was inscribed in far-apart black letters: 'ANN LEE – HATS.' In the window there were always just two hats; one on a stand, one lying on a cushion; and a black curtain with a violet border hung behind to make a background for the hats. In the two upper storeys, perhaps, Ann Lee lived mysteriously, but this no known customer had ever inquired, and the black gauze curtains were impenetrable from without.

Mrs Dick Logan and her friend Miss Ames approached the shop-front. Miss Ames had been here once before two years ago; the hat still existed and was frequently admired by her friends. It was she who was bringing Mrs Dick Logan; she hesitated beneath the names at the street corner, wrinkled up her brows, and said she hadn't remembered that Ann Lee's was so far from Sloane Square Station. They were young women with faces of a similar pinkness; they used the same swear-words and knew the same men. Mrs Dick Logan had decided to give up Clarice; her husband made such a ridiculous fuss about the bills and she had come to the conclusion, really, that considering what she had to put up with every quarter day she might have something more to show for it in the way of hats. Miss Ames, who never dealt there, agreed that Clarice *was* expensive: now there was that shop she had been to once, Ann Lee's, not far from Sloane Street—

'Expensive?' Mrs Dick said warily.

'Oh well, not cheap. But most emphatically worth it. You know, I got that green there—'

'O-oh,' cried Mrs Dick Logan, 'that *expressive* green!'

So they went to find Ann Lee.

It was an afternoon in January, and their first sensation was of pleasure as they pushed open the curtained door and felt the warm air of the shop vibrate against their faces. An electric fire was reflected in a crimson patch upon the lustrous pile of the black carpet. There were two chairs, two mirrors, a divan and a curtain over an expectant archway. No hats were visible.

'Nice interior!' whispered Mrs Logan.

'Very much *her*,' returned Miss Ames. They loosened their furs luxuriously, and each one flashed sidelong at herself in a mirror an appraising glance. They had a sense of having been sent round on approval, and this deepened in the breast of Mrs Logan as their waiting in the empty shop was prolonged by minute after minute. Clarice came rushing at one rather: Mrs Logan was predisposed to like Ann Lee for her discreet indifference to custom. Letty Ames had said that she was practically a lady; a queer creature, Letty couldn't place her.

'I wonder if she realizes we're here,' whispered Letty, her brows again faintly wrinkled by proprietory concern. 'We might just cough – not an angry cough, quite natural. You'd better, Lulu, 'cause you've got one.'

Mrs Logan really had a slight catarrh, and the sound came out explosively. They heard a door softly open and shut, and the sound of feet descending two or three carpeted steps. There was another silence, then close behind the curtain one cardboard box was placed upon another, and there was a long, soft, continuous rustling of tissue paper. One might almost have believed Ann Lee to be emerging from a bandbox. Then the curtain twitched, quivered, and swung sideways, and someone gravely regarded them a moment from the archway. 'Good afternoon,' she said serenely, and 'Good afternoon.'

Her finger brushed a switch, and the shop became discreetly brilliant with long shafts of well-directed light.

'I've come back again,' Miss Ames brought out a shade dramatically, and Ann Lee nodded. 'Yes, so I see. I'm glad, Miss Ames. I had expected you.' She smiled, and Mrs Dick Logan felt chilly with exclusion. 'And I've brought my friend, Mrs Dick Logan.'

Ann Lee, with delicately arched-up eyebrows, turned to smile.

She was slight and very tall, and the complete sufficiency of her unnoticeable dress made Mrs Dick Logan feel gaudy. Her hands were long and fine, her outspread fingers shone against her dress – on a right-hand, non-committal finger she wore one slender ring. Her face was a serene one, the lips a shade austere, and her hair was closely swathed about her head in bright, sleek bands. There was something of the priestess about her, and she suffered their intrusion with a ceremonial grace. She was so unlike Clarice and all those other women, that Mrs Logan hardly knew how to begin, and was gratified, though half-conscious of a solecism, when Miss Ames said, 'My friend would like so much to see some hats. She's rather wanting two or three hats.'

Ann Lee's eyes dwelt dispassionately on Mrs Logan's face. She looked questioningly at the eyebrows and searchingly at the mouth, then said with an assumption that barely deferred to her customer, 'Something quiet?'

Something quiet was the last thing Mrs Logan wanted. She wanted something nice and bright to wear at Cannes, but she hardly liked to say so. She put forward timidly, 'Well, not *too* quiet – it's for the Riviera.'

'Really?' said Ann Lee regretfully – 'how delightful for you to be going out. I don't know whether I have – no, wait; perhaps I have some little model.'

'I rather thought a turban – gold, perhaps?'

'Oh, a *turban* – ? But surely you would be more likely to find what you want out there? Surely Cannes—'

This made Mrs Logan feel peevish. Even if a person did look like a Madonna or something, it was their business to sell a hat if they kept a shop for that purpose. She hadn't followed Letty quite endlessly through those miserable back streets to be sent away disdainfully and told to buy her hats in France. She didn't care for shopping on the Riviera, except with her Casino winnings; the shops expected to be paid so soon, and Dickie made an even worse fuss when he saw a bill in francs. She said querulously:

'Yes, but haven't you got anything of that sort? Any goldish, sort of turbany thing?'

'I never have many hats,' said Ann Lee. 'I will show you anything I have.'

Lulu glanced across at Letty, breathing more deeply with relief at this concession, and Letty whispered, as Ann Lee vanished momentarily behind the curtain: 'Oh, she's always like that; like what I told you, queer. But the *hats*, my dear! You wait!'

When Ann Lee returned again carrying two hats, Mrs Logan admitted that there had indeed been something to wait for. These were the hats one dreamed about – no, even in a dream one had never directly beheld them; they glimmered rather on the margin of one's dreams. With trembling hands she reached out in Ann Lee's direction to receive them. Ann Lee smiled deprecatingly upon her and them, then went away to fetch some more.

Lulu Logan snatched off the hat she was wearing and let it slide unnoticed from the brocaded seat of the chair where she had flung it and bowl away across the floor. Letty snatched off hers too, out of sympathy, and, each one occupying a mirror, they tried on every single hat Ann Lee brought them; passing each one reverently and regretfully across to one another, as though they had been crowns. It was very solemn. Ann Lee stood against the curtain of the archway, looking at them gently and pitifully with her long pale eyes. Her hands hung down by her sides; she was not the sort of person who needs to finger the folds of a curtain, touch the back of a chair, or play with a necklace. If Mrs Logan and her friend Miss Ames had had either eyes, minds, or taste for the comparison, they might have said that she seemed to grow from the floor like a lily. Their faces flushed; soon they were flaming in the insidious warmth of the shop. 'Oh, *damn* my face!' groaned Miss Ames into the mirror, pressing her hands to her cheeks, looking out at herself crimsonly from beneath the trembling shadow of an osprey.

How could Lulu ever have imagined herself in a gold turban? In a gold turban, when there were hats like these? But she had never known that there were hats like these, though she had tried on hats in practically every shop in London that she considered fit to call a shop. Life was still to prove itself a thing of revelations, even for Mrs Dick Logan. In a trembling voice she said that she would certainly have *this* one, and she thought she simply must have *this*, and 'Give me back the blue one, darling!' she called across to Letty.

Then a sword of cold air stabbed into the shop, and Lulu and Letty jumped, exclaimed and shivered. The outer door was open and a man was standing on the threshold, blatant in the light against the foggy dusk behind him. Above the suave folds of his dazzling scarf his face was stung to scarlet by the cold; he stood there timid and aggressive; abject in his impulse to retreat, blustering in his determination to resist it. The two ladies stood at gaze in the classic pose of indignation of discovered nymphs. Then they both turned to Ann Lee, with a sense that something had been outraged that went deeper than chastity. The man was not a husband; he belonged to neither of them.

The intruder also looked towards Ann Lee; he dodged his head upwards and sideways in an effort to direct his line of vision past them. He opened his mouth as though he were going to shout; then they almost started at the small thin voice that crept from it to say 'Good evening.'

Ann Lee was balancing a toque upon the tips of her fingers, an imponderable thing of citron feathers, which even those light fingers hardly dared to touch. Not a feather quivered and not a shadow darkened her oval face as she replied, 'Good evening,' in a voice as equably unsmiling as her lips and eyes.

'I'm afraid I've come at a bad moment.'

'Yes,' she said serenely, 'I'm afraid you have. It's quite impossible for me to see you now; I'm sorry – I believe that hat is *you*, Mrs Logan. I'm sorry you don't care for black.'

'Oh, I do like black,' said Mrs Logan unhappily, feasting upon her own reflection. 'But I've got so many. Of course, they do set the face off, but I particularly wanted something rather sunny looking – now that little blue's perfect. How much did you . . .?'

'Eight guineas,' said Ann Lee, looking at her dreamily.

Mrs Logan shivered and glanced vindictively towards the door. Ann Lee was bending to place the toque of citron feathers on the divan; she said mildly over her shoulder, with one slight upward movement of her lashes, 'We are a little cold in here, if you don't mind.'

'Sorry!' the man said, looking wildly into the shop. Then he came right in with one enormous step and pulled the door shut behind him. 'I'll wait then, if I may.' He looked too large, with his angular blue cloth overcoat double-buttoned across the chest, and as he stuffed his soft grey hat almost furtively under his arm they saw at once that there was something wrong about his hair. One supposed he couldn't help it waving like that, but he might have worn it shorter. The shoes on his big feet were very bright. Fancy a man like that . . . Lulu allowed a note of injury to creep into her voice as she said, 'I beg your pardon,' and reached past him to receive another hat from Letty. The shop was quite crowded, all of a sudden. And really, walking in like that . . . He didn't know what they mightn't have been trying on; so few shops nowadays were hats exclusively. He didn't see either herself or Letty; except as things to dodge his eyes past – obstacles. The way he was looking at Ann Lee was disgusting. A woman who asked eight guineas for a little simple hat like that blue one had got no right to expose her customers to this.

Letty, her hair all grotesquely ruffled up with trying-on, stood with a hat in either hand, her mouth half open, looking at the man not quite intelligently. One might almost have believed that she had met him. As a matter of fact, she was recognizing him; not as his particular self but as an Incident. He – It – crops up periodically in the path of any young woman who has had a bit of a career, but Ann Lee – really. Letty was vague in her ideas of Vestal Virgins, but dimly she connected them with Ann. Well, you never knew . . . Meanwhile this was a hat shop; the least fitting place on earth for the recurrence of an Incident. Perhaps it was the very priestliness of Ann which made them feel that there was something here to desecrate.

Ann Lee, holding the blue hat up before the eyes of Lulu, was the only one who did not see and tremble as the square man crossed the shop towards the fireplace and sat down on the divan beside the feather toque. He was very large. He drew his feet in with an obvious consciousness of offence and wrapped the skirts of his overcoat as uncontaminatingly as possible about his knees. His gaze crept about the figure of Ann. 'I'll wait, if you don't mind,' he repeated.

'I'm afraid it's no good,' she said abstractedly, looking past him at the toque. 'I'm busy at present, as you can see, and afterwards I've orders to attend to. I'm sorry. Hadn't you better—?'

'It's four o'clock,' he said.

'*Four o'clock!*' shrieked Lulu. 'Good God, I'm due at the Cottinghams!'

'Oh, don't go!' wailed Letty, whose afternoon was collapsing. Ann Lee, smiling impartially, said she did think it was a pity not to decide.

'Yes, but eight guineas.' It needed a certain time for decision.

'It's a lovely little hat,' pleaded Letty, stroking the brim reverently.

'Yes, it's pretty,' conceded Ann Lee, looking down under her lids at it with the faintest softening of the lips. They all drew together, bound by something tense: the man before the fire was forgotten.

'Oh, I don't know,' wailed the distracted Mrs Logan. 'I must have that little black one, and I ought to get another dinner-hat — You know how one needs them out there!' she demanded of Miss Ames reproachfully. They both looked appealingly at Ann Lee. She was not the sort of person, somehow, that one could ask to reduce her things. There was a silence.

'It *is* four o'clock!' said the man in a bullying, nervous voice. They jumped. 'You *did* say four o'clock,' he repeated.

Ann Lee quite frightened the two others; she was so very gentle with him, and so scornfully unemphatic. 'I'm afraid you are making a mistake. On Thursdays I am always busy. Good evening, Mr Richardson; don't let us waste any more of your time. Now, Mrs Logan, shall we say the blue? I feel that you would enjoy it, though I still think the black is a degree more *you*. But I dare say you would not care to take both.'

'I'll wait,' he said, in a queer voice. Unbuttoning his overcoat, he flung it open with a big, defiant gesture as he leaned towards the fire. 'Oh, the *toque!*' they screamed; and Ann Lee darted down and forwards with a flashing movement to retrieve the frail thing from beneath the iron folds of the overcoat. She carried it away again on the tips of her fingers, peering down into the ruffled feathers; less now of the priestess than of the mother — Niobe, Rachel. She turned from the archway to say in a white voice, her face terrible with gentleness, 'Then will you kindly wait outside?'

'It's cold,' he pleaded, stretching out his hands to the fire. It was a gesture: he did not seem to feel the warmth.

'Then wouldn't it be better not to wait?' Ann Lee softly suggested.

'I'll wait today,' he said, with bewildered and unshaken resolution. 'I'm not going away *today*.'

While she was away behind the curtain, rustling softly in that world of tissue paper, the man turned from the fire to look round at the contents of the shop. He looked about him with a kind of

cringing triumph, as one who has entered desecratingly into some
Holiest of Holies and is immediately to pay the penalty, might look
about him under the very downsweep of the sacerdotal blade. He
noted without comment or emotion the chairs, the lustrous carpet,
Mrs Logan's hat, the ladies, and the mirrors opposite one another,
which quadrupled the figure of each lady. One could only conclude
that he considered Miss Ames and Mrs Logan as part of the fittings
of the shop – 'customers' such as every shop kept two of among
the mirrors and the chairs; disposed appropriately; symbolic, like the
two dolls perpetually recumbent upon the drawing-room sofa of a
doll's house. He stared thoughtfully at Miss Ames, not as she had
ever before been stared at, but as though wondering why Ann Lee
should have chosen to invest her shop with a customer of just *that*
pattern. Miss Ames seemed for him to be the key to something; he
puzzled up at her with knitted brows.

'Perhaps it would be better for us to be going?' said Miss Ames
to Mrs Logan, her words making an icy transition above the top
of his head. 'I'm afraid it's difficult for you to decide on anything
with the place crowded and rather a lot of talking.'

Mrs Logan stood turning the blue hat round and round in her
hands, looking down at it with tranced and avid eyes. 'Eight –
sixteen – twenty-four,' she murmured. 'I do think she might reduce
that little toque. If she'd let me have the three for twenty-two
guineas.'

'Not she,' said Letty with conviction.

The man suddenly conceded their humanity. 'I suppose these
are what you'd call expensive hats?' he said, looking up at Mrs
Logan.

'Very,' said she.

'Several hundreds, I dare say, wouldn't buy up the contents of
the shop, as it stands at present?'

'I suppose not,' agreed Mrs Logan, deeply bored – 'Letty, when
is she coming back? Does she always walk out of the shop like
this? Because *I* call it . . . I shall be so late at the Cottinghams, too.
I'd be off this minute, but I just can't leave this little blue one.
Where'll we get a taxi?'

'First corner,' said the man, rearing up his head eagerly. 'Round
on your left.'

'Oh, thanks,' they said frigidly. He was encouraged by this to ask if they, too, didn't think it was very cold. Not, in fact, the sort of weather to turn a dog out. 'I'm sorry if I've inconvenienced you any way by coming in, but I've an appointment fixed with Miss Lee for four o'clock, specially fixed, and you can imagine it was cold out there, waiting—' The rustling of the paper ceased; they thought the curtain twitched. He turned and almost ate the archway with his awful eyes. Nothing happened; the sleek heavy folds still hung down unshaken to the carpet. 'I've an appointment,' he repeated, and listened to the echo with satisfaction and a growing confidence. 'But I don't mind waiting – I've done so much waiting.'

'Really?' said Miss Ames, in the high voice of indifference. Determined that she must buy nothing, she was putting her own hat on again resignedly. 'She's bound to be back in a jiff,' she threw across reassuringly to Lulu, who sat bareheaded by a mirror, statuesquely meditative, her eyes small with the effort of calculation.

'I don't suppose either of you ladies,' said the man tremendously, 'have spent so much time in your whole lives trying on clothes in shops of this kind, as I've spent outside just this one shop, waiting. If any more ladies come in, they'll just have to take me naturally, for I'm going to sit on here where I am till closing time.'

Miss Ames, fluffing her side hair out in front of the mirror, repeated 'Really?' bland as a fish.

'I'm quite within my rights here,' said he, looking down now with approval at his feet so deeply implanted in the carpet, 'because you see, I've got an appointment.'

'There was no appointment, Mr Richardson,' said Ann Lee regretfully, standing in the archway.

Mrs Dick Logan, catching her breath, rose to her feet slowly, and said that she would have all three hats, and would Ann Lee send them along at once, please. It was an immense moment, and Miss Ames, who knew Dickie, thought as she heard Mrs Logan give her name and address in a clear unfaltering voice that there *was* something splendid about Lulu. The way she went through it, quarter day after quarter day ... Miss Ames glowed for their common femininity as she watched her friend pick up yet another hat and try it on, exactly as if she could have had it too, if she had wished, and then another and another. Ann Lee, writing languidly

in an order-book, bowed without comment to Mrs Logan's decision. And Letty Ames couldn't help feeling also that if Ann Lee
had wished, Lulu would have had that other hat, and then another
and another.

Mrs Logan stooped to recover her own hat from the floor. Ann
Lee, looking down solicitously, but making no movement to assist
her, meditated aloud that she was glad Mrs Logan was taking that
little black. It was so much *her*, to have left it behind would have
been a pity, Ann Lee couldn't help thinking.

As they gathered their furs about them, drew on their gloves,
snapped their bags shut, and nestled down their chins into their
furs, the two ladies glanced as though into an arena at the man
sitting on the divan, who now leaned forwards to the fire again,
his squared back towards them. And now? They longed suddenly,
ah, how they longed, to linger in that shop.

'Good afternoon,' said Ann Lee. She said it with finality.

'Good afternoon,' they said, still arrested a second in the doorway.
As they went out into the street reluctantly they saw Ann Lee,
after a last dim bow towards them, pass back through the archway
so gently that she scarcely stirred the curtains. The man beside the
fire shot to his feet, crossed the shop darkly, and went through
after her, his back broad with resolution.

There were no taxis where they had been promised to find them,
and the two walked on in the direction of Sloane Street through
the thickening fog. Mrs Dick Logan said that she didn't think she
dared show her face at the Cottinghams now, but that really those
hats were worth it. She walked fast and talked faster, and Miss
Ames knew that she was determined not to think of Dickie.

When they came to the third corner they once more hesitated,
and again lamented the non-appearance of a taxi. Down as much
of the two streets as was visible, small shop-windows threw out
squares of light on to the fog. Was there, behind all these windows,
someone waiting, as indifferent as a magnet, for one to come in?
'What an extraordinary place it was,' said Mrs Logan for the third
time, retrospectively. 'How she ever sells her things . . .'

'But she does sell them.'

'Yes.' She did sell them, Mrs Logan knew.

As they stood on the kerbstone, recoiling not without complaints from the unkindness of the weather, they heard rapid steps approaching them, metallic on the pavement, in little uneven spurts of speed. Somebody, half blinded by the fog, in flight from somebody else. They said nothing to each other, but held their breaths, mute with a common expectancy.

A square man, sunk deep into an overcoat, scudded across their patch of visibility. By putting out a hand they could have touched him. He went by them blindly; his breath sobbed and panted. It was by his breath that they knew how terrible it had been – terrible.

Passing them quite blindly, he stabbed his way on into the fog.

The Parrot

When Mrs Willesden's parrot escaped, it rocketed in a pale-green streak across the sky and settled in the chestnut tree at the foot of the garden, where it became invisible among the branches. Invisible, that is to say, to Maud Pemberty and Eleanor Fitch, who stood staring up under their hands into the glare of the morning, until Maud located his head, a vermilion blot borne up and down like a buoy, slowly, by the undulations of a lower layer of the foliage. The chestnut tree blazed all over in the sunshine with candles of wax blossom. The scent of the pollen gave Eleanor Fitch shivers; about the end of May she would pass the tree on any pretext, sighing for something that she could not remember. Maud was in love, and chestnut flowers meant nothing to her; besides, as parlour-maid, she had more to do in the house than Miss Fitch, who was only a companion.

Now they both stood looking up at the parrot piteously, fearfully; Maud who had left the window open, and Eleanor who had been cleaning the cage. They advanced towards the tree unconsciously, step by lingering step, as though attracted; still with that mesmeric upward stare.

The parrot took no notice of them. It wobbled along the branch, peevishly disentangling its wing and tail feathers from the long-fingered leaves. Its tongue was in one corner of its beak; its head turned and its eyes rolled from side to side in a mixture of ecstasy and apprehension. Once or twice it lost its balance and tilted right forward with a muffled squawk until it was hanging nearly upside down. It would recover itself, look reproachfully down at its claws, and totter along further, till another clump of leaves swept down to assault it. It wore an air of silly bravado, and looked what it was, thoroughly idiotic.

Mrs Willesden had no brothers, cousins or lovers: none certainly who were sailors, and none of these, therefore, had brought the parrot home to her from Indian seas. Dark-faced men may have dazzled it, against the purple of the ocean, with the swinging gold of their earrings, and held it up to stroke the sleek vermilion of its head. This Eleanor would have wished to believe, and Mrs Willesden even playfully asseverated; but the parrot had not, somehow, the aroma. It had no pedigree; Mrs Willesden had bought it at an auction at the other side of London: a very new-looking parrot, newer-looking even than the complete edition of Lord Lytton, or the mahogany chest of drawers. It was a guaranteed talker, but its conversation was neither entertaining, relevant, nor profane. It would mutter 'Poll, Po-oll, Pol-pol-pol' for hours, in an ecstasy of introspection, or say 'Lead, kindly Light' – just that, no more of the hymn. If one spoke to it, besought it, cursed it, wooed it, it would blink at one in a smoulder of malevolence, and say, 'Minnie? Minnie! Tom? Minnie!'

Mrs Willesden loved the parrot, and would sit beside it for hours in the afternoon. It was carried into the dining-room to meals, and its cage was placed beside her at the head of the table, on a butler's tray. Eleanor hated the parrot, and used to come down and clean its cage early in the morning before breakfast, so as to get that over. Thus it was that the parrot had escaped at a quarter past eight, before Mrs Willesden was awake, while yellow cotton blinds still unflickeringly sheathed her windows. Mrs Willesden slept late today; one did not care, one did not dare to wake her. Eleanor and Maud stood sodden-footed out in the dew, with now and then a backward glance up at Mrs Willesden's window, and their hands burnt and their fingers twitched with the desire to grab the parrot by its scaly legs and its wings and thrust it shrieking back into its cage.

Eleanor's mind went whirling round like a wheel on the hub of this moment. She knew that what had brought her here to be Mrs Willesden's companion had also brought about the escape of the parrot – her own immense ineffectuality. She knew that she was a clever girl, or she might possibly have loved Mrs Willesden; she knew that she was a wise girl, or she could not so continuously have tolerated her. She knew that she must be a nice-looking girl, or Mrs Willesden, whose sense of beauty had found its culminating expression in the parrot, would never have engaged her. She knew, however, that she could not be dangerously attractive, because although she was quite ready to marry anybody who seemed at all suitable, and thus escape from life with Mrs Willesden and the equally odious alternative of using her brains, nobody, even of the most unsuitable, had so far presented himself. She never thought about men, because she fully agreed with Mrs Willesden that this was not nice; she merely wondered sometimes when Mrs Willesden would have become a thing of the past. It was while thus wondering that she had turned away from the parrot's cage to look in a mirror, and, thus looking, had heard the unlatched door swing open and the silken sound of the flight. As things were now, Mrs Willesden might very soon become a thing of the past; and a swift nostalgia for security made the sky blur and glitter, and the chestnut candles swim.

'Well, it's no good crying, Miss,' said Maud. 'It doesn't get us out of anything, what I mean.'

'I'm not,' said Eleanor quickly. 'Poll, pretty Polly-poll, come downsey!'

'Come downsey!' echoed Maud. ('Yah, get out of that, you dirty beast!') Well, he doesn't understand, Miss. He's just stupid.'

'Go into the house and get the cage, Maud. Stick a banana between the bars, so's he can only get at it from the inside, and put it down on the grass with the door open. Go quickly and – hush!'

Maud went, and Eleanor stood staring, still mesmerically, up at the parrot, while the imagined eyes of Mrs Willesden burnt into her back. She stared up at the parrot, but Polly was preoccupied with his feat of balance and was perpetually in profile. He was not to be mesmerized, and just as Maud emerged from the house with the cage held at arm's length and the door invitingly open, he toppled forward urgently, beat for a moment with his wings, then flopped into the air. He did not rise very high this time, but after describing one or two lopsided circles, as though with wings unevenly weighted, he skimmed the top of the garden wall, glittered for a second above it in poised uncertainty, and vanished.

'There!' said Maud, and Eleanor gathered her skirts together, gave one calculating glance, and was up and on to the top of the wall like a cat.

The parrot ambled slowly through the air, with, as it were,

the jog of a fat pony translated into flight. It clumsily attempted a landing on some branches in the next garden and slid off again, its claws ripping the leaves. All along, in the pleasant irregular gardens of the road, glass-houses sparkled, flashing out rays, geraniums in the beds made neat little cubes of coral and scarlet, violas grew in great mauve cushions. A furtive young wind spilt the petals from the fruit trees on to the grass, stirred the pools they made, then crept away, frightened. Eleanor, equally furtive, knelt up on the wall, looked all round her, and tucked her skirts down. She calculated that the parrot must without fail come wheezily to earth at either the Cuthbertsons' or the Philpots'.

It could have a long wait to fly before it reached the poplars of the one garden which she could not possibly enter to retrieve it. The poplars tapered above all the trees of the gardens with a sort of elegant irresponsibility; they swayed towards one another and glittered with mirth. They rose from out of the four walls of the Lennicotts' garden, and within these walls no one in the road had set foot since the occupation of the Lennicotts.

Towards the poplars the parrot leisurely proceeded, as one in good time for an appointment, and somewhere down below them came to earth.

Mrs Willesden had told Eleanor that it was better not to ask about the Lennicotts, and that it was all very, very sad. Indeed, the less one knew the better, everybody felt, and ladies flinched as they told one another in low voices things about the Lennicotts which one did not care to say, but which demanded to be said. Mrs Willesden told Eleanor that sin was becoming, alas, very prevalent (though one did not care to talk to an unmarried girl about these things) and that she was thankful that her mother had not lived to see these days, and that her dear husband had also been spared. 'It is not even known,' she said, 'that they are the Lennicotts, but *he* is a Lennicott, and she is *called* Mrs. My library does not keep his novels, and that nice young man there looked very much surprised when I asked for them. Mrs Cuthbertson lent me a copy of one of them, but I found it very difficult to read, and so did she.'

'Was it improper?' asked Eleanor, in a low voice, winding wool quickly.

'One may be sure of that,' Mrs Willesden had replied, 'but as I
tell you, I did not finish the book; it was so very dull. As far as
I got, I did not see anything in it, and I glanced through to the
end and did not see anything either. However, I should not have
dreamed of keeping a book like that in the house with a young
girl like you about – Eleanor, you had better rewind that wool,
you are winding it too tightly . . .'

Even in London, it was said, many people would not know the
Lennicotts, so they had come here, doubtless in the hopes of making
nice friends. The road deplored the Lennicotts, and the neighbourhood envied the road. In the evenings, long shafts of blistering
whiteness streamed out from the headlamps of cars and lent an
unseemly publicity to the comings and goings of everybody's cats.
These cars drew up perpetually outside the Lennicotts' with a long
faint sound like a sniff. Though they entertained, the Lennicotts
were not rowdy; one heard only, sometimes, low excited laughter
of the kind that made one wish to stop and listen; and, very rarely,
Mrs Lennicott's voice, which was very beautiful, came floating
down among the trees of the road as she sang to her guests after
dinner.

The parrot dropped down among the poplars, and Eleanor's
heart dropped with it, like a stone. She heard a slight rattle at the
upstairs window, and knew that Mrs Willesden's blind was up, and
that soon everything would be over. She gathered herself together,
her tongue curled back in her mouth with terror, and leapt from
the top of the wall into the lane full of nettles that ran along the
backs of the gardens, past the Willesdens', past No. 17's, 18's and
19's, till it broadened out under the Lennicotts' poplars into a small
patch of common. As she turned the bend of the lane and heard
the rustle of the poplars above her, she heard also, very distinctly
and monotonously, the parrot saying 'Minnie? Minnie!' down in
the garden inside the walls. Had it encountered anybody, or was
it merely talking to itself?

Eleanor did not believe that early rising could possibly be
compatible with moral obliquity. An outraged sense of fitness was
therefore added to her astonishment when, having adjusted her
pince-nez, she found herself looking down from the top of the
Lennicotts' wall on to the unswerving centre-parting of Mrs

Lennicott's marmalade-coloured hair. The parrot sat biting its nails on one end of a pergola, and Mrs Lennicott did not notice it because she was reading a book of poetry with large print and smoking a cigarette in a long holder. She sat in a deckchair with her feet on a recumbent watering-can, and wore, as might have been expected, coloured leather shoes. When she heard the scratching sound of Eleanor's toes seeking purchase on the outer bricks, she looked up, smiled vaguely, with the sun on her gold lashes, and said, 'Good morning. Have you come to look for a tennis ball? Do come in!'

She had a long chin and a plump, oval, delicately coloured face. Her eyebrows arched very innocently, and she looked at Eleanor uncomprehendingly, but with an air of earnest effort, as though she were a verse of Georgian poetry that one could not possibly understand. 'Do come in!' she repeated.

'Thank you,' said Eleanor. 'I only wanted that parrot.' She pointed to the pergola, and Mrs Lennicott, laying her book face downwards on the grass, turned her head with interest in the same direction. Her hair was braided against her cheek. 'Really,' she said, 'is that your parrot? It is very beautiful. But do come in and take it away if you want it. I expect it is very valuable. It may have been here for some time, but I did not notice it because this garden is always full of birds, and I am very stupid about natural history.'

For the first time that morning the parrot looked straight at Eleanor; for the first time in their acquaintanceship it had a gleam of intelligence in its eye. 'Take me,' it seemed to say. 'I am an old sick bird, beaten out and weary. I have aspired and failed — it is finished. Take me.' A white sheath rolled up over its eyes; its feathers drooped.

Eleanor had an idea that if she did not breathe very deeply, if she walked lightly on the tips of her toes, taking as few steps as possible, and if she did not look quite straight at anything, especially Mrs Lennicott, she might, having entered the Lennicotts' garden, yet leave it uncontaminated. She therefore sprang from the wall, alighting on her hands and on the balls of her feet, as she had been taught at school, at the very brink of a flower bed. As she stood upright she half saw, then turned irresistibly to watch, Mrs Lennicott rise with one ripple from the deckchair and walk as

though entranced towards the pergola, holding up her hands. Her
dress hung ungirt from her bosom and swept the grass, so that its
hem was dark with dew.

'Oh, how beautiful you are!' she sighed. 'How your head flashes!
You must forgive me,' she said to Eleanor, 'but I have never looked
very closely at a parrot before.'

Polly was obviously gratified. He ducked his head and fluttered
his tail-feathers, and swayed a little from the claws. He conveyed
by a multiplicity of innuendoes that Mrs Willesden and Eleanor
were a pair of old frumps, and that even Minnie had left much
to be desired, and that he knew a woman of distinction when
he met one. Had Mrs Lennicott been allowed to engage him
further in conversation, his capture from the rear might easily
have been effected, but Eleanor was too precipitate. Her
outstretched hands cast a shadow; Polly felt them coming and
soared into the air with spread wings like a Phoenix. He squawked
derision at Eleanor, and steered a zigzag course to the verandah
drain pipe, from the pipe to an upper windowsill, from the
windowsill to a tank, from the tank to the ridge of the roof
between two chimney pots.

'Oh, how terrible for you!' cried Mrs Lennicott, in real distress.

Eleanor's cheeks burnt; little wisps of hair came down and frisked
in the light wind, tickling the back of her neck. The tides of her
spirit were slow, drawn by the slow moon of her intelligence, but
now anger stirred in her; she drew a gasp which shook her and
locked her fingers together.

'I'm going to catch that parrot,' she said, turning to Mrs Lennicott.
'I'm going to catch it so's to wring its neck.'

'*Have* you ever wrung anything's neck?' asked Mrs Lennicott in
an awed voice.

When Eleanor admitted that she hadn't, Mrs Lennicott, with
obvious relief, invited her to come into the house and catch the
parrot. 'It would be very easy,' she said, 'to get out on to the roof
from the window of my husband's room. He has often talked of
doing so when there was too much noise in the house, but the
roof is not flat enough to hold a writing-table. I don't think he is
awake, but if he were he would be delighted to help you.'

The shadow of the house fell cold on Eleanor as she left the wind and glitter and innocence of the morning behind and walked with Mrs Lennicott towards the steps of the verandah. Afterwards, there was so much lilac in the drawing-room and the place was so heavy with it that her other impressions were blurred, except that the room with its low and very many sofas lurked on sufferance round the great jutting triangle of the piano. She was still drawing shallow breaths and walking delicately, and had the sense of passing down a long low shining tunnel of wickedness, to where at the end she saw the parrot, a speck faintly visible against a familiar sky. Because it was on the west side of the house the room was in pale shadow, but beyond a great gold slab of sunshine lay across the pavement of the hall. Not thus fell the sunshine through the glass panels of a similar door on to Mrs Willesden's oilcloth.

'You are one of the thin family, aren't you?' said Mrs Lennicott. 'There are girls on bicycles – so nice-looking – with rather a sharp-looking little dog that runs behind – though I am sure he is a dear little dog, and so faithful – no, the stairs are straight ahead, through that archway. Shall I go first?'

Eleanor said no, that she was not a Philpot.

'There are a great many people in this road, aren't there? I never knew there were so many people who didn't live in London. Of course, one sees the houses, but it is difficult to realise, isn't it, that they have insides and that they really mean anything!'

Mrs Lennicott preceded Eleanor with a displaced shimmer of the skirts, a fragrant swish. She was not the sort of woman who rustles. The stair carpet crunched under one's feet with a velvety resistiveness; it had, at the first contact, a sinister sleekness. There were prints on the staircase from which Eleanor turned away quickly, tingling. It was as though the earliest darts assailed her armour. She was here in those Lennicotts' very house; its shadows and scents were surcharged for her, every contact was intolerably significant.

Then a door opened above, and Mr Lennicott came out from his bedroom on to the landing.

Eleanor stopped dead and pressed back against the wall; her shoulder caught one of the picture-frames and made it swing wildly. She shut her eyes, and at the end of that shining and inexorable tunnel the parrot quivered and receded. She was menaced; the tunnel was narrowing down upon her; she wanted to go back.

'Who in God's name!' cried Mr Lennicott.

'It's a lady come to take away a parrot, darling.'

'Parrot?' said Mr Lennicott despairingly. 'When did we get a parrot? Why didn't you pay for it? Where's all that money I gave you? I told you this would happen again. You know they came and took away the sundial. Not that I care whether you had a sundial or parrots or an apiary, but the people who come to take them away are full of moral indignation – and you know—'

'It's *her* parrot,' said Mrs Lennicott, 'and it's on the roof. Do come up,' she added, turning back to Eleanor, 'and let me introduce my husband, Miss . . . oh, I am so stupid!'

'Fitch,' whispered Eleanor, and feeling her tongue curl back in her mouth again looked up slowly. First she saw Mr Lennicott's ankles, very thin with big bones and covered with black hairs. Then came yards, it seemed, of his dressing-gowned figure, a long thin strip, bent slightly and bulging where his hands went into his pockets; then his long chin with a blue bloom on it, then his quizzical Spanish face. 'If there's anything I can do—?' said Mr Lennicott, and his teeth glimmered.

'*Is* there anything he can do?' asked Mrs Lennicott, sweeping round and leaning towards Eleanor, as she came up step by step, with such eager bright expansiveness that she almost embraced her. Her eyes were of that clear blueness which almost is not when they are empty of expression; they took colour like water. She was eager and impersonal.

The sun streamed in through the staircase window, and Mr Lennicott's dragons glowed; he might have stepped out of a cathedral window, and had indeed even that air of ornate asceticism.

'You could get out along my gutter,' he said, grasping the situation quickly, 'my room has an attic window, and from there to the ridge of the roof it's just a hoist.'

He wrapped his dressing-gown further round him with a big gesture, re-knotted the cord at the waist with an air of resolution, and, shuffling a little in his Turkish slippers, went back across the landing and held his door open for Eleanor.

'I expect the parrot isn't there any more,' said she. 'I – I expect it's gone . . . I won't mind about it today, thank you very much.'

'But it's such a *pity* to lose such a beautiful parrot!' wailed Mrs Lennicott.

'I think really I won't . . .'

'Oh, come on,' said Mr Lennicott's deep voice suddenly. 'A girl like you ought to be able to climb like a cat. No, look here, upon my word, you don't, though – I'll go up and collar the thing, and you lean out of the window and grab it.'

'You ought to put it *into* something,' said Mrs Lennicott. 'Just wait, I'll get a bandbox.' She brought a bandbox which was striped with many colours, and had a French name scrawled across the top. It was so big that Eleanor had to open her arms wide to embrace it, and tucked the lid, for better balance, under her chin. The wind was blowing in through Mr Lennicott's open window; his curtains rushed to meet them as Eleanor, contracted into an aching knot of terror, followed the be-dragoned back, leaving behind her Mrs Lennicott, the landing, and (save death) the only way of retreat. The room smelt of cigarettes and masculine unguents and had sloping ceilings. She remembered all those terrible books and pressed the bandbox closer to her chest, feeling morally as well as physically embuttressed by it.

Mr Lennicott, breathing through his teeth, grasped the window-sill and flung one leg over it on to the outside gutter. Eleanor wondered if she would have to appear at the inquest, and whether by that she would be compromised; she watched Mr Lennicott anxiously as, doubled like a brave on the warpath, he picked his way along the gutter, till he had passed the window and was out of sight.

Mrs Lennicott came in and sat on the bed, which made Eleanor feel better. She lit a cigarette and said that Trotsky never killed himself, and that it was a lovely day, and that Trotsky never took enough exercise, and that Eleanor mustn't worry. They heard a hoist and a scramble, and knew that Mr Lennicott must now be up on the roof.

'If you would hold the bandbox,' said Eleanor, 'I think I'll go too, as it's my parrot.' She didn't want the Lennicotts to think she was afraid of *that*.

'*Do*,' said Mrs Lennicott, and, with her cigarette holder cocked skywards from one corner of her mouth, relieved Eleanor of the bandbox. Eleanor, leaning towards the roof, followed Mr Lennicott along the gutter.

'Hallo-o!' hailed Mr Lennicott from above. 'That's sound. Come on, up here. Where's Piggy? Piggy coming too? It's – it's simply immense up here; you'd never believe. Come on – hoist!'

He gripped both her hands and hoisted. He was sitting astride of the roof, and Eleanor sat side-saddle, tucking down her skirts round her legs. White clouds had come up and bowled past before the wind like puffballs; the poplars swayed confidentially towards one another, then swayed apart in mirth. One of the Philpot girls was mending a bicycle down in their garden, but she did not look up. Her bowed back looked narrow and virginal; Eleanor half-laughed elatedly, and smoothed her hair behind her ears.

'And the parrot?' she said, quickly recalling herself and looking from left to right.

The wind ruffled Mr Lennicott's hair, but he sat immobile, following the clouds with his eyes and smiling to himself. 'Parrot?' he echoed, starting violently. 'What parrot? Where? . . . Oh, by Jove, yes; where is it?'

'Here,' whispered Eleanor, for the parrot had come sidling down the roof towards them, and now sat down beside her. Its feathers were dishevelled, its eyes furtive, its head, dimmed seemingly in colour, drooped a little. It looked sadder, smaller, less of a buffoon. It pecked wearily and perfunctorily at Eleanor's fingers as they closed upon it, but said nothing as she tucked it under her arm.

'Poor beast,' said Mr Lennicott. 'I believe, you know, that the other birds have been nasty to it. They don't like anything a different colour from themselves; no one ever does, you know, it's damned funny.'

He mused upon this, while Eleanor thoughtfully regarded him.

'Did you *find* the parrot. Trotsky?' inquired Mrs Lennicott, putting her head out of the window beneath them.

'No – I mean, yes!' shouted back her husband. 'We've got the parrot here – not in at all good order, but giving no trouble at all. Where's the basket?'

Mrs Lennicott leaned out perilously far, encircling the bandbox with her long smooth arms. The lid was tilted a little sideways; she placed one finger upon it to keep it thus, and gurgled with pleasurable excitement as Mr Lennicott came sliding down the roof with the parrot under his arm, and crammed the bird into the box among the tissue paper. 'Clap down the lid!' shrieked Eleanor, scarlet with excitement. Mrs Lennicott, having obeyed her, withdrew slowly into the darkness of the room, pressing the bandbox closer to her bosom, and gazing at it awfully as it began to throb with the protests of the parrot.

So that was over, and Eleanor could take the parrot home and snap the door of its cage on it, and all that hour of the day would be gone; a nothing, an irrelevancy; a lost hour that had slipped through a crack in her life and vanished. She came down from the roof nothing but an empty stomach, with an empty head above it, through which desires vaguely hurried like the clouds. She sighed as she so often sighed beneath the chestnut tree, and did not want to leave the sunny landing where Mr Lennicott, behind her, slanted up against a door-post, and Mrs Lennicott, kneeling by the bandbox, tied the lid securely down with a length of yellow ribbon. The parrot was very quiet in there; perhaps it did not want to go home either.

'This seems quite safe, I think,' said Mrs Lennicott, handing her the bandbox, 'but don't carry it by the string. I hope this hasn't been very tiring for your parrot. I didn't think it looked very well.'

Eleanor repudiated the parrot — did she then so reek of what was Mrs Willesden's? 'It's not the sort of thing *I'd* ever keep,' she said vindictively, 'I'd like to have a greyhound, or a large mastiff. It belongs to a lady, otherwise it wouldn't have mattered at all. Now I must take it home . . . I — I really ought to take it home before it begins to make a noise again . . . No, really, thank you very much, I mustn't wait for anything to eat.'

'Not fruit?' marvelled Mrs Lennicott. It was like being held back by a thousand hands, they both so evidently wished to detain her. Nobody had ever reached out for her like that so eagerly; she did not want to go back to that house of shut-out sunshine and great furniture, where the parrot was carried royally from room to room on trays, and she was nothing. But it was useless, not an inch of their way and hers lay parallel; to catch at them would mean, ultimately, only another of these wrenches. They had struck out across the open country, and it was so green there, Eleanor felt her feet aching from the high road.

All that they were suggesting, actually, was that she should go down with them to the dining-room and eat figs there, but it was not without remembrance of Proserpine, that she stood mulishly and shook her head. She had shared a roof and breasted the clouds with Mr Lennicott, and now she must be home in time to carry up the parrot and the breakfast tray into Mrs Willesden's room. How world lay overlapped with world; visible each from the other and yet never to be one! Along the wind, through the trees of the garden, came booming out the Philpots' breakfast gong.

No one spoke of meeting any more; had she, too, been a magical interlude for the Lennicotts, over which their lives would close? They went down to the garden, and the prints all down the staircase, flitting past her eyes regretfully, whispered, 'Stay, stay, stay!' And when they were out on the grass, and pointed out the path that ran to the gate standing wide to the road, fear returned to Eleanor. Should she come forth publicly out of those gates into the now awakened road, carrying this radiant bandbox?

'I think the back way would be really shorter,' murmured Eleanor.

'Back way?' said the Lennicotts.

'Over the wall . . .'

Mrs Willesden shut her windows on going to bed at nights, and it was Eleanor's duty to open them next morning, just a very little, when she brought in the parrot. Entering Mrs Willesden's bedroom for this purpose, it was difficult to believe that the winds and dews of May were a reality, or that there was running water anywhere and the shining bodies of bathers, or vigorous laughter, or open country – or roofs. The room was dim with seemly crimson curtains, and Mrs Willesden's wrappings lay ready to be put on, sheath by sheath.

'Polly's looking very well today,' said Mrs Willesden as usual, following the cage across the room with her eyes because she could not turn her head among the shawls. 'Pretty Polly, pretty little Poll-poll.'

'It got out,' said Eleanor abruptly. Mrs Willesden would have to know, lest otherwise she might find out; and she was, moreover, one contemptuously knew, a kind old lady.

'Dear me,' said Mrs Willesden, with placid admiration. 'The naughty pretty. Did he go flying far away?'

'I brought him back,' said Eleanor; 'he flew round and round the garden.'

'Looking for his banana tree and coral reefs, poor pretty boy,' sighed Mrs Willesden. 'And so you caught him, Eleanor? That was very smart of you, with nobody to help. No one knows where he mightn't have flown to: he might have met the most terrible people and never have come home again. And if strange people had caught him, even people quite respectable and honest, it would have put me in an embarrassing position — under compliment, I mean. I know it may be foolish and old-fashioned of me, but I do very much dislike being under compliment. So you caught him all alone?'

'Yes,' said Eleanor. 'He didn't give me much trouble. I — I caught him all alone.'

The parrot, rising on its perch, beat its wings and cried in a hoarse voice, 'Minnie, Minnie, *Minnie*?' It ended on a note of regret and bewilderment.

And Eleanor put down its cage quickly and walked over to the window. It was like the crowing of the cock.

The Visitor

Roger was awakened early that morning by the unfamiliar sound
of trees in the Miss Emerys' garden. It was these that had made the
room so dark the previous evening, obscuring the familiar town
lights that shone against the wall above his bed at home, making
him feel distant and magnificently isolated in the Miss Emerys'
spare-room. Now, as the sky grew pale with sunless morning, the
ceiling was very faintly netted over with shadows, and when the sun
washed momentarily over the garden these shadows became distinct
and powerful, obstructive; and Roger felt as though he were a young
calf being driven to market netted down in a cart. He rolled over
on his back luxuriously, and lay imagining this.

But the imagination-game palled upon him earlier than usual,
defeated by his returning consciousness of the room. Here was
he alone, enisled with tragedy. The thing had crouched beside
his bed all night; he had been conscious of it through the thin
texture of his dreams. He reached out again now, timidly, irresistibly to touch it, and found that it had slipped away, withdrawn
into ambush, leaving with him nothing of itself, scarcely even a
memory.

He had never slept before in anybody's spare-room; theirs at
home had been wonderful to him: a port, an archway, an impersonal
room with no smell, nothing of its own but furniture; infinitely
modifiable by the personality of brushes and spongebags, the attitude of shoe-trees, the gesture of a sprawling dress across a chair.

The Miss Emerys' spare-room had long serious curtains that
hung down ungirt beside the window, fluted into shadows. One
never touched the curtains; if one wanted to make the room dark,
one drew a blind that had a lace edge and was stamped all over
with a pattern of oak-leaves. Miss Emery, when she brought Roger
up to bed last night, tried to do this, laid one hand on the acorn
of the blind-cord, but Roger prayed her to desist and she desisted.
She understood that no one liked to see the sky from bed. She

was a sympathetic woman, and made Roger increasingly sorry for all the things he used to think about her blouses.

The furniture was all made of yellow wood, so shiny and one knew so yielding, that one longed to stab and dint it. There were woollen mats that Miss Dora Emery had made – she had even promised to teach Roger. She had promised this last night, while Roger sat beside her in a drawing-room that positively rocked and shimmered in a blinding glare of gaslight. A half-finished rug lay across her knee and rolled and slid noiselessly on the floor when she moved; the woolly, half-animate thing filled Roger with a vague repulsion. 'I'm doing the black border now,' she had explained, tweaking the clipped strands through the canvas with a crochet hook and knotting them with a flick of her wrist. 'Soon I'll be coming to the green part, the pattern, and I shall work in some touches of vermilion. You really must watch then. Roger, it will be so pretty, you'll really be amused.' Roger wondered if she would have come to the vermilion, even to the green, by the time his mother died. Miss Emery was not a quick worker. 'How much more black will there be before the pattern?' he inquired. 'Three inches,' said Miss Emery, and he measured out the distance with his finger.

There were paintings on the spare-room wall of moors with Scotch cattle, and over the chest of drawers there was a smaller picture in a green-and-gold frame called 'Enfin – Seuls'. French. It depicted a lady and gentleman holding each other close and kissing in a drawing-room full of palms; they seemed to be glad of something. The paper had a pattern on it, although Roger's father and mother had said that patterned wallpapers were atrocious. Roger looked at it, and jumped with his mind from clump to clump – they were like islands of daisies – pretending he was a frog who had been given a chance of just eight jumps to get away from a dragon.

A clock ticked out in the passage; it must be a very big one, perhaps a stationmaster's clock, given the Miss Emerys by a relation. It had no expression in its voice; it neither urged one on nor restrained one, simply commented quite impartially upon the flight of time. Sixty of these ticks went to make a minute, neither more nor less than sixty, and the hands of the clock would be pointing to an hour and a minute when they came to tell Roger what he was expecting to hear. Round and round they were moving, waiting for that hour to come. Roger was flooded by a desire to look at the face of the clock, and still hearing no one stirring in the house he crept across to the door, opened it a crack, quite noiselessly, and looking down the passage saw that the clock had exactly the same expression, or absence of expression, as he had imagined. Beyond the clock, a rich curtain of crimson velvet hung over the archway to the stairs, and a door painted pale blue stood open a little, showing the bathroom floor.

Roger had never believed that the Miss Emerys or any of the people he and his mother visited really went on existing after one had said goodbye to them and turned one's back. He had never expressed this disbelief to his mother, but he took it to be an understood thing, shared between them. He knew, of course, with his *brain*, that the Miss Emerys (as all the other people in the roads round them) went on like their clocks, round and round, talking and eating and washing and saying their prayers; but he didn't *believe* it. They were, rather, all rolled up swiftly and silently after one's departure and put away for another occasion, and if one could jump round suddenly, taking God by surprise, one would certainly find them gone. If one met a Miss Emery on one's walks, one assumed she must have sprung up somewhere just out of sight, like a mushroom, and that after one had passed her, nothingness would swing down to hide her like a curtain. Roger *knew* that all the doors round the Miss Emerys' landing opened on to rooms, or would do so if he walked through them when he was expected. But if he opened a door when he was not expected, would there be anything beyond it but the emptiness and lightness of the sky? Perhaps even the sky would not be there. He remembered the fairy tale of Curdie.

The spare-room opened off a very private little corridor that had no other door along it but the bathroom's. The Miss Emerys could not fully have realized the charm of this, or they would have taken the room for their own. Roger had an imaginary house that, when it was quite complete in his mind, he was some day going to live in: in this there were a hundred corridors raying off from a fountain in the centre; at the end of each there was a room looking out into a private garden. The walls of the gardens were so high and smooth that no one could climb over into anybody else's. When they wanted to meet, they would come and bathe together in the fountain. One of the rooms was for his mother, another for his friend Paul. There were ninety-seven still unappropriated, and now it seemed there would be ninety-eight.

Somebody in a room below pulled a blind up with a rush, and began to sweep a carpet. Day was beginning in a new house.

The Miss Emerys' breakfast-room was lovely. By the window, they had a canary in a cage, that sprang from perch to perch with a wiry, even sound. Outside, the little early-morning wind had died; the trees were silent, their leaves very still. Since there was no sun this morning, the breakfast table held without competition all the brightness, to radiate it out into the room. No sun could have been rounder or more luminous than the brass kettle genially ridiculous upon a tripod, a blue flame trembling beneath it. There were dahlias, pink and crimson, and marmalade in a glass pot shaped like a barrel cast a shadow of gold on the tablecloth. There was a monstrous tea cosy, its frill peaked intelligently; and Miss Emery smiled at Roger over the top of it. There were parrots printed on the cosy – they battled with one another – so brilliant one could almost hear them screech. Could a world hold death that held that cosy? Miss Emery had pinned a plaid bow-tie into the front of her collar. Could she have done this if what Roger expected must soon happen to Roger? Must it happen, mightn't it be a dream?

'Come in, dear,' said Miss Emery, while he revolved this on the threshold, and Miss Dora Emery, who had not come to help him to dress (perhaps she was not allowed to), forced a lump of sugar quickly between the bars of the canary's cage, and came round the table to greet him. Roger eyed her cheek uncertainly; it was pink as a peach, and against the light its curve showed downy: he wondered what was expected of him. They eyed one another with a fleeting embarrassment, then Miss Dora jerked away a chair from the table, said 'And you sit there, in Claude's place,' and pushed back the chair with him on it, pausing over him for a second to straighten a knife beside his plate.

On the table, the hosts of breakfast were marshalled into two opposing forces, and a Miss Emery from either end commanded each. The toast, eggs, bacon, and marmalade had declared for Miss Dora; but the teapot and its vassals, the cruet and the honeycomb – beautifully bleeding in flowered dish – were for Miss Emery to a man. The loaf, sitting opposite to Roger, remained unabashedly neutral. Roger looked from one Miss Emery to the other.

'Plenty of milk? I expect so; Claude always liked plenty of milk in his tea. What I always say is – little boys like what's good for them, don't you worry, grown-ups!'

'Two pieces of bacon? Look, if this egg's too soft, mop it up with your bread; I should. They *say* it isn't polite, but—'

'Yes, please,' said Roger, and 'thank you very much, I will.' What jolly ladies the Miss Emerys were!

They were looking at him anxiously; were they afraid he was not quite pleased and comfortable? Perhaps they did not often have a visitor. They were aunts; they had once had a nephew called Claude, but he had grown up and gone to India, leaving only some fishing-tackle behind him and a book about trains which had been given to Roger. Were they looking piteously at him in the pangs of baffled aunthood? But were they perhaps wondering if he *knew*, how much he knew, and whether they ought to tell him? They were ladies with bright eyes that would fill up easily with emotion, white, quick hands and big bosoms. Roger could hear them saying, 'Little motherless boy, poor little motherless boy!' and they would snatch him and gather him in, and each successively would press his head deep into her bosom, so deep that perhaps it would never come out again.

Roger shrank into himself in fearful anticipation: he must escape, he must escape, he must escape . . . Yesterday had been one long intrigue for solitude, telling a fib and slipping away from his little sisters, telling a fib and slipping away from his father. Father didn't go to work now but walked about the house and garden, his pink face horribly crinkled up and foolish-looking, lighting cigarettes and throwing them away again. Sometimes he would search anxiously for the cigarette he had thrown away, and when he had picked it up would look at it and sigh desolately to find it had gone quite out. Father was an architect: he would go into this study, tweak a drawing out of a portfolio, run to his desk with it,

pore over it, score it through; then start, look back at the door
guiltily, return to stare and stare at the drawing, push it away, and
go on walking about. Up and down the room he'd go, up and
down the room, then dart sideways as though at a sudden loophole
and disappear through the door into the garden. But he always
came back again to where Roger was; he couldn't let one alone.
His presence was a torment and an outrage. Roger disliked people
who were ridiculous, and he had never cared to look long at his
father. Father had dark-brown hair, all fluffy like a baby's, that stood
out away from his head. His face was pink and always a little curly,
his eyebrows thick and so far away from his eyes that when one
came to them one had forgotten they ought to be there. Lois and
Pamela loved him; they thought he was beautiful, so it was all quite
fair; and Roger thought *she* was wonderful, the way she had always
tolerated him and allowed him to kiss her. Always the best hour
of the day for her and Roger had been when the little girls had
gone to bed, and *he* had not yet come in. Now the pink face was
curled up tight, and the eyes were scared and horrible, and the
hands always reaching out to Roger to grab him with 'Come on,
old man, let's talk. Let's talk for a bit.' And they had nothing to
say, nothing. And at any moment this man who had no decency
might begin talking about *her*.

Now, suppose the Miss Emerys were beginning to – no, the
thing was unthinkable. And besides, perhaps they didn't even know.

'What's Roger going to do today?' Miss Emery asked her sister.

'We-ell,' said Miss Dora, considering. 'He could help you garden,
couldn't he? You know you wanted somebody to help you sort
the apples. You know you were saying only yesterday, "*If only I had
somebody to help me sort the apples!*" Now I wonder if Roger likes
sorting apples?'

'Well, I never have,' said Roger, 'but I expect it would be very
nice.'

'Yes, you'd love it,' said the Miss Emerys with enthusiasm. 'Claude
loved it, didn't he, Doodsie?' added Miss Dora. 'Do you remember
how he used to follow you about at all times of the year, even in
March and April, saying, 'Aunt Doodsie, mightn't I help you sort
the apples?' How I did tease him: I used to say, 'Now then, Mister,
I know what you're after! Is it the sorting, or the apples?' Claude

was very fond of apples,' said Miss Dora, very earnest and explana-
tory, 'he liked apples very much. I expect you do too?'

'Yes, very much, thank you.'

'Do you look forward to going back to school?' asked Miss
Emery, and her voice knew it was saying something dangerous.
Back to school ... When Mother had died, Father would send
him away to school with all the other ugly little boys with round
caps. Father said it was the best time of one's life; Father had liked
school, he had been that kind of little boy. School *now* meant a
day-school, where one painted flowers and mothers came rustling
in and stood behind one and admired. They had a headmistress,
though they were more than half of them little boys, and there
were three older than Roger. Father said this wasn't the sort of
school for a grown man of nine. This was because Father didn't
like the headmistress; she despised him and he grew fidgety in her
presence.

'Which school?' said Roger disconcertingly, when he had swal-
lowed his mouthful of bread and honey.

'We-ell,' hesitated Miss Dora, 'the one you're at now, of course,'
she said, gathering speed. 'It seems to me a very nice school; I like
to see you going out to games; and that nice girl behind you with
the red hair.'

'Yes,' said Roger, 'that's Miss Williams.' He masticated silently,
reflecting. Then he said provocatively, 'I should like to stay there
always.'

'Oooh!' deprecated Miss Dora, 'but not with little girls. When
you're a bigger boy you'll think little girls are silly; you won't want
to play with little girls. Claude didn't like little girls.'

'How long *do* you think I'll stay?' asked Roger, and watched
her narrowly.

'As long as your father thinks well, I expect,' said Miss Dora,
brightly evasive – 'Doodsie, do call poor Bingo in – or shall I? –
and give him his brekky. I can hear him out in the hall.'

Roger ignored the liver-coloured spaniel that made a waddling
entrance and stood beside him, sniffing his bare knees.

'*Why* my father?' he pressed on, raising his eyebrows aggressively
at Miss Dora.

'—Bingo-Bingo-Bingo-Bingo-*Bingo*!' cried Miss Dora suddenly, as in convulsive desperation, clapping her hands against her thighs. The spaniel took no notice of her; it twitched one ear, left Roger, and lumbered over to the fireplace, where it sat and yawned into the empty grate.

Roger spent the morning with Miss Emery, helping her sort the apples and range them round in rows along the shelves of the apple-room, their cheeks carefully just not touching. The apple-room was warm, umber and nutty-smelling; it had no window, so the door stood open to the orchard, and let in a white panel of daylight with an apple tree in it, a fork impaled in the earth, and a garden-hat of Miss Dora's hanging on the end of the fork, tilted coquettishly. The day was white, there were no shadows, there was no wind, never a sound. Miss Emery, her sleeves rolled up, came in and out with baskets of apples that were too heavy for a little boy to carry. Roger, squatting on the ground, looked them over for bruises – a bruised apple would go bad, she said, and must be eaten at once – and passed up to her those that were green and perfect, to take their place among the ranks along the shelves . . . 'That happy throng' . . . It *was* like the Day of Judgment, and the shelves were Heaven. Hell was the hamper in the musty-smelling corner full of bass matting, where Roger put the Goats. He put them there reluctantly, and saw himself a kind angel, with an imploring face turned back to the Implacable, driving reluctantly the piteous herd below.

The apples were chilly; they had a blue bloom on them, and were as smooth as ivory – like dead faces are, in books, when people bend to kiss them. 'They're cooking apples,' said Miss Emery, 'not sweet at all, so I won't offer you one to eat. When we've finished, you shall have a russet.'

'I'd rather, if I might,' said Roger, 'just bite one of these. Just bite it.'

'Well, bite then,' said Miss Emery. 'Only don't take a big one; that would be only waste, for you won't like it.'

Roger bit. The delicate bitter juice frothed out like milk; he pressed his teeth deep into the resisting whiteness till his jaws were stretched. Then in the attentive silence of the orchard he heard steps beginning, coming from the house. Not here, O God, not here! Not trapped in here among Miss Emery and the apples, when all he wanted when *that* came was to be alone with the clock. If it were here he would hate apples, and he would hate to have to hate them. He looked round despairingly at their green demi-lunes of faces peering at him over the edge of the shelves. His teeth met in his apple, and he bit away such a stupendous mouthful that he was sealed up terrifyingly. The fruit slipped from his fingers and bumped away across the floor. Not a bird or a tree spoke; Miss Emery, standing up behind him on a chair, was almost moveless – listening? The steps came slowly, weighted down with ruefulness. Something to hold on to, something to grip! . . . There was nothing, not even the apple. The door was darkened.

'The butcher *did* come, Miss. Are there any orders?' . . .

But that settled it – the apples were intolerable. Roger asked if he might go now and play in the garden. 'Tired?' said Miss Emery, disappointed. 'Why, you get tired sooner than Claude – he could go on at this all day. I'm afraid that apple disappointed you. Take a russet, dearie, look, off that corner shelf!'

She was kind; he had no heart to leave behind the russet. So he took it, and walked away among the trees of the orchard, underneath the browning leaves. One slid down through the air and clung against the wool of Roger's jersey; a bronze leaf with blue sheen on it, curled into a tired line. Autumn was the time of the death of the year, but he loved it, he loved the smell of autumn. He wondered if one died more easily then. He had often wondered about death; he had felt in *her* the same curiosity; they had peered down strangely together, as into a bear-pit, at something which could never touch them. She was older; she ought to have known, she ought to have known . . .

The grass was long and lustreless; it let his feet pass through reluctantly. Suppose it wove itself around them, grew into them and held them – Somebody's snare. He began the imagination game.

Miss Dora was leaning over the gate talking to some ladies; a mother and daughter, pink and yet somehow hungry-looking. They turned their heads at the sound of his footsteps in the grass; he dropped his eyes and pretended not to see them. They drank him in, their voices dropped, their heads went closer together. He walked past them through the trees, consciously visible, oh, every line of him conscious – this was how a little boy walked while his mother was dying . . . Yes, they had been great companions, always together. Yes, she was to die at any moment – poor little boy, wouldn't it be terrible for him! . . . He turned and walked directly away from them, towards the house. Their observation licked his back like flames.

Then he hated himself: he did like being looked at.

After lunch, Miss Dora took him down to the High Street with her to buy wool. His mouth was still sleek with apple-dumpling, his stomach heavy with it, though they had given him a magazine with horses in it, and sent him off for half an hour to digest. Now they walked by a back way; Miss Dora didn't want to meet people. Perhaps it was awkward for her being seen about with a little boy who half had a mother and half hadn't.

She walked and talked quickly, her hands in a muff; a feather nodded at him over the edge of her hat, the leaves rustled round her feet. He wasn't going to remember last autumn, the way the leaves had rustled . . . running races, catching each other up. He barred his mind against it, and bit his lip till he was quite sick. He wouldn't remember *coming in to tea* – not that.

'What's the matter, darling,' said Miss Dora, stopping short concernedly. 'Do you want to go somewhere? Have you got a pain?'

'No, oh no,' said Roger. 'I was just imagining those white mice. How awful losing them, how awful. Do go on about them, Miss Dora, go on about Claude.'

'—And when he was packing up to go back to school, *there* was the little nest, at the bottom of his play-box, and the little mother mouse, curled up, and Claude said . . .' Miss Dora continued the Saga.

When they got to the town they saw far down at the other end of the High Street the two scarlet tam-o'-shanters of Lois and Pamela, bobbing along beside the lady who had taken *them*. Somebody had given Lois a new hoop; she was carrying it. Pamela was skipping on and off the kerb, in and out of the gutter. She didn't look as if she minded about Mother a bit. Pamela was so young; she was six. He wanted to go and tell Pamela that what she was doing was wrong and horrible, that people must be looking at her out of all the windows of the High Street, and wondering how she could.

'There are the little *sisters*, Roger – rrrrun!'

People would all say,'There are those poor little children, meeting one another!' and tell each other in whispers, behind the windows of the High Street, what was going to happen. He didn't want to be seen talking to his sisters, a little pitiful group.

'Go – on, rrrrun!'

He hung back. He said he would go round and see them after tea, he thought. 'Shy of Mrs Biddle?' asked Miss Dora swiftly. He allowed her to assume it. 'Well, of course she *is* a little . . . I mean she isn't quite . . .' said Miss Dora. 'But I expect the little girls like her. And I didn't think you were a shy little boy.'

Back at the Miss Emerys' by half-past three, Roger found that it was not teatime, and that there was nothing to do, nothing to escape to. That walk with Miss Dora had shattered the imagination game; it wouldn't come back to him till tomorrow, not perhaps for two days. He leaned against an apple tree, and tried sickly to imagine Claude. A horrid little boy, a dreadful little boy; he would have pulled Roger's hair and chaffed him about playing with his mother. Mercifully, he had passed on irrecoverably into the middle years; he was grown up now and would smile down on Roger through the mists of Olympus. Roger didn't get on with other little boys, he didn't like them; they seemed to him like his father, noisy outside and frightened in. Bullies. The school he was going to would be full of these little boys. He wondered how soon he would go to school; perhaps his father was even now writing to the schoolmaster – while Mother lay upstairs with her eyes shut, not caring. Roger thought Father would find this difficult; he smiled at the thought in leisurely appreciation. 'Dear Mr Somebody-or-other, my wife is not dead yet, but she soon will be, and when she is I should like to send my little boy to your school . . . If it is not too expensive; I am not a rich man.' Roger's father often said, 'I am not a rich man,' with an air of modest complacency.

Home was not so far away from Roger as he stood in the Miss Emerys' garden. It was twenty minutes round by the road; from the top of an apple tree one should be able to see the tall white chimneys. There had been something wonderful – once – about those chimneys, standing up against the distant beech trees, dimming the beech trees, on a quiet evening, with their pale, unstirring smoke. From up high, here, one would be able to see the windows of the attics; see whether the windows were black and open, or whether the white blinds were down. If he sat from now on, high in an apple tree, he could watch those windows. Night and day, nothing should escape him. When the blinds came down gently and finally to cover them, Roger would know. There would be no need to tell him, he would be armoured against that. Then he could run upstairs to the Miss Emerys' landing, and be alone with the clock. When they came up after him, puffed with a deep-drawn breath to impart *that*, he could just turn round and say calmly, rather tiredly, 'Oh, it's all right, thank you, I do know.' Then they would look mortified and go away. Really-kind Miss Emery, really-kind Father *would* look mortified; they wouldn't like having the thing snatched away from them.

Roger gazed up into the apple tree. The branches were big and far apart, the bark looked slippery. 'I'm afraid,' he thought, and tried to drown it. He was a little boy, he was afraid of the pain of death. 'I don't dare go up, and I don't dare go back to the house. I *must* know, I can't let them tell me. Oh, help me, let them not have to come and tell me! It would be as though they saw me see her being killed. Let it not have to be!'

And now it would be and it must be, even while he deliberated and feared. Roger saw his father open the gate of the orchard and stand hesitatingly, looking round at the trees. He was hatless, his face was puckered up and scared – Oh, to run, to run quickly to somebody who would not know, who would think his mother was still alive, who need never know she was not! To be with somebody comfortable and ignorant, to grasp a cork handle through which this heat couldn't come blazing at him. Horrible footsteps, horrible grey figure coming forward again, and now pausing again desolately among the trees. 'Roger?' called the voice, 'Roger!'

Roger pressed back. He too was grey like the tree-trunks, and slimmer than they; he urged himself against one, hopelessly feigning invisibility, trying to melt. 'Roger!' came the voice continuously and wearily, 'Old man? Roger!'

Now he was coming straight towards one, he couldn't fail to see. He would drink one in and see one defenceless, and draw a big breath and say IT. No Miss Emery, no cook, no death, no refuge, and the tree shrinking away from before one.

'*Ah*, Roger!'

He thrust his fingers into his ears. 'I *know*, I *know*!' he screamed. 'Go away, I can't bear it. I know, I tell you.'

The pink face lengthened, the scared eyes of his father regarded him, as he stood there screaming like a maniac. A voice was raised, did battle with the din he made, and was defeated. Roger leaned with his arms flung round the girth of the apple tree, grinding his forehead into the bark, clamouring through the orchard. When his own voice dropped he heard how silent it was. So silent that he thought his father was dead too, lying in the long grass, till he turned and saw him beside him, holding something towards him, still standing.

He was holding out a picture-postcard; he meant Roger to take it. 'Steady, old man,' he was saying; 'steady, Roger, you're all jiggy: steady, old man!'

'What, what, what?' said Roger, staring wildly at the postcard. It was glazed and very blue; blue sea, infinitely smooth and distant, sky cloudless above it; white houses gathered joyously together by the shore, other white houses hurrying from the hills. Behind the land, behind everything, the clear fine line of a mountain went up into the sky. Something beckoned Roger; he stood looking through an archway.

'It came for you,' said Father, 'it's from Aunt Nellie; it's the Bay of Naples.'

Then he went away.

This was the blue empty place, Heaven, that one came out into at last, beyond everything. In the blue windlessness, the harmony of that timeless day, Roger went springing and singing up the mountain to look for his mother. He did not think again of that grey figure, frightened, foolish, desolate, that went back among the trees uncertainly, and stood a long time fumbling with the gate.

Joining Charles

Everybody in the White House was awake early that morning, even the cat. At an unprecedented hour in the thick grey dusk Polyphemus slipped upstairs and began to yowl at young Mrs Charles's door, under which came out a pale yellow line of candle-light. On an ordinary morning he could not have escaped from the kitchen so easily, but last night the basement door had been left unbolted; all the doors were open downstairs, for the household had gone to bed at a crisis of preparation for the morrow. Sleep was to be no more than an interim, and came to most of them thinly and interruptedly. The rooms were littered with objects that had an air of having been put down momentarily, corded boxes were stacked up in the hall, and a spectral breakfast-table waiting all night in the parlour reappeared slowly as dawn came in through the curtains.

Young Mrs Charles came across to the door on her bare feet, and, shivering, let in Polyphemus. She was still in pyjamas, but her two suitcases were packed to the brim, with tissue paper smoothed on the tops of them: she must have been moving about for hours. She was always, superstitiously, a little afraid of Polyphemus and made efforts to propitiate him on all occasions; his expression of omniscience had imposed upon her thoroughly. His coming in now made her a little conscious; she stood still, one hand on the knob of the dressing-table drawer, and put the other hand to her forehead – what must she do? Between the curtains, drawn a little apart, light kept coming in slowly, solidifying the objects round her, which till now had been uncertain, wavering silhouettes in candlelight. So night fears gave place to the realities of daytime.

Polyphemus continued to melt round the room, staring malignly at nothing. Presently Agatha tapped and came in in her dressing-gown; her plaits hung down each side of her long, kind face, and she carried a cup of tea.

'Better drink this,' said Agatha. 'What can I do?' She drew back the curtains a little more in her comfortable, common-sense way to encourage the daylight. Leaning for a moment out of the window she breathed in critically the morning air; the bare upland country was sheathed but not hidden by mist. 'You're going to have a beautiful day,' said Agatha.

Mrs Charles shivered, then began tugging a comb through her short hair. She had been awake a long time and felt differently from Agatha about the day; she looked at her sister-in-law haggardly. 'I dreamed and dreamed,' said Mrs Charles. 'I kept missing my boat, saw it sliding away from the quay; and when I turned to come back to you all England was sliding away too, in the other direction, and I don't know where I was left – and I dreamed, too, of course, about losing my passport.'

'One would think you had never travelled before,' said Agatha tranquilly. She sat down on the end of the narrow bed where Mrs Charles had slept for the last time, and shaking out Mrs Charles's garments, passed them to her one by one, watching her dress as though she had been a child. Mrs Charles felt herself being marvelled at; her own smallness and youth had become objective to her at the White House; a thing, all she had, to offer them over again every day to be softened and pleased by.

As she pulled on the clothes she was to wear for so long she began to feel formal and wary, the wife of a competent banker going to join him at Lyons. The expression of her feet in those new brogues was quite unfamiliar: the feet of a 'nice little woman'. Her hair, infected by this feeling of strangeness that flowed to her very extremities, lay in a different line against her head. For a moment the face of a ghost from the future stared at her out of the looking-glass. She turned quickly to Agatha, but her sister-in-law had left her while she was buttoning her jumper at the neck and had gone downstairs to print some more labels. It had occurred to Agatha that there would be less chance of losing the luggage (a contingency by which this untravelled family seemed to be haunted) if Louise were to tie on new labels, with more explicit directions, at Paris, where she would have to re-register. Agatha was gone, and the cup of tea, untasted, grew cold on the dressing-table.

The room looked bare without her possessions and withdrawn, as though it had already forgotten her. At this naked hour of parting she had forgotten it also; she supposed it would come back in retrospect so distinctly as to be a kind of torment. It was a smallish room with sloping ceilings, and a faded paper rambled over by roses. It had white curtains and was never entirely dark; it had so palpably a life of its own that she had been able to love it with intimacy and a sense of return, as one could never have loved an inanimate thing. Lying in bed one could see from the one window nothing but sky or sometimes a veil of rain; when one got up and looked out there were fields, wild and bare, and an unbroken skyline to emphasize the security of the house.

The room was up on the top floor, in one of the gables; a big household cannot afford a spare bedroom of any pretensions. To go downstairs one had to unlatch the nursery gate at the head of the top flight. Last time Charles was home it had been very unfortunate; he had barked his shins on the gate and shouted angrily to his mother to know what the thing was *still* there for. Louise fully realized that it was being kept for Charles's children.

During that first visit with Charles she had hardly been up to the second floor, where the younger girls slept in the old nursery. There had been no confidences; she and Charles occupied very connubially a room Mrs Ray gave up to them that had been hers since her marriage. It was not till Louise came back here alone that the White House opened its arms to her and she began to be carried away by this fullness, this intimacy and queer seclusion of family life. She and the girls were in and out of each other's rooms; Doris told sagas of high school, Maisie was always just on the verge of a love-affair, and large grave Agatha began to drop the formality with which she had greeted a married woman and sister-in-law. She thought Agatha would soon have forgotten she was anything but her own child if it had ever been possible for Agatha to forget Charles.

It would have been terrible if Louise had forgotten, as she so nearly had, to pack Charles's photograph. There it had stood these three months, propped up on the mantelpiece, a handsome convention in sepia, becomingly framed, from which the young wife, falling asleep or waking, had turned away her face instinctively. She folded back a layer of tissue paper before shutting her suitcase and poked down a finger to feel the edge of the frame and reassure herself. There it was, lying face down, wrapped up in her dressing gown, and she would have seen Charles before she looked again at his photograph. The son and brother dominating the White House would be waiting on Lyons platform to enfold her materially.

Mrs Charles glanced round the room once more, then went downstairs slowly. Through the house she could hear doors opening and shutting and people running about because of her. She felt ashamed that her packing was finished and there was nothing for her to do. Whenever she had pictured herself leaving the White House it had been in the evening, with curtains drawn, and they had all just come out to the door for a minute to say goodbye to her, then gone back to the fire. It had been more painful but somehow easier. Now she felt lonely; they had all gone away from her, there was nobody there.

She went shyly into the morning-room as though for the first time and knelt down on the rug in front of a young fire. There was a sharp smell of woodsmoke; thin little flames twisted and spat through the kindling. A big looking-glass, down to the ground, reflected her kneeling there; small and childish among the solemn mahogany furniture; more like somebody sent back to school than someone rejoining a virile and generous husband who loved her. Her cropped fair hair turned under against her cheek and was cut in a straight line over the eyebrows. She had never had a home before, and had been able to boast till quite lately that she had never been homesick. After she married there had been houses in which she lived with Charles, but still she had not known what it meant to be homesick.

She hoped that, after all, nobody would come in for a moment or two; she had turned her head and was looking out at the lawn with its fringe of trees not yet free from the mist, and at the three blackbirds hopping about on it. The blackbirds made her know all at once what it meant to be going away; she felt as though someone had stabbed her a long time ago but she were only just feeling the knife. She could not take her eyes from the blackbirds, till one with a wild flutey note skimmed off into the trees and the other two followed it. Polyphemus had come in after her and was looking out at them, pressing himself against the windowpane.

'Polyphemus,' said Mrs Charles in her oddly unchildish voice, 'have you any illusions?' Polyphemus lashed his tail.

By midday (when she would be nearly at Dover) the fire would be streaming up briskly, but by that time the sun would be pouring in at the windows and no one would need a fire at all. The mornings were not cold yet, the girls were active, and it was only because of her going away that the fire had been lighted. Perhaps Agatha, who never hurt anything's feelings, would come in and sit not too far away from it with her basket of mending, making believe to be glad of the heat. 'I don't suppose there'll be fires at Lyons,' thought Mrs Charles. Somewhere, in some foreign room tomorrow evening when the endearments were over or there was a pause in them, Charles would lean back in his chair with a gusty sigh, arch his chest up, stretch out his legs and say: 'Well, come on. Tell me about the family.'

Then she would have to tell him about the White House. Her cheeks burnt as she thought how it would all come out. There seemed no chance yet of Agatha or Maisie getting married. That was what Charles would want to know chiefly about his sisters. He had a wholesome contempt for virginity. He would want to know how Doris, whom he rather admired, was 'coming along'. Those sisters of Charles's always sounded rather dreadful young women, not the sort that Agatha, Maisie or Doris would care to know. It seemed to Charles funny – he often referred to it – that Agatha wanted babies so badly and went all tender and conscious when babies were mentioned.

'She'll make no end of a fuss over our kids,' Charles would say. The White House seemed to Charles, all the same, very proper as an institution; it was equally proper that he should have a contempt for it. He helped to support the girls and his mother, for one thing, and that did place them all at a disadvantage. But they were dear, good souls – Mrs Charles knelt with her hands on her knees and the hands clenched slowly from anger and helplessness.

Mrs Ray, the mother of Charles, suddenly knelt down by his wife and put an arm round her shoulders without saying a word. She did these impulsive things gracefully. Mrs Charles relaxed and leant sideways a little against the kind shoulder. She had nothing to say, so they watched the fire struggle and heard the hall clock counting away the seconds.

'Have you got enough clothes on?' said Mother after a minute. 'It's cold in trains. I never do think you wear enough clothes.'

Mrs Charles, nodding, unbuttoned her coat and showed a ribbed-sweater pulled on over her jumper. 'Sensible of me!' she proudly remarked.

'You're learning to be quite a sensible little thing,' Mother said lightly. 'I expect Charles will notice a difference. Tell Charles not to let you go out in the damp in your evening shoes. But I expect he knows how to take care of you.'

'Indeed, yes,' said Mrs Charles, nodding.

'You're precious, you see.' Mother smoothed back the hair from against Mrs Charles's cheek to look at her thoughtfully, like a gentle sceptic at some kind of miracle. 'Remember to write me about the flat: I want to know everything: wallpapers, views from the windows, sizes of rooms – We'll be thinking about you both tomorrow.'

'I'll be thinking of you.'

'Oh, no, you won't,' said Mother, with perfect finality.

'Perhaps not,' Mrs Charles quickly amended.

Mother's son Charles was generous, sensitive, gallant and shrewd. The things he said, the things he had made, his imprint, were all over the White House. Sometimes he looked out at Louise with bright eyes from the family talk, so striking, so unfamiliar that she fell in love with the stranger for moments together as a married woman should not. He was quiet and never said very much, but he *noticed*; he had an infallible understanding and entered deeply, it seemed, into the sisters' lives. He was so good; he was so keen for them all to be happy. He had the strangest way of anticipating one's wishes. He was master of an inimitable drollery – to hear him chaff Agatha! Altogether he was a knightly person, transcending modern convention. His little wife had come to them all in a glow from her wonderful lover. No wonder she was so quiet; they used to try and read him from her secret, sensitive face.

A thought of their Charles without his Louise troubled them all with a pang when Louise was her dearest. Charles in Lyons uncomplaining, lonely, tramping the town after business to look for a flat. The return of Louise to him, to the home he had found for her, her room upstairs already aghast and vacant, the emptiness that hung over them, gave them the sense of pouring out an oblation. The girls were heavy, with the faces of Flemish Madonnas; Doris achieved some resemblance to Charles, but without being handsome. They had cheerful dispositions, but were humble when they considered themselves; they thought Louise must have a great deal of love in her to give them so much when there was a Charles in her life.

Mrs Ray, with a groan at her 'old stiff bones', got up from the hearthrug and sat on a chair. She thought of something to say, but was not quite ready to say it till she had taken up her knitting. She had hoped to have finished this pair of socks in time to send out by Louise with his others: she hadn't been able to – Mrs Ray sighed. 'You're making my boy very happy,' she said, with signs in her manner of the difficulty one has in expressing these things.

Louise thought: 'Oh, I love you!' There was something about the hands, the hair, the expression, the general being of Mother that possessed her entirely, that she did not think she could live without. She knelt staring at Mother, all in a tumult. Why be so lonely, why never escape? She was too lonely, it couldn't be borne; not even for the sake of the White House. Not this morning, so early, with the buffeting strangeness of travel before her, with her wrists so chilly and the anticipation of sea-sickness making her stomach ache. The incommunicableness of even these things, these little ills of the body, bore Mrs Charles down. She was tired of being brave alone, she was going to give it up.

It is with mothers that understanding and comfort are found. She wanted to put down her head on a bosom, this bosom, and say: 'I'm unhappy. Oh, help me! I can't go on. I don't love my husband. It's death to be with him. He's grand, but he's rotten all through—' She needed to be fortified.

'Mother—' said Louise.

'Mm-mm?'

'If things were not a success out there – If one weren't a good wife always—' Mother smoothed her knitting out and began to laugh; an impassable, resolute chuckle.

'What a *thing*—' she said. 'What an idea!'

Louise heard steps in the hall and began kneading her hands together, pulling the fingers helplessly. '*Mother*,' she said, 'I feel—'

Mother looked at her; out of the eyes looked Charles. The steady, gentle look, their interchange, lasted moments. Steps came hurrying over the flags of the hall.

'I can't go—'

Doris came in with the teapot. She wasn't grown up, her movements were clumsy and powerful, more like a boy's. She should have been Charles. Her heavy plait came tumbling over her shoulder as she bent to put down the teapot – round and brown with a bluish glaze on it. Sleep and tears in the dark had puffed up her eyelids, which seemed to open with difficulty: her small eyes dwindled into her face. '*Breakfast*,' she said plaintively.

Rose, the servant, brought in a plate of boiled eggs – nice and light for the journey – and put them down compassionately.

'Even Rose,' thought Mrs Charles, getting up and coming to the table obediently because they all expected her to, 'even Rose—' She looked at the breakfast-cups with poppies scattered across them as though she had not seen them before or were learning an inventory. Doris had begun to eat as though nothing else mattered. She took no notice of Louise, pretending, perhaps, to make things easier for herself, that Louise were already gone.

'Oh, Doris, not the *tussore* tie with the *red* shirt.' Whatever the White House might teach Mrs Charles about common sense, it was her mission to teach them about clothes. 'Not,' said Mrs Charles, with bravado rising to an exaggeration of pathos, 'not on my last day!'

'I dressed in the dark; I couldn't see properly,' said Doris.

'You won't get eggs for breakfast in France,' said Maisie with a certain amount of triumph as she came in and sat down.

'I wonder what the flat'll be like?' said Maisie. 'Do write and tell us about the flat – describe the wallpapers and everything.'

'Just think,' said Doris, 'of Charles buying the furniture! "*Donnez-moi une chaise!*" "*Bien, Monsieur.*" "*Non. Ce n'est pas assez comfortable pour ma femme.*"'

'Fancy!' said Maisie, laughing very much. 'And fancy if the flat's high up.'

'There'll be central-heating and stoves. Beautiful fug. She

actually won't be chilly.' Mrs Charles was always chilly: this was a
household joke.

'Central heating is stuffy—'

Doris broke away suddenly from the conversation. 'Oh!' she said
violently, 'Oh, Louise, you are *lucky*!'

A glow on streets and on the pale, tall houses: Louise walking
with Charles. Frenchmen running in blousey overalls (Doris saw),
French poodles, French girls in plaid skirts putting the shutters
back, French ladies on iron balconies, leaning over, watching
Charles go up the street with Louise and help Louise over the
crossings; Charles and Louise together. A door, a lift, a flat, a
room, a kiss! 'Charles, Charles, you are so splendid! Mother loves
you and the girls love you and I love you—' 'Little woman!' A
French curtain fluttering in the high, fresh wind, the city under
the roofs – forgotten. All this Doris watched: Louise watched
Doris.

'Yes,' smiled Louise. 'I *am* lucky.'

'Even to be going to France,' said Doris, and stared with her
dog's eyes.

Louise wanted to take France in her two hands and make her
a present of it. 'You'll be coming out soon, Doris, some day.' (It
was not likely that Charles would have her – and did one, anyhow,
dare let the White House into the flat?)

'Do you really think so?'

'Why not, if Mother can spare you?'

'*Louise!*' cried Maisie reproachfully – she had been sitting
watching – 'you aren't eating!'

Agatha, sitting next to her, covered up her confusion with gentle,
comforting noises, cut the top off an egg and advanced it coaxingly.
That was the way one made a child eat; she was waiting to do the
same for Charles's and Louise's baby when it was old enough.
Louise now almost saw the baby sitting up between them, but it
was nothing to do with her.

'You'll be home in *less* than the two years, I shouldn't be surprised,'
said Mother startlingly. It was strange, now one came to think of
it, that any question of coming back to the White House had not
been brought up before. They might know Mrs Charles would be

coming back, but they did not (she felt) believe it. So she smiled at Mother as though they were playing a game.

'Well, two years at the very least,' Mother said with energy.

They all cast their minds forward. Louise saw herself in the strong pale light of the future walking up to the White House and (for some reason) ringing the bell like a stranger. She stood ringing and ringing and nobody answered or even looked out of a window. She began to feel that she had failed them somehow, that something was missing. Of course it was. When Louise came back next time she must bring them a baby. Directly she saw herself coming up the steps with a child in her arms she knew at once what was wanted. Wouldn't Agatha be delighted? Wouldn't Maisie 'run on'? Wouldn't Doris hang awkwardly round and make jokes, poking her big finger now and then between the baby's curling pink ones? As for Mother – at the supreme moment of handing the baby to Mother, Louise had a spasm of horror and nearly dropped it. For the first time she looked at the baby's face and saw it was Charles's.

'It would do no *good*,' thought Mrs Charles, cold all of a sudden and hardened against them all, 'to have a baby of Charles's.'

They all sat looking not quite at each other, not quite at her. Maisie said (thinking perhaps of the love-affair that never completely materialized): 'A great deal can happen in two years,' and began to laugh confusedly in an emotional kind of way. Mother and Agatha looked across at each other. 'Louise, don't forget to send us a wire,' said Mother, as though she had been wondering all this time she had sat so quiet behind the teapot whether Louise would remember to do this.

'Or Charles might send the wire.'

'Yes,' said Louise, 'that would be better.'

Polyphemus, knowing his moment, sprang up on to Mrs Charles's knee. His black tail, stretched out over the tablecloth, lashed sideways, knocking the knives and forks crooked. His one green eye sardonically penetrated her. *He* knew. He had been given to Charles as a dear little kitten. He pressed against her, treading her lap methodically and mewing soundlessly, showing the purple roof of his mouth. 'Ask Charles,' suggested Polyphemus, 'what became of my other eye.' 'I know,' returned Mrs Charles silently. '*They* don't, they haven't

been told; you've a voice, I haven't – what about it?' 'Satan!' breathed
Mrs Charles, and caressed fascinatedly the fur just over his nose.

'Funny,' mused Agatha, watching, 'you never have cared for
Polyphemus, and yet he likes you. He's a very transparent cat; he
is wonderfully honest.'

'He connects her with Charles,' said Maisie, also enjoying this
interchange between the wife and the cat. 'He's sending some kind
of a message – he's awfully clever.'

'Too clever for me,' said Mrs Charles, and swept Polyphemus
off her knee with finality. Agatha was going as far as the station;
she went upstairs for her hat and coat. Mrs Charles rose also, picked
up her soft felt hat from a chair and pulled it on numbly, in front
of the long glass, arranging two little bits of hair at the sides against
her cheeks. 'Either I am dreaming,' she thought, 'or someone is
dreaming me.'

Doris roamed round the room and came up to her. 'A book
left behind, Louise; *Framley Parsonage*, one of your books.'

'Keep it for me.'

'For two years – all that time?'

'Yes, I'd like you to.'

'Doris sat down on the floor and began to read *Framley Parsonage*.
She went into it deeply – she had to go somewhere; there was
nothing to say; she was suddenly shy of Louise again as she had
been at first, as though they had never known each other – perhaps
they never had.

'Haven't you read it before?'

'No, never, I'll write and tell you, shall I, what I think of it?'

'I've quite forgotten what *I* think of it,' said Louise, standing
above her, laughing and pulling on her gloves. She laughed as
though she were at a party, moving easily now under the smooth
compulsion of Somebody's dreaming mind. Agatha had come in
quietly. 'Hush!' she said in a strained way to both of them, standing
beside the window in hat and coat as though *she* were the traveller.
'Hush!' She was listening for the taxi. Mother and Maisie had gone.

Wouldn't the taxi come, perhaps? What if it never came? An
intolerable jar for Louise, to be deprived of going; a tear in the
mesh of the dream that she could not endure. 'Make the taxi come
soon!' she thought, praying now for departure. 'Make it come soon!'

Being listened for with such concentration must have frightened the taxi, for it didn't declare itself; there was not a sound to be heard on the road. If it were not for the hospitality of *Framley Parsonage* where, at this moment, would Doris have been? She bent to the pages absorbedly and did not look up; the leaves of the book were thin and turned over noisily. Louise fled from the morning-room into the hall.

Out in the dark hall Mother was bending over the pile of boxes, reading and re-reading the labels upside down and from all aspects. She often said that labels could not be printed clearly enough. As Louise hurried past she stood up, reached out an arm and caught hold of her. Only a little light came down from the staircase window; they could hardly see each other. They stood like two figures in a picture, without understanding, created to face one another.

'Louise,' whispered Mother, 'if things should be difficult – Marriage isn't easy. If you should be disappointed – I know, I feel – you do understand? If Charles—'

'Charles?'

'I do love you, I do. You would tell me?'

But Louise, kissing her coldly and gently, said: 'Yes, I know. But there isn't really, Mother, anything to tell.'

Charity

When Rachel had done showing Charity the garden, they both
sat down in a wheelbarrow beside the flowering currant-bush,
swung their legs exaggeratedly, and looked away from each other.
There was still another hour before tea. The fact was, they were
still rather strange to one another in the relation of guest and
hostess. All the effects Rachel had planned for this afternoon had
come off; yet somehow not quite come off, because there was an
incalculable strangeness about Home today that had altogether
surprised her. Nothing seemed as usual. By the time they were
halfway round the house she was beginning to feel, each time she
opened a door, 'Perhaps I am letting Charity in for more than I
know?' When they looked into the bogey-hole under the stairs,
and she told Charity by way of a joke that they kept the family
ghost there, she felt horribly afraid. Even the currant-bush began
to be affected; it smelt so hot and sharp that she felt she ought to
explain it in some way. The zumming and bump of bees in and
out of it filled up the silence embarrassingly. It seemed equally
unlifelike to mention the bees and to ignore them, so she laughed
aloud to herself unnaturally and kicked the wheel of the barrow.

Yet the strangeness perhaps lay in Charity. She wore a flowery
hat from under which her nose came out at an unexpected angle,
and when she took her hat off she patted her hair. When she talked
to Father or Mother she had 'a manner'. She had got out of the
train (backwards) in a bottle-green dress much longer than usual.
Rachel had understood at once that there need be no fear of her
not being a success at Home; on the other hand, she did not seem
to be so much impressed by it all as one had expected. Her gaze
ate things up and diminished them. Her own home and her
unknown relations kept like a shadow behind her. She might almost
have been one of the Little Daughters of Your Age that Mother
invited to tea. Just now, as they slowly paraded the borders, Rachel
had caught herself wishing that they were back in the garden at

school. *There* it would have been thrilling to be walking about with Charity, arm in arm . . . She did not show her the Secret Place . . .

For this her heart smote her. 'Did you know,' she said, 'that I had rabbits of my own now?'

'Show!' said Charity.

With a lovely feeling of release they rushed off.

Rachel had been praying days ahead that Adela might be out for tea that first afternoon. Yet even when the gong sounded she could not be sure. She thought it better to prepare the ground, so said to Charity coming across the hall, 'You will laugh when you see my sister!'

'I thought she was grown up,' said Charity, looking down thoughtfully into a brass pot that held, besides a palm, several of Father's and Adela's cigarette-ends.

'Still, she's pretty mad,' said Rachel cautiously. She punched Charity in the small of the back to make her go first through the door, Charity punched her back, and they scuffled together on the threshold quite naturally, as at school. But Rachel was noticing how the dining-room and the round white table in the afternoon light looked less like themselves than like their own reflection in a looking-glass. Mother and Father made a smiling pattern one on each side of it. What a cheery pair of little girls!

They sat down: Mother and Father, not too apparently watching them, talked to each other. They broke off now and then to say encouraging things to the Little Friend, who sat with her chin tucked in, taking long drinks and smiling politely. Having dining-room tea in the holidays gave Rachel the un-familiar and pleasant feeling of this houseful of grown-up people pivoting round on herself. Nobody else liked it; there were plain kinds of dripping-cake and gingerbread that nobody else cared for; Father would drink his two cups straight off and go away quickly; Adela would cry out, '*Must* we all watch this child eat?' cross her legs and jerk back her chair. Sitting thus, she would smoke and say, 'Oh lord! *Oh* lord!' and at last take Mother by the arm and march her out through the French window into the garden. Mother would go with her frowning and laughing, very much flattered, torn in herself and reluctant. Then it would be dreary sometimes, though not unprofitable, being left alone with the cakes.

Father was going over, for Charity's benefit, all his usual rather silly questions and jokes about school. 'Do they cane you?' he kept asking her. 'Do they make you talk Latin? Do you have dormitory feasts?' Charity gave little giggles. 'Ooh, Major Monstrevor, you *are* . . .!' She ate a refined tea, and did not want jam, she said, because it was sticky. Rachel was proud of her father's appearance, she thought he looked 'soldierly'; but she could not bear him to talk too much. In an access of nervousness and with some idea of causing a distraction, she leant over and said to her mother, 'Where's Adela? Isn't she in?'

Her heart went up into her throat at the question, and stayed there till Mother, absent-minded, brought herself to reply, 'Oh, Adela? Tennis.'

This was an answer to prayer, but it might be more awful than ever when Adela did come in. To hear her talk of her tennis made one hot all over: she might have been Suzanne at least: one did not know where to look.

Mother came out with the inevitable. Getting up, she beamed at them. 'And what are you going to do with yourselves?' said Mother.

There was an absolutely blank moment: everybody looked at Rachel. Rachel remembered that *this* was the afternoon she had been saving herself up for since the middle of term; she could have wept. If only she could be back at school again, telling Charity . . . But *this* was Charity, looking at her aloofly with critical little clear pale eyes. Charity waiting to be entertained. It was an absolutely blank moment. 'Oh, *I* dunno,' said Rachel. 'Just mouch round . . .'

Mother smiled helpfully; the smile stayed on a minute or two while her thoughts wandered.

'Rabbits?' said Father.

'She's seen the rabbits . . .'

So he took them into the study and showed Charity his butterfly collection. He took down cabinet after cabinet of the poor, brittle, bright-coloured creatures that one would rather die than touch. Rachel loathed the butterflies and the way they would all quiver suddenly on their pins as though coming alive again; she was certain

Charity loathed them too, but she felt grateful to Father. To make things go off well she exclaimed loudly at them as though she hadn't seen them before, and asked their names eagerly. She hoped Charity didn't remember what she had once said about Father's butterflies, on their way to gym. Charity, who didn't like her own father, had said that fathers were the limit. Rachel had agreed at once, though with a feeling of shock, and, seeking round for some shortcoming of her father's, thought of his collection. Wasn't it atrociously cruel, she had said, to stick a butterfly, still quite living, through with a pin! Anyhow, when she had said 'atrociously cruel!' she hadn't *meant* anything to do with Father.

He thought of something important, put away the butterfly-cabinets suddenly, and turned his back on the two of them, bored. So Rachel pushed Charity through the door (she seemed to have been pushing Charity through doors all day, but no solution yet offered itself), and they went back to the garden and played French-cricket there with a tennis ball.

Charity played a brilliant game and couldn't be got out. Rather flushed, she began to enjoy herself, and soon with her eyes (apparently) quite tight shut she was scornfully knocking Rachel's bowling all over the place. At last she sent the tennis ball in at the drawing-room window and knocked over a pot of azaleas.

'Crikey!' she said. 'Will They mind? Let's tell Them afterwards . . . I call this a silly old game!'

The rude way she said this made Rachel see light. It was this politeness that had been the matter all day. Inspired, she shouted, 'Silly fool yourself!' and came charging at Charity full tilt, in the role of Laughing Tomahawk. Charity, unprepared, lost her balance forthwith and rolled over. She lay kicking at Rachel with both feet for a moment or two, and it seemed as if things were going all right. Then she jumped up suddenly (that green frock!), stood dusting herself, and said in a cold voice, 'Shut up; I wish you wouldn't.' She was an absolute stranger; the green frock had pleats down the side and bobbly brass buttons. *What* one must have looked like, with one's scarlet yelling mouth, being Laughing Tomahawk! . . . Rachel was quenched.

'Shall we climb up,' she said, 'and sit on the roof of the bicycle shed?'

'I don't mind,' said Charity. 'Do you often?'

Rachel did. It was here that she read her books, designed cath-edrals, made a new will every holidays, and kept the key to a terribly secret cipher under a flowerpot. It was here that she would lie pulling an elder-branch up and down above her head like a punkah, and dinting the roof with her heels while she thought about Charity. She felt embarrassed as she hoisted up Charity into this ring of terribly secret thoughts; she wished that she had gone up first to get the place into order. Sometimes the thoughts would simply be conversations, or sometimes the school was on fire, or there was nearly a bathing fatality. Sometimes there was a war on, and, as none of the men were brave enough, they were both going to fight.

'This must be awfully bad for the roof,' said Charity, jumping about. 'Just look at those dints. Do They mind?' But Rachel took out the cipher, and suddenly, effortlessly, unknowingly, like falling asleep at last when one has been trying and trying, they were together again. The evening went terribly fast.

Presently they heard a bicycle being rattled along and branches brushing against a bicycle wheel. Adela coming home. Adela's red felt hat was pulled right over her eyes like a sombrero; the top of her looked Spanish, and the rest, muffled up to the mouth, like an Antarctic explorer. She came back from tennis like this in the hottest weather because, one could only suppose, it looked rather professional. She managed to look languid and sinister, even pushing a bicycle down a narrow path through syringa bushes. 'Crikey!' said Charity audibly when she appeared.

Adela looked up at them darkly from under her hat, but kept her chin in her scarf and said nothing. They both rolled over on to their stomachs, and watched her over the edge of the roof while she put her bicycle away.

'You know that's bad for the roof,' said Adela in her dead-sounding voice as she came out again.

('There!' said Charity to Rachel.)

'*Are* you,' said Adela, 'Faith, or Hope?' Charity giggled. She did not know that Adela had been talking about her, before she came, as the Charity Child, and asking Mother in Rachel's presence to have her thoroughly disinfected. 'You never know,' she had said, 'with Charity Children . . .'

Standing still in the path underneath them, like a pillar of salt in the six o'clock sunlight, Adela began to unwind (very guardedly, for fear of pneumonia) some of her wrappings. Her chin came out, chalky white like the tip of her nose, and her long thin jaw like rather a beautiful crocodile's. She grinned to herself; the joke was for neither of them, but she did not mind them seeing she was amused. 'I've heard the most *terrible* things about you,' she said, looking at Charity, and, shaking her head in a horrified way, walked away through the bushes. She left behind a fatal gash in the peace of the afternoon. When they kicked the roof it gave out a dungeony, clanking sound, and down in the shed underneath Adela's bicycle rattled.

Charity could not give her mind to the cipher again; she was very pink. 'What *have* you been telling her?' she asked in an agitated, pleased voice. Rachel said, 'Nothing'; she never told Adela anything. 'Well, I must say I didn't expect her like *that*,' said Charity sharply.

Adela did not seem to Rachel to have gone off so badly. This revived a particular hope that the awfulness of Adela might be simply her own delusion, and that she would seem just an Elder Sister to any one else. 'She isn't really so bad,' she said comfortably, deep in the cipher.

'Well, I must say . . . She isn't what I'd call very Good Style.'

Rachel was so angry, she did not know with whom, that she was hardly able to speak.

People were coming to dinner, so Rachel and Charity were to have 'a tray' in the spare-room. This felt very select, especially when one spread a lace handkerchief over the table in the window and imagined this was a restaurant; though there had been an uncomfortable moment when Rachel saw Charity unpack two beautiful evening dresses and hang them up in the wardrobe without saying a word. Was this, she wondered, the only house in the world where girls of twelve didn't come down to dinner? The spare-room was a magnificent room (like in somebody else's house), all mirrors; they danced a pyjama ballet surrounded by their reflections. The room got so dusky that when the tray with their poached eggs was brought in and put down they did not see it, and forgot that supper was there.

They sat in the windowsill, outside, told each other stories and listened to the rooks going to bed. There would be a sudden cry, a tree shaken, and the sky would be dark with them; then calling to one another again and again, they would drop back into the branches. Fewer rooks rose each time, and this gave one a feeling of great peacefulness, as though the whole earth were being hushed-up and reassured. These were the evenings that Rachel missed most when she went back to school.

The happiness that she had been waiting for all day seemed to have something to do with light behind the trees, the rooks, and the dry chintzy smell of the curtains when she leant back her head against them into the room. Also, there is something very heroic about dangling one's legs at a height.

Suddenly they remembered supper and dived into the darkness to look for the poached eggs. They lit one candle, and Charity, who could be very funny, sat languishing in the light of it, fluttered her lashes and ate off the tip of her fork. Rachel was a Guardsman, very adoring, and kept offering her champagne and cocktails. 'A *mushroom* cocktail,' she said coaxingly, and they both thought that sounded delicious. They imagined cocktails to be little red things like prawns, that sat at the bottom of glasses with their tails turned up.

Rachel, still in the character of Guardsman, jumped up, flung an arm round Charity's neck and kissed her violently. 'Oh, be *care*ful, Captain de Vere,' squeaked Charity; 'you are dripping champagne from your moustache ... *Oh*, my Reveille and Rossiter!' She mopped the champagne from Captain de Vere's moustache off the front of her pyjama-jacket, and wrung out her handkerchief into her plate.

Then she stiffened up and pushed Rachel away. The expression was wiped off her face suddenly, leaving it blank. 'Do *listen*,' she snapped out, listening herself all over. Rachel heard nothing at all for a moment; it was creepy, as though Charity were hearing a ghost. To encourage herself and hear better she lighted more candles, padding round the room in her bare feet and trying not to shake the matchbox. All she heard then was Adela moving about next door, pulling drawers open and pushing them shut with a rattle. For a moment she wondered what Adela could be doing at midnight

– she felt like midnight, miles from the ordinary, delirious, rather guilty: then she remembered the gong hadn't gone yet; it couldn't be more than eight. That could only be Adela dressing for dinner.

When Charity heard this she got up and swaggered about the room. It is wonderful what one can do on cocoa and a little imagination. She made Rachel feel as a matter of course that everybody else in the house was their enemy.

'Let's make a raid,' said she; 'let's tie up Her door handle!'

'Coo . . .' wavered Rachel, greatly attracted.

'No, let's go in and pretend to be sick on Her bed.'

'But Mother'd—'

'Who cares for your mother?'

They took off the ropes from the waists of their dressing-gowns and crept into the passage. Adela's door was ajar and her lights lighted; she was humming, and seemed to be prowling about like a panther. As though she had heard them, she pounced and appeared in her doorway. She was tall, and every inch of her glared in the gaslight. Rachel immediately curled up inside like a woodlouse, because she felt Adela was going to 'rasp'. They stood there at bay rather foolishly, the ropes of their dressing-gowns coiled up in their hands like lassoes. But Adela's best 'Evening' manner had been finally arranged and put on with her pearls and her earrings; she wasn't going to take it off again, even for them.

'What the devil—' she began pleasantly, as though to her own friends.

Having nothing ready they stood curling up their bare toes, each wondering what the other was going to do. Evening dress still filled Adela's mind as she stood above them; frowning down as though they were not there, she touched delicately, inquiringly, one long earring after the other with the tip of a finger, and, with head a little sideways, screwed one tighter. Having done this she shook her head, at first very cautiously, but though the earrings wagged violently they did not come off. Relief at this made Adela still more pleasant. 'What *do* you want?' she said, and raising her eyebrows smiled despairingly, as though she must be very kind to a little idiot sister.

Charity moved. 'We came,' she said in an awed and breathy voice, 'to ask if you would come in and say goodnight to us?'

'Soppy,' said Adela, pleased. The gold fringe round her dress swung as she stepped back into her room to close a cupboard door and turn the light off. Saved, it seemed that they were.

'You have got a nerve!' said Rachel in a shaky whisper. But Charity's features rolled up into an appalling 'face'. 'Come on; come now!' said Rachel, quite unnerved and tugging at the skirt of Charity's dressing-gown. '*Back* from the jaws of death, *Back* from the gates of Hell,' she was saying to herself, half aloud. She knew she must be what they all called 'very excited.' She was so excited that something throbbed in her ears, and she wanted to scream and rush back across the passage before a something that was worse than Adela put out a long arm and grabbed her into the dark room. She wanted to slam the spare-room door in the Enemy's face and barricade it, perhaps with the wardrobe. 'You won't get us,' she was prepared to call out, 'not if you burn the house down.' She felt like staying up all night. She tugged with all her might at Charity's dressing-gown.

'Leave go!' An unknown, scornful person flashed round suddenly. A dressing-gown was wrenched from her. 'Let *go*, you fool!' Full of wild suspicion and enmity, lost to one another, they scuffled, skidding on the oilcloth. Rachel cried, half sobbing from breathlessness, 'No, listen, Charity . . . Charity, don't be a beast.' Charity grew a year older each moment, her protests grew shriller and more reasonable . . . 'No, seriously, *listen*, Charity . . .'

'It's you that are the beast,' said Charity in a remote voice, as Adela showed up again in the dark doorway. With a wave, as though they had been sparrows quarrelling, Adela dispersed them. She put an arm round Charity's shoulders, and they walked off into the spare-room. 'My friend and I,' their two back views, short and tall, said of each other.

'*You* must go to bed,' said Adela, looking back. '*You're* excited.'

Rachel sat on her bed in the dark and thought over her day. Her door was ajar, and she heard a continuous murmur and mumble and laugh coming out of the spare-room. Then Adela came out, keeping on the same smile with which she had said goodnight to Charity, to do for the visitors down in the drawing-room. She paused at the top of the stairs, touched her earrings again, and shook out the fringe of her dress. Then she turned the gas low and went down. 'Well, I just hope,' thought Rachel, 'she *likes* being tucked up by Adela. I've never known any one tuck up so rottenly.' She felt contemptuous and, in a queer sort of way, happier than she had been all day. She knew Charity would be expecting her back, and presently, sure enough, she heard 'Coo-ee?'

'Coo-ee, Coo-ee,' Charity kept repeating, every few seconds. Rachel lay with her eyes shut, taking no notice, and then there began later a puzzled and angry silence. 'I shall go to sleep,' thought Rachel, beginning to count sheep. Then she began to believe she heard Charity sobbing. She lay listening for the irregular vague sounds, watching the circle of light from the gas-bracket wobble and fade on the ceiling over the spare-room door. When she was nearly asleep, Charity, hugging her elbows, crept out and stood on the landing.

'Oh, I can't sleep,' moaned Charity. 'Oh, I'm so homesick. Oh, I'm so lonely in there. Oh, what a *horrible* way to behave to a visitor . . .'

'Homesick?'

'Of course,' said Charity, shivering in a dignified way. 'Wouldn't you be homesick, away from your father and mother?'

Uninvited, she groped through the dark room and got into Rachel's bed, sobbing and shivering.

'Well, I must say, Charity,' said Rachel, making room for her, 'I don't understand you at all.'

The Jungle

Towards the end of a summer term Rachel discovered the Jungle. You got over the wall at the bottom of the kitchen garden, where it began to be out of bounds, and waded through knee-high sorrel, nettles and dock, along the boundary hedge of Mr Morden's property until you came to a gap in the roots of the hedge, very low down, where it was possible to crawl under. Then you doubled across his paddock (this was the most exciting part), round the pond and climbed a high board gate it was impossible to see through into a deep lane. You got out of the lane farther down by a bank with a hedge at the top (a very 'mangy' thin hedge), and along the back of this hedge, able to be entered at several points, was the Jungle. It was full of secret dog-paths threading between enormous tussocks of bramble, underneath the brambles there were hollow places like caves; there were hawthorns one could climb for a survey and, about the middle, a clump of elders gave out a stuffy sweetish smell. It was an absolutely neglected and wild place; nobody seemed to own it, nobody came there but tramps. Tramps, whose clothes seem to tear so much more easily than one's own, had left little fluttering tags on the bushes, some brownish newspaper one kicked away under the brambles, a decayed old boot like a fungus and tins scarlet with rust that tilted in every direction holding rainwater. Two or three of these tins, in some fit of terrible rage, had been bashed right in.

The first time Rachel came here, alone, she squeezed along the dog-paths with her heart in her mouth and a cold and horrible feeling she was going to find a dead cat. She knew cats crept away to die, and there was a sinister probability about these bushes. It was a silent July evening, an hour before supper. Rachel had brought a book, but she did not read; she sat down under the elders and clasped her hands round her knees. She had felt a funny lurch in her imagination as she entered the Jungle, everything in it tumbled together, then shook apart again, a little altered in their relations to each other, a little changed.

At this time Rachel was fourteen; she had no best friend at the moment, there was an interim. She suffered sometimes from a constrained, bursting feeling at having to keep things so much to herself, yet when she compared critically the girls who had been her great friends with the girls who might be her great friends she couldn't help seeing that they were very much alike. None of them any more than the others would be likely to understand . . . The Jungle gave her a strong feeling that here might have been the Perfect Person, and yet the Perfect Person would spoil it. She wanted it to be a thing in itself: she sat quite still and stared at the impenetrable bramble-humps.

On the last day of term Rachel travelled up in the train with a girl in a lower form called Elise Lamartine, who was going to spend the holidays riding in the New Forest. Elise had her hair cut short like a boy's and was supposed to be fearfully good at French but otherwise stupid. She had a definite quick way of doing things and a thoughtful slow way of looking at you when they were done. Rachel found herself wishing it weren't the holidays. She said, off-hand, as she scrambled down from the carriage into a crowd of mothers: 'Let's write to each other, shall we?' and Elise, beautifully unembarrassed, said, 'Right-o, let's!'

During the holidays Rachel became fifteen. Her mother let down her skirts two inches, said she really wasn't a little girl any more now and asked her to think about her career. She was asked out to tennis parties where strange young men had a hesitation about calling her anything and finally called her Miss Ritchie. Her married sister Adela promised that next summer holidays she'd have her to stay and take her to 'boy and girl dances'. 'Aren't I a girl now?' asked Rachel diffidently. 'You oughtn't to be a girl in that way till you're sixteen,' said Adela firmly.

Rachel had one terrible dream about the Jungle and woke up shivering. It was something to do with a dead body, a girl's arm coming out from under the bushes. She tried to put the Jungle out of her mind; she never thought of it, but a few nights afterwards she was back there again, this time with some shadowy person always a little behind her who turned out to be Elise. When they came to the bush which in the first dream had covered the arm she was trying to tell Elise about it, to make sure it *had*

been a dream, then stopped, because she knew she had committed
that murder herself. She wanted to run away, but Elise came up
beside her and took her arm with a great deal of affection. Rachel
woke up in a gush of feeling, one of those obstinate dream-taps
that won't be turned off, that swamp one's whole morning,
sometimes one's day. She found a letter from Elise on the
breakfast-table.

Elise wrote a terrible letter, full of horses and brothers. So much
that might have been felt about the New Forest did not seem to
have occurred to her. Rachel was more than discouraged, she felt
blank about next term. It was impossible to have a feeling for
anyone who did so much and thought nothing. She slipped the
letter under her plate and didn't intend to answer it, but later on
she went upstairs and wrote Elise a letter about tennis parties.
'There has been talk,' she wrote, 'of my going to boy and girl
dances, but I do not feel keen on them yet.'

'Who is your great friend now?' asked Mother, who had come
in and found her writing. She put on an anxious expression whenever she spoke like this, because Rachel was a Growing Daughter.

'Oh, no one,' said Rachel. 'I'm just dashing off something to
one of the girls.'

'There was Charity. What about Charity? Don't you ever write
to her now?'

'Oh, I like her all right,' said Rachel, who had a strong sense
of propriety in these matters. 'I just think she's a bit affected.' While
she spoke she was wondering whether Elise would get her remove
or not. Rachel was going up into IVA. It would be impossible to
know anybody two forms below.

Next term, when they all came back, she found Elise had
arrived in IVB (one supposed on the strength of her French),
but she was being tried for the Gym Eight and spent most of
her spare time practising for it. Rachel looked in at the Gym
door once or twice and saw her doing things on the apparatus.
When she wasn't doing things on the apparatus Elise went about
with the same rather dull girl, Joyce Fellows, she'd been going
about with last term. They sat together and walked together and
wrestled in the boot-room on Saturday afternoons. Whenever
Rachel saw Elise looking at her or coming towards her she

would look in the other direction or walk away. She realized how the holidays had been drained away by imagination, she had scarcely lived them; they had been wasted. She had a useless, hopeless dull feeling and believed herself to be homesick. By the end of the first fortnight of term she and Elise had scarcely spoken. She had not been back again to the Jungle, of whose very existence she somehow felt ashamed.

One Sunday, between breakfast and chapel, they brushed against each other going out through a door.

'Hullo!' said Elise.

'Oh – hullo!'

'Coming out?'

'Oh – right-o,' said Rachel, indifferent.

'Anywhere special? I know of a tree with three apples they've forgotten to pick. We might go round that way and just see—'

'Yes, we might,' agreed Rachel. They went arm in arm.

It was early October, the day smelt of potting-sheds and scaly wet tree-trunks. They had woken to find a mist like a sea round the house; now that was being drawn up and the sun came wavering through it. The white garden-gate was pale gold and the leaves of the hedges twinkled. The mist was still clinging in sticky shreds, cobwebs, to the box-hedges, the yellow leaves on the espaliers, the lolling staggering clumps of Michaelmas daisies; like shreds of rag, Rachel thought, clinging to brambles.

Elise's apple tree was halfway down the kitchen-garden. They looked up: one of the apples was missing. Either it had fallen or some interfering idiot had succeeded in getting it down with a stone. The two others, beautifully bronze, nestled snugly into a clump of leaves about eight feet up. The girls looked round; the kitchen-garden was empty.

'One could chuck things at them,' said Rachel, 'if one didn't make too much row.'

'I bet I could swing myself up,' said Elise confidently. She stepped back, took a short run; jumped and gripped a branch overhead. She began to swing with her legs together, kicking the air with her toes. Every time she went higher; soon she would get her legs over that other branch, sit there, scramble up into standing position and be able to reach the apples.

'How gymnastic we are!' said Rachel with the sarcastic admiration which was *de rigueur*. Elise half-laughed, she hadn't a breath to spare. She stuck out her underlip, measured the branch with her eye. Her Sunday frock flew back in a wisp from her waist; she wore tight black stockinette bloomers.

'– *Elise*' shrieked a voice from the gate. 'Rachel *Ritchie*! Leave that tree alone – what are you doing?'

'Nothing, Miss Smyke,' shouted Rachel, aggrieved.

'Well, don't,' said the voice, mollified. 'And don't potter! Chapel's in forty minutes – don't get your feet wet.'

Elise had stopped swinging, she hung rigid a moment, then dropped with bent knees apart. 'Damn!' she said naturally. Rachel said 'dash' herself, sometimes 'confound'. She knew people who said 'confound' quite often, but she had never had a friend of her own who said 'Damn' before. 'Don't be profane,' she said, laughing excitedly.

Elise stood ruefully brushing the moss from her hands 'Damn's not profane,' she said. 'I mean, it's nothing to do with God.' She took Rachel's arm again, they strolled towards the end of the kitchen-garden. 'Are you getting confirmed next term?'

'I think I am. Are you?'

'I suppose I am. Religion's very much *in* our family, you see. We were Huguenots.'

'Oh, I always wondered. Is that why you're called—'

'– Elise? Yes, it's in our family. Don't you like it?'

'Oh, I *like* it . . . But I don't think it suits you. It's such a silky delicate kind of a girlish name. You, you're too—' She broke off; there were people you couldn't talk to about themselves without a confused, excited, rather flustered feeling. Some personalities felt so much more personal. 'You ought to have some rather quick hard name. Jean or Pamela . . . or perhaps Margaret – *not* Marguerite.'

Elise was not listening. 'I ought to have been a boy,' she said in a matter-of-fact, convinced voice. She rolled a sleeve back. 'Feel my muscle! Watch it – look!'

'I say, Elise. I know of a rather queer place. It's near here, I discovered it. I call it the Jungle, just to distinguish it from other places. I don't mean it's a bit exciting or anything,' she said rapidly, 'it's probably rather dirty; tramps come there. But it is rather what

I used to call "secret".' She was kicking a potato down the path before her, and she laughed as she spoke. Lately she had avoided the word 'secret'. Once, at the end of a visit, she had shown a friend called Charity a 'secret place' in their garden at home, and Charity had laughed to the others about it when they were all back at school.

'Which way?'

'Over the wall – you don't mind getting your legs stung?'

The nettles and docks were rank-smelling and heavy with dew. One was hampered by Sunday clothes; they tucked their skirts inside their bloomers and waded through. 'It's a good thing,' said Rachel, 'we've got black stockings that don't show the wet. Brown are the limit, people can see a high-water mark.' The wet grass in Mr Morden's paddock squashed and twanged, it clung like wet snakes as they ran, cutting their ankles. She pulled up panting in the lane below. 'Sure you're keen?' said Rachel. 'There may be blackberries.'

When they came to the Jungle she pushed in ahead of Elise, parting the brambles recklessly. She didn't mind now if she *did* find a dead cat: it would be almost a relief. She didn't look round to see what Elise was doing or seemed to be thinking. They were down in a hollow, it was mistier here and an early morning silence remained. A robin darted out of a bush ahead of her. It was an even better place than she had remembered; she wished she had come here alone. It was silly to mix up people and thoughts. Here was the place where the dead girl's arm, blue-white, had come out from under the bushes. Here was the place where Elise, in the later dream, had come up and touched her so queerly. Here were the rags of her first visit still clinging, blacker and limper . . . the same boot—

'Like a nice boot?' she said facetiously.

Elise came up behind her, noisily kicking at one of the tins. 'This is an awfully good place,' she said. 'Wish *I'd* found it.'

'It isn't half bad,' said Rachel, looking about her casually.

'Do you like this sort of thing – coming here?'

'I bring a book,' said Rachel defensively.

'Oh, that would spoil it. I should come here and make camp fires. I should like to come here and go to sleep. Let's come here together one Saturday and do both.'

'I think sleeping's dull,' said Rachel surprised.

'I love it,' exclaimed Elise, hugging herself luxuriously. 'I can go to sleep like a dog. If wet wouldn't show too much on the back of my dress I'd lie down and go to sleep here now.'

'My dear – how *extraordinary*!'

'Is it?' said Elise, indifferent. 'Then I suppose I'm an extraordinary person.' She had stopped in front of a bush; there were a few blackberries, not very good ones; just like a compact, thick boy in her black tights she was sprawling over the great pouffe of brambles, standing on one foot, balancing herself with the other, reaching out in all directions. But for that way she had of sometimes looking towards one, blank with an inside thoughtfulness, one couldn't believe she had a life of her own apart from her arms and legs. Rachel angrily doubted it; she crouched beside the bush and began eating ripe and unripe blackberries indiscriminately and quickly. 'I am a very ordinary person,' she said aggressively, to see what would come of it. She wondered if Elise had a notion what she was really like.

'No, you're not,' said Elise, 'you're probably clever. How old are you?'

'I was fifteen in August. How old—'

'I shall be fifteen in March. Still, it's awful to think you're a whole form cleverer than I am.'

'I'm not clever,' said Rachel quickly.

Elise laughed. 'One queer thing,' she said, 'about being clever is that clever people are ashamed of it . . . Look what worms some of these brains here are – I say, if I eat any more of them I shall be sick. They're not a bit nice really, they're all seed, but I never can help eating things, can you?'

'Never,' said Rachel. 'At home I often used to eat three helpings – I mean of things like *éclairs* or pheasant or treacle tart – our cook makes it awfully well. I don't now that I have started staying up to late dinner. That makes an awful difference to what one eats in a day, helpings apart.'

'I'd never eat three helpings because of my muscles. I mean to keep awfully strong, not get flabby like women do. I know all the things men don't eat when they're in training. Do you?'

'No. Do you stay up to late dinner?'

'We don't have late dinner,' said Elise scornfully. 'We have supper and I've stayed up to that ever since I was eight.'

Elise's people must be very eccentric.

They were seen coming breathless across the garden twenty minutes late for chapel and found Miss Smyke at the door with a flaming sword. 'What did I say?' asked Miss Smyke, rhetorical. 'What did I *tell* you? It's no use going into chapel now,' she said spitefully (as though they would want to). 'They're at the Te Deum. Go up and change your stockings and stay in your dormitories till you're sent for.' She turned and went back into chapel, looking satisfied and religious.

Being punished together was intimate; they felt welded. They were punished more severely than usual because of Elise, who had a certain way with her under-lip . . . She had a way with her head, too, that reminded Rachel of a defiant heroic person about to be shot. It didn't come out, mercifully, that they had broken bounds; the Jungle remained unmenaced. They were ordered apart for the rest of the day (which sealed them as 'great friends') and Rachel, usually humiliated by punishment, went about feeling clever and daring. On Monday evening she kept a place beside her for Elise at supper, but after some time saw Elise come in arm in arm with Joyce Fellows and sit down at another table. She looked away. After supper Elise said, 'I say, why didn't you come? Joyce and I were keeping a place for you.'

Term went on, and it was all rather difficult and interesting. Rachel was a snob; she liked her friends to be rather distinguished, she didn't like being 'ordered about' by a girl in a lower form. That was what it amounted to; Elise never took much trouble about one, her downright manner was peremptory: when she said, 'Let's—' it meant (and sounded like), 'You can if you like: *I'm* going to.' Whenever they did things together it ended in trouble; Rachel began to wish Elise wouldn't stick out her lip at people like Casabianca and look down her nose. Mistresses spoke scornfully about 'Going about with the younger ones'. They never asked her to 'influence' Elise, which showed that they knew. IVB seemed a long way down the school, yet Elise would swagger ahead of one along passages and throw back, without even looking: 'Buck up:

do come on!' Then there was Joyce Fellows; a silly, blank-faced, rather unhappy 'entourage'.

One evening in prep Charity did a drawing on a page of her notebook, tore it out and passed it across to Rachel. It was called 'Jacob (Rachel's Rajah)', and was a picture of Elise in trousers hanging upside down from a beam in the gym roof and saying, in a balloon from her mouth, 'Buck up, come here, I'm waiting.' Rachel couldn't climb ropes and hadn't a good head when she did get to the top of things, so this was unkind. The name was stupid but the drawing was rather clever. Rachel showed it to Elise at supper and Elise turned scarlet and said, 'What a darned silly fool!' She hadn't much sense of humour about herself.

The next evening there was a drawing of a figure like two tennis balls lying on Charity's desk. (Charity's figure was beginning to develop feminine curves at an alarming rate.) Charity looked, laughed and picked the drawing up with the very tips of her finger and thumb. 'Of course I don't *mind* this,' she said, 'but I suppose you know your beastly little common friend has no business in our form-room?'

Rachel's cheeks burnt. It wouldn't have mattered a bit if the drawing had been clever, but Elise couldn't draw for toffee: it was just silly and vulgar. 'I don't know why you should think it was you,' she said, 'but if the cap fits—'

Later she rounded on Elise. 'If you did want to score off Charity you might have invented a cleverer way.'

'*I* don't pretend to be clever,' said Elise.

'I'd never have shown you the Jacob one if I'd thought you were going to be such a silly serious ass,' stormed Rachel.

Elise stared with her wide-open pale grey eyes that had, this moment, something alert behind them that wasn't her brain. 'You knew that wouldn't be my idea of a funny joke,' she said, 'didn't you?'

Rachel hesitated. Elise, with tight lips, made a scornful little laughing sound in her nose.

'As a matter of fact,' said Rachel, 'I didn't think it mattered showing you what all my friends in my form think. You know you have got into a fearfully bossy way with everybody.'

'I don't know what you're talking about,' said Elise. 'I don't s'pose you do either. What do you mean by "everybody"? I never take any notice of anybody unless I happen to like them, and if they think I'm bossy I can't help it. It's not me who's bossy, but other people who are sloppy?'

'Do you think I'm sloppy?'

'Yes, you are rather sloppy sometimes.'

It was at supper, a dreadful place to begin a conversation of this sort. Rachel and Elise had to remain side by side, staring at the plates of the girls opposite, biting off and slowly masticating large mouthfuls of bread-and-jam. Then Rachel half-choked over a mouthful, turned away quickly and flung herself into the conversation of two girls on the other side. They all three talked 'shop' about algebra prep. Elise just sat on there, perfectly natural and disconcertingly close. When Rachel peeped round she did not notice. She sat badly, as always, her head hunched forward between her shoulders, and Rachel knew her lip was out and had a feeling that she was smiling. When grace was over they pushed back their chairs and bolted out in different directions. Out in the hall everybody was crowding up to the noticeboard. Rachel turned away and went into the classroom and sat at her desk. When the others had gone she came out and looked at the noticeboard. The lists for the next match were up and Elise was in the Lacrosse Eleven.

The last Sunday but one, in the afternoon, Rachel went back to the Jungle. It was December, goldenly fine; the trees were pink in the afternoon light, rooks circled, grass was crisp in the shadows from last night's frost. She had started out in an overcoat with a muffler up to her nose and rabbit-skin gloves, but soon she untwisted the muffler and stuffed the gloves into her pocket. The lovely thin air seemed to have turned warmer; her breath went lightly and clearly away through it. The wall, the hedge, the gate of the paddock gave her a bruised feeling.

She stumbled across the paddock, tripping up on the long ends of her muffler, with her unbuttoned overcoat flapping against her legs. 'It will be a good end to this kind of a term,' she thought. 'If Mr Morden catches me.'

It really hadn't been much of a term. She hadn't worked, she hadn't been a success at anything, she hadn't made anyone like her.

The others in IVA had been nice to her since she 'came back', but they forgot her unintentionally; they had got into the way of doing things together in twos and threes since the beginning of term and she got left out – naturally. She felt lonely, aimless, absolutely inferior; she tried a lot of new ways of doing her hair, designed a black velvet dress for herself and looked forward to going home. She brought names, Charity's and the other girls', rather unnaturally into her letters so that Mother shouldn't suspect she was being a failure. She felt so sick for Elise that she prayed to be hit by a ball on the head every time she went out to Lacrosse.

Elise had the most wonderfully natural way of not seeing one. She said 'Sorry' when she bumped into one in the passage, shared a hymn-book in chapel when they found themselves side by side, and when she caught up and passed one going out to the playing-field side-glanced indifferently as though one were one of the seniors. She had got her colours after her third match; no one under fifteen had ever got their colours before. All the important people were taking her up and talking about her. IVA agreed that they would not have minded, they'd have been glad, if she'd only been humble and nice to begin with and not such an absolutely complacent pig. They never talked about her in front of Rachel and Rachel never mentioned her.

Down in the lane there were deep ruts; she walked between them on crumbling ridges. A dog was barking somewhere at Mr Morden's, snapping bits out of the silence, then letting it heal again. The bank to the Jungle was worn slippery; Rachel pulled herself up it from root to root. The Jungle was in shadow; the grass had fallen like uncombed hair into tufts and was lightly frosted. 'It's nice to come back,' said Rachel. 'I never was really *here* that last time, it's awfully nice to come back.' She bent down, parting the brambles; the leaves were purple and blackish; some rotting brown leaves drifted off at her touch.

Coming out from the brambles, an arm was stretched over the path. 'Not, O God, in this lonely place,' said Rachel – 'let there not be a body!'

She was shaken by something regularly, put up a hand to her heart with the conscious theatrical movement of extreme fear and found it thumping. The hand lay a yard ahead of her – she could

have taken three steps forward and stepped on it – the thumb bent,
the red, square-tipped fingers curling on to the palm.

'Elise, is this you?' whispered Rachel. She waited, plucking leaves
from the bramble, hearing the dog bark, then went round to where
Elise was lying in a valley between the brambles.

Elise lay half on her side, leaning towards the arm that was flung
out. Her knees were drawn up, her other arm flung back under
her head which rested, cheek down, on a pile of dead leaves as on
a pillow and was wrapped up in a muffler. The muffler was slipping
away from her face like a cowl. Down in the sheltered air between
the bushes she was flushed by sleep and by the warmth of the
muffler. She was Elise, but quenched, wiped-away, different; her
mouth – generally pressed out straight in a grudging smile – slack-
ened into a pout; thick short lashes Rachel had never noticed
spread out on her cheeks. Rachel had never looked full at her
without having to pass like a guard her direct look; her face now
seemed defenceless. Rachel stood looking down – the only beautiful
thing about Elise was the cleft in her chin. She stood till her legs
ached, then shifted her balance. A twig cracked; Elise opened her
eyes and looked up.

'I told you I'd come here and sleep,' she said.

'Yes – isn't it fearfully cold?'

Elise poked up her head, looked round and lay back again,
stretching luxuriously. 'No,' she said, 'I feel stuffyish. Have you just
come?'

'Yes. I'm going away again.'

'Don't go.' Elise curled up her legs to make room in the valley.
'Sit down.'

Rachel sat down.

'Funny thing your just coming here. Have you come much?'

'No,' said Rachel, staring into the brambles intently as though
she were watching something that had a lair inside them moving
about.

'I brought Joyce Fellows once; we came in here to smoke cigars.
I hate smoking – Joyce was as sick as a cat.'

'How *beastly*!'

'Oh, I don't suppose there's anything left now, we covered it
up. Anyhow, I shall never smoke much. It's so bad for the wind.'

'Oh, by the way,' said Rachel, 'congratulations about your colours.'

Elise, her hands clasped under her head, had been lying looking at the sky. 'Thanks so much,' she said, now looking at Rachel.

'Aren't we mad,' said Rachel uneasily, 'doing this in December?'

'Why shouldn't we if we're warm enough? Rachel, why shouldn't we? – Answer.'

'It'll be dark soon.'

'Oh, dark in your eye!' said Elise, 'there's plenty of time . . . I say, Rachel, I tell you a thing we might do—'

Rachel wound herself up in her muffler by way of a protest. She had a funny feeling, a dancing-about of the thoughts; she would do anything, anything. ''Pends what,' she said guardedly.

'You could turn round and round till you're really comfy, then I could turn round and put my head on your knee, then I could go to sleep again . . .'

The round cropped head like a boy's was resting on Rachel's knees. She felt all constrained and queer; comfort was out of the question. Elise laughed once or twice, drew her knees up higher, slipped a hand under her cheek where the frieze of the overcoat tickled it.

'All right?' said Rachel, leaning over her.

'Mm – *mmm*.'

The dog had stopped barking, the Jungle, settling down into silence, contracted a little round them, then stretched to a great deep ring of unrealness and loneliness. It was as if they were alone on a ship, drifting out . . .

'Elise,' whispered Rachel, 'do you think we—'

But the head on her knees had grown heavy. Elise was asleep.

The Dancing-Mistress

About half-past three at the end of November a sea-fog came up over the edge of the cliff and, mounting the plate-glass windows, filled the Metropole ballroom with premature twilight. The fantastic trees in the garden sank in like a painting on blotting-paper; the red roofs of surrounding houses persisted an hour in ever-ghostlier violet and faded at last. Below the gold ceiling the three chandeliers draped in crystal flowered reluctantly into a thin batch of lights: the empty floor of the ballroom was pointed with yellow reflections.

The door of the ladies' cloakroom kept creaking and swinging, gusts of chatter came out from the little girls being unpeeled from their wraps. Inside was a shuffle of feet on the muffling carpet, water gushing in basins, a clatter of ivory brush-backs on marble slabs. The mothers and governesses wanted elbow-room for their business with combs, for the retying of sashes and tugging of woolly gaiters from silk-clad legs. With their charges, they overflowed into the corridor. Here, all along, it was chilly and rustling with muslins; Shetlands and cardigans were flung over the radiators; little girls sat in rows on the floor to put on their dancing-sandals. Miss James, the dancing-mistress, hurrying past in her fur coat with her dispatch-case, with her frail forward slant like a reed in the current, was obliged to pick her way over their legs. This she did with stereo-typed little weary amused exclamations: her pianist followed in silence, a sharper, more saturnine profile against the brocaded wallpaper.

Miss James and the pianist went into the ballroom, where they opened their dispatch-cases behind the piano and, holding the mirror for one another, dusted over their faces with large soft puffs. The pianist moistened the tips of her fingers to flatten her hair back; it was polished against her skull like a man's. Miss James took the mirror and, biting her lip, glanced once more at herself in the oval with a slanting, fleeting, troubled kind of reproach.

The pianist looked up at the chandeliers, then scornfully out at the mist. 'I'm so glad we've got back to artificial – it seems much more natural, I think. – I say *sure* you don't feel too rotten?'

'Not as rotten as all that, I suppose,' said Miss James, indifferent. She had taken two classes already today; before the second she had declared a headache.

Miss Joyce James had begun as a pupil of Madame Majowski's; she worked for her now. Six days a week she went all over the country giving lessons; in the mornings she got up early to perfect her dancing at Mme Majowski's studio. She had eight dancing dresses like clouds, in gradations of beauty, a black satin tunic for studio practice, and besides these and the fur coat to cover them nothing at all but a cloth coat-and-skirt that looked wrong in the country and shabby in town. She was twenty-one, pretty but brittle and wax-like from steam-heated air. All day long she was just an appearance, a rhythm; in studio or ballroom she expanded into delicate shapes like a Japanese 'mystery' flower dropped into water. Late at night, she stopped '*seeming*' too tired to 'be'; too tired to eat or to speak; she would finish long journeys asleep with her head on the pianist's shoulder: her sister received her with Bovril and put her to bed. Her eyebrows tilted outwards like wings; over her delicate cheekbones looked out, slightly tilted, her dreamy and cold eyes in which personality never awakened.

Miss James and Miss Peel the pianist sat for some minutes more in the window-embrasure behind the piano, side to side in jaded intimacy like a couple of monkeys. There was a radiator beside them. Miss Peel, having shivered out of her coat, kept spreading out her hands to the radiator, chafing them gently together, then spreading them out again, drawing in a reserve of warmth through the hands for her whole body. Her thin shoulder blades rippled the silk of her dress as she bent forward. Miss James kept her eyes on the door, watching the children in, vacantly counting. As each came in its name jumped back to her memory as though a ticket had clicked up over its head. Though her mind was blank of this party of children from Wednesday to Wednesday, she never hesitated or was confused between the Joans and Jeans, the Margerys or the Mollies.

The little girls swung themselves in through the glass doors in

twos and threes and skidded over the floor. The mothers and governesses sat down in groups round the walls with a resigned look of
un-expectation. Their murmuring made a fringe round the silence,
they nodded across at each other. The ballroom was gaunt in the
vague smoky daylight, like a large church.

Three minutes before the class was due to begin, the hotel
secretary appeared in the doorway, looking towards the piano. Miss
Peel was sorting her music; she paused for a moment. 'There's
Lulu,' she murmured.

'I know,' said Miss James.

Lulu, Romano-Swiss, fervent and graceful, looked away from
them guiltily, looked round the room officially, switched on a dozen
more lights. Miss James picked up a valse and frowned at it. She
sighed, she was so tired. Two more little girls squeezed in past the
secretary's elbow. The door swung to with a sigh.

'He's gone,' said Miss Peel and went back to her music.

'I know,' said Miss James.

A quarter to four. They both glanced at their wristwatches,
sighed and admitted the hour. The dancing-mistress came round
the piano, the pianist sat down in front of 'Marche Militaire', shook
back a slave-bangle up either arm, and waited, her eyes on Miss
James who stood at the top of the room and looked down steadily
into a looking-glass at the bottom.

'Good afternoon!' she said, silvery. The little girls ran forward,
shaking out their dresses. 'Fall in for the March! Grizelda leading
. . . Skirts out, right foot pointed . . . GO! . . . *Right*, left – right
– right – right – Heads *well* up – *that's* right! . . . Skirt, Phyllis . . .
Toes, Jean! . . . Oh, *toes*, Margery – Margery, what *are* you doing
. . . *to-o-o-es!*'

Miss Peel spanked out the 'Marche Militaire'. Grizelda, impec-
cable, head erect, face blank, toes pointed quiveringly, led the
twenty-five twice round the room and up the centre. Then they
divided, ones right, twos left, met again, came up in twos, in fours,
and then spaced out for the exercises. That was that.

The five positions: they performed like compasses. First . . .
second . . . third . . . fourth . . . fifth! For each a chord, a shock of
sound tingling out into silence. The dancing-mistress kept them in
the fifth position and melted down between the lines to look.

Margery Mannering never did anything right. Her week was darkened by these Wednesdays. She was perfectly certain Miss James hated her — Miss James did. She was an overdressed little girl who belonged to a grandmother. She had red sausage-curls tied up with lop-eared white bows and spectacles that misted over, blinding her, when she got hot. She stood crooked forward anxiously. A coldness fingered its way down her spine as Miss James came softly to her down the room in her blue dress that fell into points like a hyacinth-bell and fluted out.

'Now, Margery . . . Margery Mannering. What are you doing *now*?'

They looked hard at each other; all the rest waited. Margery thought, 'She'd like to kill me.' Miss James thought, 'I would like to kill her — just once.' Her face had a hard wistfulness. 'Just *think*,' she gently invited. The girls in front turned round. Margery looked at her feet. Just feet, they were, like other people's; boat-like in dancing-sandals. Oh, she had taken the *third* position!

'Yes,' said Miss James and nodded. 'Now do you see? . . . Now you can take those positions again by yourself. — Music, please — Go!' The chords clanged vindictively, like choppers falling. '*Now* do you see?'

Margery had pretty-child affectations that sat forlornly upon her. Now she flung back her hard curls; they bounced on her back. She peered up through misted spectacles like a plump small animal in the bite of a trap — like a rat, perhaps, that no one decently pities.

'Yes, Miss James.'

'Then please remember,' said Miss James, and walked away. The unrealized self in her made itself felt, disturbing her calm with a little shudder of pleasure. A delicate pink touched her cheekbones, she thought of Lulu, she was almost a woman.

Next the springing exercises, so graceful, from which the few little boys were excluded. Rows and rows of little girls kicking the air pointedly, showing the frills on their underclothes, waving their bent arms and fluttering fingers apart and together, tossing their heads. There were gleaning movements, throwing and catching movements, movements that should have scattered roses about the room. Miss Peel played 'Oh where, and oh where, has my little dog gone!' with a kind of saturnine prance.

Grizelda and Lois and Cynthia, Jean Jones and Doris excelled at varying movements; they were set to dance by themselves, to show the others. When someone was dancing alone as a glory the music was different, Margery Mannering thought; the choppers became curling feathers, fluttering in towards one and waving out.

The skipping began and finished; they passed the exercises with ribbons and Indian clubs. The fancy dances began. Little Cynthia was Spain itself in the Spanish dance; the grown-ups sighed at her, she was so sweet. Miss James told her that *next* Wednesday she could come, if she liked, with some castanets. Grizelda and Doris were best in the Irish Jig; so saucy, quite Irishly saucy. The Gavotte made two more couples illustrious; they were given the floor to themselves. 'If one could only teach you to curtsey,' Miss James sighed. If she could only, only teach them to curtsey. They went down on themselves all skewered; feet got lost behind them; knees stuck out in front.

'Just *look*, children: watch me' . . . But they all stood round sceptical; they knew they would never be able to curtsey like that. She sank with bowed head; with arms curved before her she melted into the floor. She flowed down into it and; flowing up again, stood. 'If I had a dress like that . . .' Doris thought. 'She's not like a person at all,' thought Jean Jones.

The hotel secretary stood looking in through the glass door. His eyes came a little nearer together, his face was intent. Miss Peel played a slow ripple; in her mind Miss James was curtseying.

After the fancy dancing there was an interval. The little girls flocked and slid to the chairs round the wall. Margery Mannering went back and sat by her grandmother's maid, who was knitting a bedsock. 'Got into trouble again, I see,' said the grandmother's maid and wetted her thin lips. 'You did ought to have practised that Spanish dance.' 'You mind your own business,' said Margery, who was rude to servants. She slid along three empty chairs and sat by herself. She watched Miss James go round the room, congratulating the mothers of little girls who had been dancing nicely. Governesses she did not congratulate; she was too tired.

Cynthia sat with her mother just beyond Margery Mannering; they were holding each other's hands excitedly and talking about castanets. Cynthia never seemed bare of being loved, it was round

her at school, everywhere, like a sheath. Miss James came round
to them, smiling. Margery watched, her head well back on her
thick neck, playing with one of her ringlets, and Miss James felt
something catch at her, going by. She had again that shudder of
life in her; a quick light came into her eyes. 'Don't kick that chair,'
she said, put on her smile again and went on.

Miss Peel was back at the radiator. 'How d'you feel?' she said.
'Must you go round all those hags? Are you bad?'

'I suppose I'll get through . . . Did you hear me killing that
Mannering child?'

'Which one?'

'Oh, you *know*. The red one.' She laughed a little and sat stroking
one of her arms. 'She makes me feel awful . . . I – I don't know
how it is.'

'Has she got anyone with her?'

'Only a maid.'

'Perhaps she'll die,' said Miss Peel brightly, and ran her eye over
a foxtrot.

'Oh, she couldn't,' said Miss James, startled. She couldn't do
without Margery Mannering; she wanted to kill her. She got up
and said: 'Now all take your partners for the waltz.'

'Lulu's been back,' said Miss Peel hurriedly. 'When are you going
to see him?' Miss James shrugged her shoulders and walked off.
The music began.

By this time the fog had been stained to solid darkness; the
windows were slabs of night. The chandeliers were in full flower.
Children went round and round, smoothly spinning; the tall
looking-glass at the end of the room doubled them into a crowd;
they were doubled again on the outside darkness. She could not
think why nobody came to draw the curtains. When she felt him
again at the door, looking in at her with that straight level look
of desire, she went towards him, pulled open the door, and said,
'Do please draw the curtains. The room looks so ugly; the mothers
don't like it. People can see in.'

'You will give up your train, just once, just tonight?' he said.
'Yes?'

'No, I can't, I'm tired; I've got a headache. Besides, you know
Peelie's here; she wouldn't go home alone.'

He skirted the floor and went round to the three windows, touching a cord somewhere so that the curtains trembling with movement slid over them noiselessly. Returning, he brushed Miss Peel's back as she played. 'I want her tonight,' he said over her shoulder. 'We all three have supper together – Yes? I put you both into the 8.40. Yes? Dear Peelie, yes?'

She nodded, in time with the music.

'Dear Peelie – *good*!'

She wriggled her shoulders, he hurried away.

'All arranged,' he said joyously. 'I get a taxi immediately. We all three had supper together down by the Pier.'

'Go away,' Joyce James whispered. 'You're dreadful; you'll ruin me – *One* two three, *one* two three. *Time*, Jean and Betty, time, time! What are you doing! – Mollie, don't talk while you're dancing! Margery Bates, remember you're a gentleman; what does a gentleman do with his hands? . . . *Toes*, Margery Mannering: *why* don't you *dance* on your *toes*?'

Lulu saw something wrong at the end of the room; the chairs were pushed crooked; he went to arrange them. Again he brushed past her. 'Till then, I keep watching. You are so beautiful. I would give my soul, my body, all that I have . . .'

She walked away, clapping her hands together – '*One* two three, *one* two three,' watching the couples go round. Then she suddenly cried to the music, to all the children: 'STOP!'

Of course it was Margery Mannering. She did not know how to waltz; she went bumping and hopping round on the flat of her feet, with her partner all limp. Miss James went over in silence and took her partner away.

'I shall have to take you myself. – All you others sit down for a moment. – We shall go on till I've taught you. And will you please *try*, Margery. You see you are wasting everyone else's time – Music, please!'

All alone on the empty floor, Miss James waltzed with Margery Mannering. They did not speak; they heard one another's breathing; the girl's light, the child's loud and painful. The thump of Margery's heart was like the swelling and bursting of great black bubbles inside her: now the bubbles were in her throat. Her hot body sagged on Miss James's cold bare arm. Her eyes, stretched with physical fear like a rabbit's, stared through the clouding spectacles at the mild white hollow of Miss James's throat. From her spectacles, light flashed up sharply into her partner's face as they circled under the chandeliers. Miss James's hand like a cold shell gripped the hot hand tighter.

'She really is patient and good,' said the mothers, nodding. 'She's so thorough.' They congratulated themselves. 'Look at the pains she takes with that poor little stupid. Wonderful; she keeps smiling.'

And indeed, she was smiling. Lulu watched through the door; his eyes got larger and darker and closer together, his face came closer up to the glass. Miss Peel played on mechanically; she watched him watching.

'I'm giddy,' said Margery suddenly.

'It's no good. I shall keep you on till you've learnt.'

In the taxi, the girls leant back silently. Lulu, his back to the driver, sat watching the town lights flash over their faces. The fog was lifting, but the taxi went slowly through spectral streets like a blind snorting animal. Sometimes the driver pulled up with a jar; the girls nodded forward, the window-frames rattled. Joyce's close-fitting hat was pulled over her eyebrows; her half-hidden face was impassive. Peelie sat with her hat on her knees, she looked over Lulu's head, sombrely humming. Joyce rolled her head with a sigh and an impatient movement; Peelie and Lulu both reached for the window-strap; Lulu was first there and let down the window. Mist came curling in, the air freshened; the taxi had turned down through the old town and the lonely crying of sirens came from the harbour. 'They're awful,' Joyce shuddered.

'She is tired,' said Peelie to Lulu across her.

'She will be better after supper.'

'She won't eat,' said Peelie, discouraging.

'Won't you eat dinner?' said Lulu, imploring. He touched Joyce's knee, left a hand there. Peelie eyed the hand sharply. Joyce took no notice. Peelie's foot felt a gentle pressure. 'That's my foot.' 'Oh, so sorry, Peelie.' The taxi crawled past a terrace of balconied houses and sharply drew up.

The 'Star' Private Hotel was modest and friendly. It was six o'clock; they went in and sat in the lounge. Peelie was pleased at

Lulu's discretion; *here* they would meet no one who'd recognize Lulu and Joyce and go away talking to make scandal about the Metropole dancing class. It did not do for Lulu, who showed ladies into their bedrooms, or Joyce who spent hours in clumsy men's arms, to be patently man and woman; their public must deprecate any attraction. Poor Lulu was also distressingly beautiful; the shabby other visitors kept turning round to look – at the grace of his height, his dark-ivory forehead (foreign men do so much more with a forehead), the ripple-back of his hair, his gaze of shy ardency Joyceward, narrowed by low straight lids. He went off to order the supper – just supper, they said, fish or something, with coffee to follow. Peelie shook Joyce's arm suddenly.

'Do wake up,' she said. 'Can't you really love anyone?'

'I didn't want to – you brought me . . . Well then, give me my powder-puff.'

'You've got heaps on – it's colour you want. Haven't you got—'

'No, you know I don't have any; Majowski hates it.'

'You may be thankful Lulu's Swiss. He wouldn't let you just sit there yawning if he were an Italian.'

'No. He's going to keep an hotel – isn't it awful. With two private funiculars. On the top of a glacier or something. Oh well, *he* won't melt any glaciers!' Joyce changed a yawn to a laugh; she laughed weakly, ruefully, almost in spite of herself, biting in her mouth at one corner and shrugging her slight shoulders.

'What are you laughing for?' said Lulu, coming back. They did not answer; he showed them into the dining-room. The room was empty, not a waitress there. He guided them to their table with an arm lightly round Joyce's waist; as he pulled her chair out she had to step back closer against him. Peelie's hard unabashed eyes contemplated them curiously. Each conscious of the two others they waited, then something in Peelie's eyes made it impossible, shameful for him not to press Joyce closer and kiss her twice on the cheek, high up, where the patch of colour sometimes appeared. Peelie laughed, Joyce laughed uncertainly, Lulu uneasily smiled: they sat down. Joyce unfastened her coat and let it slide down her shoulders, showing her neck and the soft rucked top of the hyacinth dress. Her eyes glittered under the hanging lights with their cold white shades.

'Did you see me killing that child?' she asked Lulu, eagerly turning. 'You were there at the door, you must have seen. Wasn't I dreadful – Peelie thinks I was dreadful.'

'Which child?' he said, while his eyes asked doubtfully, 'Who's there? What's there? *Are* you, at all? I want you.'

'Tell him, Peelie.'

'That fat Mannering child with red hair, she means. I only said: "Don't hate her so's the others can notice."'

'But I do hate her, don't I? Isn't it awful of me. I made her waltz till she cried. But I did teach her.'

Peelie eyed her exaltedness. 'She's quite awake now,' she said, congratulatory, to Lulu. 'I dare say she's quite hungry.' But soon the film crept back, Joyce faded like the roofs into this afternoon's mist; she let her hand lie coldly in Lulu's under the table. As Jean Jones had thought, she was not like a person at all.

When supper was finished they strolled back towards the harbour to look for a taxi. The salt air was milder, lamps made pale stains on the mist. It was high tide; under the mist, to their left, the dark, polished water sucked hard-lipped at the embankment. The edge of the road was protected by chains slung from posts; Peelie went to look over, stood idly clanking and swinging the chain with her knee.

'I wonder what you two would do next if I fell in and never bobbed up again.'

'Oh, *Peelie!*'

'Well, I won't – not *this* woman. All the same, I do wonder . . .'

Her meditation, tinged with contempt for them, broke up sharply when, hearing no more behind her, she turned to see where they were. Lulu had caught Joyce out of the lamplight . . . He was not so unlike an Italian. They stood as one figure till with a gasp he stepped back from her. Joyce stood vaguely, huddling up her coat-collar and looking round for Peelie. They started towards each other under the lamp. Peelie thought: 'Now what's coming?' but all Joyce said was: 'We must get that taxi. I can't go any further. Oh, Peelie, I'm *dead!*'

It was a long drive from the harbour up to the Central Station. No one spoke. Lulu's hands hung between his parted knees; he kept wringing and chafing his hands together. Joyce slipped deeper, deeper into her great fur collar, a swerve of the taxi flung her on Peelie's shoulder; she did not stir, she leaned there inert, asleep. Peelie slipped an arm along the back of the seat; supporting her; this was how they were going to travel home. Light from a picture-palace blared in, disturbing them like a trumpet-blast, on to the small set face of the sleeper, her hat pushed down unevenly over one eye. Lulu, startled, cried out: 'It's not fair!'

'Hush! . . . Nothing's fair.'

'In six weeks I go back to Switzerland. What does she care? – Nothing. And still you are having her day after day.'

'You and I, you and she, she and I, we'll forget each other anyhow – that's nature.'

'Don't you care?'

'Not so much.'

'Peelie . . .'

'Um?'

'*Peelie* . . . I . . . let me just . . .'

She beckoned. Two or three minutes were taken up by a cautious shuffling, balancing, edging; they rose and changed places like people passing each other in a boat. She sustained Joyce's weight till his arm touched her own, supplanting it, under Joyce's shoulders. Joyce never stirred, never woke; she lay quiet under their movements, their whispers and anxious breathing.

'Don't touch her head, you'll wake her – *don't*, Lulu; just let it roll – I do – it finds its own place. Just keep your arm – so – loosely; keep your hand on her other side so's she won't flop back . . . You'll be as stiff as hell in a few minutes – I am, always. Don't try moving, that's worse; just relax . . .'

Joyce sighed; her sleeping body crept closer against him, her head rolled into the hollow of his shoulder – 'found its own place'. She sighed again with her cheek on his breast; she was comfortable here. Lulu's face came down, scarcely breathing; his chin was just over her little black hat.

Joyce smiled. A new life, the self's, moulded her lips in a soft line. Her face was all broken up, vivid in sleep . . . She was dancing with Margery Mannering. 'I'll kill you, I'll kill you,' she said like a knife. Something burst behind Margery's stretched eyes; she fainted . . . Joyce smiled in her sleep.

The Disinherited

Autumn had set in early. While the days were still glowing, the woods took on from a distance a yellow, unreal sheen, like a reflection from metal; their fretted outlines hardened against the blond open hills that the vibrations of summer no longer disturbed. In the early mornings, dew spread a bright white bloom between long indigo shadows; the afternoon air quickened, but after sunset mists diluted the moon. This first phase of autumn was lovely; decay first made itself felt as an extreme sweetness: with just such a touch of delicious morbidity a lover might contemplate the idea of death.

Later the rain came, and there were drenching monotone days; the leaves, rotting uncoloured, slid down through the rain. Mid autumn set in mild, immobile and nerveless; the days had unclear margins, mists webbed the gardens all day, the sun slanting slowly through them to touch the brown pear trees and pale yellow currant-leaves, here and there a marigold or a sodden rose. There was no wind, and the woods stood heavily tense; against their darkness, in the toneless November evenings, the oaks were still yellow and shed a frightening glare. Everything rotted slowly. The dark, rain-swollen rivers flowed fast between bleaching sedges, with leaves caught on the current. After the rain, an unlit grey sky bound the earth, and pools threaded the grass and lay unglittering inside the brittle reeds. Now and then the skies were disturbed by a high-up swift rustling sigh: the summer birds flying south. The shredded last leaves still clung to the trees, as though they would not fall: eternity seemed to have set in at late autumn. Some way into November, a wind sprang up at nights.

Marianne Harvey was not aware of the autumn to which her friend Davina was becoming a prey. Since August, Marianne had been cheerfully busy, without a moment for any kind of reflection; the Harveys were nesting over again, after twelve years of marriage, making a new home. But all those weeks Davina Archworth had been idle with a melancholy and hollow idleness, with all day to kick the wet leaf-drifts and watch the birds go.

The Harveys had left London and come up to live on the new building estate, in a freshly built white rough-cast house with a touch of priggishness in its architecture. The estate, on a hill dominating from some distance a university city, was exclusive; lots here could only be purchased on the distinct condition that houses of a fixed value were to be put up. You undertook not to keep chickens, put up a frame garage or hang out clothes. Into the tone of this niceness the Harveys easily fell. Few houses had gone up so far; those there were stood apart, like Englishmen not yet acquainted, washed by clear upland air and each in its acre of wiry grass that had lost its nature, being no longer meadow and not yet lawn. Half-made roads, like the first knowing cuts of a scalpel, mapped the flank of the hill out, up to the concrete water-tower upon its crest. No buses approached, and there were and would be no shops.

At the foot of this genteel hill, at the river level, the old village frowsted inside its ring of elm trees, mouldy and snug. Its lichened barn-roofs were yellow, and from the church spire the weathercock now and then shot out one sharp gold ray; from the tower there came up, climbing the hill on Sundays, ponderous chimes. A clot of thin smoke hung melting in watery river light over the roofs of the village; after sunset a few dark lights outlined the three-cornered green. A wide pitch-black by-pass road with white kerbs swept south round the foot of the hill, cutting off the old village from the new building estate. On the far flank of the village the stretching brick-red tentacles of the city made their advance over water-meadows tufted with lines of willow; far off, the brittle city spires pricked at the skyline. The small, shallow river on which the village was built ran into another, grand one: a beetle-green gasometer stood at this point, and there was a steel bridge over which London expresses rumbled and rang. Sometimes a swan, disturbed, sailed up the backwater.

It enraged Davina that the new estate (no affair of her own, as she had not been asked to live there) should not have any shops. Naturally aristocratic, she loathed refinement. She especially liked little shops to be just a minute away from wherever she might be living, shops that are cheesy and mixed and stay open on Sundays, where you buy cigarettes, peppermints, shoelaces, picture papers, sardines, purgative pills and writing compendiums with pictures on the outside. She liked chatting late across counters in the dark lamplight and charming unauthorized people into selling her stamps. She had that kind of restless feeling for Marianne that makes one critical; she therefore despised Marianne's habit of shopping by telephone, which put her, she thought, out of touch with reality. The whole new estate with its rawness, its air at once hygienic and intellectual, revolted Davina. All the same, she was up there constantly, dropping in at all times of the day to see Marianne Harvey. Attraction, propinquity and, on Davina's part, idleness fostered this funny alliance.

Davina had come to live in the old village with and on her aunt – or, strictly, her uncle's widow – Mrs Walsingham Archworth. Her existence was temporary; though she had few prospects she was, or had been till lately, hoping for better times. Her aunt's house had been the manor, and Mrs Archworth, though she had by now disposed of all other property, still looked on herself as patroness of the village. Her house, backed by an ilex and flanked by lines of clipped hollies, had a high, narrow face, with dark inanimate windows, and looked like the frontispiece to a ghost-story. Inside, however, it was kindly, crimson and stuffy. Its front windows looked down a lawn, through wrought-iron gates, on to the village green, where the lime trees shed their leaves early ... Davina could not enjoy living here, on her aunt; mortification and dullness ravaged her. But, at twenty-nine, she had no more money of any kind; she had run through her capital; love-affairs and her other expensive habits had ruined her. To earn was out of the question: she had no idea what to do. In an agony of impatience, she waited about indefinitely. Something that should have occurred – she was not sure what – had not occurred yet, and became every day more unlikely. She remained, angry, immobile, regretting that circumstances over which she had had really, at one time, every control, should have driven her into exploiting her aunt's affection.

This was too easy. In looks as well as in temperament Davina resembled her dead uncle, who, melancholy and dashing, had hung up his hat in this house with a gracious despondent gesture and had been loved to distraction by his dull, pink wife throughout the years of their marriage, in return for which he had given her scarcely a smile. Davina herself had, further, just that touch of the sombre romantic about her that appeals to all other women, even to relatives. She was adored by her aunt, now a puffy, huffy, formal, bewildered, charmless elderly widow. Davina was tall, with a head set strikingly on a dark-ivory neck; her springy dark hair, shortish, was tucked back behind her ears. Her features, well cut, were perhaps rather pronounced, but her sombreness and her unwilling smile could be enchanting. She could command that remarkable immobility possible only to nervously restless people, when only her dark eyes' intent and striking glitter betrayed the tension behind. She moved well, with an independent and colt-like carriage; her manner was, for a young woman's, decided, a shade overbearing, intimidating to lovers whom her appearance beguiled. Had she had sphere, space, ease of mind, she might have been generous, active and even noble; emotion need only have played a small part in her life. She was a woman born to make herself felt.

As things were, hurt pride distorted her memories; an inflamed sense of self isolated her; miscarried projects darkened her whole view. Her thoughts were almost all angry. 'If I had money—' she said again and again. She walked miles a day, clicking her third left-hand finger angrily on her thumb, pacing the fields with a long nervy mannish stride. In this countryside she was a stranger; in the mild academic city she cared to know nobody. Friends, it appeared, had forgotten her. Indoors she smoked, kicked the fire up, tore the plots from crime novels, and switched the wireless scornfully on and off.

Mrs Archworth was sorry to see the hill she had known all her life, and sometimes walked with her husband, cut up for building plots. For several months this had made her huffy, distressed. She had to admit, however, that times were changing, and after some searchings of heart she decided to call on the newcomers. So her heavy Daimler ploughed uphill one afternoon through the mud of the half-made roads, swerving past rubble and bouncing her on the springs. Alas, the new houses were draughty, with sweating plaster, and she returned with a chill: it was unfortunate that she had found anybody at home. Marianne, for her part, had been gratified by Mrs Archworth's visit, for she took her to be county. It was in returning the call that Marianne had met Davina for the first time: she was shown by the parlourmaid into a morning-room dense with smoke and loud with the wireless, from which Davina, glowering, found no way to escape.

Six days after that, on the ridge of the hill by the water-tower, they met again. Marianne, hatless, was exercising two dogs. Her thick honey-fair hair, ruffling away from her forehead, glinted in afternoon sunshine that fell on the unspoilt country beyond the hill. Rivery twists of mist lay along the river below. This was the first phase of autumn, the air agitating and sweet. When Marianne saw Davina she blushed with pleasure and shyness. They walked on the skyline, between the brambles that still gave out a morningish smell of dew: Marianne invited Davina back to her house for tea . . . She was house-proud, and led this new friend with a touch of emotion up the path to the porch, across the ambitious raw garden. Davina, however, looked neither to right nor left: indoors, she did give one glance of surprise rather than pleasure round the Harvey living-room, artfully pale and bare, where through steel-framed windows blue-pink afternoon light flooded the walls and waxy expanse of floor. It all looked to Davina nullish, with, here and there, the stigmata of intellectual good taste. The hearth was bare, but steam heating drew out sweat from the plaster while, to Davina's senses, devitalizing and parching the air. Ranged round the cold brick hearth, three low chairs with sailcloth cushions invited a confidence everything else forbade. A clock ticked, but the room had no pulse.

'My husband's not here,' said Marianne, looking uncertain. Davina simply said, 'Oh.' They sat down to tea.

'I am fifteen years younger than Matthew,' Marianne said later, apropos of something else.

Matthew had lately retired from the Civil Service owing to ill health. However, he felt better now. At the same time his aunt had died, leaving Matthew more money, so he had decided to live where he liked, and to build. Sentiment had drawn him back to the scene of his happiest years, Marianne having agreed that it

would be interesting to live near a university. He was honorary
secretary to a society here; in addition to this, he had some phil-
anthropic work in connection with which he was quite often away.
He was a member of the senior common-room of his college, and
dined in hall three times a term. Once or twice a week the Harveys
would dine early and motor into the city to attend the meetings
of learned societies or soirées given by the Art Club. Life here was
full of interest, Marianne said. Moreover, Matthew and Marianne
were happy in each other's affection. After twelve years of marriage
his wife still charmed him with her serenity, mild good spirits and
love of home. And she had more than this: he took pride in that
touch of the farouche about her beauty; she was big-limbed, wide-
browed, and looked like a diffident goddess, but her eyebrows
turned up to her temples like impatient wings and her alive hair
in honey-dark ringlets fell every way. Her fairness and uncertain
manner made her seem still quite young: in his friends here she
stirred up a dusty sentiment. All this was dear to Matthew, who
craved little more than refreshment: he was not a passionate man.
Living closely, since they came back here, with the ghost of his
own adolescence, raising the old evocations from the same poetry
– out of one book slipped a grass-blade twenty-five years old, from
another a pressed fritillary – taking the same river-walks, he saw
how his friends grew greyer, how their sentiments creaked, and,
with dismay for himself, dreaded to desiccate. He clung to his
wife's ever-freshness, her touch of the vine-leaf . . . Cautious, well-
read, tolerant, and inclined to be prosy, Matthew had fluffy pepper-
and-salt hair thinning away from the temples, a rather too constant
kind smile, and a nose veined at the bridge; he wore shell-rimmed
spectacles with gold hook-on side-pieces, a Norfolk jacket of
antique cut, and grey flannel trousers that always bulged at the
knee. He and Marianne had two sons, Edwin and Luke; Luke had
just joined Edwin at a preparatory school. When the boys came
back for their first Christmas in the new home they would be
taken for walks by their father, who would describe his youth here
and make them familiar with the antiquities of the city.

Davina had never learned how a poor relation behaves. She exacted,
grumbled and ordered the servants around, walked mud into carpets,

and stayed in bed overtime, rang bells all day long, and, till recently, took out the car when she chose. Her aunt's maids admired Davina's lordly habit of being unfair: their own mistress, with her affronted, muddled and rather tippeting manner, they had well in control . . . From the first, however, there had been trouble with the chauffeur.

Prothero, the chauffeur, lived in the coachman's room above what had been the stables, up a built-in staircase at the end of the yard. His window faced the Manor back-bedroom windows. He had been with Mrs Archworth four months, a few weeks more than Davina, having been engaged after good old Robinson died. He had come with a first-rate character; none of his former employers could write too highly of him. He was forbiddingly faultless, a careful driver; he did not grumble, make love to the maids or expect beer. Mrs Archworth could never be certain why she did not like him better, or why his proximity while he was tucking her into the car, his way of receiving orders, even the set of his shoulders and back of his ears as he drove, should fill her with a resentful uneasiness. There was something unlikely about him and she mistrusted the odd. Between his flat peaked blue cap and his blue collar his face was always shadowless, abstract, null; a face remembered as being unmemorable. The only look he gave you was level and unmoving. Though she got all she paid for, she could not feel he was hers. Her cook was 'my cook', but he remained 'the chauffeur'. His manner had not that alacrity to which she was accustomed; always on the polite side of surly, he was at the same time unsmiling and taciturn. Here, however, he was, and she dreaded change as in some way an ally of death . . . So that she liked to think his oddness was simply his surname; such an unusual name for a chauffeur, everyone said.

But one point against Prothero Mrs Archworth *could* fix: he burnt light too late. Her own nights were often disturbed by a windy form of dyspepsia; her long bedroom extended the depth of the house, and it was annoying to see, through the blind of her back window, Prothero's light still burning, behind the screen of the ilex, till one or two o'clock. It became her nervous habit to court the annoyance, to wake again and again to see if this were still so. Mrs Archworth would lie rigid with anger and speculation.

Finally, one morning, flushing with apprehension, she protested against this use of her electricity. Prothero bowed. That night, at ten o'clock, he flicked off his hanging light with sardonic promptness: a dimmer glow succeeded: he sat up by candlelight. She had to suppose, with an obscure sense of frustration, the candles might be his own. Night after night, as she still peered through the ilex, not a shadow moved on his blind. She suspected him, all the same, of bringing in women – but the yard gates were bolted and there was never a sound from the dog.

His life at the edge of this household of women remained inscrutable. But one thing they could all see: he could not do with Davina. She would take out the car when it pleased her, without a word to Prothero: she brought it in always dirty and sometimes late. Then one night she found the gates bolted against her; two days after that he had locked the garage. Davina went, stormy, for Prothero. No one knew what occurred, but after that she no longer took out the car. No word from either side reached Mrs Archworth direct. During this friction between her niece and her chauffeur she behaved like a terrified ostrich. After that week, things had quieted down for a bit.

One night in early November, Prothero, in reply to a whistle repeated on a rising note and each time with less caution, opened his door at the head of the built-in staircase and came halfway down, cigarette in his mouth. The stairs creaked as he padded, and came to a stop silently. Davina stood in the arch at the foot of the staircase, with Marianne Harvey behind her out in the yard. Their figures were silhouetted against a patch of yard lamplight. Both the young women were hatless and wore heavy overcoats. Against the night sky, clotted and dense, the papery ilex shivered; night wind, with a sinister flitter of dead leaves, raced round the yard, whose cobbles dappled away into leathery bat's-wing darkness beyond the lamp.

The two stood looking up; the staircase creaked again, and Prothero still said nothing. Davina advanced with a nervous swaggering movement and put one foot on the stairs. She began: 'Look here—'

He said uncivilly: 'Well?'

She dug her hands into her pockets. 'I want some more money,' she said with a casual air.

He shifted his cigarette. 'What,' he said, '*now*? Tonight?'

'Naturally,' said Davina, with some impatience. Outside the archway Mrs Harvey stepped back and glanced uneasily round her into the dark, as though she did not care at all for her company. An unseen smile hung in the dark of the stairs; Prothero let his cigarette drop and ground it out with his heel. 'For heaven's sake,' she said, '*hurry*'; and shifted her foot. The deliberate and endless silence was painful to Marianne. 'Right,' he said. 'Come on up.'

He turned back into his room, and Davina, with automatic swiftness and energy, went springing upstairs after him. His door stayed ajar; vibrations of heat from the stove came down through the arch to the horrified Marianne. Looking up at the dark sky, she fought for a feeling of everybody's nonentity. The clock in the church tower, not far away, struck nine: before the last stroke finished Davina was down again. She caught Marianne by the elbow and ran her across the yard. They paused by the lamp a minute; Davina held a crackling note close up to Marianne's face. 'That is that,' she said.

Wincing away from the note, with its smell of delinquency, Marianne, not for the first time, wished herself safe at home. But the wish was the merest moment's frightened retraction and not sincere: Marianne's heart was set on this evening's pleasure, this fantastic setting-out. In these weeks of knowing Davina her faculty for disapproval seemed to be all used up. She was under a spell. She blamed herself, and knew Davina despised her, for being too shy or too sly to ask Matthew for money before he started for London, where he would stay tonight.

She said faintly, 'Oh, how you *could* . . .'

Her friend looked satirical. She had seen Marianne's recoil from the servant's money. On the subject of class, she knew, Marianne felt as awkwardly and obscurely as people do about sex. Marianne said: 'But why not go to your aunt?'

'You have no idea of what's impossible and what's not! It would make *me* sick to ask Matthew — However, that's your affair. Now, for God's sake, my good girl, don't waste any more time!'

Marianne's brain hummed with frightening anticipation. Leaving the yard, they crept like a couple of cats round the unlit flank of the house, between the wall and the spiny flutter of hollies. Round at the front, an inch-wide slit of bright light fell on Davina's smile: secrecy quickened their breath as they stopped a minute to look in between the drawing-room curtains at Davina's aunt at bridge with three of her neighbours. In the dense red-shaded lamplight sealed in by the pane the two ladies' lace jabots, the two gentlemen's shirt-fronts, stood out like tombstones: the intent quartette, the glazed cabinets and woolly white rugs, all looked embedded in something transparent, solid and hot, like clarified red wax. Not a sound came through the pane. The two turned and crept away down the dark lawn.

Outside the gates, Marianne's coupé had been run up on to the rough grass of the green, with its lights out. Its air was lurking and crookish. They got in, and Marianne ran the car bumpily off the grass and away down a lane between blank end-walls of cottages, on to the by-pass road. Marianne's heart went up as they slid clear of the walls that had stared amazed in her headlights: the sweeping black irresistible river of road sucked at her will like a current; their speed heightened; with a swing of lights they swept south. Davina eyed the speedometer. 'Hurry,' she said.

Marianne had a flicker of spirit. 'If you bully me, I'll go home.'

'Let me *drive*—'

'No.'

'Oh, very well, Mrs Harvey.'

'This is a good beginning,' said Marianne, sore.

'Left!' said Davina sharply, and held to the lights of the dashboard, as they approached a crossroads, a vague little pencilled map. After some minutes she said: 'If it makes you feel any better, he's not a chauffeur; he's a crook.'

'Don't be silly,' said Marianne. An impassable wall of good humour divides any lady from fact. But she could not resist saying, 'Besides, how do you know?'

'I know he knows I know. He's lying low here. I've seen his photograph somewhere – something once happened.'

'You get ideas in your head from reading those frightful books.'

'But things do happen, you know,' said Davina calmly. Sliding down in her seat and eyeing the flying darkness, she fingered the note in her pocket with cautious pleasure, like someone hugging a thought. Meanwhile Marianne thought of a smart little Jewish girl she used to go to tea with when she was nine years old and living at Dulwich. That little girl had declared there was a dead baby strapped up in a trunk in her family's cistern loft. After tea in the frightening Gothic house, they had crept up to the door, but Marianne would not go in, hearing with horror the cistern inside gurgle. But later her mother told her the little Jewish girl was not a lady, and ever since then Marianne had thought of the extraordinary with contempt. Pressing her chin down in the folds of her muffler, she made up her mind to ask no more about Prothero.

Prothero's pound note was soon changed, for Marianne had not filled up the car and they had to pull up for petrol: she ran the car into the bay of a filling station. While the man unlocked the pump, Marianne got out a minute, restlessly, from the car. Behind them, the last lights of streets were strung along the horizon; the thin glow above a provincial city hung on the sky. Marianne felt her face turned for ever to the unknown. But flight was life to Davina, with nothing to leave behind.

A friend's unknown friends are daemons or demigods with frightful attributes. Marianne's heart sank at the thought of the meeting ahead. The night air was uncalming and anxious: no moon but a rolling hurry of clouds: a circle of rotting flower-stalks outside the petrol station shivered under their headlights in the dark wind.

They drove on.

A glittering Neon sign like wolves' eyes read: OPEN ALL NIGHT, at which thought a dry weariness pervaded the brain. 'We shan't be staying *all* night,' said Davina easily. Here they were, and they tore up the pencilled map and scattered the scraps on the wind.

The roadhouse stood at the crossroads, its row of Christmas-card windows shedding a fictitious glow. Four wide black roads had been levelled into the hill, and met in a kind of circus inside the clay banks of the cutting. The roadhouse stood high up; to the porch you mounted some steps up the high embankment; a car park was scooped out fifty yards further on. The wind moaned cheerlessly over the down behind, but the scene had a hard air of late night merriment, like a fixed grin . . . In the porch, Marianne pulled off a gauntlet to tuck back a strand of hair; Davina whipped out her lipstick and gave herself new, bright lips. 'We were once rather in love.'

But inside there was no one. A long row of swinging lanterns bobbed in their own horrid light as they pushed open the door. The lounge was empty and bald as the inside of a band-box, glazed with synthetic panelling. The chairs were askew, empty, with flattened cushions; ashtrays sent up a cold fume; the place wore an air of sudden, sheepish vacuity, as though a large party had just got up and gone out. The barman leaned, yawning, just inside the bar shutter. When they came in, he took no notice. Davina's friends had not come.

Davina, who had sauntered in with a smile on her fine reddened lips, dropped the smile and looked round her, utterly at a loss.

'Perhaps we are early,' said Marianne.

'No.'

'Perhaps they are late?'

'They can't be later than us.'

'Perhaps they've given us up?'

'They know I am always late——' Davina broke off, crossed the room, and angrily questioned the barman. No, no one had asked for her; no one had waited; no one had telephoned. Sitting down by the shutter, she snapped out an order for bitter. 'I can't drink beer,' said Marianne, as it was brought.

'You'd better,' Davina said with a hollow look.

Marianne fingered her glass. 'This seems a funny place to be meeting anyone in . . .'

'Well, we're not, you see. Does that make it all right?'

A clock struck ten; someone bumped down the bar shutter and locked it. The barman came for their glasses. So that was that.

After some time Marianne said: 'You know, we can't wait all night.'

'I don't see why not.'

Lighting a cigarette, Davina said no more. An uneasy silence set in. Marianne, watching her friend's lips pulling at the cigarette, the once bold dark eyes that now crept to the door then dropped quickly to cover their mortification, felt pity go through her heart with a shameful pang. She also was mortified, and could have easily wept. She only half knew now all she had hoped of tonight. Girlish delicious expectancy went sour inside her. She was tragically sold. She had been, from the first, imposed on by something about Davina – her dashingness, curtness and air of experience. In these last weeks, Marianne's consciousness had been extended deliciously, painfully. A segment of bright unknown world had fallen across her path, where it shed prisms. Only she knew what formless excitement had racked her lately.

But where was Tonight?

Seeing Davina sitting, so much at a loss, with 'Forgotten' pasted across her, too proud to look up, Marianne felt the world contract again. In the next room, someone put a wailing blues on the gramophone. Marianne wished she were home, with her feet on the hot pipes and the cat on her stomach. Out here, draughts raced round the floor.

Davina shot up and said: 'I shall telephone!'

They drove on again. 'I'll tell you one thing,' Davina was saying. 'Somebody's double-crossed me. Unless Oliver's lying – and I don't think he'd be lying – I ought to have got his message at aunt's today.'

'Plans are changed?' quavered Marianne.

'Yes, don't you *see*—' said Davina. Her spirits, however, were up. She sat smiling and silent, looking along the headlights. Things had changed for the better. They had swung east at the crossroads, always further from home. After more miles of flying hypnotic light, Davina said it ought to be anywhere now. 'Any time now, on your right . . .' On their right, they crept in between two Palladian lodges, unlit and staring, the wide gates standing apart. Beech-trunks raced past their lights and a sleek wettish avenue spattered under the tyres: three more gates were hooked back.

The immense façade of the house rushed glaring on to their headlamps: between high white-shuttered windows pilasters soared out of sight above an unlit fanlight like patterns of black ice. Reaching across Marianne, Davina touched the horn, which sent up that face of coldness its peevish cry. The cry repeated – 'They can't even *hear*!' she groaned. But then the fanlight amazingly sprang into light, the hall door burst open on a perspective of pillars, and, with so much thrusting and force that this seemed a muffled riot, dark people shot out, surrounded the car, and pulled open both doors at once. Marianne ducked in a sweep of night air. Davina, peering, said: 'Oliver?'

'I've g-got this all to myself!' exclaimed an excitable voice.

'Where's Thingummy?'

'O-o-oh, he never turned up.'

'So he's not here,' said a woman.

'I am furious,' said Davina.

'That's too bad,' said Oliver, pulling Davina out of the car with a glass in his other hand. 'Never mind, you're here now.'

'It was too bad,' agreed someone. 'However, here we all are.'

They trooped back into the hall. A stout, speechless man who had pulled Marianne through the other door of the car looked at her in the light, closely, to see what he had got. He seemed satisfied. Indoors, the immense cold hall, all chequered pavement and pillars, wore an air of outrage, ravished by steps and voices. One door stood open, and light peered in at the glacial sheeted outlines of furniture and a chandelier that hung in a bag like a cheese and glittered inside the muslin. A chill came from the hearthstones; the house was masterless. Along a pathway of drugget over the marble, at a quick muffled shuffle as though conducting a funeral secretly, the revellers passed down the hall to a door at the far end. They shot through with a rush, each unwilling to be the last, and shut the door defiantly on the echoing house.

'Outside there gives you the creeps,' said the only woman who spoke. Davina's friend Oliver, dishevelled, fair, aquiline, and unnaturally tall, turned and shook hands with Marianne. 'I didn't see you,' he said. 'I'm so glad you came. I hope you had no trouble; I went down just now and opened the gates myself. Do you know if the sheep got out? They are grazing sheep; things are not what they used to be.'

Smoke and human stuffiness thickened the air of this room with its dead undertone of chill on which a snapping wood fire had little effect. It was a high, shabby, gilt-and-white octagonal anteroom, the naked shutters of three windows fortified by iron bars. Bottles crowded a top-heavy ornate table under the chandelier;

panels of tarnished mirror kept multiplying the company, and on a red marble column a Psyche balanced with one hand over a breast. Oliver said: 'I brought her in here for company: I always liked the girl.' On a settee, pulled across the hearth at an angle, an enormous congested old lady slept with her feet apart, letting out stertorous breaths. Her wool coatee was pinned over the heaving ledge of her bust with a paste brooch in the form of a sailing-ship, and at each breath this winked out a knowing ray. Her hands, chapped and knouty, lay in the trough of her lap. Half under her skirts a black pair of kitchen bellows lay on the marble fire-kerb. There was not much more furniture in the room.

'That is Mrs Bennington, who takes care of me. She's so nice,' said Oliver. He rinsed a glass out at a siphon and brought Davina a drink. 'It's a nice house, too,' he said, ''till you get used to it.'

'It's all right once one's got here. Why not suggest this in the first place?'

'You see, I thought there'd be Thingummy.'

'Well, you certainly muddled things,' said Davina with less rancour, her nose inside her glass. When he and she had been younger, handsome, high-spirited, and still with something to spend, they had been in love, and expected to marry one day. Their May had been blighted. Now, each immobile from poverty, each frozen into their settings like leaves in the dull ice of different puddles, they seldom met. They had the dregs of tenderness left for each other, but, each time they met, less to say. It was best to meet in a crowd, as they met tonight. Tonight the crowd was not large, but things might have been worse.

Oliver shook the dregs from another glass and absently rinsed it, meanwhile looking at Marianne. He said to Davina: 'Will she enjoy herself?'

'She has a deadly life. Her standard is not high.'

'She looks most beautifully shy,' Oliver said wistfully.

Marianne felt very shy. The more the room settled down, the more strongly she felt she had no place here. She stood with a hand on the mantelpiece, looking blindly about with her wide-apart troubled eyes. The stout man who had her in charge snatched the glass Oliver had been so vaguely holding, filled it, and brought it to Marianne. 'Now you'll feel better,' he said. His name was

Purdon. Marianne could not explain that she did not like whisky. The smell of spirits repelled and interested her; her nostrils quivered; she drank. '*That's* better,' said Purdon, and bustled up with a chair. Marianne sat down blinking and holding her glass. As though she had been a refugee, her coming in had seemed to constitute some kind of emergency.

'Where are we?' she said.

'Ah, *that's* just the fun,' said Purdon. 'Where we've no call to be!'

'As much call as anyone else,' said the platinum blonde oldish girl, Miriam. She knelt by the kerb and, pulling the bellows from under Mrs Bennington's skirts, began to puff at the fire. She coaxed the flames up knowingly; firelight flapped on her face and up Marianne's knees. An un-English man in a crimson high-necked pullover reached his drink from the floor and resettled himself on the settee, one arm around Mrs Bennington, with an air of content. These were all the people there really were in the room. The party resumed its tenor, illicit but not defiant. A low-spirited intimacy, an innocent kind of complicity, made itself felt. Little seemed worth saying, everything understood. What was said strayed up like bubbles from depths of interiority. They had the flat, wise air of a party of bandit children with their bravado put off, gathering in a cellar.

Marianne looked into her glass; where had all that gone? Her dilated eyes swam round the smoky gilt-and-white room with its tarnished reaches of mirror. She met Oliver's look that was like something swimming desperately on a heaving tide of light. Her throat pricked and she pulled at the scarf she still wore. She exclaimed to the fat man: 'This is nicer than where we were!'

'More homey?' he said nicely. She let him unwind her scarf and drape it about the Psyche. 'That poor girl,' he said, 'gives me the shivers.'

'It feels homey all right to me,' said Miriam, withdrawing her head from the grate. She wiped bellows-black from her fingers on to her black velvet skirt and went on: 'Which may throw some light on my pedigree, now that I come to think.'

No one knew who her father was; he might have been almost anyone. Owing her unkind and scandalous mother no duty, Miriam was always glad to air this uncertainty: it gave her a feeling of space and sometimes, to her mind, a slightly divine quality. She was herself a shady and bitter very good-hearted girl whom everyone liked and nobody seemed to want.

All Oliver's friends were like this. He was, like Davina, an enemy of society, having been led to expect what he did not get. His father had sold himself up and Oliver had had from him little but bad advice. Oliver despised the rich and disliked the poor and drank to the bloody extinction of the middle classes. He wished to call no man brother, and disbelieved with ferocity in himself. The old order left him stranded, the new offered him no place. He lived as he could, and thought well of Davina for settling herself on her aunt. His own relations had, under the suavity of their aspect, a mean kind of canniness, and were not to be imposed upon: they did what they could by imposing him on their friends. Perverse bad manners and clumsiness disqualified Oliver for the profession of being a guest, by which otherwise he might have victualled and housed himself. He had once or twice, on his uncle's recommendation, catalogued country-house libraries; his work was impatient, showy and incorrect, but no one had said so so far, for fear of offending his uncle. He was an ungracious beggar, and, handicapped by a stammer, uncertain health and excitable sensibility, an embarrassment to himself. With his height and fairness he was, in an overcast kind of way, magnificent-looking: a broken-spirited Viking. He was capable of fantastically disinterested affections. Not having been born for nothing into a privileged class, he was, like Davina, entirely unscrupulous.

Lord Thingummy – so Oliver called him, and it is good enough for the purposes of this tale – possessed a fine, mouldy, unreadable library. Inflated, one night at his club, by intellectual pride, he had let himself be persuaded by Oliver's uncle as to the existence, down at his house in the country, of possible unknown treasures in calf and vellum, and induced to hire Oliver to explore and catalogue these. For this he gave Oliver twenty pounds and his victuals. Lord Thingummy had been disposed to join Oliver for a few days in the country; but yesterday he had wired to put off. The very thought of the place had been too damp, for him. His caretaker, Mrs Bennington, was put in charge of Oliver, with instructions not to make him too comfortable, for one had heard of Oliver as a dilatory chap . . . Lord Thingummy was thus, tonight, the party's unconscious host.

The man on the settee in a crimson pullover was a White Russian with little stake in the future. Tonight he was on a holiday; as a rule he lived rather drearily with a woman of means who had a feeling for Russians, in a maisonette just off Addison Road. Miriam was a girl he and Oliver knew. The stout man, Purdon, was a dentist who had won five thousand pounds in an Irish Sweep and shut up his surgery till this should all be spent: he regretted nothing. Tomorrow he went back to work. He was overflowing with friendliness and had bought the drinks for tonight.

Thingummy, said Oliver, was so damned mean he had had the heating turned off and taken the key of the cellar. The library, where he had said he had no doubt Oliver would be happy browsing about, smelt of must. 'He had the n-nerve,' said Oliver, 'to send me down here to live on chops in this ice-house. May his soul rot like his books!'

Purdon explained to Marianne by what a remarkable stroke of luck they all came to be here. When she understood, she had only one thought: she was agonized – the angry earl would appear. Her brain stopped like a clock; she had met few peers. She said unsteadily: 'I must be going home.'

'Rats,' said Purdon. Nobody else heard.

Davina and Oliver pulled cushions on to the parquet and sat with their shoulders against a corner of the settee. She said: 'How is the catalogue?'

'Getting on fast; I'm so anxious to get away.'

'Where shall you go next?'

'How should I know?'

'You might come and stay with my aunt.'

'That would depend,' he said. 'I must have a look at her first.'

Miriam tittered: 'He's put in the names of the stuck-on books on the doors.'

'He's as likely to read those as any others,' said Oliver.

Marianne trembled and stood up, eyeing her empty glass. She thought: 'Where am I?' put down her glass, and began to finger her way along the mantelpiece's swags and medallions. She thought the marble throbbed. In despair, she sat carefully down again, gripping the scrolled gold chair-arms. Looking across for Davina, she met Oliver's eyes once more. He immediately got up and came to her side. 'I've forgotten your name,' he said.

'Marianne,' she said. 'But I've got to be going home.'

He exclaimed in distress: 'Aren't you happy?'

She hesitated. 'I feel lost.'

'Why do you say that?' said Oliver miserably.

Her uncertain look turned away from him to the fire; he saw her cheeks burn and her trembling, obstinate grip on the arms of the chair. Feeling unutterably miserable and guilty, he turned and said to Davina: 'Don't let her go!'

'She's worn out,' said Davina, 'naturally.' Mortification came flooding back to her; she plucked angrily at a carnation she had taken from one of her aunt's vases and stuck in her buttonhole. 'That place was awful,' she said. '*You* simply thought, "No doubt they'll turn up here somehow." Message? I got no message. You seem to expect one to know where you are by instinct! People like you waste one's life!'

'Your aunt ought to be on the telephone.'

'You just hate trouble,' she said.

'Well, don't make it,' said Oliver.

'Please don't quarrel,' said the Russian. Their angry dialogue took place across the room. Through some seconds of silence Mrs Bennington wheezed.

'I took the message,' said Miriam, 'I, in my little fly – I mean, in my little car: I took the message. Purdon and I drove up to your aunt's house on the way from buying the drink. We snooped around the front lawn and just felt we couldn't face it, so we went round to the back and you still weren't there. They said you weren't anywhere. So we left word with a man who was polishing up a Daimler—'

'That is so,' said Purdon. 'We left word with the chauffeur.'

'We left word very particularly,' said Miriam. '*Don't* come where we said, we said, come straight to Thingummy's, here, because he's not here, so we can be. We even drew you a map,' said Miriam earnestly.

Davina pulled the carnation to pieces. 'I'd like to believe you,' she said, 'but I got no message.'

'Then somebody double-crossed you,' said Miriam.

*　　*　　*

By half-past ten Mrs Archworth's evening was over. The parlourmaid
let out the retired Indian Civilian and his wife and the retired
admiral, who pattered away round the green, with its dim lamps,
to their cottages past the church. In the drawing-room the parrakeet, disturbed by the sudden silence, fidgeted under its red baize
cover. Mrs Archworth turned two of the lamps out and stooped
for a good night chat with the Pekinese. The parlourmaid came
in to take out the tray of glasses.

'Shall I shut up, madam?' she said.

'Not till Miss Davina is in. She is dining at Mrs Harvey's; she
won't be late. No doubt they will see her home. You must leave
the door on the latch and come down later to bolt it.'

Kissing the Pekinese between the eyeballs, Mrs Archworth
handed it over regretfully to the parlourmaid; she picked up her
lozenge-box, her patience cards, and a paper-knife, and, with her
usual air of unfocused indignation – for she seldom expected to
sleep – went up to bed. The parlourmaid followed her up with a
glass of hot water. Shaking her nightly powder into the glass and
watching the water cloud, the aunt awaited, on the stretch and
uneasy, Davina's step on the gravel. Outside two red rings of lamplight the darkness showed flat and empty; her thoughts groped
around in it ignorantly, like tentacles, asking what everybody was
doing, where everybody might be. She did not regret, however,
that she was not on the telephone. Her axiom had been always:
People can come to see one, or else people can write.

At ten o'clock to the minute Prothero lit four candles stuck into
bottles and with satiric promptness flicked out the hanging light.
So that Mrs Archworth, peering out later through her back
window-curtains, found his blind pallid. His room, a manservant's,
with match-boarded ceiling, glazed cotton blind and fibre matting,
was bare; the furniture showed by candlelight mean outlines on
the whitewash. The man had no belongings; the place seemed to
be to let. His chauffeur's tunic hung huddled against the back of
the door. The stove through its mica front shed a dull red glow
on the matting. The wind had dropped; inside its walls and high
locked gates the yard down there was as still and deep as a well.
Not a draught stirred those thin sheets of close-written paper

shuffled over his table. Reaching the four candles closer to his left
elbow, he went on writing again.

His hand with the twitching pen went rushing from line to
line at a fever-high pace. He did not once pause. The pen rushed
the hand along under some terrific compulsion, as though something, not thought, vital, were being drained out of him through
the point of the pen. Words sprang to their places with deadly
complicity, knowing each other too well . . . Once or twice when
a clinker fell in the stove, or the outside staircase unaccountably
creaked as though a foot were upon it, he looked up, the tyrannic
pen staggered, he looked round the room with its immutable
fixtures as though he were a ghost—

— grave to the N.N.E. of the church tower in the sunk bit by
the wall. No stone yet as it's too soon, the earth is too soft, but
a wire wreath frame left with some stalks of some sort of flowers,
they were quite dead. Last month you must have got soaked
through to what was your heart, rain comes hard on a grave with
the earth not set yet. So now you must do without company. I
went once.

You said once you thought you should like to die in a ward,
for company. As much as you thought, you thought that. Well I
was there. But you never thought much of that. Whatever you did
want it wasn't that, whatever you did want you didn't seem to be
getting. I never did know what you did want and I don't think
you did. What you did get you didn't want, that was me. But you
got what you didn't want. You got that and now I don't want any
more.

I don't want you any more because I don't want any more. I
don't want more of all that so I don't want you or see you. I don't
see your eyes that you thought as much as you thought I should
not forget. If you could think now you could not think how much
I never want you and how much I forget. I don't go back to the
bungalow. If you could see you could see how much I forget that
time. You could see I don't see the picture of dogs' heads and the
pink dotted curtain flapping or standing still or the moth bumping
round the whole time or the magazine with the girl's face by your
feet on the bed. You tried with eyes to say I should always see

them but you were wrong. They are in a list, I can say them but
I can't see them.

The bungalow is shut up, the papers call it a love nest but what
you got there does no good to that kind of place. No woman
would go there now and no one but a fool woman would have
gone there in the first place. You said that yourself first thing when
I came, it was no good, it was mouldy, the trees drip on the roof
and over the edge of the roof, that made green smears, the press
was musty inside where you hung your dress and it was you said
the sheets had a musty smell. If you wanted to be by the river you
should have been by the river and not a field off, and then that
might not have been such a lonely place. For all I know no one
goes there and as I do not see it it may not be there, for all I
know.

Now I don't want all that any more, now I don't want, I get
on fine here with no more ants in my brain. The old woman's all
right. She gets what she wants. I shut her into the hearse, it is like
a hearse, with her rug and her dog and we go bumping along. My
ears stick out like you said under my cap and the buttons have
crests, a fist with a knife, and I click my heels when she talks. I
give satisfaction here if you know what that means but you do
not know what that means. She gets her money's worth.

I always was what I am, now I am what I always was, what you
said that time. Flunkey. I like what I am, a free man. Up here I'm
as snug as a monk with a stove with two hours' fuel, no pictures,
no pictures of dogs. The bed squeaks when I turn so I lie still like
you lie, only it's broader, with your arms down at your sides. My
stairs are my stairs and no one comes up, if I did want they would
come. I have that money you had, that was my money you had,
a bad debt after all I did. The girl owes me seven pound ten and
six, so I buy the kisses now. All the fun's in the deal now I know
what I don't want.

They say when you've done what I've done you go back. But
that's not true. I went once where you are to be sure you are there,
but I don't go where we were that last time. I don't act any way
they would think I would act. I act my own way now, only I act
that way because it is my way. If I don't know what I will do, how
can they know what I will do? I act now before I think, and I

don't think after I act. I act how I like. You always knew what I would do, so I always had to do that. Now no one knows, I don't know, I act.

Love was just having to act in the one way. There was just one way we could go, like both being in a tram. We acted the way we had to. Slippings-off just us two and fake names and quarrels and all that fun. They all go that same way. Where the tram didn't take the points, where the bump was, was your way with that money you had. You had all the money. The clink in your gold chain bag that you always watched and always kept by your hand and the wallet you brought out when the bills came, smiling because it was you had the money to spend but not liking to spend your money and smiling at me that knowing way and pushing the notes back that we didn't want yet. You could pay for the fancies you had with all that money you had. Our bed smelt of all your money. I was a fool then to love you the way I did, I gave more than you paid for, you saw I was a fool and that you paid for a fool. You were not the big business man's daughter for nothing, Anita, and not the great big business man's wife.

No one saw so no one knew, we met first of all in the train so no one knew we had met, we didn't write letters, you were very smart that way, you were very sly. I saw you were no good. Your husband was a strict man. For some time we tricked your husband all over the place in a hurry, then you said there was no time, we had to have more time, we had to have some place. What with being so plotty, so damned smart, so careful no one would see us who would remember, a different place every time – that was not value, you thought. You had to have more time, you said. What did you have to have more time for? You'd torn me up by that time, in that first month, what more did you want? You went off and leased that bungalow in a fake name. By that time I was poison to you, and you were to me. It rained that first day that was the last time, when you told me I had to come there. I left my car in the garage outside the town up the river and then I walked down in the rain to where you were. I felt like lead, the wind bent the trees back on the hill on the far side, the rain hit the river, it was all dark grey like a photograph. No one was out, I didn't meet anyone. I felt like a stone. When I came round the trees I saw that was the place and I hated the place with trees dripping on the roof and streaks on the white gate. It looked a hole for a toad. When I came up the path a window blew open, a pink dotted curtain blew out in the wet. Your arm came out after the curtain and shut the window so I knew you were in there waiting. The trees up there lashed about. You had seen me, of course. Then, at that time, I couldn't see any way out. There was no air in the house. Though the place was alone with nobody going by you drew the pink curtain as soon as I came in. The whole time the windows rattled, the rain got lashed down by the trees on our roof.

At sunset the wind stopped and then the rain stopped, I got up and opened the window. There was a yellow light near the river, it was hot because it was July, now the wind had stopped and then everything steamed. The steam made everything hot, moths came out and bumped on the windows as it was getting darker, musty smells came out of the walls of the room where we were. We were done in by then. You began crying and I went off to open a can of corned beef to eat. I shut the door but you opened it, you went on talking at me while I was opening the can and that note came in your voice like the needle skidding on the inside of a record when the record is done. When I didn't answer you came into the kitchen the way you were and asked for a cigarette. I said I hadn't a cigarette, I'd been looking for yours. Then you said what you said. So I went out and walked.

I walked along by the river and didn't meet anyone, I thought I wouldn't go back but my hat was there and you had to have some answer to what you had said. I saw you had me bought up. A motor salesman who didn't do big business and didn't have money and started to have tastes he didn't have money for. A war gentleman after the war, you'd have liked me then in the war. I could see how things were. A man with the sort of face everybody forgot, that you said you mostly forgot. I walked some time by the same bit of the river. I didn't go far.

When I came back you had lit the lamp by the bed and lay smoking and reading a magazine with a girl's face on the front, you knew I would come back. I came and stood the other side of the lamp to wait till you had finished your magazine story. You stretched your arms past your head and yawned and arched up your back, then you smiled the way you smiled and said you'd been nervous. You said how much you liked company, like you had always said. But when I didn't say anything but just waited, without noticing you, you turned over slowly as though you were so comfortable and slid your hand slowly between your cheek and the pillow and said that again slowly. You said that again. You said what you meant. You said what you'd said before. I saw a red mist where your face was, just a mist on the pillow. I took the pillow and smothered you.

The moth bumped about the whole time I leaned on the pillow, then flew into the curtain. The picture of dogs' heads was over the bed and the magazine stayed by your feet on the bed, when you didn't move any more it was still there. Your eyes were looking at me when I lifted the pillow. I took the note-case out of your gold handbag and took your pearls off the table and took your rings and I left the lamp by you to burn out. I left fingerprints, I suppose. I took no trouble. I had taken trouble enough. I banked on no one knowing I knew you. I rubbed your face powder off the mirror with my elbow and had a good look, I thought at least I'd remember my own face. I went out leaving the door on the latch. You stayed there, that was all you knew. You stayed alone.

I took the gold bag that you always kept by your hand and dropped it in the river along the bank. Clouds came up again but everything was quite quiet, it was dark then. Walking away for always from where you were I didn't feel like me yet. Two swans went by but I didn't meet anyone by the river. It was past ten, I came to the town with the garage, I passed the cinema then, they were all coming out. I joined in with them all and walked to the garage along with some people, we all took our cars out. I drove south towards Newhaven, and pulled up the car by a wood and slept for a bit, then I drove on. I put up the car at Newhaven when it was light and crossed by the day boat the way it had been arranged. I was crossing to France that day on the firm's business anyhow. In Paris I sold your pearls and two of your rings, I kept the third I liked best. I was at Le Mans when I saw they'd found you, then the firm sent me on to Lyons and I saw your face in the papers, you were the bungalow crime, the French papers had

you in because you were young and pretty and it looked like a
man. It seemed funny to think I knew you when I saw you in
those papers. Your husband covered our tracks, he thought more
of being so strict than of hanging anybody, he was just like you
always said. He said you'd taken the bungalow for yourself for a
rest cure and he had been going to join you. That didn't help the
police so they fixed robbery for the motive and pulled in a tramp
but the fingerprints didn't fit, then they went after a deserter from
Aldershot, they're not so sharp as they say. For all everyone knew
I might not have been born.

This seemed odd to me, when I knew for the first time I had
been born and knew who I was now. I felt grand those weeks and
fit to lift a ton weight with nothing to lift but pennies. I felt so
grand I didn't know what to do. I was all alone. I didn't get thick
with anybody for fear of talking when there was only the one
thing I wanted to tell anybody. My head stayed very good and I
saw the sense of things I never had seen the sense of. Everything
got simple. So I began to like life and want a run for my money,
else what was the good of being the way I was? So I wasn't taxing
my good luck any more, I thought I would stage a get-out and
start new, the chance came when the firm sent me to Marseilles.
Mutts disappear there every day.

A man came along there that was what I wanted, a drunk,
Prothero, a chauffeur who'd been sacked from a villa near Antibes,
he'd drunk all his money in Marseilles, he was so tight he sold me
his passport for two hundred francs and threw in his references for
fifty more. His face fitted mine all right. I said if he'd meet me
again I'd give him the fifty francs that I hadn't on me the first
time; he turned up blind again. I walked him down by the quays
where there weren't so many lamps and then nudged him over
into the harbour, he wasn't giving a damn for what happened next
anyhow, so that was all right by him, he sank like a stone. I went
back to his place and checked out his luggage, I left mine where
it was in my hotel. The hotel people reported me missing, they
found my papers and passport along with my luggage and wrote
back to the firm. I wasn't just then owing the firm anything, so
they didn't worry, they concluded I'd been one more of those fool
English who get themselves done in in the pleasure quarter and

aren't heard of again. The French police poked round but they get sick of the English. I hadn't any family to make trouble, nobody cared so everyone let things drop. My photograph was in the French papers and in the English papers, and it must have been funny for people to think they had known me. No one remembered my face. No one went into mourning, no one felt that way. After a bit I came back to England and began to put Prothero's references into action. I was anxious to lie low, so applied here. The old woman considered herself lucky. So I got on without you, you see. You lie expecting me back, I don't come back.

You never considered yourself lucky. You considered you'd saddled yourself with a fool but you had to have me, I was a fool to love you that way, you were quite right. We are quit of each other, if that was what you wanted you got what you wanted, it was what I wanted, perhaps all the time we were wanting the same thing, and now I've got that I don't want anything more. You thought I had to have you, as much as you thought you thought that. You thought that when you said what you said then, and you thought that under the pillow. When I took the pillow off that was in your eyes. Well, unthink that. If I thought you thought that still, if I thought you lay thinking that where you are now, I'd break right through, I'd tear anything down to get at you and tear the thought out, I'd tear up the sunk earth. Yes, it makes me mad to see you don't see that I don't see you or want you, that you don't see when these stairs creak outside that I don't think 'Here she is,' that I lie as still as you lie with my bed not creaking any more than your sunk earth and don't think, 'She was here once.' If I were to write, '*I love you, I cannot bear this, I want you, come back*' – you might be tricked. You might come back to see me see you, then you would see me not see you, you would unthink the thought you thought under the pillow, as much as you thought. Yes, look, if I tricked you this way, you'd come back, you could not not come back, you could never resist that. Yes, so look, I'll trick you I'll write loud, like a scream would be if anyone was in the dark with nothing (but I am not in the dark) I'll write so loud you will hear though you can't hear, *Anita*—

The pen charged in his hand. Dragging his hand down to the foot of the paper, in staggering charging characters it wrote – '*Anita, I love you Anita, Anita, where are you? I didn't mean that, that was not me, I didn't, I can't bear you away. I see your eyes on my pillow, I can't lie alone, I cannot get through the night, come back, where are you, I won't hurt you, come back, come back, come back—'*

Prothero dropped the pen as though it were burning. He watched it, frightfully animate, roll to the edge of the table and over the edge. He stared at his right hand and spread out the fingers slowly; they reasserted his will. Shutting his eyes, he screwed round full to the light of the four candles a blank-lidded square fair face clammy with sweat. His hands meanwhile groped over the table, gathering up by feel the close-written sheets. Rising, an automatic and mindless movement, he flung open the lid of the stove with a pothook and thrust the papers in, heard for a minute the hot red roar of the stove, then dropped the lid on the roar.

So his nights succeeded each other. At the back of the Manor House, through the ilex, a light was still burning in Mrs Archworth's room. Downstairs, behind the red kitchen blind, a sleepy, indignant maid sat up for Davina. The village clock struck midnight with rolling strokes.

The wreathed gilt clock above Marianne's head struck midnight with brittle chimes, at which the air quivered like something stretched too tight. The chandelier glittering high up exhausted itself on the smoke, light losing quality as the evening wore on, and a sluggish chill crept over the party's wearied over-acute senses like a miasma. With drifts of cigarette ash in the lap of her black velvet skirt, Miriam sat talking introspectively to nobody in particular; she did not drink any more. The Russian played cat's cradle with a bit of gold cord from a chocolate-box. Purdon sat on a highish chair with his legs crossed, yawning at the chandelier. Mrs Bennington slept on.

'You see, I'm that way,' went on Miriam. 'I don't believe in anything. I don't believe anything really exists, you see.'

The Russian slipped the gold cord off the tips of his fingers and, frowning with concentration, started over again. 'But look here,' said Purdon, 'if you're not going to believe in anything, you have to have something not to believe *in*.'

'*I* don't have to,' said Miriam. 'I can believe in nothing. I always could; I was always funny that way.'

'Do you believe in progress?' said the Russian.

'Everything's talk,' said Miriam, 'and what does all that come to? I see through it.'

'I don't, either,' said the Russian.

'And look at all this fuss all the time. Every time you pick up a paper there's a fuss about something. What I want to know is, what are they getting at? Have you any idea?' she said to Davina.

'No,' said Davina.

'I dare say you've never thought; I dare say you're right, too. What do *you* do?'

'Nothing,' replied Davina. 'I can't.'

'Oh, well,' said Miriam kindly, 'perhaps you've got money?'

'No, not now.'

'Dear me,' said Miriam, 'none of us have any luck. If you'd had a hundred pounds I'd have taken you into partnership. I'm looking round for a partner. Or, strictly, I'm looking round for a hundred pounds, but I wouldn't mind a partner; it would be company. Have you heard about me?'

'No. What?'

'I keep a tea-and-cake parlour called The Cat and Kettle. If you like cakes it's all right, but it puts you off them. It's not far from here, at Warring – on the river, you know. I've got check blinds and an inglenook and olde-oak beams and a cat; it's nice till you get used to it. I do Devonshire Teas at one and six and Dainty Teas *à la carte*. I lose on the Devonshires, mostly; you've no idea how much a person can eat to spite you. Still, it's a draw, and you've got to consider that. I wouldn't mind so much if it weren't for the black beetles; I always think they try and run up my legs. My cat eats them, but you should see how they multiply; however, don't tell me a cat's not faithful. I bake the stuff myself; I'm a real home girl, I am; there's plenty of use for a gas-oven without putting one's head in it, as I always tell the girls. Every now and then my hand goes right out; I don't mind telling you, you could knock a man down with some of my gingerbread. But people would eat a boot if it was home made. They like getting caraways into their teeth and spitting out burnt currants; it feels like the old home. I've had customers drive thirty miles to see the dear old black kettle sit on the hob and kid themselves I made the tea out of it.

Neurotic, that's what they are. I get mostly courting couples; the girls like it; there's something about that kettle that brings a man to the point. He mashes my comb honey about and goes soppy about his mother; it makes you sick. You'd think it would make a girl sick, but a girl goes through worse than that, as I always say. However, no times like the old times − Look in next time you're passing,' she said to Davina.

'I never am,' said Davina. 'I haven't got a car.'

'Well, you won't miss much,' said Miriam without rancour. 'It's a hole of a place where I am. Dishwater fogs all the winter and a slow motion High Street with no one about all day but the dear vicar. In summer it's like the inside of a hot pipe and you can't hear yourself think. Cars in a screaming jam all down the street, and punts jammed down the river till you couldn't drown a kitten between, and couples tie up all night, with ukuleles and portables, to the bank under my yard wall. You never know what goes on. It wouldn't be *your* cup of tea.'

'You know,' said Purdon to Miriam, 'you ought really to marry me.'

'Yes,' sighed the Russian, 'that's what I always say.' He put his head down on Mrs Bennington's shoulder and dropped the twist of gold cord despondently into her lap.

All this time, Oliver had been standing above Marianne, leaning against the mantelpiece. He had said nothing since the clock struck, but now he turned and said eagerly to Marianne: 'Come for a turn.'

The fire had 'caught' and danced fluttering up, throwing pink light on the kerb: Marianne sat so close that a faint smell of wool scorching came from her skirt. She fixed her eyes on the smiling, familiar flames and felt more herself. Once or twice with a sleepy unconscious movement she leaned her forehead against the cold marble upright of the mantelpiece. Remotely she had heard midnight strike on the gilt clock. All the time she was aware with some apprehension of Oliver standing silently tall above her, like a tree that might fall. When he did speak, she looked away from him round the room with her frightened eyes: everything seemed to vacillate. The table toppling with bottles seemed to be balancing anxiously, splaying its gilt claw feet out on the parquet like an animal on the ice.

'Won't you come?' said Oliver.

'It's so late. It's so cold.'

'We will walk round the house.'

He opened the door; she rose and, unwinding her scarf from the Psyche, walked through the door ahead of him in a dream. The others said nothing. Like children in a large temple the two walked through the hall and up the bare white stone staircase, ascending to meet themselves in a darkish mirror at the head of the first flight. Here the staircase divided and rose in two sweeps like antlers against the high wall that was hung each side of the mirror with pastoral tapestries. From the head of each flight ran a gallery, waxy and dark. The house's great vacant height and resounding unlit perspectives weighed upon Marianne. As they went from room to room she heard Oliver's fingers tap in the dark on the wall for the light switch, then Italianate ceilings and sheeted icebergs of furniture sprang into cold existence. 'Think of living here!' she said.

'Where *do* you live?'

She began to explain. But she was held up by something ardent and curious in his manner, the impatience with which, shaking his lock of fair hair back, he stared through her outline, not seeming to listen. What she was saying trailed off into unimportance. Tonight and his presence tightened their hold on her spirit; the everyday became cloudy and meaningless and, like a tapestry, full of arrested movement. At the tapestry she looked down – for they had come back to the gallery. She stood fixing her eyes on the subfusc temples on hills and the nymphs trailing dead garlands, inanimate in brown gloom.

'Shan't I see you again, then?'

She did not know what to say.

'You tell me you're married,' Oliver said accusingly.

Coming in tonight with Davina, quite unexplained, she had seemed to him as disconnected from fact as an angel or goddess. Her lost face, mild wild air, and, once or twice as they groped through the dark house, her anxious touch on his arm, had set up in him a violent solicitude. Now, outraged by what she had only begun to tell him, he exclaimed excitedly: 'Damn the natural affections!'

'Oh, you mustn't say that!'

'They are a ramp,' said Oliver. One angry hand on her elbow, he wheeled her right about to face a pair of heavily moulded doors. He flung one of these open on a resounding void, announcing: 'The grand saloon.' They went in. He flicked at a half-dozen switches but no light came. 'The bulbs are all gone; he's as poor as a rat,' said Oliver.

Reflections from outside touched the glass fronts of cabinets; a white path of canvas drugget led off into the dark. The room sounded enormous. He pulled the sheet from a sofa and they sat down; behind them the door swung to with a heavy click and Marianne caught a breath. Oliver swooped on her two hands in the dark and kissed the side of her cheek as she leaned wildly away.

'This isn't the way to behave—'

'It's how I behave!' he said with a touch of hysteria.

'I'd rather go home.'

'I've been missing you all my life!'

'We can't meet again now!'

'For God's sake don't play-act!' said he.

Excitement with Oliver took its most crippling form. Her wrists encircled in his tyrannic clutch, Marianne heard his hurried breathing check and gather into a sob. A tear, then another, splashed on the back of her hand. Speechless, he let go her hands to dash the tears from his face. In the large unknown room a ring of autumnal silence, sealike and desolate in its unbounded nature, bore in on Marianne their distance from everything fixed.

'What's the matter?' she said.

'You're the last straw.'

'Haven't you got any home?'

'Damn, damn,' said Oliver at a fresh burst of tears. Fumbling and trembling, she thrust her cambric handkerchief into his hand. She put her arm round him, his head slid on to her shoulder, the sofa shook with a sob and he swore again.

'Why do you keep saying that?'

'This is not how I feel,' he said angrily.

'What can I do?'

Davina and Paul, the Russian, left the restless ante-room a few minutes later; they went for a turn, too, and wandered about the mansion, upstairs and down, knocking ash off their cigarettes. It was very cold; Davina stopped in the hall to put on her overcoat. They could see from lights on upstairs that the other two must be somewhere, and were uncertain whether to join them or not. They opened and shut doors without much curiosity. They sat down on a chest in the gallery, and Paul said how much mistaken Miriam was, not marrying Purdon, not believing in anything. Then he said he thought the end of the world would soon come.

'No doubt it's high time,' said Davina. 'But don't let's talk of it.'

'Who is your friend?'

'Marianne? She has a dull life. But look here, Paul: about me – I never know what to do.'

'Wait for something to happen.'

'I hate having no power. Tonight, for instance, I'm furious with someone.'

Not understanding, he looked at her sympathetically, got up and opened one of the grand saloon doors. They stood on the threshold and stared in at the dark. He said: 'The lights are not working.'

'Never mind, it's only a room.' They both turned away.

'All the same, we ought to find Oliver. It's high time Mrs Bennington went to bed.'

Next morning, pale milky sunshine flooded the façade of Lord Thingummy's house. In a bedroom behind the parapet Mrs Bennington, fully dressed under the eiderdown, lay breathing spirituously. The solitary housemaid, having risen at nine, opened the shutters all over the house, and long shafts of misty sunshine slid through the rooms. Patiently stooping, she picked up the cigarette-ends stamped out on the floors. In the grand saloon she sheeted up again an unsheeted sofa and picked up a lady's handkerchief and a striped woollen scarf. Downstairs, in the ante-room, the gilt clock had stopped at ten minutes to four: the hearth was white with cold wood-ash. The housemaid flung up a window and let out on to the morning the stale, cold fumes that hung like lead in the air. She sniffed each of the bottles and swept up some broken glass: a cigarette had burnt out in the trough of a brocade cushion. Fine dust lay everywhere; the sleepy housemaid bumped vaguely

round with her broom, swirling the dust up and letting it settle
again.

The housemaid's steps in the hollow house, her violence with
the shutters and the knock of her broom, woke Oliver up. He
woke saying 'She's gone,' and lay sprawled rigidly sideways across
his bed with his eyes shut, unwilling to wake, while thoughts of
his own ignobility raced through his brain . . . The grass of the
park rolled fawn-pale to the horizon in the veiled sunshine; the
lake stretched bright white against a brown belt of trees, fringed
with papery pale windless reeds. A swan slowly turned on the
lake and a man on horseback rode along the bare skyline: nothing
else moved. The outdoor world lay reflected in the dark glass of
Oliver's mind as he lay, with his eyes shut, sideways across his
bed; he groaned at the still morning scene as though he stood
at his window. For himself he could see no reason. He had,
unwillingly, deluded her with his tears; one cannot weep all the
time. He longed to see himself otherwise, like any other man,
with a sound and passionate core. He thought of the grand
saloon with alarm and pity, as though she lay dead in there.
Opening his eyes a moment on the accusing daylight, he rolled
over to reach for his first cigarette . . . He never finished Lord
Thingummy's catalogue.

A thin veil of river-mist lay on the Archworth garden. Davina
woke late, looked at the unclear trees, and thought: 'At least we
are honest.' Getting up, she found she had circles under her eyes:
one did not grow any younger. She thought with relief of last
night's pleasure, because it was over, because it had been so slight.
She and her friends had come to the same sad age when one can
change no longer, and only become more oneself. They could
enthral and bluff each other no longer – but still, to meet is to
meet. They had made some kind of hearth, and its warmth remained.
Oliver with his dispirited Viking air, at once gallant and craven,
and Paul with his placid and disenchanted smile, were renewed in
her heart; she pictured Miriam on her high heels stepping over
the beetles this morning and Purdon re-opening his surgery with
a sigh. Combing back her springy dark hair and making up her
mouth with pomegranate lipstick – alas! for no one – Davina

thought of them kindly, regretting their premature autumn. 'We are not so bad,' she thought.

She went to her aunt's room.

Mrs Archworth sat propped up in bed in a hug-me-tight trimmed with marabou. Beside the hot bedroom fire the Pekinese snored and dribbled. As Davina tapped on the door and came in smartly, resentment fought with affection on her aunt's face: 'I was a little anxious—' Mrs Archworth began.

'But just you wait till you hear—'

Mrs Archworth could not resist that flashing dark look. Poor plain pompous fussy old woman, no one else was at pains to fascinate her these days. She shifted her feet in bed, making room for Davina to sit, and patted the eiderdown with an uncertain smile. Davina explained with more than usual vividness how, Marianne's car having broken down, on a drive after dinner, outside unknown gates, the two had been for some hours the guests of Lord Thingummy.

'He would be kindness itself,' said her aunt. 'I once danced with him. And we dined there once, I remember, not long after your uncle and I were married. I am glad you should be making friends in the neighbourhood. This house, Davina, I'd like you to understand, is to be yours when I die.'

Davina said, startled: 'That's very good of you.'

Her aunt, with a wry and oddly dignified smile, said: 'My dear, I shall not need it.'

Marianne drove to meet Matthew at the 12.33 from London. The down platform was crowded, and for a moment or two of uncertain feeling she thought he had missed the train. Then he came ambling her way with light on his spectacles. His overcoat flapped and he carried a small dispatch-case. 'How is my girl?' he said, as they made their way through the barrier.

She was disorientated; she did not know. At home, she had not renewed the water in the bowls of chrysanthemums; it was a greenish colour, and stank faintly. The dogs, not yet exercised, fawned rather pointedly on the returning pair. The cat ran to meet them with its tail straight up; turned for no reason and ran away again. Mild unclear morning light filled the new white house with its evenly heated rooms. Matthew Harvey never kissed in a station, so halfway across the hall he put down his dispatch-case, closed the door to the kitchen, and kissed his wife. Colour rushed up her face, but he did not see.

He returned a book to the shelf and looked through a pile of letters. Meanwhile Marianne's look trailed wearily round the living-room, as though it were she who were just back from a journey and could still find no place to rest.

'I think,' said Matthew, 'I must get my glasses changed.'

'Changed?' said Marianne, starting.

'My glasses, yes,' said Matthew, leaning back in his chair and looking at her with affection. Then he stooped to pick up an end of white cotton from a hand-woven rug. He rolled this into a cocoon and flicked it into the fire. 'A bit of white cotton,' he said, 'but I picked it up.'

She stood with her back to him, looking out of the window, and said: 'The weathercock's pointing the other way.'

'The wind must have changed,' he said pleasantly.

She looked downhill, over the raw garden terraces, at the tops of the village trees with, in their heart, the glinting veering gold bird. Over the Archworths' chimneys a whorl of white smoke immobilized. Far off, across the flat water-meadows, the creeping red streets waited: beyond, a crowd of pale spires pricked the stooping grey sky. The world reflected itself in the vacant glass of her mind. Her hands, on which tears had fallen, vaguely clenched and unclenched in the pockets of her tweed coat.

'It is good to be back,' observed Matthew.

She did not reply.

'What's the matter?' he said. 'You're not quite yourself.'

'Perhaps I have got a slight chill.'

Davina looked over the net blind of Mrs Archworth's window, down into the yard. There was no one about in the yard, least of all Prothero. Biting her lip, she stared down at the white cobbles, the cement incline to the garage, the drifted leaves. A flush of angry intention appeared on her cheekbones. 'What's that?' exclaimed Mrs Archworth, struck by her rigid attitude. But the bedroom door had shut sharply: Davina was gone.

Inside its kennel, the foolish yard dog stirred with a rustle, dragging its chain in the straw; the pigeons rose wheeling on noisy
wings. Davina slid back the garage door on its rollers, but found
only the Daimler's wide polished back. The cook looked out of
the back door and said that if it was Prothero anyone wanted, he
had gone out.

'Why should he do that?'

'I couldn't tell you, I'm sure, miss. We're so independent, we
are.'

Davina swung round and went out through the yard gate, down
the lane to the village. Her tremendous anger made the village
spread round the green, with its porches, dark little shop-fronts
and stooping gables, look like a stage scene, a scene set for today.
The raggy grass of the green was shredded with dead lime leaves,
a smell of woodsmoke hung in the still air. Her look darted round
the green; she had only one thought: 'He's gone.' That thought was
bitter.

But Prothero came out of the grocer's opposite, with a felt hat
pulled down over his forehead and a packet of candles under his
arm. He stood in the shop door, not seeing Davina. Then, with
his swinging, leisurely, damned independent stride, he started back
round the green to the house again. Davina cut back before him
to the mouth of the lane. She waited; they came face to face and
Prothero pulled up patiently.

'Well?' said he.

'What about that message?'

'What about that money?'

'That's no way to talk – whoever you are.'

'It was good enough for you last night – whoever I am.'

She said contemptuously: 'I was in a hurry.'

'Oh, come,' said he, 'we had quite a pleasant chat.'

His light eyes and her dark eyes met implacably. Davina, driving
her hands down into her pockets, said: 'They gave you a message
for me. What became of it?'

'If your friends want to leave messages, they should go to the
front door, not hang round the yard like tinkers. I'm not here to
take messages; I am a busy man.'

'You'll be dismissed for this. You forget yourself.'

'I should like to,' he said, smiling without pleasure. 'But what would your aunt say to our little bill? I wouldn't upset her now you've feathered your nest so nicely. Besides, we should miss each other, I dare say.'

'That's blackmail,' she said. 'You're a crook, aren't you?'

'I got even with someone.'

'That was grand,' she said bitterly.

'Yes, I'm right on top of the world.' He looked up at the weathercock.

'You must be mad,' she said, looking at him intently. 'Else why spoil my evening? Why make an enemy of me? Suppose I gave you away?'

'You wouldn't do that if you could. For one thing, you haven't the guts, and it wouldn't get you anywhere. Spoil your evening?' He looked at her incuriously. 'How you do set your heart on things!'

'A monkey trick,' she said scornfully. 'Oh, you're a great man!'

'Mmn. I do what I want. And I take what I want, I don't hang about for it. I wonder it doesn't sicken a girl like you, hanging about here, waiting. You'd better get out. I'm through. Don't keep coming after my money; it's not my money you want. I know your sort. Well, I'm through with all that. I'm buying not selling, these days. You keep your place, Miss Archworth, and I'll keep mine. You can't have it both ways. Good day.'

Nodding, he walked away from her down the lane. She followed him, at a distance, through the yard gates. He was mad, in plain terms – her own. She watched him, with fascination, cross the yard to his staircase. It was true she had, in some strange fashion, fed her own pride by the hasty sale of her kisses, feeling set free of herself each time those anonymous lips without pleasure had claimed her own, or those unseeing abstract cold eyes lit on her face. She went to the archway and called up the hollow staircase: 'Who *are* you?'

'My own man,' he said, and shut his door vigorously. Flakes of plaster slid from the staircase wall, and the steps creaked into silence after his tread. Davina felt in her pocket but found no cigarette. She called. 'I'm going,' and turned back to the house.

In the drawing-room, she filled up her case from the

cigarette-box put out last night for the admiral and the Indian Civilian. The parrakeet wobbled on its perch; upstairs, she heard her aunt beginning to move about; she leaned on the mantelpiece thinking about Prothero: free men do not boast . . . She decided to walk up, now, at once, to the Harveys', to tell Marianne she was going away, would be quite gone in a week. But Matthew would be at home.

Davina walked up the hill, but not to the Harveys'; straight up between the ruts of the half-made road; then she struck out across the grass to the water-tower. Along the brambly skyline she walked rapidly, clicking her finger against her thumb and thinking: 'If I had money . . .'

She saw that events led nowhere, crisis was an illusion, and that passions of momentary violent reality were struck off like sparks from the spirit, only to die. One could precipitate nothing. One is empowered to live fully: occasion does not offer. The whole panorama of life seemed spread out under this hill: between the brambles, hitting an old tin can with her stick idly, Davina stood still to stare . . . Downhill from the tower the gentlemanly new houses reflected the autumn daylight in steel-framed windows. As the sky sharpened with clouds and over the landscape the morning darkened, the skyline spires went leaden, the gasometer and the far-off curve of the river took on a wary glint. An almost inaudible hum of wind rising began below in the trees.

Davina decided to throw off her dashing character and ask her aunt for the money to repay Prothero. Two men came uphill her way, stopped and debated: they were surveyors coming to peg out a new road.

The Last Night in the Old Home

Annabelle, who had been searching about upstairs, pinching the corners of mattresses as though they ought to hold guineas and opening and shutting drawers, discovered a pair of gloves in the blue room wardrobe. So she came down to ask everyone whose these could be. From room to room she went: everyone soon learned to dread her step.

'It seems a pity,' she said, 'that they should be sold *with* the wardrobe. They are nice gloves – look.' They were fine suède gloves for narrow hands, worn at the fingertips, doing up at the wrists with small pearl buttons. 'Someone should have the good of them.'

'Perhaps they're Delia's,' said Henry, her present victim.

'She says no. Hers don't *button* up.'

'I should keep them yourself.'

'Oh, no, Henry, I mustn't; besides, look, they are too small.'

Henry could have screamed. Throughout the house, disappearing in dusk, there reigned an unnatural silence that first he could not account for: all the clocks had been let run down. You cannot auction a ticking clock. The silence echoed, for against the dusty feet of tomorrow all carpets had been rolled up. Here in the morning-room hung a smell of stale note-paper; his mother had taken the family letters – from school, from London, from India – out of the bureau drawers to be read aloud. Now, thank God, they were burnt. Only the best, the jauntiest and most eloquent, had been put away in dispatch-cases. All Adrian's had been kept, because he was dead. (With the dispatch-cases no one knew what to do.) Had Henry been dead, his might have acquired some kind of morbid value. As it was, they put up a poor show at the hearing by mother and sisters and had been unostentatiously burnt. Absent or present, he was constrained with his family: too civil, nervous. He was humiliated by Annabelle's oddness, that all the others took calmly. His embarrassment was unforgivable: Annabelle was not 'afflicted'; she simply did not grow up. Inside the big, bustling form of a woman she was a girl of ten. So she remained their home-girl.

After Annabelle, Delia looked into the morning-room. 'How funny it is,' she said briskly, 'with all the pictures down!' Smoke had dimmed, sun faded, the wallpaper; fresh flowery squares stared oddly.

Delia always put balm on the rawest of situations by saying something quite brilliantly superficial. She had been clicking round on her high heels, applying this happy touch to the family's nerves, all today and yesterday. Quite beautiful, she had married and left home young: she cared for no one at all. Henry liked her the best of them; she was as gay as a stranger; between these two convention was comfortably present. 'There's a fire,' she said, 'in the library.'

'Who's in there?'

'Mother and father and poor dear John.'

'Doing what?'

'That's the difficulty,' she said brightly; 'there's nothing much they *can* do. Oh, mother is trying to rub out the places where we all used to be measured against the door.'

Something more than her constant wish to be social accounted for Delia's brightness: she felt a profound relief. Something let go of her conscience. Delia was no good; to her husband, who bored her, she had for years been unfaithful; she was as light as a little cat. With home still going on here, some fiction of innocence had always unnerved her. Now mother and father and Annabelle would be people in a hotel; the cuckoo-clock, the scrap screen, the big chintz chairs rumpled by dogs, would all be auctioned tomorrow and carted away. There *it* went – pouf! Its grip relaxed on her spirit . . . Delia asked Henry to give her a cigarette, and, balancing with a hand on his shoulder as they stood over the grate cold with papery ashes, she began to tell him, amazingly, all about her life. Once or twice she glanced defiantly round the morning-room. Henry, having had no idea she was such a bad woman, violently registered shock.

She concluded: 'I've always wanted to ask you – do you have love-affairs?'

He looked at her queerly, 'No,' he said.

'How *wise*, but how silly.'

Annabelle went into the kitchen, where cook, for her final credit, was giving a final scrub to the copper and zinc saucepans, then ranging them back in their lots on the dresser and tables. All the other servants had wept and gone. Annabelle turned the handle of the mincing-machine and looked regretfully into a colander. 'Oh, dear,' she sighed. Cook took the mincing-machine firmly away from Annabelle and put it back on a shelf.

'I used to make cakes here, usen't I?'

'You did indeed, miss, and very nice cakes they were. Now let that strainer alone, there's a good girl!'

'Cook, whose gloves *can* these be? No one seems to care.'

No doubt, said cook, they had belonged to a visitor. Her eyes, always watery in their scorched lids from the heat of so many fires, looked smaller and dull, like a dead porcupine's; it was hard to tell if she had been crying. Tomorrow she was going straight on to another gentleman's family. If she felt at all, it was angry sorrow for John. He was her darling: it seemed a direct hit at cook that it should be John who had ruined the family. He had a way with him. He never told cook how much, these days, he detested apricot jam, or that her puddings and cakes made him flatulent.

Decency had required John's presence at the obsequies of the home. He felt this unduly hard; his parents' brave brightness affected him. Their silence from all reproach became sinister, like the silence of clocks. He felt prickly all over and drank a good deal of whisky. When Henry told him that, rationally, this was for the best, that the old place had no place now they were all grown up and there were no grandchildren, and that their parents would do much better out of this valley climate, John became very angry. He felt that it was in spirit Henry who ruined the home. Hard-hit, John felt really innocent. Not once had he been deliberate: if mess-bills ran up, horses he backed turned out rotten, cards he held worthless and women he loved exacting, was John to blame? He told himself he had had no real fun. It had always helped him to think of his old home; after a thick night it made him feel good and squashy.

The marks where the children were measured would not rub off the door; John suggested scratching them out with a pocket-knife, but his mother said that would spoil the paint. So he left the library, where the books were stacked up in lots, and went upstairs to look out of the landing window. Here the garden poplars were visible through the dusk, but he saw more plainly his figure reflected against the sky. He turned from the window; the gas was lit on the landing; outside the nursery door John saw the rocking-horse. So mounted, John as a little fellow had charged impressively, hurling himself on enemies. But, when you got off, those red-painted nostrils were always scoffing away. Maddened, John kicked the rocking-horse.

The rocking-horse, stirrups flying, bumped noisily on its rollers. 'Oh, you *mustn't*!' screamed Annabelle, darting out of the nursery, the suède gloves still in her hand. Kneeling, she crooned on the horse's neck. 'Darling . . . poor darling . . . Wicked, unkind John!'

'Damn!' muttered John, unnerved.

Annabelle heard him. Wild with affront, she scrambled heavily to her feet with a cowlike movement and dashed down the naked stairs. 'Mother, mother,' she wailed. Her mother came out of the library. 'Oh, mother, John said "Damn" to me!'

'Never mind,' said her mother, patting the convulsed home-girl.

'He *looked* so awful.'

'We must be kind to him.'

All the doors were open. Henry and Delia glanced at each other; she smiled at a crease in her sleeve, he fumbled a cigarette out and went quite white. They both felt home had lasted a day too long. John came downstairs; his hand shook on the banisters. He looked in at Delia, mouth twisted as though he wanted to laugh, then pushed past into the dining-room where the decanters were.

'He's right,' said Delia. 'I think I should like one too.'

'Our horse,' Annabelle wailed, 'our old darling horse . . .'

'This is intolerable,' said Henry. But their mother looked at him with expressionless eyes over Annabelle's heaving shoulder. 'Never mind,' she murmured, and Henry knew that he had been ordered away.

Only the drawing-room, where they were all always polite, remained unentered, untroubled. It was prepared for tomorrow, its last occasion, when crowds would bid for the piano, the sofas, the clock. The rugs were rolled up and numbered, the chairs stood in rows; statues' unwearied arms upheld unlit lamps on the mantelpiece.

Twilight came in through the unshuttered windows, hung in drops from the chandeliers, and shone in the mirrors.

A wind came up; creepers began to tap on the south windows; draughts crept through the house, fluttering here and there a ticket on objects already bespoken. A door slammed upstairs. Henry went up to shut the windows; the rocking-horse was still rocking. A straw from some packing-case blew past his feet in the dark, which was melodramatic.

Her Table Spread

Alban had few opinions on the subject of marriage; his attitude to women was negative, but in particular he was not attracted to Miss Cuffe. Coming down early for dinner, red satin dress cut low, she attacked the silence with loud laughter before he had spoken. He recollected having heard that she was abnormal — at twenty-five, of statuesque development, still detained in childhood. The two other ladies, in beaded satins, made entrances of a surprising formality. It occurred to him, his presence must constitute an occasion: they certainly sparkled. Old Mr Rossiter, uncle to Mrs Treye, came last, more sourly. They sat for some time without the addition of lamplight. Dinner was not announced; the ladies by remaining on guard, seemed to deprecate any question of its appearance. No sound came from other parts of the Castle.

Miss Cuffe was an heiress to whom the Castle belonged and whose guests they all were. But she carefully followed the movements of her aunt, Mrs Treye; her ox-eyes moved from face to face in happy submission rather than expectancy. She was continually preoccupied with attempts at gravity, as though holding down her skirts in a high wind. Mrs Treye and Miss Carbin combined to cover her excitement; still, their looks frequently stole from the company to the windows, of which there were too many. He received a strong impression someone outside was waiting to come in. At last, with a sigh they got up: dinner had been announced.

The Castle was built on high ground, commanding the estuary; a steep hill, with trees, continued above it. On fine days the view was remarkable, of almost Italian brilliance, with that constant reflection up from the water that even now prolonged the too-long day. Now, in continuous evening rain, the winding wooded line of the further shore could be seen and, nearer the windows, a smothered island with the stump of a watchtower. Where the Castle stood, a higher tower had answered the island's. Later a keep, then wings, had been added; now the fine peaceful residence had French windows opening on to the terrace. Invasions from the water would henceforth be social, perhaps amorous. On the slope down from the terrace, trees began again; almost, but not quite concealing the destroyer. Alban, who knew nothing, had not yet looked down.

It was Mr Rossiter who first spoke of the destroyer – Alban meanwhile glancing along the table; the preparations had been stupendous. The destroyer had come today. The ladies all turned to Alban: the beads on their bosoms sparkled. So this was what they had here, under their trees. Engulfed by their pleasure, from now on he disappeared personally. Mr Rossiter, rising a note, continued. The estuary, it appeared, was deep, with a channel buoyed up it. By a term of the Treaty, English ships were permitted to anchor in these waters.

'But they've been afraid of the rain!' chimed in Valeria Cuffe.

'Hush,' said her aunt, 'that's silly. Sailors would be accustomed to getting wet.'

But, Miss Carbin reported, that spring there *had* already been one destroyer. Two of the officers had been seen dancing at the hotel at the head of the estuary.

'So,' said Alban, 'you are quite in the world.' He adjusted his glasses in her direction.

Miss Carbin – blonde, not forty, and an attachment of Mrs Treye's – shook her head despondently. 'We were all away at Easter. Wasn't it curious they should have come then? The sailors walked in the demesne but never touched the daffodils.'

'As though I should have cared!' exclaimed Valeria passionately.

'Morale too good,' stated Mr Rossiter.

'But next evening,' continued Miss Carbin, 'the officers did not go to the hotel. They climbed up here through the trees to the terrace – you see, they had no idea. Friends of ours were staying here at the Castle, and they apologized. Our friends invited them in to supper . . .'

'Did they accept?'

The three ladies said in a breath: 'Yes, they came.'

Valeria added urgently, 'So don't you *think*—?'

'So tonight we have a destroyer to greet you,' Mrs Treye said quickly to Alban. 'It is quite an event; the country people are coming down from the mountains. These waters are very lonely; the steamers have given up since the bad times; there is hardly a pleasure-boat. The weather this year has driven visitors right away.'

'You are beautifully remote.'

'Yes,' agreed Miss Carbin. 'Do you know much about the Navy? Do you think, for instance, that this is likely to be the same destroyer?'

'*Will they remember?*' Valeria's bust was almost on the table. But with a rustle Mrs Treye pressed Valeria's toe. For the dining-room also looked out across the estuary, and the great girl had not once taken her eyes from the window. Perhaps it was unfortunate that Mr Alban should have coincided with the destroyer. Perhaps it was unfortunate for Mr Alban too.

For he saw now he was less than half the feast; unappeased, the party sat looking through him, all grouped at an end of the table – to the other, chairs had been pulled up. Dinner was being served very slowly. Candles – possible to see from the water – were lit now; some wet peonies glistened. Outside, day still lingered hopefully. The bushes over the edge of the terrace were like heads – you could have sworn sometimes you saw them mounting, swaying in manly talk. Once, wound up in the rain, a bird whistled, seeming hardly a bird.

'Perhaps since then they have been to Greece, or Malta?'

'That would be the Mediterranean fleet,' said Mr Rossiter.

They were sorry to think of anything out in the rain tonight.

'The decks must be streaming,' said Miss Carbin.

Then Valeria, exclaiming. 'Please excuse me!' pushed her chair in and ran from the room.

'She is impulsive,' explained Mrs Treye. 'Have *you* been to Malta, Mr Alban?'

In the drawing-room, empty of Valeria, the standard lamps had been lit. Through their ballet-skirt shades, rose and lemon, they gave out a deep, welcoming light. Alban, at the ladies' invitation, undraped the piano. He played, but they could see he was not pleased. It was obvious he had always been a civilian, and when he had taken his place on the piano-stool – which he twirled round three times, rather fussily – his dinner-jacket wrinkled across the shoulders. It was sad they should feel so indifferent, for he came from London. Mendelssohn was exasperating to them – they opened all four windows to let the music downhill. They preferred not to draw the curtains; the air, though damp, being pleasant tonight, they said.

The piano was damp, but Alban played almost all his heart out. He played out the indignation of years his mild manner concealed. He had failed to love; nobody did anything about this; partners at dinner gave him less than half their attention. He knew some spring had dried up at the root of the world. He was fixed in the dark rain, by an indifferent shore. He played badly, but they were unmusical. Old Mr Rossiter, who was not what he seemed, went back to the dining-room to talk to the parlourmaid.

Valeria, glittering vastly, appeared in a window.

'Come *in*!' her aunt cried in indignation. She would die of a chill, childless, in fact unwedded; the Castle would have to be sold and where would they all be?

But – 'Lights down there!' Valeria shouted above the music.

They had to run out for a moment, laughing and holding cushions over their bare shoulders. Alban left the piano; they looked boldly down from the terrace. Indeed, there they were: two lights like arc-lamps, blurred by rain and drawn down deep in reflection into the steady water. There were, too, ever so many portholes, all lit up.

'Perhaps they are playing bridge,' said Miss Carbin.

'Now I wonder if Uncle Robert ought to have called,' said Mrs Treye. 'Perhaps we have seemed remiss – one calls on a regiment.'

'Patrick could row him out tomorrow.'

'He hates the water.' She sighed. 'Perhaps they will be gone.'

'Let's go for a row now – let's go for a row with a lantern,' besought Valeria, jumping and pulling her aunt's elbow. They produced such indignation she disappeared again – wet satin skirts and all – into the bushes. The ladies could do no more: Alban suggested the rain might spot their dresses.

'They must lose a great deal, playing cards throughout an evening for high stakes,' Miss Carbin said with concern as they all sat down again.

'Yet, if you come to think of it, somebody must win.'

But the naval officers who so joyfully supped at Easter had been, Miss Carbin knew, a Mr Graves, and a Mr Garrett: *they* would certainly lose. 'At all events, it is better than dancing at the hotel; there would be nobody of their type.'

'There is nobody there at all.'

'I expect they are best where they are . . . Mr Alban, a Viennese waltz?'

He played while the ladies whispered, waving the waltz time a little distractedly. Mr Rossiter, coming back, momentously stood: they turned in hope: even the waltz halted. But he brought no news. 'You should call Valeria in. You can't tell who may be round the place. She's not fit to be out tonight.'

'Perhaps she's not out.'

'She is,' said Mr Rossiter crossly. 'I just saw her racing past the window with a lantern.'

Valeria's mind was made up: she was a princess. Not for nothing had she had the dining-room silver polished and all set out. She would pace around in red satin that swished behind, while Mr Alban kept on playing a loud waltz. They would be dazed at all she had to offer – also her two new statues and the leopard-skin from the auction.

When he and she were married (she inclined a little to Mr Garrett) they would invite all the Navy up the estuary and give them tea. Her estuary would be filled up, like a regatta, with loud excited battleships tooting to one another and flags flying. The terrace would be covered with grateful sailors, leaving room for the band. She would keep the peacocks her aunt did not allow. His friends would be surprised to notice that Mr Garrett had meanwhile become an admiral, all gold. He would lead the other admirals into the Castle and say, while they wiped their feet respect-fully: 'These are my wife's statues; she has given them to me. One is Mars, one is Mercury. We have a Venus, but she is not dressed. And wait till I show you our silver and gold plates . . .' The Navy would be unable to tear itself away.

She had been excited for some weeks at the idea of marrying Mr Alban, but now the lovely appearance of the destroyer put him out of her mind. He would not have done; he was not handsome. But she could keep him to play the piano on quiet afternoons.

Her friends had told her Mr Garrett was quite a Viking. She was so very familiar with his appearance that she felt sometimes they had already been married for years – though still, sometimes, he could not realize his good luck. She still had to remind him the island was hers too . . . Tonight, Aunt and darling Miss Carbin had so fallen in with her plans, putting on their satins and decorating the drawing-room, that the dinner became a betrothal feast. There was some little hitch about the arrival of Mr Garrett — she had heard that gentlemen sometimes could not tie their ties. And now he was late and would be discouraged. So she must now go halfway down to the water and wave a lantern.

But she put her two hands over the lantern, then smothered it in her dress. She had a panic. Supposing she should prefer Mr Graves?

She had heard Mr Graves was stocky, but very merry; when he came to supper at Easter he slid in the gallery. He would teach her to dance, and take her to Naples and Paris . . . Oh, dear, oh, dear, then they must fight for her; that was all there was to it . . . She let the lantern out of her skirts and waved. Her fine arm with bangles went up and down, up and down, with the staggering light; the trees one by one jumped up from the dark, like savages.

Inconceivably, the destroyer took no notice.

Undisturbed by oars, the rain stood up from the water; not a light rose to peer, and the gramophone, though it remained very faint, did not cease or alter.

In mackintoshes, Mr Rossiter and Alban meanwhile made their way to the boathouse, Alban did not know why. 'If that goes on,' said Mr Rossiter, nodding towards Valeria's lantern, 'they'll fire one of their guns at us.'

'Oh, no. Why?' said Alban. He buttoned up, however, the collar of his mackintosh.

'Nervous as cats. It's high time that girl was married. She's a nice girl in many ways, too.'

'Couldn't we get the lantern away from her?' They stepped on a paved causeway and heard the water nibble the rocks.

'She'd scream the place down. She's of age now, you see.'

'But if—'

'Oh, she won't do that; I was having a bit of fun with you.' Chuckling equably, Mrs Treye's uncle unlocked and pulled open the boathouse door. A bat whistled out.

'Why are we here?'

'She might come for the boat; she's a fine oar,' said Mr Rossiter wisely. The place was familiar to him; he lit an oil-lamp and, sitting down on a trestle with a staunch air of having done what he could, reached a bottle of whisky out of the boat. He motioned the bottle to Alban. 'It's a wild night,' he said. 'Ah, well, we don't have these destroyers every day.'

'That seems fortunate.'

'Well, it is and it isn't.' Restoring the bottle to the vertical, Mr Rossiter continued: 'It's a pity you don't want a wife. You'd be the better for a wife, d'you see, a young fellow like you. She's got a nice character; she's a girl you could shape. She's got a nice income.' The bat returned from the rain and knocked round the lamp. Lowering the bottle frequently, Mr Rossiter talked to Alban (whose attitude remained negative) of women in general and the parlour-maid in particular . . .

'*Bat!*' Alban squealed irrepressibly, and with his hand to his ear – where he still felt it – fled from the boathouse. Mr Rossiter's conversation continued. Alban's pumps squelched as he ran; he skidded along the causeway and balked at the upward steps. His soul squelched equally: he had been warned, he had been warned. He had heard they were all mad; he had erred out of headiness and curiosity. A degree of terror was agreeable to his vanity: by express wish he had occupied haunted rooms. Now he had no other pumps in this country, no idea where to buy them, and a ducal visit ahead. Also, wandering as it were among the apples and amphoras of an art school, he had blundered into the life room: women revolved gravely.

'Hell,' he said to the steps, mounting, his mind blank to the outcome.

He was nerved for the jumping lantern, but halfway up to the Castle darkness was once more absolute. Her lantern had gone out; he could orientate himself – in spite of himself – by her sobbing. Absolute desperation. He pulled up so short that, for balance, he had to cling to a creaking tree.

'Hi!' she croaked. Then: 'You *are* there! I hear you!'

'Miss Cuffe—'

'How too bad you are! I never heard you rowing. I thought you were never coming—'

'Quietly, my dear girl.'

'Come up quickly. I haven't even seen you. Come up to the windows—'

'Miss Cuffe—'

'Don't you remember the way?' As sure but not so noiseless as a cat in the dark, Valeria hurried to him.

'Mr Garrett —' she panted. 'I'm Miss Cuffe. Where have you been? I've destroyed my beautiful red dress and they've eaten up your dinner. But we're still waiting. Don't be afraid; you'll soon be there now. I'm Miss Cuffe; this is my Castle—'

'Listen, it's I, Mr Alban—'

'Ssh, ssh, Mr Alban: *Mr Garrett has landed.*'

Her cry, his voice, some breath of the joyful intelligence, brought the others on to the terrace, blind with lamplight.

'Valeria?'

'Mr Garrett has landed!'

Mrs Treye said to Miss Carbin under her breath, 'Mr Garrett has come.'

Miss Carbin, half weeping with agitation, replied, 'We must go in.' But uncertain who was to speak next, or how to speak, they remained leaning over the darkness. Behind, through the windows, lamps spread great skirts of light, and Mars and Mercury, unable to contain themselves, stooped from their pedestals. The dumb keyboard shone like a ballroom floor.

Alban, looking up, saw their arms and shoulders under the bright rain. Close by, Valeria's fingers creaked on her warm wet satin. She laughed like a princess, magnificently justified. Their unseen faces were all three lovely, and, in the silence after the laughter, such a strong tenderness reached him that, standing there in full manhood, he was for a moment not exiled. For the moment, without moving or speaking, he stood, in the dark, in a flame, as though all three said: 'My darling . . .'

Perhaps it was best for them all that early, when next day first lightened the rain, the destroyer steamed out – below the extinguished Castle where Valeria lay with her arms wide, past the boathouse where Mr Rossiter lay insensible and the bat hung masked in its wings – down the estuary into the open sea.

The Man of the Family

'Dear William,' Mrs Peel kept exclaiming. '*Isn't* William wonderful?'
She was his Aunt Luella, and because his talk was beyond her, and
she could not always grasp what he was saying, she kept casting
bright sceptical glances around the lunch-table. Her blonde shell-
rimmed spectacles gave these glances a twinkle. Lady Lambe, his
Aunt Héloïse, however, listened intently; she made little flapping
gestures at the butler when he offered her things, as though she
could not bear to be distracted. When she noticed the *soufflé* the
others were eating she recalled the butler with an apology.

After each interruption William would raise his voice half a
tone and continue patiently. He was on his way across London
from Oxford. Patsey, beside him, sat with her hands on her lap
twisting her rings about when she was not eating and taking no
part in the talk. She was not modern at all and always seemed
discouraged. Pretty Rachel sat smiling into the bowl of glass fruit,
on which green sunshine, reflected back from the Regent's Park
trees, twinkled and slid. The trees were in full June light, the dining-
room in shadow. The table was round, with no 'head', so that any
difficulty in placing William had been avoided.

Aunt Héloïse was also a Liberal: at the last three elections she
had stood for Parliament: she meant to keep on standing. She
was not original, but she was sound and receptive; when she
came down to Oxford he took her to debates at the Union.
Rachel Lambe never came with her mother; she said they all
made her feel so terribly old (she was twenty-four). He too
seldom saw her; she went out a great deal and seemed to have
numerous friends; when they met she, though so naïve, contrived
to be very mysterious. She had bronzy-gold hair, parted down
the centre, that rippled smoothly against the line of her cheeks,
and a smile – subtle, gentle, malicious – that sent curves up under
her eyes: a da Vinci smile. An extraordinary daughter for one of
one's aunts to have had.

William always lunched at his Aunt Luella's on his way across London. The Regent's Park house was his *pied-à-terre*; he could put up here even when the family were out of town, and bring friends in to meals – had he wished. Aunt Luella was an irritating, attractive woman; she was thin as a lath, wore a perpetual string of brown amber, and dressed to tone in with it. Her taste in interior decoration made him blush, but she kept an excellent table. She called him 'the man of the family' or 'the head of the family' (which he in fact was), and scoffed away gently at him. She scoffed at herself, her daughter and everyone else. Patsey was thirty-two, and looked like her mother's sister. She was statuesque, expensively dressed, and null; she had been engaged twice, but nothing had come of it. Quite a lot of life (he often longed to point out) was before her; interests still offered, but Patsey seemed blind to them. Her tomboyish name was unsuitable; Patsey was painfully womanly.

When William and Aunt Héloïse had settled the Government finally, they cleared their throats and there was a benign pause. Aunt Luella blinked. The butler came round with the Camembert. 'Do they *teach* you politics at Oxford?' Rachel said vaguely. William did not reply; he readjusted himself and turned sideways to Patsey.

'Well, Patsey, how goes it?' he said at last, genially.

She started violently. 'Goes what?' she said, flustered. 'It? Oh, very well, thank you. I've been having a lovely time.'

'Good,' said William. 'Splendid.'

'I've been helping at fêtes,' Patsey explained conscientiously. 'I went to the Chelsea Flower Show. I've been ever so many times to the Academy.'

'Splendid,' said William drearily. 'Nothing like going around. A man I know meant to go to the Academy only the other day, but I don't think he ever did.'

She looked at him, sidelong, out of her doglike brown eyes.

'I *adore* the Academy,' Rachel put in in her deep voice. 'I went to the private view and saw everyone. I *adore* the Academy.'

'Rachel "adores" anything to do with clothes,' said her mother. It was gratifying to her, as a plain intellectual woman to have produced something so pretty and frivolous. Yet neither 'pretty' nor 'frivolous' suited Rachel; they hung foolishly as pink muslin on her queer personality.

'Aren't I futile?' said Rachel, smiling down at her peach.

There certainly was no brandy like Aunt Luella's. William slid back in his chair with a good feeling inside. Catching her eye, he bowed an acknowledgment. 'And, oh, *William*,' said she, leaning suddenly forward. 'If you're not too busy today I'd love a little talk some time. Business.'

Business was Aunt Luella's forte. She loved to settle down at it for a stretch and bemuse William with documents. In her morning-room, with gold curtains and beetle-green walls blistered over with bluish patches like scum on a pool, he had put in hours of claustrophobia and torment. The shining shagreen accoutrements of her desk disappeared early under a sea of parchments – deeds, securities, settlements – God could hardly know what. Dispatch-boxes yawned and pink tape littered the floor. When he was of age she meant him to be a Trustee – he felt even now she was fattening him up for one. She ran in and out of documents like a spider, at demoniacal speed. 'Of course,' she would say, 'I've really no *head* for these things. One's a lone woman – but don't let me bother you. Only it is such a help to talk things out with a man. Your father was marvellous; no one could know what a help to me! But you must be *sure* now and don't let me waste your time.'

Escape was always impossible. 'I wish I took after father,' William would mutter, scrubbing his hands through his hair.

'I think you've a *wonderful* grasp of things,' she would always say brightly. These were the only occasions when she took him – or anything – seriously. He never could think what the woman thought she was getting at – showing off, merely? He could bet any amount she hadn't allowed Uncle Henry within sight of those boxes; she had so thoroughly kept Uncle Henry down. William hated, however, to be a beast in any way about Aunt Luella.

This afternoon, however, no tin boxes appeared. She burrowed vaguely in one writing-table drawer, giving William time to finish his coffee and light one more of her excellent cigarettes. He wondered sadly if Rachel would have gone by the time she had finished; he had thought it might be pleasant to walk back with Rachel across the Park. He jumped when Aunt Luella, twisting round on her chair, leaned vivaciously towards him and, swinging out her string of beads on one finger, said: 'It's about *Patsey*. Didn't you notice her?'

'N-not particularly.'

'She's been looking really quite brilliant. The thing is: Patsey's just going to be engaged again – I don't say *married*, because really I'm getting so superstitious about the poor darling. Engaged. Well, she is now, really, only I mean it isn't announced.'

'How terribly nice,' said William, clattering down his coffee-cup. 'Shall I go and congratulate her?'

'*Just* one moment . . . He's really, the dearest old charming thing; "Chummy," we call him – his name's Everard. So *nice*, so nice-looking, such nice people. Patsey and I are delighted with him. It's ideal – just one thing's a pity. He is divorced, poor dear.'

'Oh . . . Did it, or had it done to him?'

'Oh, *did* it, of course. The wife was a little baggage. He's been worn to a shadow, had no sort of life. He wants somebody absolutely reposeful. Patsey's the very thing. It's lovely to see them together. Only people do ask such silly questions, and talk. "Wasn't he divorced?" they say, as if poor Chummy hadn't come out of it splendidly. So I just thought I'd tell you before you spoke to Patsey, so's you couldn't ask anything awkward. Not that you would. We're all quite full of it – Aunt Héloïse, Rachel, and all. Only do remember, it isn't really *announced*.'

Up in the Chinese drawing-room, Patsey and Rachel sat one at each end of a sofa, each glancing over a copy of *Vogue*. Rachel had the more recent. Aunt Héloïse sat in an upright chair by the window reading *The Times* thoroughly. Patsey kept re-settling her cushions behind her, and Rachel re-crossing her legs; the room was full of the amiable drooping silence of relatives who have nothing special to say. When William entered, all three of them brightened up. Rachel leaned back with her hands propping her head; Patsey, pinkly self-conscious, shuffled *Vogue* off her knee, then pulled it back and began to scan the advertisements.

William, congratulations nicely delivered, stayed looming above them, hands in his pockets. Rachel meanwhile gazed up at him, not unkindly. He was a nice-looking fairish youth, intelligent but bothered-looking. He had even some prestige; his own friends thought he disproved that one couldn't be brilliant *and* solid. 'I shall hope to meet Everard,' he was saying to Patsey encouragingly. He remembered how, centuries ago, when he was still at his prep school, Patsey had come down one afternoon in the car, very much engaged, very pink, very conscious, with her first young man, Gerald, very pink also. She seemed to be nearly always in this condition. 'Chummy's coming to tea,' she said proudly, with that old deprecating, absurd, rather touching glow in her cheeks. 'You *will* stay, won't you? I thought we might all get tickets for something tomorrow night.'

'Um-m,' said William. He glanced at Rachel – it rather depended on her. But Rachel did not respond: he was disconcerted at catching a flash of glances across him. Rachel and Rachel's mother were making faces – or something subtler: 'expressions' – at one another.

'I'm terribly much afraid,' he said, scenting danger, 'I can't be in town for more than a night this time. I'm so sorry, Patsey. But I'd love to stay for tea.'

Rachel could not stay for tea: she was seldom available. She must get back she said; she had some wretched people coming. Aunt Héloïse had a committee meeting at three. Lady Lambe had four afternoon committees a week, and on those afternoons Rachel was at home to friends. Lady Lambe and her daughter lived in Walpole Street, Chelsea. Rachel, getting up thoughtfully, invited William to walk just across the Park with her. 'I think Regent's Park's so shady; one never knows. Last time I got spoken to by a boy on a scooter, and today I was followed by a repulsive Airedale. We parted out on the doorstep; it's probably waiting still. I hate dogs, you know.'

'Oh, poor old fellow,' cried Patsey; 'he must have got lost!' Rachel thought this quite likely; she patted the top of Patsey's head, kissed her hand to her mother, and went out, followed by William, who felt pleased.

Rachel walked beautifully; people kept turning to look at her. Her blue dress fled back from her figure in the light wind and the waves of her gold hair flickered against her cheeks. William wore the grey flannels and brown hat in which he had left Oxford. He decided that if Rachel should happen to ask him to come back to tea with her, Chummy might well keep. She walked in an absent silence, but he felt she had something special to say. He glanced at her once or twice, then said at a venture: 'What do *you* think of this person – this Everard?'

She looked past him at the lake and said casually, 'I *don't* think about him, but I know him, of course.'

'Oh, you do? Doesn't he bear thinking about?'

'Oh, I don't know whether he'd *bear* it – he's just not worth the effort. I don't think often.'

'Aunt Luella and Pat seem pleased.'

'Yes, poor dears,' agreed Rachel, and wrinkled up her nose. 'Aren't women all pathetic?'

This had not struck him. 'So long as *they're* pleased,' he said, 'I don't think we need think twice of it. Patsey's obviously got to marry someone.'

'Oh, I know,' agreed Rachel. 'Babies and that sort of thing. But she can't, I'm afraid, marry Chummy – so this has got to be stopped.'

William pulled up short; his mind reeled. Rachel came to a stop too, and stood eyeing him calmly.

'Why on earth? What's the matter with it? Or do *you* want to marry him?'

This sounded unkind, but seemed to him only fair. Such awkward clashes often occurred in novels. But Rachel shook her head definitely. 'Though I'd do quite a lot,' she said, 'for a really good home. But that, as a matter of fact, is exactly what Everard's after himself. I don't want to sound a brute, you know, William, but of course Aunt Luella and Patsey are very well off; what you'd call "warm". Everard values his comforts. After the first lunch he must have seen points about Patsey, and after two or three dinners and door-to-doors in the Daimler the best of her really nice character must have been perfectly clear. I don't mean that he probably isn't quite fond of her by this time – who wouldn't be, of Patsey? She's the dearest old slug.'

'Still, if they're both pleased,' William repeated. 'And, after all, people have to have *some* reason to marry. Aunt Luella may not be strong as a mother, but she's a born mother-in-law. Think what a time Chummy'll have with those black boxes!'

'That's just it. The poor woman's such a hopeless fool about money. She's as timid as a fowl by herself, and wouldn't re-invest tuppence, but she's probably been chatting to him about securities and he'll have been telling her she's the perfect woman of business. You know how weak her head is. I wouldn't mind him messing Aunt Luella's money about and losing it for her — she's got far too much — if he weren't also going to mess up Patsey's affections. But I cannot see why any one man should do both.'

Rachel said this so weightily that he stared.

'Do you hate him?' he asked. 'Or just know him fearfully well?'

'Wellish,' said Rachel. 'At least, I suppose you might say so. We nearly went abroad.'

They walked at uneven speed in the shade of the beeches, heads close for discretion's sake and talking in low tones. People veered to avoid them, for they looked anxious and pretty, like a young couple in love. Even William's friends, had they passed, might have thought this of him. Rachel paused at an empty seat and looked down at it hopelessly; William dusted a patch with his handkerchief and they both sat down. He stuck his feet out and glared at the toes of his shoes. Rachel brought out a mirror, studied her mouth, and applied a little more red.

'It was when I first grew up,' she said. 'I was fearfully bored. You know how hard up we were till grandfather died. Mother'd dropped all her friends who weren't on the right committees, and I never saw anyone, and had nothing to wear if I did. Mother never thought about anything but saving European children, and I used to take pleats in Patsey's cast-offs and wish I could die. Everyone seemed to be having a marvellous time, though I don't suppose they were really. Then a girl asked me down at the last moment to fill up a gap in a Hunt Ball party; Aunt Luella stood me a frock and I easily picked up Everard. I thought I was made.

'He seemed to be quite an experience. I had always suspected I must be all right really, but I never quite knew how nice I could be. He hadn't then come to the end of his wife's money, so he gave me a slap-up time. I wasn't a bit particular in those days. I saw he had mouldy patches, but that didn't bother me, till I met somebody else — but I hadn't then. Then he said, "Come abroad," and I didn't see why not. I'm sorry, William, but morals are like clothes and I'd scrapped one lot and hadn't found others to suit me. He said we'd

go in his car. Mother was going to Serbia on a hunt of some kind.
We fixed our start for the day after she was going – three weeks
ahead. But in those three weeks Everard lost colour. One way and
another . . . His wife put him on an allowance, and he got careful
– not to say slightly morbid if he thought he was spending too
much. So when he did take one out, he wanted his money's worth.
He's not stupid, exactly; he's got a tongue. That's where I went right
off him. In fact, he's not a nice man. That's where Patsey's heart
would come in. You may think me cynical, William, but I honestly
do believe that manners (or people not having them) undermine
happiness far quicker than morals. A person, specially not a person
like Patsey, can't expect her husband always to stay in her pocket,
but she does expect him to be polite when he's there. It's these little
remarks with an edge – you know, spiteful, cutting. He'd skin Patsey
alive. He can't leave a person in peace once he doesn't like their
face or thinks they're not keen on his. He never *hurt* me: you see,
I wasn't really attached to him; but he merely annoyed me rather. I
"kept him under observation" (as they say about measles), and when,
the very last day, he turned nasty at having to pay an extra seven-
and-six on my passport, I simply went home. I went down to Aunt
Luella in Wales and wired from there that our trip was off, on
grounds of economy.

'Now mind you, William, those three weeks he was in love with
me and wanting me more than anything, and still he couldn't help
being nasty. What he's wanting now is the key to Aunt Luella's
black boxes – and, I dare say, the key of the cellar. What chance
has Patsey got once they've settled him in?'

'You mean,' said William anxiously, 'that there's a distinction
between being nasty and being simply immoral?'

'I do, of course,' said Rachel, with some impatience. 'Now you
do see why this marriage is impossible?'

Her recital had given William all sorts of queer feelings. However,
he felt he knew Rachel very much better. His theory that this sort
of thing only happened to other people's relations broke down.
'What a lot goes on,' he thought. 'And how calmly women take
it.' He felt Rachel underrated his own sex. All the same, he had
this new, intimate feeling about her. 'But I can't quite see what
you're going to do,' he said.

'It's a question of what you are going to do,' she said. 'You see, you will be expected to take a line about this.'

'My dear girl—'

'Why else do you think I told you?' said Rachel languidly, opening her eyes very wide.

'What do you expect me to do?' he asked. 'Rush back and kick Everard, shouting "Swine, swine, swine, swine?"'

Sitting with hands folded on her turquoise-blue bag, she shrugged her shoulders in absolute detachment. Beyond the Park, the white walls of Aunt Luella's house twinkled behind the screen of a drooping branch. Rachel's cheeks went up into charming curves; she was smiling at William.

'If you did,' she said, 'it wouldn't come off. Aunt Luella would blink and twiddle her beads and say "Listen to William; isn't he wonderful!" and Patsey and Everard would go on chastely squeezing each other's hands. I'm afraid you can't be direct. Besides, you really can't give them chapter and verse. Mother would be so upset. Besides, I don't want Everard made an idiot of. He's right according to his lights. The last thing I want is to score off the poor old thing. He did do me one good turn; he pulled me out of my hole, and, as I say, he did seem to be an experience. No, William, don't shoot him up. All we have to work for is the protection of Patsey. He must be quietly blighted. That's up to you, I feel. As the man of the family, you really do carry some weight with Aunt Luella. Simply be rather heavy. Tell her . . . tell her you've heard the most shocking things about Everard at Oxford. Say they're being said everywhere. If the worst comes to the worst, I'll support you, of course. But I think I should make the worst worse. You see, it's awkward for mother; she loathes Chummy instinctively; I think she must have some jungle instinct about him. But seeming to crab Patsey's marriage when she hasn't got me off— And whenever she tries to say anything about Everard, Aunt Luella goes off like an alarm clock.'

'Oxford,' said William annoyed. 'Who in God's name would have heard of Chummy there? He's quite obscure, isn't he?'

'Oh, I suppose you all gossip,' said his cousin, indifferent. 'Like men always do.' She laid her gloved hand with the diamond bracelet over his for a moment. 'William,' she said, 'be effective. I count on you absolutely. Do go back and be effective at once, *now*. Then

come round and let's go out to dinner and hear how effective
you've been.'

Shaking out her blue dress with a gesture, his cousin was gone.
The June sun seemed to William paler; a very slight shiver went
down his back.

As William paced round the morning-room, waiting for Aunt
Luella, he asked himself once more what this fuss was about. He
tried to pull out an antique-looking book from a rack, to discover
this opened, revealing a vanity-box. He brushed his nose nervously
over some prim yellow roses which were scentless and which,
unbalanced, flopped heavily from the vase. He seated himself
abruptly in an armchair which, mounted on springs, sank under
him. Unnerved, he stood up with his back to the empty grate,
repeating that values were relative. He glared at the children racing
around in the Park and thought what a pity it was that the race
need go on.

His Aunt Luella sent urgent messages, wanting to know why
he wouldn't join them for tea. Perhaps she would never come.
Suppose she sent Everard?

Then he heard her plunging along in that characteristic way,
her necklace swinging against her belt-buckle. She shot in with
the light on her spectacles, glittering at him reproachfully. 'William,
you're *too* naughty! You mustn't be such a shy boy. Chummy is
most disappointed. I never heard—'

'It's not that,' said her nephew. 'I never have been a shy boy. I've
got heaps to say when I'm let get a word in edgeways. I've got
heaps to say about Everard. Aunt Luella, this marriage—'

'– *Dear* Everard!' she exclaimed, and, as Rachel had said, went
off like an alarm clock. Going on talking, she put out a hand for
William's and made him sit down by her on the window-seat.
'Dear Chummy,' she finished, 'I do admire him so. Happiness makes
him *solemn.*'

'He may have cause to be solemn. Do you really *know*, Aunt
Luella, that he is in every way a suitable husband for Patsey?'

'Almost anyone would be – anyone *nice*. She'd make anyone
into a good husband. That's her gift, I've always thought. It's sheer
bad luck that it's never come into play. Dear Patsey . . .'

'I'm sorry,' said William, standing up with an effort. 'I'm afraid I've got to be a bit of a brute. It's up to me – I mean there seems no one else – I mean, as a man – I'm afraid Everard *isn't* nice. He won't do. Certain things have come to my knowledge— We must face facts.'

'Don't talk,' said his aunt with asperity, 'about what you know nothing about.'

'I'm sorry,' repeated William, 'but I've been given to understand—'

'My dear boy, you're too young to understand anything.'

'I merely happen to know,' said her nephew, scarlet, 'that he made improper suggestions to a young girl.'

'*My-dear-boy*—' said his aunt. She looked from his chin to his shoes, blinked quickly behind her glasses, let out a small smothered hysterical sound like a whinny, then pressed her handkerchief violently to her lips. She was leaning back with her shoulder against the shuter: the shutter shook. William thrust his hands deep into his pockets and feelingly looked away from her.

The shutter still shook, and small noises exploded from his aunt's handkerchief. 'Aunt Luella,' said William, 'do pull yourself together. We've got to do something, haven't we?'

Aunt Luella meekly lowered her handkerchief from a mouth twisted in uncontrollable mirth. 'Dear William,' she faltered, 'I'm so awfully sorry. But you were so dramatic. Now, *who's* been giving our poor Rachel away?'

William froze by the table, opening the shagreen blotter. 'Oh so you've found out?'

'I know,' his aunt said grimly, 'the real *facts* of the matter. Who's been telling you fairy tales? . . . I suppose,' she darted out at him, 'Rachel has?'

William nodded cautiously. Aunt Luella stared into the air between them. 'Oh!' she exclaimed. 'The *unscrupulous* girl she is!'

William gulped. 'I laughed for a moment,' his aunt explained indignantly. 'William, of course you are *wax* in that girl's hands. All boys are. Of course you don't know Rachel! If there ever was "still water!" Just one mass of jealous subtlety. She cannot bear to see Patsey happy this way. We all know she stops at nothing. But even so—'

'Didn't it rather shock you?'

'Shock me! My dear boy, at your age you cannot *imagine* what that poor Everard's been through. She's been his bad angel. Of course, she made a dead set at him. If ever a girl tried to wreck a man! And Chummy, being so conscientious and good all the time, trying to live his miserable marriage down. Told me? Of course he told me; he was so splendid about it, trying to shield that little minx all the way through. He was so distressed for us all when she walked in one day and he found she was Patsey's cousin. *She* never turned a hair. Of course he told me; Chummy and I are *friends*! He said he did feel, as things were, that I ought to know. But Chummy doesn't bear malice!'

'Anxious to get in first,' observed William gloomily.

His aunt, glaring, continued. '"I only want," poor Everard said, "to shield Patsey. We must think first of her." That was of course what we both felt. And of course we kept poor dear Héloïse out of it. Though I must say it's what she deserves. Always saving Serbian children and looking superior. I could have told her Rachel would come to no good. But, really, her spite surprises me. And her effrontery. My first instinct was, of course, never to have her here again. But then dear Patsey'd have wondered. She asked him to take her abroad *in his wife's car*!'

'Aunt Luella,' said William, 'you shock me. How can you believe a swine who talks like that about Rachel! How can you let a person like that marry your Patsey!'

'I know the girl only too well,' his aunt said with gloomy triumph. 'For years I've seen this coming. I'm sorry for *you*, William. I don't like to disillusion a boy of your age. I wouldn't like you to feel you have made a fool of yourself.'

(Of this she gave small indication.) 'But there's only Rachel to thank. No, I'm not angry. I'm merely sorry for you.'

It struck William, whose relations with Aunt Luella had up to now been affable, suave and pleasant, that they were now in the thick of a raging row. She was rather certainly hating him. He felt like the dog in the Anstey story that inconveniently dug up the shot poodle. The familiar air of her beetle-green room reproached him. The cigarette-box recalled sharply arrears of her hospitality, their pleasant chats about documents. He gazed at his aunt, whose mauve colour rose steadily: he had never seen Aunt Luella change colour before. His heart dropped an inch.

'My God,' he thought, 'am I wrong?' He couldn't believe this was normal family life. 'Is this mother love?' he wondered, and pictured a large red hen. Or could there be something subtler, nearer the quick, as it were, the matter with Aunt Luella? 'Confound all women,' he thought. He said obstinately: '*I* think Rachel comes out of this well. I'm sorry her name was ever brought into this. She simply wanted to save you and Patsey from—'

'She didn't,' snapped Aunt Luella; 'she wanted to wreck the marriage.' Frantic with indignation, she tugged at her amber string; the string snapped and the beads clattered about the floor. This gave William the sense of a last catastrophe; he went hopelessly down on his knees to gather the beads up.

'Stop crawling about,' said his aunt, 'and listen to me, William. I could have never believed that even a boy of your age could be so clumsy and stupid. You act like a child of five. You make it difficult for me ever to have you or Rachel about in this house again. If it were not for your Aunt Héloïse, I should advise you not to see Rachel again. She's an extremely bad influence.'

'Here are six of your beads,' said William with dignity. 'You'd be sorry to lose them. As it happens, I'm dining with her tonight.'

'Will you *listen* to what I'm saying?'

'I'm sorry this . . . outbreak . . . should have occurred, Aunt Luella. I'd no idea I'd upset you. But I can't regret having spoken. You seem to me on the verge of a fearful mistake. I feel bound, as the man of the family—'

'Man? My dear child, you've only just left school. Yes, I quite see you're sorry. But you really should learn you're too young to meddle with things. We won't say any more about it, only please try and remember another time that you don't know *every*thing yet. Now do go and flatten your hair down and wash your face and get cool. Then come and have tea and talk nicely to Patsey and Everard. Of course, we'll forget this. I'm sure you meant very well.' She approached and patted his shoulder.

William turned to the door. His aunt, now only too normal, looked after him quizzically. 'Yes, run along with you,' she said. 'And don't be so silly again. Stop; just come back and give your

old auntie a kiss . . . There, *now* we're right again, aren't we? . . .
Dear old William. How nice that we don't, as a family, ever have
grievances.'

His aunt's kiss still damp on his cheek, he succeeded in leaving
the room.

William rang up the Ivy to book a table for two. As he crossed
the landing he heard, through the drawing-room door above a rich
male voice talking affably. He heard a tinkle of glass and excited,
delighted laughter from Aunt Luella and Patsey.

'Well, if I *must*—' said the voice with beautiful resignation.

'Yes, you *must*, Everard; mustn't Everard, mummy?'

'Of course he must. Come along, don't be silly, Chummy!'

'Well, if I *must* . . .' William heard a siphon go off.

'Mummy, where's that other table? It's higher.'

'No, wait, Chummy – let me!'

'Well, if you really *will* insist . . .' Someone moved a table up
for Everard's drink. 'No, let me light it!' cried Patsey. Later, she
dropped the matchbox. The Man of the Family was very much in
possession.

'It really doesn't much matter,' thought William. 'They're all
fools.'

Tears, Idle Tears

Frederick burst into tears in the middle of Regent's Park. His mother, seeing what was about to happen, had cried: 'Frederick, you *can't* – in the middle of Regent's Park!' Really, this was a corner, one of those lively corners just inside a big gate, where two walks meet and a bridge starts across the pretty, winding lake. People were passing quickly; the bridge rang with feet. Poplars stood up like delicate green brooms; diaphanous willows whose weeping was not shocking quivered over the lake. May sun spattered gold through the breezy trees; the tulips though falling open were still gay; three girls in a long boat shot under the bridge. Frederick, knees trembling, butted towards his mother a crimson, convulsed face, as though he had the idea of burying himself in her. She whipped out a handkerchief and dabbed at him with it under his grey felt hat, exclaiming meanwhile in fearful mortification: 'You really haven't got to be such a *baby*!' Her tone attracted the notice of several people, who might otherwise have thought he was having something taken out of his eye.

He was too big to cry: the whole scene was disgraceful. He wore a grey flannel knickerbocker suit and looked like a schoolboy; though in fact he was seven, still doing lessons at home. His mother said to him almost every week: 'I don't know what they will think when you go to school!' His tears were a shame of which she could speak to no one; no offensive weakness of body could have upset her more. Once she had got so far as taking her pen up to write to the Mother's Advice Column of a helpful woman's weekly about them. She began: 'I am a widow; young, good tempered, and my friends all tell me that I have great control. But my little boy –' She intended to sign herself 'Mrs D., Surrey.' But then she had stopped and thought no, no: after all, he is Toppy's son . . . She was a gallant-looking, correct woman, wearing today in London a coat and skirt, a silver fox, white gloves and a dark-blue toque put on exactly right – not the sort of woman you ought to see in a Park with a great blubbering boy belonging to her. She looked a mother of sons, but not of a son of this kind, and should more properly, really, have been walking a dog. 'Come on!' she said, as though the bridge, the poplars, the people staring were to be borne no longer. She began to walk on quickly, along the edge of the lake, parallel with the park's girdle of trees and the dark, haughty windows of Cornwall Terrace looking at her over the red may. They had meant to go to the Zoo, but now she had changed her mind: Frederick did not deserve the Zoo.

Frederick stumbled along beside her, too miserable to notice. His mother seldom openly punished him, but often revenged herself on him in small ways. He could feel how just this was. His own incontinence in the matter of tears was as shocking to him, as bowing-down, as annulling, as it could be to her. He never knew what happened – a cold, black pit with no bottom opened inside himself; a red-hot bellwire jagged up through him from the pit of his frozen belly to the caves of his eyes. Then the hot, gummy rush of tears, the convulsion of his features, the terrible, square grin he felt his mouth take all made him his own shameful and squalid enemy. Despair howled round his inside like a wind, and through his streaming eyes he saw everything quake. Anyone's being there – and most of all his mother – drove this catastrophe on him. He never cried like this when he was alone.

Crying made him so abject, so outcast from other people that he went on crying out of despair. His crying was not just reflex, like a baby's; it dragged up all unseemliness into view. No wonder everyone was repelled. There is something about an abject person that rouses cruelty in the kindest breast. The plate-glass windows of the lordly houses looked at him through the may trees with judges' eyes. Girls with their knees crossed, reading on the park benches, looked up with unkind smiles. His apathetic stumbling, his not seeing or caring that they had given up their trip to the Zoo, became more than Mrs Dickinson, his mother, could bear. She pointed out, in a voice tense with dislike: 'I'm not taking you to the Zoo.'

'Mmmph-mmph-mmph,' sobbed Frederick.

'You know, I so often wonder what your father would think.'

'Mmmph-mmph-mmph.'

'He used to be so proud of you. He and I used to look forward to what you'd be like when you were a big boy. One of the last things he ever said was: "Frederick will take care of you." You almost make me glad he's not here now.'

'Oough–oough.'

'What do you say?'

'I'm t-t-trying to stop.'

'Everybody's looking at you, you know.'

She was one of those women who have an unfailing sense of what not to say, and say it: despair, perversity or stubborn virtue must actuate them. She had a horror, also, of the abnormal and had to hit out at it before it could hit at her. Her husband, an R.A.F. pilot who had died two days after a ghastly crash, after two or three harrowing spaces of consciousness, had never made her ashamed or puzzled her. Their intimacies, then even his death, had had a bold naturalness.

'Listen, I shall walk on ahead,' said Frederick's mother, lifting her chin with that noble, decided movement so many people liked. 'You stay here and look at that duck till you've stopped that noise. Don't catch me up till you have. No, I'm really ashamed of you.'

She walked on. He had *not* been making, really, so very much noise. Drawing choppy breaths, he stood still and looked at the duck that sat folded into a sleek white cypher on the green, grassy margin of the lake. When it rolled one eye open over a curve, something unseeing in its expression calmed him. His mother walked away under the gay tree-shadows; her step quickened lightly, the tip of her fox fur swung. She thought of the lunch she had had with Major and Mrs Williams, the party she would be going to at five. First, she must leave Frederick at Aunt Mary's, and what would Aunt Mary say to his bloated face? She walked fast; the gap between her and Frederick widened: she was a charming woman walking by herself.

Everybody had noticed how much courage she had; they said: 'How plucky Mrs Dickinson is.' It was five years since her tragedy and she had not remarried, so that her gallantness kept on coming into play. She helped a friend with a little shop called *Isobel* near where they lived in Surrey, bred puppies for sale and gave the rest of her time to making a man of Frederick. She smiled nicely and carried her head high. Those two days while Toppy had lain dying she had hardly turned a hair, for his sake: no one knew when he might become conscious again. When she was not by his bed she was waiting about the hospital. The chaplain hanging about her and the doctor had given thanks that there were women like this; another officer's wife who had been her friend had said she was braver than could be good for anyone. When Toppy finally died the other woman had put the unflinching widow into a taxi and driven back with her to the Dickinsons' bungalow. She kept saying: 'Cry, dear, cry; you'd feel better.' She made tea and clattered about, repeating: 'Don't mind me, darling: just have a big cry.' The strain became so great that tears streamed down her own face. Mrs Dickinson looked past her palely, with a polite smile. The empty-feeling bungalow with its rustling curtains still smelt of Toppy's pipe; his slippers were under a chair. Then Mrs Dickinson's friend, almost tittering with despair, thought of a poem of Tennyson's she had learnt as a child. She said: 'Where's Frederick? He's quiet. Do you think he's asleep?' The widow, rising, perfectly automatic, led her into the room where Frederick lay in his cot. A nursemaid rose from beside him, gave them one morbid look and scurried away. The two-year-old baby, flushed, and drawing up his upper lip in his sleep as his father used to do, lay curved under his blue blanket, clenching one fist on nothing. Something suddenly seemed to strike his mother, who, slumping down by the cot, ground her face and forehead into the fluffy blanket, then began winding the blanket round her two fists. Her convulsions, though proper, were fearful: the cot shook. The friend crept away into the kitchen, where she stayed a half-hour, muttering to the maid. They made more tea and waited for Mrs Dickinson to give full birth to her grief. Then extreme silence drew them back to the cot. Mrs Dickinson knelt asleep, her profile pressed to the blanket, one arm crooked over the baby's form. Under his mother's arm, as still as an image, Frederick lay wide awake, not making a sound. In conjunction with a certain look in his eyes, the baby's silence gave the two women the horrors. The servant said to the friend: 'You would think he knew.'

Mrs Dickinson's making so few demands on pity soon rather alienated her women friends, but men liked her better for it: several

of them found in her straight look an involuntary appeal to themselves alone, more exciting than coquetry, deeply, nobly exciting:
several wanted to marry her. But courage had given her a new
intractable kind of virgin pride: she loved it too much; she could
never surrender it. 'No, don't ask me that,' she would say, lifting
her chin and with that calm, gallant smile. 'Don't spoil things.
You've been splendid to me: such a support. But you see, there's
Frederick. He's the man in my life now. I'm bound to put him
first. That wouldn't be fair, would it?' After that, she would simply
go on shaking her head. She became the perfect friend for men
who wished to wish to marry but were just as glad not to, and
for married men who liked just a little pathos without being
upset.

Frederick had stopped crying. This left him perfectly blank, so
that he stared at the duck with abstract intensity, perceiving its
moulded feathers and porcelain-smooth neck. The burning, swirling
film had cleared away from his eyes, and his diaphragm felt relief,
as when retching has stopped. He forgot his focus of grief and
forgot his mother, but saw with joy a quivering bough of willow
that, drooping into his gaze under his swollen eyelids, looked as
pure and strong as something after the Flood. His thought clutched
at the willow, weak and wrecked but happy. He knew he was now
qualified to walk after his mother, but without feeling either guilty
or recalcitrant did not wish to do so. He stepped over the rail – no
park keeper being at hand to stop him – and, tenderly and respect-
fully, attempted to touch the white duck's tail. Without a blink,
with automatic uncoyness, the duck slid away from Frederick into
the lake. Its lovely white-china body balanced on the green glass
water as it propelled itself gently round the curve of the bank.
Frederick saw with a passion of observation its shadowy, webbed
feet lazily striking out.

'The keeper'll eat you,' said a voice behind him.

Frederick looked cautiously round with his bunged-up eyes.
The *individual* who had spoken sat on a park bench; it was a girl
with a dispatch case beside her. Her big bony knee-joints stuck
out through her thin crêpe-de-chine dress; she was hatless and her
hair made a frizzy, pretty outline, but she wore spectacles, her skin
had burnt dull red; her smile and the cock of her head had about

them something pungent and energetic, not like a girl's at all. 'Whatcher mean, eat me?'

'You're on his grass. And putting salt on his duck's tail.'

Frederick stepped back carefully over the low rail. 'I haven't got any salt.' He looked up and down the walk: his mother was out of sight, but from the direction of the bridge a keeper was approaching, still distant but with an awesome gait. 'My goodness,' the girl said, 'what's been biting *you*?' Frederick was at a loss. 'Here,' she said, 'have an apple.' She opened her case, which was full of folded grease-paper that must have held sandwiches, and rummaged out an apple with a waxy, bright skin. Frederick came up, tentative as a pony, and finally took the apple. His breath was still hitching and catching; he did not wish to speak.

'Go on,' she said, 'swallow: it'll settle your chest. Where's your mother gone off to? What's all the noise about?' Frederick only opened his jaws as wide as they would go, then bit slowly, deeply into the apple. The girl re-crossed her legs and tucked her thin crêpe-de-chine skirt round the other knee. 'What had you done – cheeked her?'

Frederick swept the mouthful of apple into one cheek. 'No,' he said shortly. 'Cried.'

'I should say you did. Bellowed, I watched you all down the path.' There was something ruminative in the girl's tone that made her remark really not at all offensive; in fact, she looked at Frederick as though she were meeting an artist who had just done a turn. He had been standing about, licking and biting the apple, but now he came and sat down at the other end of the bench. 'How do you do it?' she said.

Frederick only turned away: his ears began burning again.

'What gets at you?' she said.

'Don't know.'

'Someone coming it over you? I know another boy who cries like you, but he's older. He knots himself up and bellows.'

'What's his name?'

'George.'

'Does he go to school?'

'Oh, lord, no; he's a boy at the place where I used to work.' She raised one arm, leaned back, and watched four celluloid bangles, each of a different colour, slide down it to her elbow joint, where they stuck. 'He doesn't know why he does it,' she said, 'but he's got to. It's as though he saw something. You can't ask him. Some people take him that way: girls do. I never did. It's as if he knew about something he'd better not. I said once, well, what just *is* it, and he said if he *could* tell me he wouldn't do it. I said, well, what's the *reason*, and he said, well, what's the reason not to? I knew him well at one time.'

Frederick spat out two pips, looked round cautiously for the keeper, then dropped the apple-core down the back of the seat. 'Where'd's George live?'

'I don't know now,' she said, 'I often wonder. I got sacked from that place where I used to work, and he went right off and I never saw him again. You snap out of that, if you can, before you are George's age. It does you no good. It's all the way you see things. Look, there's your mother back. Better move, or there'll be *more* trouble.' She held out her hand to Frederick, and when he put his in it shook hands so cheerfully, with such tough decision, that the four celluloid bangles danced on her wrist. 'You and George,' she said. 'Funny to meet two of you. Well, goodbye, Henry: cheer up.'

'I'm Frederick.'

'Well, cheer up, Freddie.'

As Frederick walked away, she smoothed down the sandwich papers inside her dispatch case and snapped the case shut again. Then she put a finger under her hair at each side, to tuck her spectacles firmly down on her ears. Her mouth, an unreddened line across her harshly-burnt face, still wore the same truculent, homely smile. She crossed her arms under the flat chest, across her stomach, and sat there holding her elbows idly, wagging one foot in its fawn sandal, looking fixedly at the lake through her spectacles, wondering about George. She had the afternoon, as she had no work. She saw George's face lifted abjectly from his arms on a table, blotchy over his clerk's collar. The eyes of George and Frederick seemed to her to be wounds, in the world's surface, through which its inner, terrible unassuageable, necessary sorrow constantly bled away and as constantly welled up.

Mrs Dickinson came down the walk under the band of trees, carefully unanxious, looking lightly at objects to see if Frederick

were near them: he had been a long time. Then she saw Frederick
shaking hands with a sort of girl on a bench and starting to come
her way. So she quickly turned her frank, friendly glance on the
lake, down which, as though to greet her, a swan came swimming.
She touched her fox fur lightly, sliding it up her shoulder. What a
lovely mother to have. 'Well, Frederick,' she said, as he came into
earshot, 'coming?' Wind sent a puff of red mayflowers through the
air. She stood still and waited for Frederick to come up. She could
not think what to do now: they had an hour to put in before they
were due at Aunt Mary's. But this only made her manner calmer
and more decisive.

Frederick gave a great skip, opened his mouth wide, shouted:
'Oo, I say, mother, I nearly caught a duck!'

'Frederick, dear, how silly you are: you couldn't.'

'Oo, yes, I could, I could. If I'd had salt for its tail!' Years later,
Frederick could still remember, with ease, pleasure and with a sense
of lonely shame being gone, that calm, white duck swimming off
round the bank. But George's friend with the bangles, and George's
trouble, fell through a cleft in his memory and were forgotten
soon.

The Needlecase

The car was sent to the train – along the straight road between dykes in the late spring dusk – to bring back Miss Fox, who was coming to sew for a week. Frank, the second son of the house, had come suddenly back from town; he was pleased to find the car there, which was more than he hoped, but appalled to see Miss Fox, in black, like a jointed image, stepping in at the back. Frank had, and wished to have, no idea who she was. So he sat in front with the chauffeur, looking glumly left at the willows and dykes flitting by, while Miss Fox, from the back, looked as fixedly out at willows and dykes at the other side of the road. No one spoke. They turned in at the lodge gates and the avenue trees closed in.

When the car drew up at the hall door, Frank got out and shouted. It embarrassed him having come home, and he did not want to explain. His sister Angela, sitting up at her window, heard, shot downstairs, and flung her arms round his neck, nearly knocking him over, like far too big a dog, as though he had been away two years instead of two days. This pleasure she overexpressed was perfectly genuine; Angela was effusive because she was often depressed; she could not be bothered being subtle with Frank, whom she knew far too well, and whose chagrins she often shared. So she kept up this rowdy pretence that everything was for the best.

'Had-a-good-time?' she said.

'No.'

'I'm sure you did really,' said Angela.

'No doubt you know best,' said Frank. 'Who in God's name's that in there?'

'Oh, that's Miss *Fox*,' explained Angela, peering into the car, where Miss Fox sat like an image, waiting to be let out. Angela rang the bell wildly for someone to come and cope. The chauffeur carried Frank's bag and the sewing-woman's strapped-up brown paper suitcase up the wide steps. The front of the house loomed

over them, massive and dark and cold: it was the kind of house
that easily looks shut up, and, when shut up, looks derelict. Angela
took Frank's arm and they went indoors, into the billiard-room,
the only place they could be certain of meeting nobody else. The
room had a dank, baizey smell, and a smell of cold anthracite from
the unlit stove: four battered green shades hung low over the
sheeted table. It was not cheery in here. Frank sat on the fender-
stool with his shoulders up and stared through his sister Angela
heavily, uninvitingly. Had he wished to be quite alone he would
not, however, have shouted.

'What did you do?' said Angela.

'Nothing special,' Frank said. He had been up to London to
meet a man who might get him a job if he liked the looks of him,
and the man clearly had not. The man had seen Frank to do Arthur
a good turn: unfortunately the brothers did not resemble each
other. Everyone liked Arthur. And Frank had stayed up in London,
and had hoped to stay longer, because of a girl, but that had been
a flop too: he had run through his money; that was why he was
home. Angela had the good sense to ask no more. Leaning against
the table and screwing her left-hand white coral earring tighter
(she always looked rather well) she said nonchalantly: 'The Applebys
have been over. Hermione's after Arthur. They want us for tennis
on Monday. The vet. came about Reno; he says it's nothing – oh,
and mother has heard from Arthur; he's coming down Friday week
and bringing his new girl. So then mother wired to hurry on Miss
Fox. She's going to make us all over – first the drawing-room
covers, then mother's black lace, and then do up Toddy and me
– cut some dresses and run up some tennis frocks. She's our one
hope for the summer. No doubt she sews like hell, but we really
couldn't look worse. Could we, Frank? I mean, could we?'

'Yes,' said Frank. 'I mean, no.'

'We heard of her through Aunt Doris,' said Angela, chatting
away. 'She's one of the wonderfully brave – she's got a child to
support that she shouldn't have. She trained somewhere or other,
so I suppose she *can* make. She's been on these rounds for years,
going down in the world a bit. She seems dirt cheap, so there must
be something fishy. She used to work, years ago, for the
Fotheringhams, but Aunt Doris only got on to her after she fell.'

'You surprise me,' said Frank, yawning drearily, wanting a drink more than anything in the world.

Miss Fox's arrival, though perfectly unassuming, had left quite a wake of noise: she had been taken up and put somewhere, but doors went on opening and shutting, Frank's mother stood out in the hall giving directions, and his elder sister Toddy began shouting for Angela. As Frank crossed the hall his mother broke off to give him her vivid mechanical smile and say, 'Oh, you're *back*.' The house – far too big but kept on for Arthur, who was almost always away but liked to think of it there – had many high windows and a white stone well staircase that went, under a skylight, up and up and up. This would have been an excellent house for someone else to have lived in, and heated; Frank and Angela could then have visited comfortably there. As it was, it was like a disheartened edition of Mansfield Park. The country around it was far too empty and flat.

Miss Fox was not to work tonight; they left her to settle in. But Toddy was in such a hurry to get in first with her things that she slipped upstairs, unobtrusively, as soon as dinner was over. She found Miss Fox still smoking over her supper tray. She was of that difficult class that has to have trays all the time. Too grand for the servants, she had to be fed in her room – one of those top bedrooms in any Georgian house with high ceilings and windows down by the floor. It looked rather bleak in the light of two hanging bulbs. A massive cheval glass, brought from downstairs today, reflected Miss Fox's figure sitting upright at the table. Deal presses stood round the walls, dress-boxes tottered in stacks and two dressmaker's dummies – one stout and one slimmer – protruded their glazed black busts. A sewing-machine with a treadle awaited the dress-maker's onslaught. In the grate, a thin fire rather uncertainly flapped. What should be done had been done to acclimatize Miss Fox. But her purpose here could be never far from her mind, for she rigidly sat at the table where she would work. A folded-back magazine was propped on the coffee-pot: when Toddy came in she lifted her eyes from this slowly, but did not attempt to rise.

Her meek, strong, narrow, expressionless face, with heavy eyelids, high cheekbones and secretive mouth, framed in dusty fair hair brushed flat and knotted behind, looked carven under the bleak overhead light. Its immobile shadows were startling. Toddy thought: 'She's important.' But this was absurd.

Toddy kicked the door to behind her and stood stock still, a cascade of tired dance dresses flung over one arm, two bales of gingham for tennis frocks balanced under the other. Success this forthcoming summer was deadly important, for Toddy was now twenty-four. She felt Miss Fox held her fate in the palm of her hand. So she stood stock still and did not know how to begin. She had quieter manners, a subtler air than Angela, but was in fact a rather one-idea girl.

'I hope you have all you want,' she said helplessly.

'Yes, thank you, Miss Forrester.'

'I mustn't disturb you tonight. But I thought you might like some idea—'

'Show me,' said Miss Fox politely, and pushed her chair back from the table.

'My red tulle is ripped right round. It caught on a spur—'

She stopped, for Miss Fox was looking at her so oddly, as though she were a ghost, as though it were terror and pleasure to see her face. Toddy's looks were not startling, but were, like her brother Arthur's, pleasant enough. No one, no man, had been startled this way before.

'It caught on a spur,' she said, on a rising note.

Miss Fox's eyes went quite blank. 'Tch-tch-tch,' she said, and bent quickly over the stuff. She had unpacked and settled in – Toddy saw, looking round – screens hid her bed and washstand, the facts of her life, away, but one or two objects had appeared on the mantelpiece, and a fine, imposing work-basket stood at her elbow. Toddy, who loved work-baskets, had a touch of the jackdaw, so, while Miss Fox was examining the martyred red dress, she flicked back the hinged lid of the basket and with innocent, bird-like impertinence routed through its contents. All sorts of treasures were here; 'souvenir' tape-measures, tight velvet emery bags, button-bags, a pin-cushion inside a shell, scissors of all sorts in scabbards – and oh, such a needlecase! 'As large as a family Bible,' said Toddy, opening it, pleased. And, like a family Bible, it had a photo stuck inside. 'Oh, what a nice little boy!' – '*Thank you,*' exclaimed Miss Fox, and with irresistible quickness, a snatch, had the needlecase back. The movement so surprising, it seemed not to have happened.

'That looked such a dear little boy,' Toddy went on, impenitent.

'My little nephew,' Miss Fox said impenetrably.

It was odd to think she had a child, for with such a nun-like face she had looked all wrong, somehow, smoking a cigarette. The dusty look of her hair must be the effect of light, for Toddy, standing above her, looked down and saw how well brushed her hair was. Her fingers looked as though they would always be cold, and Toddy dreaded their touch on her naked spine when the time would come to try on her evening dresses. And felt frightened alone with her, at the top of this dark, echoing house. They saved light everywhere, you had to grope up the stairs, for this well of a house drank money. So its daughters, likely to wither, had few 'advantages'. Everyone knew, Arthur knew, that Arthur must marry money. Toddy was sick of the sacrifice. She was in love this year, baulked all the time, and her serene, squarish face concealed a constant, pricking anxiety.

'I've *got* to look nice,' she said suddenly.

'I'll do all I can,' said Miss Fox, flashing up once again that odd, reminiscent look.

'How *like* you, Toddy,' Angela cried at breakfast.

'What was like Toddy?' Frank asked, scrawling a maze among the crumbs by his plate. He seldom listened to what his sisters were saying, but sat on at table with them because he had nowhere special to go next.

'Creeping up there, then poking about in her things. You really might give the poor old creature a break.'

'She's not so old,' said Toddy, serene. 'And the child looked about seven.'

'What was it like?'

'I only saw curls and a collar – I tell you, she snatched it away.'

'What child?' said Frank. He pushed his cup across vaguely and Angela gave him more coffee, but it was cold.

'The child she had,' said Toddy.

'Oh God,' said Frank, 'is she fallen?' But he did not care in the least.

'I told you she was, last night,' said Angela, hurt.

That morning, Miss Fox was put in the drawing-room to work. Bales of chintz were unrolled and she cut out the new covers, shaping them over the backs of the chairs with pins. In cold, windy April sunlight she crawled round and round the floor, with pins in her mouth. The glazed chintz looked horribly cold. Frank, kept so short of money, not only thought the rosy-and-scrolly pattern itself obscene, but found these new covers a frenzied extravagance. But now Arthur's most promising girl was coming to stay, and must at all costs be impressed. If she did marry Arthur, she'd scrap these covers first thing. Any bride would. Frank leaned in the doorway, letting a draught in that rustled under the chintz, to watch Miss Fox at work on her thankless task. She magnetized his idleness. Their silence was fascinating, for if he spoke she would have to spit out those pins. The drawing-room was full of tables covered with photographs: Arthur at every age. He watched Miss Fox dodge the tables and drag her lengths of chintz clear.

Then she sat back on her heels. 'How fast you get on,' Frank said.

'I give my whole mind to it.'

'Don't your hands get cold, touching that stuff?'

'They may do; I'm not particular.'

She put pins back in her mouth and Frank wondered how she had ever been seduced. He picked up her big scissors idly and snipped at the air with them. 'This house is like ice,' he said. 'Do you know this part of the world?'

She was round at the back of the sofa and nothing came for some time; she must be eyeing the pattern and chewing the pins. Then her voice came over the top. 'I've heard speak of it. It seems very quiet round here.'

'*Quiet*—' began Frank.

But, hearing his voice, his mother looked in and said with her ready smile: 'Come, Frank, I want you a moment. We mustn't disturb Miss Fox.'

That same afternoon, the sun went in. Sharp dark clouds with steely white edges began bowling over the sky and their passing made the whole landscape anxious and taut. Frank went out riding with

Angela; the wind, coming up and up, whistled among the willows; the dykes cut the country up with uneasy gleams. The grass was still fawn-coloured; only their own restlessness told them that it was spring. It *was* quiet round here. They jogged tamely along, and Angela said she saw no reason why things should ever happen, and yet they did. She wished they saw more of life. Even Miss Fox in the house was *something*, she said, something to talk about, something going on. 'And of course I do need those clothes. But when we *are* all dressed up, I don't know where we're to go. Oh hell, Frank. I mean, really.' She rode hatless, the wind stung her cheeks pink: Frank bitterly thought that she looked like some Academy picture about the Morning of Life.

'Do you think Arthur'll marry that girl?'

'I dare say he'll try,' said Frank.

'Oh, come. You know, Frank, our Arthur's a big success . . . It's terrible how we wonder about Miss Fox. Do you think we are getting prurient minds? But the idea's fantastic.'

'Fantastic,' Frank agreed, feeling his own despondency ironed into him. Angela shot off and galloped across the field.

That night, in a wind direct from the Ural mountains, the house began to creak and strain like a ship. The family sat downstairs with as few lights on as possible. It was Angela who slipped up to talk to Miss Fox. The handsome work-basket was present but hasped shut, and Angela, honourably, turned her eyes from it. She really did want to talk. She sat on the rug by the grate; the wind puffed down the chimney occasional gusts of smoke that made her eyes smart. Miss Fox sat at the table, puffing away at a cigarette with precision. Perhaps she was glad of company. Nothing showed she was not. Her head, sculptured by shadows, was one of the finest heads that Angela had ever seen.

'You must see a lot of funny things, going from house to house.'

'Well yes, I do. I do see some funny things.'

'Of course, so do hospital nurses. But people must be much funnier trying on clothes. And some families are mares' nests. I wish you'd tell me . . .'

'Oh well, that would hardly do.'

'You know nurses aren't discreet . . . My brother Frank thinks you're a witch.'

'Gentlemen will have their fun,' said Miss Fox, with an odd inflec-
tion, as though she were quoting. Meeting Angela's eye, she smiled
her held-in, rigid smile. Angela thought with impatience of gentlemen's fun that they must have – and, in this connection, of Arthur,
who had his share. She heard the wind gnaw at the corners of this
great tomb of a house that he wouldn't let them give up.

'It's all right for Arthur,' she said.

'Those photographs in the drawing-room – they are all your
Mr Arthur?'

'Of course,' said Angela crossly.

'Miss Toddy favours him, doesn't she?'

Angela hugged her knees and Miss Fox got no answer to this.
So the sewing-woman reached out her cold hand across the table,
shook out of the packet and lit with precision another thin cigarette. Then: 'I've seen Mr Arthur,' she said.

'Oh yes, I've seen Mr Arthur. He was staying one time in a
lady's house where I worked. There were several young gentlemen
there, and I wasn't, of course, in the way of hearing their names.
They were a big party, ever so gay and high-spirited, dodging all
over the house, they used to be, every night, and in and out of
my workroom, playing some game. I used to be sitting alone, like
I sit here, and they used to stop for a word as they went through,
or sometimes get me to hide them. Pleasant, they all were. But I
never did catch any names. Mr Arthur took a particular fancy to
one of my dummies, and asked me to lend it him to dress up for
some game. I should have known better; I ought to have known
my place.

'But it was eight years ago. The last night, I let him take the
dummy away. They did laugh, I heard. But there was an accident
and Mr Arthur let it drop on the stairs. The pedestal broke and some
of the skirt-wires bent. He came back, later, to tell me how sorry
he was. He *was* sorry, too. He said he'd make it all right. But he
went off next day, and I suppose something happened to put it out
of his head. My lady was not at all pleased, as she had had the
dummy made to her own figure, and her figure was difficult. I didn't
work there again.'

'How like him!' exclaimed his sister, savagely reclasping her
hands round her knees.

Miss Fox, immensely collected, let out a cloud of smoke. 'He meant no harm,' she said stonily.

Frank came upstairs in the dark, feeling his way by the handrail and calling, 'Angela?' It gave him the creeps when anyone disappeared. And downstairs Toddy was fumbling on the piano. 'Here,' called Angela. Frank knocked once, and came in. 'You look very snug,' he said, rather resentfully. This room's being inhabited gave the house a new focus. Soon they would all be up here. He came and stood by the fire and watched his sister rocking and hugging her knees. He saw by her face that he had cut in on a talk. His own superfluity bit him.

'Miss Fox once knew Arthur, Frank.'

'A ladder's run right down your stocking,' said Frank with angry irrelevance.

'Damn,' said Angela vaguely.

'Best catch it up,' said Miss Fox.

She looked from Frank to Angela. There was a pause. Then, in the most businesslike way, she put down her cigarette, opened her work-basket, glanced at Angela's stocking and, matching it with her eye, drew a strand from a mixed plait of darning silks. Then she took out the big black needlecase. 'Mr Frank . . .' she said. He went over and, taking the case, brought it across to Angela. She knelt upon the hearthrug; he rested a hand on her shoulder and felt the shoulder go stiff. 'What a lot of needles,' she said mechanically. She and Frank both stared at the photograph of the child. They saw, as Toddy had seen, its curls and its collar. Like Arthur's collar and curls in old photographs downstairs. And between the collar and curls, Arthur's face stared back again at the uncle and aunt.

'I should take a number five needle,' said Miss Fox calmly.

'I have,' said Angela, closing the needlecase.

'Ladders down stockings break one's heart,' said Miss Fox.

The Easter Egg Party

Their object was to restore her childhood to her. They were simple and zealous women, of an integrity rooted in flawless sentiment; they bowed to nothing but their own noble ideas, and flinched from nothing but abandoning these. They issued the invitation on an impulse but awaited the answer with no drop in morale. They did not shrink from facts, for they attended committees for the good of the world – most facts, however, got to West Wallows a little bit watered down: such things did happen, but not to people one knew. So that when their eye was drawn – they were unmarried sisters, with everything in common, and had, in regard to some things, one eye between them – when their eye was drawn by a once-quite-familiar name to an obscure paragraph in their daily paper, their hearts (or their heart) stopped. The case was given in outline, with unusual reticence. When they saw what had either happened or nearly happened – they were not quite clear which – to the little girl of a friend they had known as a little girl, shyness and horror drove a wedge between them; they became two people whose looks could not quite meet. Across the breakfast table of their large cottage, in the half-acre garden already gladey and glittering with the first greens of spring, they failed to discuss the matter. After a day of solitary side-by-side reflection it came up with them in its happier practical aspect: 'Could one *do* anything now? . . . Is there any way one could help?'

Eunice and Isabelle Evers were both just over fifty: their unperplexed lives showed in their faces, lined only by humour, and in their frank, high foreheads. They were Amazons in homespuns, Amazons, without a touch of deprivation or pathos; their lives had been one long vigorous walk. Like successful nuns, they both had a slightly married air. An unusual number of people in Gloucestershire knew and respected them, and they cut ice in the village of West Wallows. They thought the world of children, of any children; and children, in consequence, thought the world of them: they were past mistresses at blowing that bubble world that is blown for children by children-loving grown-ups – perhaps, also the dearest of their own pleasures lay there. If they had any fantasies, these centred round ponies and bread-and-jam on the beach, and they still received intimations of immortality.

Therefore, any unspeakable thing happening to any child was more upsetting to them than if they had been mothers. It was against their natures to judge Dorothea (the friend they had known as a little girl) in any way. All the same, across what line, into what world had she wandered in these years since her marriage, since they had lost sight of her, that her little girl should be exposed to such things as this? Dorothea's marriage had failed. Must one own she failed as a mother? They knew, vaguely, Dorothea was 'on the stage' – though one never saw her name on the programme of any play.

Dorothea's answer to their invitation took so long in coming that they had begun to fear she was out of reach. But when she did answer, Dorothea accepted with alacrity. She said that it really was truly sweet of them, and she only hoped they would find Hermione good. 'She's really as good as gold, but she's always rather reserved. I am sure it might do her good to be away from me for a bit; you see, I am really very upset these days. I suppose that's only natural; my nerves have always been awful, and now *this* coming, on top of everything else. It's nearly killed me, of course. I suppose one will get over it. Well, it really is dear of you; you always were such dears. *Oh*, how far away all those happy days seem now! . . . I will send Hermione down on April 12th. Yes, I think she's fond of animals; at all events you could try. Of course she's never had any, poor little soul.'

So they began to prepare for Hermione.

West Wallows was more than a village: it was a neighbourhood. From the wide street branched roads that led past the white gates of many homes. The rector was tactful and energetic, the squire unusually cultivated; there were a number of moderate-sized dwellings – some antique, some quite recently built. Inexpensive sociability, liberal politics, shapely antique family furniture, 'interests', enlightened charity set the note of the place. No one was very rich; nobody was eccentric, and, though few people hunted, nobody wrote letters against blood sports. The local families harmonized with the pleasant retired people who had settled here. Probably few neighbourhoods in England have such a nice atmosphere as West Wallows. In the holidays all the children had a jolly time . . . The Easter holidays were in progress now, and this created a slight predicament: how much should Hermione be with other children?

The Misses Evers decided to wait and see.

They decided to wait for grace and see what line things took. They hinted at nothing to anyone. In the week before Hermione came, the tortoiseshell cat Barbara was persuaded to wean her two patchy kittens, who learnt to lap prettily from an Umbrian saucer. The honeysuckle up the south front of the cottage unfolded the last of its green shoots, and in the garden and in the strip of orchard the other side of the brook daffodils blew their trumpets.

The first afternoon was windy. Every time a sucker of honeysuckle swung loose and tapped the window Hermione jumped. This was the only sign she gave of having grown-up nerves. She was not quite a pretty child; her face was a long, plump oval; her large dark-grey eyes were set rather close together, which gave her an urgent air. Her naturally curly dark hair had grown too long for a bob and swung just clear of her shoulders. She sat in the dark glass dome of her own inside world, just too composedly eating bread and honey. Now and then she glanced, with mysterious satisfaction, at the bangles on one or the other of her wrists.

'This is honey from our own bees, Hermione.'

'Goodness.'

'It tastes quite different from other honey, we think.'

'Yes; Mummy said you kept bees. Do you keep doves too?'

Eunice glanced at the white forms that whirled rather frighteningly over the wind-teased garden. 'Those are the next-door pigeons; they keep on flying over, so we have the fun of them.'

'The next-door cat in London keeps getting into our larder. I do hate cats.'

'Oh, but you must like Barbara — and she's got two kittens.'

'Cats always do that, don't they?'

After tea Eunice took her up to what was to be her room, the spare-room over the porch, snug as a ship's cabin and frilly with sprigged stuff. She showed her the sampler worked by another little girl of eleven, just a hundred years ago, and some framed photographs of Italy. 'That's Assisi, where St Francis lived.'

'Goodness,' said Hermione, biting her thumb vaguely. She looked through the loops of dotted muslin curtain at the tops of the apple trees. 'It's just like on a calendar,' she said. She sat on the bed, with her tongue feeling round one cheek, while Eunice unpacked her two suitcases for her. 'Oh, what pretty clothes and things,' said Eunice deprecatingly. 'But I don't think you'll have a chance to wear most of them here. You'll want to wear old clothes and simply tumble about.'

'I haven't got any old clothes. Mummie gives them away.'

In her tweed skirt, with her knotted oak walking-stick, lifting her forehead to the sweet spring air Isabelle, next morning, swung down the village street, and Hermione walked beside her, changing step now and then with a queer little dancing hop. In her raspberry-woollen dress, her turn-up hat with the Donald Duck clip and her long, white, carefully pulled-up socks, the child looked like a stage child halfway through a tour: nothing would tone her down. Isabelle pointed out the village pond with its white ducks, the saddle-back church tower, the Beacon on the top of the steep, green, nursery-rhyme hill, the quaint old sign of the Spotted Cow, which made all children laugh – Hermione did not smile. A street is a street, and the point of a street is, people: looking boldly up, she challenged whoever passed with her dusky, gelatinous dark-grey eyes. It was their attention she wanted; she collected attention like twists of silver paper or small white pebbles. Her search for attention was so arduous that she gave less than half her mind to whatever Isabelle said. Whenever Isabelle turned into a shop, Hermione would ferret along the counter. In the chemist's she said she would like to buy that green celluloid box to keep her toothbrush in.

'Have you brought your pocket-money?' said Isabelle brightly.

'Oh – but I haven't any.'

'Then I'm afraid the green box will have to wait,' said Isabelle still more brightly, with an inspiring smile. She did not approve of

buying hearts with small gifts: besides, one must teach Hermione
not to 'hint'. Hermione gave the green box a last look, the first
fully human look she had spent on anything since she came to
West Wallows. She slowly dragged her eyes from it and followed
Isabelle out of the chemist's shop.

'This afternoon,' said Isabelle, 'we'll go primrosing.'

'I think those lambs are pretty,' said Hermione, suddenly pointing
over a wall. 'I should like a pet lamb of my own; I should call it
Percy.'

'Well, perhaps you can make a friend of one of these lambs. If
you go every day very quietly into the field—'

'But I want it to be my own; I want to call it Percy.'

'Well, let's call "Percy", and see which of them comes . . . Percy,
Percy, Percy!' called Isabelle, leaning over the wall. None of the
lambs took any notice: one of the sheep gave her a long, reproving
look. Hermione, meanwhile, had frigidly walked away.

Eunice and Isabelle took it in turns to what they called take
Hermione out of herself. They did not confess how unnerved they
sometimes were by their sense of intense attention being focused
on nothing. They took her in to see the neighbour who kept the
pigeons; Eunice taught her to climb the safe apple trees; Isabelle
took her out in a pair of bloomers and dared her to jump the
brook. Hermione jumped in and was pulled out patient and very
wet. They borrowed a donkey for her, and the run of a paddock,
but she fell off the donkey three times. This child stayed alone the
whole time and yet was never alone; their benevolent spying on
her, down the orchard or through windows, always showed them
the same thing – Hermione twirling round her silver bangles at
some unseen person, or else tossing her hair. They took her primrosing three times; then they took her bird's nesting in the Hall
grounds. In the great hollow beech hedges, in the dense ivy, the
secret nests excited her: she stood up on tiptoes; her cheeks flamed.
But all this waned when she might not touch the eggs. She could
not understand why. The glossy blues, the faint greens, the waxy
buff-pinks, the freckles seemed to her to be for nothing: while the
sisters, breathless, held apart the branches she now looked only
glumly into the nests. When they found a brood of fledglings she

ran six yards back and said: 'Ugh! Fancing leaving eggs just for *that*!'

'But they're alive, dear. Next Spring they'll be singing away, like all the birds we hear now, or laying eggs of their own.'

'Well, I don't see why.'

The sisters bound each other to silence with quick glances.

Hermione said: 'I'd sooner have sugar eggs.'

It was from this rather baffling afternoon that the idea of the Easter egg party arose.

Hermione ought now, they felt, if ever, to be fit for younger society. Perhaps she might find friends – how they doubted this! At all events, one must see. And since she was to meet children, why should she not meet all the West Wallows children at once? About a quite large party there should be something kind and ambiguous: if she failed to hit it off with Maisie or Emmeline, she might hit it off with Harriet or Joanna. (The fact was, they felt, in a way they rather dreaded to face, that in a large party she would stand out less.) The Misses Evers were well known for their juvenile parties, but up to now these had always been held at Christmas, when guessing games could be played, or at Midsummer, when they got permission for their young guests to help to make someone's hay. An Easter party was quite a new idea and looked like running them in for more expense – they did not jib at this, but they dreaded the ostentation. Isabelle bicycled into Market Chopping and bought three dozen sweet eggs – a little reduced in price, as Easter was just over. Some were chocolate, wrapped in brilliant metallic paper; some were marzipan, with the most naturalistic freckles; some were cardboard, containing very small toys. That same afternoon, Eunice, at her bureau, wrote out invitations to the fourteen young guests, ranging in age from fourteen down to six. As she addressed each envelope she would pause, to give Hermione, entrancedly doing nothing on the sofa beside her, a biography of each possible child.

The afternoon of the party was, happily, very fine. From three o'clock on the garden gate clicked incessantly: unaccompanied by grown-ups the guests in their coloured jerseys or very clean blouses came up the path – to be mustered by Eunice and Isabelle on the patch of lawn by the sundial. They were already tanned or freckled by the spring sun, and all wore an air of stolid elation. 'Now, finding *ought* to be keeping,' said Isabelle, 'but we think that if any one of you people finds more than three, he or she might hand the rest back, to go at the end to some other person who may not have been so clever.'

Eunice put in: 'And we shall be giving a prize: this Easter rabbit' (she held up a china ornament) 'to whoever hands in most eggs by the end of the afternoon.'

Isabelle took up: 'They are hidden about the garden and in the orchard the other side of the stream. To make things just a little easier we have tied a piece of pink wool *somewhere near* every place where an egg is. And whoever finds each egg must untie the pink wool, please, or it will be so difficult. Now, are we all here? Oh, no: we are still waiting for Poppy. The moment she's here I'm going to blow this whistle, then – off with you all! At five o'clock I shall blow the whistle for tea.'

At this moment the late-comer bolted in at the gate, whereupon Isabelle blew the whistle piercingly. The children – the boys were small, the girls larger-sized, some of them quite lumpy – glanced at each other, tittered and moved off. For some distance they stayed in compact formation, like explorers advancing in dangerous territory; though all the time their sharp eyes were glancing left and right. Then, in the glittering sunshine of the garden, shreds of pink wool began to be discerned. One by one children bounded off from the others, glancing jealously round to see that no one was on their tracks.

Hermione had lagged a little behind the party that moved off. She had been introduced to all the children by name, but after the 'how-d'you-do's no one had spoken to her. She had secured by the wrist the only other child that tagged behind the party, a small, dumb little boy: she gripped this child by the wrist as though he were not human – he appeared in some way to give her countenance. From the beginning she had been difficult: she had been reluctant to come down from her room at all: from the lawn below Eunice had called and waved; Hermione had answered but not come. Ghostly just inside her shut window, or like a paper figure pasted against the glass, she had watched strange children invade the garden she knew. She had gone on like a kitten that somehow gets up a tree, panics, and cannot be got down again – till Eunice ran up to dislodge her with some well-chosen words. But alas, once one had got her on to the lawn, her up-a-tree air only became more noticeable. She shook hands with a rigid arm, on which all the bracelets jumped. She looked straight at everyone, but from a moody height: what was evident was not just fear or shyness but a desperate, cut-off haughtiness. In her eyes existed a world of alien experience. The jolly, tallish girls with their chubbed hair, the straddling little boys with their bare knees, apt to frown at the grass between their sandshoes, rebounded from that imperious stare. Either she cared too much or she did not care a fig for them – and in either case they did not know how to meet her.

Sloping south to the brook, the garden was made devious by swastika hedges: it was all grots and plots. Japanese plums caught light in their ethereal petals; flowering currants sent out their sweet, hot smell. The waving shreds of pink wool made round themselves centres of magnetic attraction in which children hummed and jostled, like the bees round the currants. The garden, the orchard became tense with the search: now and then yelps of triumph struck their silence like sharp bells. By the end of a half-hour everyone seemed to have found at least one egg. Children met to compare their spoils, then pounced jealously off again.

Only Hermione and the doomed little boy that she would not let go of had not yet found an egg. She sometimes shifted her grip on his hot wrist. In her haze of self-consciousness, weighted by that deep-down preoccupation, she moved too slowly, dragging the little boy. Once or twice she did see pink wool, but when she got to the spot it was always being untied by the child who had found the egg. Disgraced by their failure, she and the little boy said not a word to each other; they moved about in silence of deepening animosity. Now they stood on the bridge, between the garden and orchard: Hermione looked from one shore to the other with eyes that held incredulity and despair. She had not found *any* egg.

Without warning the little boy went rigid all over, braced himself against the rail of the bridge, threw open his cave of a mouth and yelled: 'Oh *Mais-see*, I wanner go with you!'

A girl bustling contentedly through the orchard, three bright eggs shining on the palm of her hand, stopped and lifted her nose like a mother dog. Then she approached the bridge. 'I say,' she said to Hermione, 'would you mind letting my little brother go? He'd like to look by himself.'

'He and I are looking together.'

'Oh. How many have you each found?'

'Somebody else always finds the ones we are looking for.'

'Good gracious,' said Maisie, 'then haven't you found *any*? Someone says that Harriet's got six, and everyone else here has found at least two. Do you mean to say poor Simon hasn't got *any*? . . . Never mind, Simon; come and look with me. *We'll* soon find some.'

'I don't see why he should. Why should I be the only person left who hasn't got any egg?'

'Well, I can't help that, can I? You'd better look more properly . . . Come along Simon.'

Hermione let him go.

When she found herself quite alone on the bridge she shaded her eyes (because the sun was descending) to peer at the round, white object under one apple tree. It was a panama hat, last seen on the girl Harriet: now it sat on the grass. As though something inside her answered a magnet, Hermione left the bridge and ran to that apple tree. The general search had ebbed back to the garden: in the orchard no one shouted; no one swished through the long grass – the place was deserted suddenly. Hermione knelt down, cautiously raised the hat, and saw the clutch of six super-natural eggs – two gold, one red, one silver and two blue. They lay tilted together in their nest in the grass. Trembling with satisfaction, she regarded them steadily. Then she made a pouch of her skirt and gathered the eggs up into it. Clumsily, cautiously rising, she made off at a trot for a hedge that cut off the orchard from Church Lane.

She was not missed till the five o'clock whistle sounded and the children trooped in through the french window for tea. Then Eunice and Isabelle combined to pass the contretemps over as smoothly as possible. While Eunice poured out, and kept the chatter going, Isabelle, with the whistle, slipped out for a thorough look. Sadly, sadly, she saw some trampled daffodils – the nicer the set of children, the larger their feet. When she got to the end of the orchard she saw the gap forced through the hedge, and her heart sank.

The big scandal only broke at the end of tea-time, when Eunice began to check up the eggs found. Throughout tea the outraged Harriet had not suffered in silence: there had been a good deal of mumbling at her end of the table, but Eunice did not know what the matter was. When the loss came out Eunice put two and two together with disheartening rapidity – so did everyone else. Speaking looks were cast by the West Wallows children at the place where Hermione did not sit. There was nothing for it but to present the china rabbit to Harriet with as much haste, and still as much pomp, as possible and to suggest we should now all play prisoners' base on the lawn.

Seven strokes from the church clock fell on the sad, clear evening. The Easter egg party guests had been sent home an hour ago; the sisters had returned from their desperate search up and down the village, in the fields, in the near woods. Something made Eunice go up to Hermione's room – there *was* Hermione, sitting on the bed. She must have slipped back while nobody was about. In the deep dusk she was sitting across the bed, legs stuck out and back stuck to the wall, in the attitude in which one props up a doll. She was, presumably, waiting: the moment the door opened, she said, without looking up: 'I want to go home now.'

'But Hermione—'

'Mummy said I needn't stay if I didn't like it. She said I could come straight home.'

'Dear, this isn't because you think *we* are . . . upset about anything?'

'I can't help *what* you are,' said Hermione, quite dispassionate. 'Couldn't you get some other girl to stay with you? There's nothing for me to do here; I mean, I can't do anything. And all those girls were awful to me today; nobody cared if I found an egg or not. That girl Maisie wouldn't let me play with her brother. No one has ever been so awful to me as they all were; they took all the eggs, and I never found even one. And you never let me talk, all the time, you never let me touch anything. You keep on making me take an interest in things, and you never take the slightest interest in me. Mummy said you were interested in me, but now

I don't believe her. I feel just as if I was dead, and I do want to go home. Oh, and I took those six old eggs.'

'Well, hush now, dear: we're all tired. Hop into bed, like a good girl, and I'll bring you some biscuits and milk. Would you like me to bring up one of the kittens too?'

'No, thank you; your kittens scratch. Well, can I go home tomorrow?'

'We'll see about that tomorrow.'

Eunice sighed and went downstairs. She filled a beaker with milk and put out a plate of biscuits, then she looked into the parlour for a word with Isabelle. The lamps were lit, but the curtains were not drawn yet: outside there was a dark twitter of birds. Isabelle, reading the look on her sister's face, came round the table, saying: 'Oh, Eunice . . .'

'I know,' Eunice said. 'It apparently can't be helped. Her mind's set now on going home. I wonder whether she'd better . . .'

'Eunice, that's not like you!' cried Isabelle, with a burst of their old heroic energy.

'I know,' said Eunice, putting down the biscuits. Absently, she began to sip the milk. 'But you see, this is really not like anything else. There are times when being like one's self, however much one's self, does not seem much help. Well, there it is, Isabelle. We've always known life was difficult, but I must confess, till today I'd never really believed it. I don't see quite where we failed: she *is* a child, after all.'

'I suppose, once a child has been the centre of things . . .'

'Oh, look – I'm drinking this milk. It really was for Hermione.'

Hermione left next day: perhaps it was for the best. They never speak of her to the children at West Wallows, and the West Wallows children do not ask about her. The sisters seldom speak of her even between themselves; she has left a sort of scar, like a flattened grave, in their hearts. It rained the day she left, but cleared up again at sunset. When Isabelle, in her gum-boots, walking in the orchard, found the six Easter eggs under the original apple tree, the chocolate under the paper had gone to a pulp, and the gold and colours of the paper had run.

Reduced

The Carburys' two little girls, Penny and Claudia, went upstairs again with their governess, Miss Rice, as soon as lunch was over; their steps could be heard retreating along the pitch-pine gallery round the hall. The visitors were disappointed – Mrs Laurie liked children and Frank Peele had been hoping to see more of the governess. Rain drummed on the hall skylight; still smoking their host Godwin Carbury's rather musty cigarettes, the grown-ups allowed themselves to be driven into the library. Here no chair invited you, the uninviting books must have been bought in lots, and looked gummed in the shelves. It could have been a pretty September day; the plum tree leaves in the tilting orchards round were bright yellow, but for days the Forest of Dean had been clouded and sodden.

Mrs Laurie, who was vivacious and had married at nineteen, and Mrs Carbury, who was muddled and dim, had been friends years ago in India when they were both young girls. They had kept in touch, Mrs Carbury having no other vivacious friend, life having taught Mrs Laurie that there was no knowing when anybody devoted might not come in useful – besides, she had always been sorry for Mima.

Mima's life had been unrewarding. She returned flatly from India after her friend's wedding, and it had not been till she was twenty-seven or eight that she met Godwin Carbury, who at forty was looking round for a wife. He had the reputation of being the most unpopular man in his part of the country, and that reputation followed him up to London. He was careful, savagely careful, about money and not careful enough about seeing this was not known. Added to this, he had a dour self-importance. It was understood that economy kept him single as long as his mother had lived to keep house at Pendlethwaite. Possibly Mima saw something in him that no one else saw; she was anxious to 'settle' suitably, and not herself accustomed to being liked. At all events, they married, and had had after some years these two thin, remote little girls. They had few neighbours at Pendlethwaite and Godwin's peculiarities cut them off more and more from anybody there was. Whatever misgivings she had, Mima pandered to him blindly. On her own account she had just a little money, so once or twice a year she came up to London, gazed into shop windows, met Mrs Laurie (now widowed) and bought reduced coats and shoes for the little girls. She had begun lately to talk of giving up London; the girls' education would be a heavy expense, she said.

It surprised Mrs Laurie to find herself at Pendlethwaite, but she had been at a loose end, with nowhere to go for a week. So she thought, 'Try the Carburys', and had written to Mima. She was a shiftless woman, maintaining herself by the exercise of a good deal of charm: she could say daring things without sounding impertinent, and determined to get a little fun out of Godwin – apart from this, she did not expect very much.

Pendlethwaite was not a lovable house. Built about 1880 of unpleasing maroon brick, it creaked inside with pitch-pine; its church-like windows peered narrowly at the smiling landscape round; its grounds darkened a valley with belts of laurel and stiff, damp-looking clumps of unindigenous firs. The house looked dedicated to a perpetual January: sunnier seasons beat back from its walls. The bloomy red plums and mellow apples bending the boughs this month were pagan company for it. Indoors, there was no electricity; panels absorbed the lamplight; before October, no fires were lit till night. It had not even the insidious charm of decay, for Godwin had great ideas of keeping things up: the laurels were kept clipped, the thrifty meals served formally . . . Mrs Laurie had been diverted to find that she had a fellow guest, but this did not see her far. Frank Peele, just back on leave from Siam, was Mima's second cousin. He must have asked himself here because he had to be somewhere; she thought he was not a man you would scramble to entertain. At about thirty, he was a haggard schoolboy – shambling, facetious, huffy, forlorn, melancholic, with perhaps (she feared most of all) a romantic soul. She supposed Mima must enjoy being even sorrier for him than she need be for herself . . . Entertaining on this scale must be a plunge for the Carburys. Mrs Laurie could almost hear Godwin saying to Mima: 'Well then, in for a penny, in for a pound.' He went through with his duties as host with glum correctness. 'But if one stayed a day too long he'd cut off supplies.' As it was, his rigid economies hit you everywhere.

The one startling un-economy was the governess. Mrs Laurie, though unhappily childless, knew an expensive governess when she saw one. Miss Rice's technique was perfect. Her first appearance, at lunch, took Nella's breath away with its unobtrusiveness. Penny and Claudia – their dark eyes set close in, tucking their long, fair hair back behind their shoulders primly – clearly revolved round her. 'Those two little mice adore her,' thought Mrs Laurie, recalling the composed retreat after lunch: three people going back to a world of their own. But the adoration was kept within nice bounds. 'How does Mima *keep* the woman in this mausoleum? She might be anywhere. Mima can't be such a fool as I thought . . . I must find out.'

In the library, she lost no time in doing this. In the bow window, Frank Peele with his hands in his pockets stood looking out unexpectantly at the rain; Mima poured out thin coffee; Godwin glumly handed the cups round. Mrs Laurie said affably: 'So you got a governess? Last time we met, you were busy looking for one.'

'Yes, oh yes. We did,' Mima said in her flustered way.

'Miss Rice came in May,' said Godwin firmly.

'She seems a great success . . .'

Frank Peele grunted.

'When she first came in,' went on Mrs Laurie, 'I felt certain I'd seen her somewhere. I wonder where she was before? She's startlingly good-looking, but in such a tactful way. Hag-ridden – but that's the life, I suppose.'

'She appears content with us,' said Godwin, handing the sugar to Mrs Laurie bitterly. 'Mima, what are your plans for this afternoon?' His wife looked blank.

'Our guests should be entertained.'

'It struck me,' said Frank, wheeling round, 'as one of the few faces I had not seen before.'

'Really?' said Godwin.

Mima touched the coffee-tray clumsily; everything on it skidded. Did she not want Cousin Frank to fall for the governess? The nicest women like having unattached men around. 'She must be full of brains,' said Mrs Laurie vaguely.

'She teaches wonderfully; she's got the children on so. They seem to be learning everything.'

'Can we have them all down after tea to play Up Jenkin or something?'

'They do preparation then,' said Godwin repressively. ('Set,' thought his guest, 'on getting his money's worth.') Mima's eyes, oddly overwrought in her pink, creased face, stole to meet her husband's. 'Frank,' Godwin continued, 'I could show you those maps now.' Clearly, any discussion of Miss Rice was closed.

'Not today, thanks,' said Frank, 'I've got a crick in my neck.' Godwin, after one more forbidding look at Mima, left them, shutting the door reprovingly. Frank loafed along the bookshelves, pulled out *Monasteries of the Levant*, and folded himself in a chair with an air of resigned discomfort. A man with a book is practically not present. Mrs Laurie whipped out her *petit point* and the two women, pulling their chairs together zestfully, settled down for a talk. Rain streamed down the windows, paper rustled inside the cold grate.

Mima saw so few friends that talk went to her head like wine. Evenly sing-song, the women's voices began rising and falling. After half an hour, Frank's book slipped on to his knee; his head rolled back, jaw dropping; he let out a sharp snore. 'Really . . .' exclaimed Mima, stopping the talk to titter. 'A tropical habit,' said Mrs Laurie. This was better than Frank with a book, they were quite alone. She hopped back to her topic.

'Mima, what's Godwin got up his sleeve about Miss Rice?'

'Miss Rice? – nothing,' Mima said, over-acting.

'His one wicked extravagance?'

'No,' faltered Mima. 'That's just the point – she's not.'

'A bargain? You amaze me. Can she be at all fishy?'

'My dear Nella – she's good with the children, isn't she?' Mima fixed her friend with such oddly imploring eyes that Mrs Laurie, startled, put down her work: 'She's made princesses of them,' she said extravagantly. 'How wise you have been, Mima!'

'You do really think so? Godwin and I wanted the best we could get, you see: he has such ideas for Penny and Claudia.'

'It does him credit,' said Mrs Laurie warmly.

'I suppose so—' blurted out Mima — then, looking wretched, put her hand to her cheek. 'I've never quite liked — I mean if she — I can't help wondering—'

'Why did Godwin snap me up when I said I thought I knew her face?'

'We'd hoped no one would think that,' said Mima surprisingly. 'As a rule, you see, almost nobody comes here, and in every other way she seemed quite ideal: she is. In the ordinary way, we never could have afforded her. It did seem such an opportunity. You see, we could not offer a high salary.'

'That would narrow things down . . .'

'It did. All the ones I had interviewed were so vulgar and pushing, besides seeming to know nothing at all. The agency woman said, "For that, what can you expect?" I was in despair.'

'Oh? So then—?'

'I came round more and more to Godwin's idea. As he said, it was practically a charity. It did seem unfair that the thing should count against her. When she had paid for her defence she hadn't a penny, and no other future, of course. And she was acquitted.'

'What on earth do you mean?'

Looking thoroughly frightened, Mima caught herself up. 'Oh dear,' she said, 'and I swore never to speak of it. Nella, will you swear to let this go no further? It's such a relief to tell you: it's on my mind the whole time. You see, Godwin had followed all the evidence carefully. The witnesses gave her such magnificent testimonials, almost all her former employers were called. Even the Prosecution didn't make out she wasn't a good *governess*. And after all, she was cleared. (If only they'd found who'd done it . . .)'

'Begin at the beginning.'

'Well . . . Do you ever read murder trials?'

'Hardly ever miss one.'

'Do you remember that Sir Max Rant dying suddenly?'

'Mima — she's not *Henrietta Post*?'

'Sssh — sssh,' whispered Mima, glancing Frank's way cautiously. Then she nodded at Nella with frightened, important eyes.

Mrs Laurie stared, galvanized, at her hostess. Then: 'She's lucky to be alive,' she said. 'It was touch and go.'

'He was a dreadful old man, apparently. At the very worst, they said nothing against her *morals*.'

'No wonder she's haunted-looking. That was an appalling ordeal . . . But, after that, how on earth—?'

'Godwin got me to write to her three weeks after the trial, offering her a new life and twenty-five pounds a year . . .'

'Godwin is on the spot! Well, they're your children, not mine – *Henrietta Post*!'

Immovably, without batting a closed eyelid, Frank said, 'Who is Henrietta Post?'

'Miss Rice's hands are cold again,' said Penny.

Claudia went on painting a moment longer, then, balancing her brush on the glass jar of paint-water, which gave out a prussic smell and had a red sediment, looked intently across the table at Penny, who stood by Miss Rice's chair, chafing her right hand. Their governess, with her book propped on the table, her pale cheek on her left hand, read on, smiling unnoticingly. Once she withdrew her hand from Penny's to turn over a page.

'Whatever will she do in winter?' said Claudia.

'There'll be fires then.'

'This fire never burns much.' They shared the same desperate thought: 'Suppose our darling should leave us?'

This afternoon, the black chill of the grate focused your fancy as firelight might have done. The schoolroom had a faded sea-blue wallpaper cut into by pitch-pine presses and two doors: not a colour warmed it; the high windows looked into a rain-blurred hill. Miss Rice had put nothing of her own on the mantelpiece, along which marched a file of plasticine animals modelled by the little girls. About the room were products of other hobbies good governesses encourage children to have – on the windowsill a nursery-garden in pots: pink-cheeked 'Bubbles' and 'Cherry Ripe' looked queerly down at the bleak room where these three people were living as best they could.

Miss Rice put away the book and with it her happy, forgetful smile – the book had been *Emma*. 'Have you stopped painting?' she said.

She had given them for their subject a Greek temple. Claudia's

temple had a sunset behind it, Penny had filled in the columns
with Mediterranean blue. Miss Rice came round and looked. 'A
sunset like that would make reflections on white stone, Claudia.
Penny, on such a fine day there would be shadows.' They saw.
She always thought of something they had not thought of: they
wrinkled up their foreheads in ecstatic despair. 'Penny, if you are
stopping, wash that blue off your paint-brush.'

'Are paints poison?'

'Sometimes. Well, are you cold, too?'

They would admit nothing that could distress her.

'Then push the table back and get the skipping-ropes out.'

The little girls were alike, though there were two years between
them, as though they could not decide to part in any particular.
There was not much difference in size, as though Penny had waited
for Claudia. Their voices were pitched on the same persuasive note;
when their vehement dark eyes met they seemed to consult. What
they thought of being alive their parents would never know; their
characters were like batteries storing something up. Before Miss
Rice was here, the doctor's sister had come in every morning to
give them lessons. They had known before how to read and write,
so all they had learnt from the doctor's sister was what everyone
else knew: just why their house was avoided, how bitterly father
was laughed at and mother pitied because of him. They learnt that
it was wretched to be themselves. They marked the contempt with
which every morning she bicycled up their avenue, and how
insolently she ate what there was at lunch. Her raspy fingertips,
the pearls screwed tight in her fleshy ears, her horse sense, all
seemed part of her power to mortify them. She was the world and
they prayed she might die, but she married. After that they waited,
in armour. Then came Miss Rice.

'If you want to keep warm you must hurry,' said Miss Rice.

Claudia unwound the skipping-ropes and they took one each:
they stood with their arms out, gripping the handles eagerly. 'One,
two, three – go!' The ropes zip-zipped on the oilcloth. Penny
stumbled at fifty-six, but Claudia kept in and skipped seventy-eight:
her toes bounced and bounced, her hair flopped, her eyes started
out of her head. At last the rope caught her toe. 'That's the record,'
said Miss Rice, 'but Penny may beat it next time.' Both breathless

they knelt on the hearthrug, life tingling up through them from their toes to their cheeks.

'If you skipped,' said Claudia, 'you might skip a hundred.'

'The rope is too short,' said Miss Rice.

'What else used you to do – dance?'

'Yes, once.'

They had never seen anyone dancing except in pictures of ballrooms; they preferred to imagine Miss Rice not on the crook of an arm but floating alone around a floor, with her ageless, shining white face, unfrivolous as an angel. At this happy moment, near her and warm from skipping, they felt on the edge of the story she did not tell . . . But *she* looked down at the skipping-ropes on the floor. 'Better put those away,' she said. Except when she was reading she never stayed quiet long: something they could feel creep up behind her chair would make her speaking eyes go suddenly cold and dark as the grate. Against this their love was powerless. This dreadful expectation seemed wrong in their darling – mother without her worries would not be anyone, father was there to stare and bite his moustache, but she seemed to them born to inherit light . . . Feeling their enemy here now the children, helpless, got up to put the skipping-ropes back in the press.

'Someone's coming!' said Penny. They heard the baize door at the far end of their passage swing to behind somebody, then a man's step. A knuckle rapped the door once, unconfidently: Miss Rice and the children waited. 'Come in,' she said.

Frank Peele peered round the door. 'Oh?' he said. 'May I come in? Sorry, I was exploring. Looking for secret passages. Exercise before tea.' Miss Rice smiled composedly. 'So here you all are,' he went on. He looked at the table. 'Painting?'

'Yes.'

'What a day!' he said to Miss Rice humbly. 'Very cheery up here, though. You believe in fresh air?' Then he saw that both windows were bolted: what he felt were the draughts. Miss Rice had moved to the table where she had been reading; Frank dropped into the wicker chair with a creak. The children shut their paint-boxes up. 'Must be getting on tea time,' remarked Frank.

'Are you hungry, Cousin Frank?' said Claudia gently.

Frank looked relieved at hearing someone say something. 'I

don't deserve tea; I slept like a log in the library. Your mother and Mrs Laurie complain I snored.' He looked round the schoolroom wistfully, like a dog. 'They were talking nineteen to the dozen. When I dropped off they were well away about India; when I came to it was one Henrietta Post.'

Penny laughed. 'Who's Henrietta Post?' she said.

'Don't ask me,' said Frank. 'Miss Rice, who's Henrietta Post?'

Miss Rice pondered while the clock ticked several seconds and a cart rattled off into silence behind the wet orchards. The children turned to see how she took Frank's joke. She looked twice at him with steady, considering dark eyes. 'Surely you know?' she said at last.

'I don't know a soul,' said Frank, 'I've been in Siam.'

'But you get the papers there, don't you?'

'She's a celebrity, is she?'

'She was accused of murder,' said Miss Rice, as though giving a history lesson, 'tried last spring, acquitted, but never properly cleared. So she disappeared, hoping to be forgotten.'

'Good God,' exclaimed Frank. 'Where would a woman go to, after a show like that?'

'She is fortunate to be anywhere.'

'Stop: it's coming back!' Frank said, delighted to have a topic. 'Wasn't she that governess? The old swine whose house she was in had been making up to her, so when someone did him in they tried to fix it on her. I remember I thought at the time—'

Miss Rice's marked unresponse reminded Frank where he was. Chidden, he stopped awkwardly, with a glance at the children. *They* sat stone-still, clasped hands thrust down between their knees; you could not possibly tell what was going on in their heads, which were both turned intently away from their governess. Frank kicked himself. But for the life of him he couldn't stop blurting out: 'She was very good-looking, wasn't she?'

'You never saw any photographs?'

'Out where I am I only get *The Times*, you see. No pretty pictures in it.'

'I see.'

Frank went on violently: 'I know I thought at the time what a shocking, unfair thing to happen to any woman!' . . . Miss Rice

with her cold smile looked thoughtfully into the grate as though
there were a fire burning there: she said nothing more. Her charges'
agonized tension became startling. Frank hummed and beat a
nonplussed tattoo on his knee. They were waiting to see the last
of him. Whatever brick one had dropped, they were all very odd
up here . . .

This wet autumn evening closed in so early that the children had
to stop work and wait for the lamp to come; when Mrs Carbury
looked in they were all in the dark. 'Why, whatever are you doing?'
she said nervously. 'Where's Miss Rice? Why doesn't she ring for
the lamp?'

'It never comes any sooner.'

'Father wouldn't like you wasting your time like this. Where is
Miss Rice?'

'In her room,' Penny said, so indifferently that there seemed to
be something foolish about the fuss. At this point a band of light
appeared in the passage; the housemaid brought in the lamp and
Mima saw her daughters facing each other like images across the
table of lesson books, their unchildish eyes dark in the sudden
lamplight. She sat down, acting calm while the housemaid was in
the room; all the same, her manner made the girl so jumpy that
she went away again without drawing down the blinds. Mrs Carbury
sat eyeing the other door; the children's bedroom opened off the
schoolroom and Miss Rice's room was beyond, connecting with
theirs. Her relief at not finding the governess was tremendous: all
the same, she felt she was being defied.

'Does she always leave you to do preparation alone?'

'She's tired,' said Claudia. 'Cousin Frank was up here.'

'Oh? . . . Well, tell her I want to speak to her. Then you can
leave your lessons, just for this evening, and go downstairs; Mrs
Laurie says she will play games with you.'

The children looked at their books without stirring, and Mima
for the first time felt mutiny in the air . . . Mima had had to brace
herself to come in; twice already since tea she had started up to
the schoolroom, then turned back before the baize door to that
wing. Ever since her revelation to Mrs Laurie she had been in a
fearful state: the way Mrs Laurie took it brought her own most

persistent throttling fears to the top: 'Henrietta Post . . . Well, they're your children, not mine.' What Nella said was what anybody who knew would say. Mima had shrunk back from the schoolroom door, feeling: 'No, I really cannot face her.' Then she had been forced to think: 'But that is the woman my children are with the whole time . . .' Once she had gone as far as Godwin's study to tell him he must agree to send Miss Rice away tomorrow, but the way he had looked up at her settled that. 'Nothing has changed since I agreed to engage her.' Mima knew too well that her husband found her a fool. 'I will give her notice first, then tell Godwin. It won't be so bad with Nella in the house here. Nella will back me up. *But when Godwin hears I've told Nella?* . . . He said before she came to stay: "Suppose your friend is inquisitive?" . . . What are they doing up there? What does she say to them? What goes on the whole time? My own children are strangers; they don't like being downstairs now. *What was it the prosecution said about influence?*'

Mima raised her voice. 'Run along now at once, children: Mrs Laurie is waiting.'

'We would much rather not, mother.'

'Then you're very ungrateful. Besides, I have got something to say to Miss Rice – Penny and Claudia, don't look at each other like that! It's rude to look at each other when mother speaks!'

'Miss Rice is tired,' repeated Claudia gently.

'If you give us the message,' said Penny, 'we'll tell her.'

'No, I want to talk to Miss Rice,' said Mima, her voice unnatural.

'Do you, mother?' said Penny. 'You don't generally.'

The wicker chair Mima sat in creaked convulsively. 'When we're alone again you may learn to make your mother happy. You may understand mother then and not be unkind to her. Tomorrow, Miss Rice will be going away, children.'

Penny and Claudia looked at the chair their mother now sat in, then up at *Emma* left on the edge of the mantelpiece. Claudia looked at their row of young plants in the windowsill, sharp in the lamplight against the rain-lashed dark outside, Penny at the wrinkled rug where that afternoon they had knelt at their darling's feet. Then their gentle, vehement dark eyes, meeting, paused to consult again. They said in their quiet voices: 'Then we will go too.'

Summer Night

As the sun set its light slowly melted the landscape, till everything
was made of fire and glass. Released from the glare of noon, the
haycocks now seemed to float on the aftergrass: their freshness
penetrated the air. In the not far distance hills with woods up their
flanks lay in light like hills in another world – it would be a pleasure
of heaven to stand up there, where no foot ever seemed to have
trodden, on the spaces between the woods soft as powder dusted
over with gold. Against those hills, the burning red rambler roses
in cottage gardens along the roadside looked earthy – they were
too near the eye.

The road was in Ireland. The light, the air from the distance, the
air of evening rushed transversely through the open sides of
the car. The rims of the hood flapped, the hood's metal frame
rattled as the tourer, in great bounds of speed, held the road's
darkening magnetic centre streak. The big shabby family car was
empty but for its small driver – its emptiness seemed to levitate it
– on its back seat a coat slithered about, and a dressing-case bumped
against the seat. The driver did not relax her excited touch on the
wheel: now and then while she drove she turned one wrist over,
to bring the watch worn on it into view, and she gave the mileage
marked on the yellow signposts a flying, jealous, half-inadvertent
look. She was driving parallel with the sunset: the sun slowly went
down on her right hand.

The hills flowed round till they lay ahead. Where the road bent
for its upward course through the pass she pulled up and lighted
a cigarette. With a snatch she untwisted her turban; she shook her
hair free and threw the scarf behind her into the back seat. The
draught of the pass combed her hair into coarse strands as the car
hummed up in second gear. Behind one brilliantly-outlined crest
the sun had now quite gone; on the steeps of bracken in the
electric shadow, each frond stood out and climbing goats turned
their heads. The car came up on a lorry, to hang on its tail,

impatient, checked by turns of the road. At the first stretch the driver smote her palm on the horn and shot past and shot on ahead again.

The small woman drove with her chin up. Her existence was in her hands on the wheel and in the sole of the foot in which she felt through the sandal, the throbbing pressure of the accelerator. Her face, enlarged by blown-back hair, was as overbearingly blank as the face of a figure-head; her black eyebrows were ruled level, and her eyes, pupils dilated, did little more than reflect the slow burn of daylight along horizons, the luminous shades of the half-dark.

Clear of the pass, approaching the county town, the road widened and straightened between stone walls and burnished, showering beech. The walls broke up into gateways and hoardings and the suburbs began. People in modern building estate gardens let the car in a hurry through their unseeing look. The raised footpaths had margins of grass. White and grey rows of cottages under the pavement level let woodsmoke over their half-doors: women and old men sat outside the doors on boxes, looking down at their knees; here and there a bird sprang in a cage tacked to a wall. Children chasing balls over the roadway shot whooping right and left of the car. The refreshed town, unfolding streets to its centre, at this hour slowly heightened, cooled; streets and stones threw off a grey-pink glare, sultry lasting ghost of the high noon. In this dayless glare the girls in bright dresses, strolling, looked like colour-photography.

Dark behind all the windows: not a light yet. The in-going perspective looked meaning, noble and wide. But everybody was elsewhere – the polished street was empty but cars packed both the kerbs under the trees. What was going on? The big tourer dribbled, slipped with animal nervousness between the static, locked cars each side of its way. The driver peered left and right with her face narrow, glanced from her wristwatch to the clock in the tower, sucked her lip, manoeuvred for somewhere to pull in. The A.A. sign of the hotel hung out from under a balcony, over the steps. She edged in to where it said *Do Not Park*.

At the end of the hotel hall one electric light from the bar shone through a high-up panel: its yellow sifted on to the dusty

desk and a moth could be seen on the glass pane. At the door end
came in street daylight, to fall weakly on prints on the oiled walls,
on the magenta announcement-strip of a cinema, on the mahogany
bench near the receptionist's office, on the hatstand with two
forgotten hats. The woman who had come breathlessly up the steps
felt in her face a wall of indifference. The impetuous click of her
heeled sandals on the linoleum brought no one to the receptionist's
desk, and the drone of two talkers in the bar behind the glass panel
seemed, like the light, to be blotted up, word by word. The little
woman attacked the desk with her knuckles. 'Is there nobody there
– I say? Is there nobody *there*?'

'I am, I am. Wait now,' said the hotel woman, who came impassively through the door from the bar. She reached up a hand and
fumbled the desk light on, and by this with unwondering negligence
studied the customer – the childish, blown little woman with
wing-like eyebrows and eyes still unfocused after the long road.
The hotel woman, bust on the desk, looked down slowly at the
bare legs, the crumple-hemmed linen coat. 'Can I do anything for
you?' she said, when she had done.

'I want the telephone – want to put through a call!'

'You can of course,' said the unmoved hotel woman. 'Why not?'
she added after consideration, handing across the keys of the
telephone cabinet. The little woman made a slide for the cabinet:
with her mouth to the mouthpiece, like a conspirator, she was
urgently putting her number through. She came out then and
ordered herself a drink.

'Is it long distance?'

'Mm-mm . . . What's on here? What are all those cars?'

'Oh, this evening's the dog racing.'

'Is it?'

'Yes, it's the dog racing. We'd a crowd in here, but they're all
gone on now.'

'I wondered who they were,' said the little woman, her eyes on
the cabinet, sippeting at her drink.

'Yes, they're at the dog racing. There's a wonderful crowd. But
I wouldn't care for it,' said the hotel woman, fastidiously puckering
up her forehead. 'I went the one time, but it didn't fascinate me.'

The other forgot to answer. She turned away with her drink,

sat down, put the glass beside her on the mahogany bench and began to chafe the calves of her bare legs as though they were stiff or cold. A man clasping sheets of unfurled newspaper pushed his way with his elbow through the door from the bar. 'What it says here,' he said, shaking the paper with both hands 'is identically what I've been telling you.'

'That proves nothing,' said the hotel woman. 'However, let it out of your hand.' She drew the sheets of the paper from him and began to fold them into a wad. Her eyes moved like beetles over a top line. 'That's an awful battle . . .'

'What battle?' exclaimed the little woman, stopping rubbing her legs but not looking up.

'An awful air battle. Destroying each other,' the woman added, with a stern and yet voluptuous sigh. 'Listen, would you like to wait in the lounge?'

'She'd be better there,' put in the man who had brought the paper. 'Better accommodation.' His eyes watered slightly in the electric light. The little woman, sitting upright abruptly, looked defiantly, as though for the first time, at the two watching her from the desk. 'Mr Donovan has great opinions,' said the hotel woman. 'Will you move yourself out of here?' she asked Mr Donovan. 'This is very confined – *There's* your call, now!'

But the stranger had packed herself into the telephone box like a conjuror's lady preparing to disappear. '*Hullo?*' she was saying. 'Hullo! I want to speak to—'

'—You are,' the other voice cut in. 'All right? Anything wrong?'

Her face flushed all over. 'You sound nearer already! I've got to C—.'

The easy calm voice said: 'Then you're coming along well.'

'Glad, are you?' she said, in a quiver.

'Don't take it too fast,' he said. 'It's a treacherous light. Be easy, there's a good girl.'

'You're a fine impatient man.' His end of the line was silent. She went on: 'I might stay here and go to the dog racing.'

'Oh, is that tonight?' He went on to say equably (having stopped, as she saw it, and shaken the ash off the tip of his cigarette), 'No, I shouldn't do that.'

'Darling . . .'

'Emma . . . How is the Major?'

'He's all right,' she said, rather defensively.

'I see,' he said. 'Everything quite O.K.?'

'In an hour, I'll be . . . where you live.'

'First gate on the left. Don't kill yourself, there's a good girl. Nothing's worth that. Remember we've got the night. By the way, where are you talking?'

'From the hotel.' She nursed the receiver up close to her face and made a sound into it. Cutting that off she said: 'Well, I'll hang up. I just . . .'

'Right,' he said – and hung up.

Robinson, having hung up the receiver, walked back from the hall to the living-room where his two guests were. He still wore a smile. The deaf woman at the table by the window was pouring herself out another cup of tea. 'That will be very cold!' Robinson shouted – but she only replaced the cosy with a mysterious smile. 'Let her be,' said her brother. 'Let her alone!'

The room in this uphill house was still light: through the open window came in a smell of stocks from the flower beds in the lawn. The only darkness lay in a belt of beech trees at the other side of the main road. From the grate, from the coal of an unlit fire came the fume of a cigarette burning itself out. Robinson still could not help smiling: he reclaimed his glass from the mantelpiece and slumped back with it into his leather armchair in one of his loose, heavy, good-natured attitudes. But Justin Cavey, in the armchair opposite, still look crucified at having the talk torn. 'Beastly,' he said, 'you've a beastly telephone.' Though he was in Robinson's house for the first time, his sense of attraction to people was marked, early, by just this intransigence and this fretfulness.

'It is and it's not,' said Robinson. That was that. 'Where had we got to?' he amiably asked.

The deaf woman, turning round from the window, gave the two men, or gave the air between them, a penetrating smile. Her brother, with a sort of lurch at his pocket, pulled out a new packet of cigarettes: ignoring Robinson's held-out cigarette case he frowned and split the cellophane with his thumbnail. But, as though his sister had put a hand on his shoulder, his tension could be almost seen to relax. The impersonal, patient look of the thinker appeared in his eyes, behind the spectacles. Justin was a city man, a black-coat, down here (where his sister lived) on holiday. Other summer holidays before this he had travelled in France, Germany, Italy: he disliked the chaotic 'scenery' of his own land. He was down here with Queenie this summer only because of the war, which had locked him in: duty seemed to him better than failed pleasure. His father had been a doctor in this place; now his sister lived on in two rooms in the square – for fear Justin should not be comfort-able she had taken a room for him at the hotel. His holiday with his sister, his holiday in this underwater, weedy region of memory, his holiday on which, almost every day, he had to pass the doors of their old home, threatened Justin with a pressure he could not bear. He had to share with Queenie, as he shared the dolls' house meals cooked on the oil stove behind her sitting-room screen, the solitary and almost fairylike world created by her deafness. Her deafness broke down his only defence, talk. He was exposed to the odd, immune, plumbing looks she was for ever passing over his face. He could not deflect the tilted blue of her eyes. The things she said out of nowhere, things with no surface context, were never quite off the mark. She was not all solicitude; she loved to be teasing him.

In her middle-age Queenie was very pretty: her pointed face had the colouring of an imperceptibly fading pink-and-white sweet-pea. This hot summer her artless dresses, with their little lace collars, were mottled over with flowers, mauve and blue. Up the glaring main street she carried a *poult-de-soie* parasol. Her rather dark first-floor rooms faced north, over the square with its grass and lime trees: the crests of great mountains showed above the opposite façades. She would slip in and out on her own errands, as calm as a cat, and Justin, waiting for her at one of her windows, would see her cross the square in the noon sunshine with hands laced over her forehead into a sort of porch. The little town, though strung on a through road, was an outpost under the mountains: in its quick-talking, bitter society she enjoyed, to a degree that surprised Justin, her privileged place. She was woman enough to like to take the man Justin round with her and display him; they went out to afternoon or to evening tea, and in those drawing-rooms of tinted lace and intently-staring family photographs, among octagonal tables and painted cushions, Queenie, with her cotton gloves in her lap, well knew how to contribute, while Justin talked, her airy, brilliant, secretive smiling and looking on. For his part, he was man enough to respond to being shown off – besides, he was eased by these breaks in their *tête-à-tête*. Above all, he was glad, for these hours or two of chatter, not to have to face the screen of his own mind, on which the distortion of every one of his images, the war-broken towers of Europe, constantly stood. The immolation of what had been his own intensely had been made, he could only feel, without any choice of his. In the heart of the neutral Irishman indirect suffering pulled like a crooked knife. So he acquiesced to, and devoured, society: among the doctors, the solicitors, the auctioneers, the bank people of this little town he renewed old acquaintanceships and developed new. He was content to bloom, for this settled number of weeks – so unlike was this to his monkish life in the city – in a sort of tenebrous popularity. He attempted to check his solitary arrogance. His celibacy and his studentish manner could still, although he was past forty, make him acceptable as a young man. In the mornings he read late in his hotel bed; he got up to take his solitary walks; he returned to flick at his black shoes with Queenie's duster and set off with Queenie on their tea-table rounds. They had been introduced to Robinson, factory manager, in the hall of the house of the secretary of the tennis club.

Robinson did not frequent drawing-rooms. He had come here only three years ago, and had at first been taken to be a bachelor – he was a married man living apart from his wife. The resentment occasioned by this discovery had been aggravated by Robinson's not noticing it: he worked at very high pressure in his factory office, and in his off times his high-powered car was to be seen streaking too gaily out of town. When he was met, his imperturbable male personality stood out to the women unpleasingly, and stood out most of all in that married society in which women aspire to break the male in a man. Husbands slipped him in for a drink when they were alone, or shut themselves up with him in the dining-room. Justin had already sighted him in the hotel bar. When Robinson showed up, late, at the tennis club, his manner with women was easy and teasing, but abstract and perfectly automatic. From this had probably come the legend that he liked women 'only in one way'. From the first time Justin encountered Robinson, he had felt a sort of anxious, disturbed attraction to the big, fair, smiling, offhand, cold-minded man. He felt impelled by Robinson's unmoved physical presence into all sorts of aberrations of talk and mind; he committed, like someone waving an anxious flag, all sorts of absurdities, as though this type of creature had been a woman; his talk became exaggeratedly cerebral, and he became prone, like a perverse person in love, to expose all his own piques, crotchets and weaknesses. One night in the hotel bar with Robinson he had talked until he burst into tears. Robinson had on him the touch of some foreign sun. The acquaintanceship — it could not be called more — was no more than an accident of this narrowed summer. For Justin it had taken the place of travel. The two men were so far off each other's beat that in a city they would certainly not have met.

Asked to drop in some evening or any evening, the Caveys had tonight taken Robinson at his word. Tonight, the night of the first visit, Justin's high, rather bleak forehead had flushed from the moment he rang the bell. With Queenie behind his shoulder, in muslin, he had flinched confronting the housekeeper. Queenie, like the rest of the town ladies, had done no more till now than go by Robinson's gate.

For her part, Queenie showed herself happy to penetrate into what she had called 'the china house'. On its knoll over the main road, just outside the town, Bellevue did look like china up on a mantelpiece — it was a compact, stucco house with mouldings, recently painted a light blue. From the lawn set with pampas and crescent-shaped flower beds the hum of Robinson's motor mower passed in summer over the sleepy town. And when winter denuded the trees round them the polished windows, glass porch and empty conservatory sent out, on mornings of frosty sunshine, a rather mischievous and uncaring flash. The almost sensuous cleanness of his dwelling was reproduced in the person of Robinson — about his ears, jaw, collar and close clipped nails. The approach the Caveys had walked up showed the broad, decided tyre-prints of his car.

'Where had we got to?' Robinson said again.

'I was saying we should have to find a new form.'

'Of course you were,' agreed Robinson. 'That was it.' He nodded over the top of Justin's head.

'A new form for thinking and feeling . . .'

'But one thinks what one happens to think, or feels what one happens to feel. That is as just so happens – I should have thought. One either does or one doesn't?'

'One doesn't!' cried Justin. 'That's what I've been getting at. For some time we have neither thought nor felt. Our faculties have slowed down without our knowing – they had stopped without our knowing! We know now. Now that there's enough death to challenge being alive we're facing it that, anyhow, we don't live. We're confronted by the impossibility *of* living – unless we can break through to something else. There's been a stop in our senses and in our faculties that's made everything round us so much dead matter – and dead matter we couldn't even displace. We can no longer express ourselves: what we say doesn't even approximate to reality; it only approximates to what's been said. I say, this war's an awful illumination; it's destroyed our dark; we have to see where we are. Immobilized, God help us, and each so far apart that we can't even try to signal each other. And our currency's worthless – our "ideas", so on, so on. We've got to mint a new one. We've got to break through to the new form – it needs genius. We're precipitated, this moment, between genius and death. I tell you, we must have genius to live at all.'

'I am certainly dished, then,' said Robinson. He got up and looked for Justin's empty glass and took it to the sideboard where the decanters were.

'We have it!' cried Justin, smiting the arm of his chair. 'I salute your genius, Robinson, but I mistrust my own.'

'That's very nice of you,' said Robinson. 'I agree with you that this war makes one think. I was in the last, but I don't remember thinking: I suppose possibly one had no time. Of course, these days in business one comes up against this war the whole way through. And to tell you the truth,' said Robinson, turning round, 'I do like my off times to *be* my off times, because with this and then that they are precious few. So I don't really think as much as I might – though I see how one might always begin. You don't think thinking gets one a bit rattled?'

'I don't think!' said Justin violently.

'Well, you should know,' said Robinson, looking at his thumbnail. 'I should have thought you did. From the way you talk.'

'I couldn't think if I wanted: I've lost my motivation. I taste the dust in the street and I smell the limes in the square and I beat round inside this beastly shell of the past among images that all the more torment me as they lose any sense that they had. As for feeling—'

'You don't think you find it a bit slow here? Mind you, I haven't a word against this place but it's not a place I'd choose for an off time—'

'—My dear Robinson,' Justin said, in a mincing, schoolmasterish tone, 'you seem blind to our exquisite sociabilities.'

'Pack of old cats,' said Robinson amiably.

'You suggest I should get away for a bit of fun?'

'Well, I did mean that.'

'I find my own fun,' said Justin, 'I'm torn, here, by every single pang of annihilation. But that's what I look for; that's what I want completed; that's the whole of what I want to embrace. On the far side of the nothing – my new form. Scrap "me"; scrap my wretched identity and you'll bring to the open some bud of life. I *not* "I" – I'd be the world . . . You're right: what you would call thinking does get me rattled. I only what you call think to excite myself. Take myself away, and I'd *think*. I might see; I might feel purely; I might even love—'

'Fine,' agreed Robinson, not quite easy. He paused and seemed to regard what Justin had just said – at the same time, he threw a glance of perceptible calculation at the electric clock on the mantelpiece. Justin halted and said: 'You give me too much to drink.'

'You feel this war may improve us?' said Robinson.

'What's love like?' Justin said suddenly.

Robinson paused for just less than a second in the act of lighting a cigarette. He uttered a shortish, temporizing and, for him, unnaturally loud laugh.

Queenie felt the vibration and turned round, withdrawing her arm from the windowsill. She had been looking intently, between the clumps of pampas, down the lawn to the road: cyclists and walkers on their way into town kept passing Robinson's open gate.

Across the road, above the demesne wall, the dark beeches let
through glitters of sky, and the colour and scent of the mown lawn
and the flowers seemed, by some increase of evening, lifted up to
the senses as though a new current flowed underneath. Queenie
saw with joy in her own mind what she could not from her place
in the window see – the blue china house, with all its reflecting
windows, perched on its knoll in the brilliant, fading air. They are
too rare – visions of where we are.

. When the shock of the laugh made her turn round, she still
saw day in Robinson's picture-frames and on the chromium fingers
of the clock. She looked at Robinson's head, dropped back after
the laugh on the leather scroll of his chair: her eyes went from
him to Justin. 'Did you two not hit it off?'

Robinson laughed again, this time much more naturally: he
emitted a sound like that from inside a furnace in which something
is being consumed. Letting his head fall sideways towards Queenie,
he seemed to invite her into his mood. 'The way things come out
is sometimes funny,' he said to Justin, 'if you know what I mean.'

'No, I don't,' Justin said stonily.

'I bet your sister does.'

'You didn't know what I meant. Anything I may have said about
your genius I do absolutely retract.'

'Look here, I'm sorry,' Robinson said, 'I probably took you up
all wrong.'

'On the contrary: the mistake was mine.'

'You know, it's funny about your sister: I never can realize she
can't hear. She seems so much one of the party. Would she be fond
of children?'

'You mean, why did she not marry?'

'Good God, no – I only had an idea . . .'

Justin went on: 'There was some fellow once, but I never heard
more of him. You'd have to be very oncoming, I dare say, to make
any way with a deaf girl.'

'No, I meant my children,' said Robinson. He had got up, and
he took from his mantlepiece two of the photographs in silver
frames. With these he walked down the room to Queenie, who
received them with her usual eagerness and immediately turned
with them to the light. Justin saw his sister's profile bent forward

in study and saw Robinson standing above her leaning against the window frame. When Robinson met an upward look from Queenie he nodded and touched himself on the chest. 'I can see that – aren't they very like you?' she said. He pointed to one picture then held up ten fingers, then to the other and held up eight. 'The fair little fellow's more like you, the bold one. The dark one has more the look of a girl – but he will grow up manly, I dare say . . .' With this she went back to the photographs: she did not seem anxious to give them up, and Robinson made no movement to take them from her – with Queenie the act of looking was always reflective and slow. To Justin the two silhouettes against the window looked wedded and welded by the dark. 'They are both against me,' Justin thought. 'She does not hear with her ears, he does not hear with his mind. No wonder they can communicate.'

'It's a wonder,' she said, 'that you have no little girl.'

Robinson went back for another photograph – but, standing still with a doubtful look at Queenie, he passed his hand, as though sadly expunging something, backwards and forwards across the glass. 'She's quite right; we did have a girl,' he said. 'But I don't know how to tell her the kid's dead.'

Sixty miles away, the Major was making his last round through the orchards before shutting up the house. By this time the bronze-green orchard dusk was intense; the clumped curves of the fruit were hardly to be distinguished among the leaves. The brilliance of evening, in which he had watched Emma driving away, was now gone from the sky. Now and then in the grass his foot knocked a dropped apple – he would sigh, stoop rather stiffly, pick up the apple, examine it with the pad of his thumb for bruises and slip it, tenderly as though it had been an egg, into a baggy pocket of his tweed coat. This was not a good apple year. There was something standardized, uncomplaining about the Major's movements – you saw a tall, unmilitary-looking man with a stoop and a thin-nish, dropping moustache. He often wore a slight frown, of doubt or preoccupation. This frown had intensified in the last months.

As he approached the house he heard the wireless talking, and saw one lamp at the distant end of the drawing-room where his aunt sat. At once, the picture broke up – she started, switched off

the wireless and ran down the room to the window. You might
have thought the room had burst into flames. 'Quick!' she cried.
'Oh, gracious, quick! – I believe it's the telephone.'

The telephone was at the other side of the house – before he
got there he heard the bell ringing. He put his hands in his pockets
to keep the apples from bumping as he legged it rapidly down the
corridor. When he unhooked on his wife's voice he could not help
saying haggardly: 'You all right?'

'Of course. I just thought I'd say good night.'

'That was nice of you,' he said, puzzled. 'How is the car running?'

'Like a bird,' she said in a singing voice. 'How are you all?'

'Well, I was just coming in; Aunt Fran's in the drawing-room
listening to something on the wireless, and I made the children
turn in half an hour ago.'

'You'll go up to them?'

'Yes, I was just going.' For a moment they both paused on the
line, then he said: 'Where have you got to now?'

'I'm at T— now, at the hotel in the square.'

'At T—? Aren't you taking it rather fast?'

'It's a lovely night; it's an empty road.'

'Don't be too hard on the car, she—'

'Oh, I know,' she said, in the singing voice again. 'At C— I did
try to stop, but there was a terrible crowd there: dog racing. So I
came on. Darling . . .?'

'Yes?'

'It's a lovely night, isn't it?'

'Yes, I was really quite sorry to come in. I shall shut up the
house now, then go up to the children; then I expect I'll have a
word or two with Aunt Fran.'

'I see. Well, I'd better be pushing on.'

'They'll be sitting up for you, won't they?'

'Surely,' said Emma quickly.

'Thank you for ringing up, dear: it was thoughtful of you.'

'I was thinking about you.'

He did not seem to hear this. 'Well, take care of yourself. Have
a nice time.'

'Good night,' she said. But the Major had hung up.

In the drawing-room Aunt Fran had not gone back to the

wireless. Beside the evening fire lit for her age, she sat rigid, face turned to the door, plucking round and round the rings on her left hand. She wore a foulard dress, net jabot and boned-up collar, of the type ladies wear to dine in private hotels. In the lamplight her waxy features appeared blurred, even effaced. The drawing-room held a crowd of chintz-covered chairs, inlaid tables and wool-worked stools; very little in it was antique, but nothing was strikingly up-to-date. There were cabinets of not rare china, and more blue-and-white plates, in metal clamps, hung in lines up the walls between water-colours. A vase of pink roses arranged by the governess already dropped petals on the piano. In one corner stood a harp with two broken strings – when a door slammed or one made a sudden movement this harp gave out a faint vibration or twang. The silence for miles around this obscure country house seemed to gather inside the folds of the curtains and to dilute the indoor air like a mist. This room Emma liked too little to touch already felt the touch of decay; it threw lifeless reflections into the two mirrors – the walls were green. Aunt Fran's body was stranded here like some object on the bed of a pool that has run dry. The magazine that she had been looking at had slipped from her lap to the black fur rug.

As her nephew appeared in the drawing-room door Aunt Fran fixed him urgently with her eyes. '*Nothing wrong?*'

'No, no – that was Emma.'

'What's happened?'

'Nothing. She rang up to say good night.'

'But she had said good night,' said Aunt Fran in her troubled way. 'She said good night to us when she was in the car. You remember, it was nearly night when she left. It seemed late to be starting to go so far. She had the whole afternoon, but she kept putting off, putting off. She seemed to me undecided up to the very last.'

The Major turned his back on his aunt and began to unload his pockets, carefully placing the apples, two by two, in a row along the chiffonier. 'Still, it's nice for her having this trip,' he said.

'There was a time in the afternoon,' said Aunt Fran, 'when I thought she was going to change her mind. However, she's there now – did you say?'

'Almost,' he said, 'not quite. Will you be all right if I go and shut up the house? And I said I would look in on the girls.'

'Suppose the telephone rings?'

'I don't think it will, again. The exchange will be closing, for one thing.'

'This afternoon,' said Aunt Fran, 'it rang four times.'

She heard him going from room to room, unfolding and barring the heavy shutters and barring and chaining the front door. She could begin to feel calmer now that the house was a fortress against the wakeful night. 'Hi!' she called, 'don't forget the window in here' – looking back over her shoulder into the muslin curtains that seemed to crepitate with dark air. So he came back, with his flat, unexpectant step. 'I'm not cold,' she said, 'but I don't like dark coming in.'

He shuttered the window. 'I'll be down in a minute.'

'Then we might sit together?'

'Yes, Aunt Fran: certainly.'

The children, who had been talking, dropped their voices when they heard their father's step on the stairs. Their two beds creaked as they straightened themselves and lay silent, in social, expectant attitudes. Their room smelled of toothpaste; the white presses blotted slowly into the white walls. The window was open, the blind up, so in here darkness was incomplete – obscured, the sepia picture of the Good Shepherd hung over the mantelpiece. 'It's all right,' they said, 'we are quite awake.' So the Major came round and halted between the two beds. 'Sit on mine,' said Di nonchalantly. 'It's my turn to have a person tonight.'

'Why did Mother ring up?' said Vivie, scrambling up on her pillow.

'Now how on earth did *you* know?'

'We knew by your voice – we couldn't hear what you said. We were only at the top of the stairs. Why did she?'

'To tell me to tell you to be good.'

'She's said that,' said Vivie, impatient. 'What did she say truly?'

'Just good night.'

'Oh. Is she there?'

'Where?'

'Where she said she was going to.'

'Not quite – nearly.'

'Goodness!' Di said; 'it seems years since she went.' The two children lay cryptic and still. Then Di went on: 'Do you know what Aunt Fran said because Mother went away without any stockings?'

'No,' said the Major, 'and never mind.'

'Oh, *I* don't mind,' Di said, 'I just heard.' 'And I heard,' said Vivie: she could be felt opening her eyes wide, and the Major could just see, on the pillow, an implacable miniature of his wife's face. Di went on: 'She's so frightened something will happen.'

'Aunt Fran is?'

'She's always frightened of that.'

'She is very fond of us all.'

'Oh,' burst out Vivie, 'but Mother likes things to happen. She was whistling all the time she was packing up. Can't *we* have a treat tomorrow?'

'Mother'll be back tomorrow.'

'But *can't* we have a treat?'

'We'll see; we'll ask Mother,' the Major said.

'Oh yes, but suppose she didn't come back?'

'Look, it's high time you two went to sleep.'

'We can't: we've got all sorts of ideas . . . *You* say something Daddy. Tell us something. Invent.'

'Say what?' said the Major.

'Oh goodness,' Vivie said; '*something*. What do you say to Mother?'

He went downstairs to Aunt Fran with their dissatisfied kisses stamped on his cheek. When he had gone Di fanned herself with the top of her sheet. 'What makes him so disappointed, do you know?'

'I know, he thinks about the war.'

But it was Di who, after the one question, unlocked all over and dropped plumb asleep. It was Vivie who, turning over and over, watched in the sky behind the cross of the window the tingling particles of the white dark, who heard the moth between the two window-sashes, who fancied she heard apples drop in the grass. One arbitrary line only divided this child from the animal: all her senses stood up, wanting to run the night. She swung her legs out of bed and pressed the soles of her feet on the cool floor. She got right up and stepped out of her nightdress and set out to walk the house in her skin. From each room she went into the human order seemed to have lapsed – discovered by sudden light, the chairs and tables seemed set round for a mouse's party on a gigantic scale. She stood for some time outside the drawing-room door and heard the unliving voices of the Major and aunt. She looked through the ajar door to the kitchen and saw a picked bone and a teapot upon the table and a maid lumped mute in a man's arms. She attempted the front door, but did not dare to touch the chain: she could not get out of the house. She returned to the schoolroom, drawing her brows together, and straddled the rocking-horse they had not ridden for years. The furious bumping of the rockers woke the canaries under their cover: they set up a wiry springing in their cage. She dismounted, got out the box of chalks and began to tattoo her chest, belly and thighs with stars and snakes, red, yellow and blue. Then, taking the box of chalks with her, she went to her mother's room for a look in the long glass – in front of this she attempted to tattoo her behind. After this she bent right down and squinted, upside down between her legs, at the bedroom – the electric light over the dressing-table poured into the vacantly upturned mirror and on to Emma's left-behind silver things. The anarchy she felt all through the house tonight made her, when she had danced in front of the long glass, climb up to dance on the big bed. The springs bounced her higher and higher; chalk-dust flew from her body on to the fleece of the blankets, on to the two cold pillows that she was trampling out of their place. The bed-castors lunged, under her springing, over the threadbare pink bridal carpet of Emma's room.

Attacked by the castors, the chandelier in the drawing-room tinkled sharply over Aunt Fran's head.

She at once raised her eyes to the ceiling. 'Something has got in,' she said calmly – and, rising, made for the drawing-room door. By reflex, the Major rose to stop her: he sighed and put his weak whisky down. 'Never mind,' he said, 'Aunt Fran. It's probably nothing. I'll go.'

Whereupon, his Aunt Fran wheeled round on him with her elbows up like a bird's wings. Her wax features sprang into stony prominence. 'It's never me, never me, never me! Whatever *I* see, whatever I hear it's "nothing", though the house might fall down. You keep everything back from me. No one speaks the truth to me but the man on the wireless. Always things being said on the telephone, always things being moved about, always Emma off at the end of the house singing, always the children hiding away. I am never told, never told, never told. I get the one answer, "nothing". I am expected to wait here. No one comes near the drawing-room. I am never allowed to go and see!'

'If that's how you feel,' he said, 'do certainly go.' He thought: it's all right, I locked the house.

So it was Aunt Fran's face, with the forehead lowered, that came by inches round Emma's door. She appeared to present her forehead as a sort of a buffer, obliquely looked from below it, did not speak. Her glance, arriving gradually at its object, took in the child and the whole room. Vivie paused on the bed, transfixed, breathless, her legs apart. Her heart thumped; her ears drummed; her cheeks burned. To break up the canny and comprehensive silence she said loudly: 'I am all over snakes.'

'So this is what . . .' Aunt Fran said. 'So this is what . . .'

'I'll get off this bed, if you don't like.'

'The bed you were born in,' said Aunt Fran.

Vivie did not know what to do; she jumped off the bed saying: 'No one told me not to.'

'Do you not know what is wicked?' said Aunt Fran – but with no more than estranged curiosity. She approached and began to try to straighten the bed, her unused hands making useless passes over the surface, brushing chalk-dust deeper into the fleece. All of a sudden, Vivie appeared to feel some majestic effluence from her aunt's person: she lagged round the bed to look at the stooping, set face, at the mouth held in a curve like a dead smile, at the veins in the downcast eyelids and the backs of the hands. Aunt Fran did not hurry her ceremonial fumbling; she seemed to exalt the moment that was so fully hers. She picked a pillow up by its frill and placed it high on the bolster.

'That's mother's pillow,' said Vivie.

'Did you say your prayers tonight?'

'Oh, *yes*.'

'They didn't defend you. Better say them again. Kneel down and say to Our Lord—'

'In my skin?'

Aunt Fran looked directly at, then away from, Vivie's body, as though for the first time. She drew the eiderdown from the foot of the bed and made a half-blind sweep at Vivie with it, saying: 'Wrap up, wrap up.' 'Oh, they'll come off – my snakes!' said Vivie, backing away. But Aunt Fran, as though the child were on fire, put into motion an extraordinary strength – she rolled, pressed and pounded Vivie up in the eiderdown until only the prisoner's dark eyes, so like her mother's, were left free to move wildly outside the great sausage of padded taffeta, pink.

Aunt Fran, embracing the sausage firmly, repeated: 'Now say to Our Lord—'

Shutting the door of her own bedroom, Aunt Fran felt her heart beat. The violence of the stranger within her ribs made her sit down on the ottoman – meanwhile, her little clock on the mantelpiece loudly and, it seemed to her, slowly ticked. Her window was shut, but the pressure of night silence made itself felt behind the blind, on the glass.

Round the room, on ledges and brackets, stood the fetishes she travelled through life with. They were mementoes – photos in little warped frames, musty, round straw boxes, china kittens, palm crosses, the three Japanese monkeys, *bambini*, a Lincoln Imp, a merry-thought pen-wiper, an ivory spinning-wheel from Cologne. From these objects the original virtue had by now almost evaporated. These gifts' givers, known on her lonely journey, were by now faint as their photographs: she no longer knew, now, where anyone was. All the more, her nature clung to these objects that moved with her slowly towards the dark.

Her room, the room of a person tolerated, by now gave off the familiar smell of herself – the smell of the old. A little book wedged the mirror at the angle she liked. When she was into her ripplecloth dressing-gown she brushed and plaited her hair and took out her teeth. She wound her clock and, with hand still trembling a little, lighted her own candle on the commode, then switched off her nephew's electric light. The room contracted round the crocus of flame as she knelt down slowly beside her bed – but while she said the Lord's Prayer she could not help listening, wondering what kept the Major so long downstairs. She never felt free to pray till she had heard the last door shut, till she could relax her watch on the house. She never could pray until they were *all* prostrate – loaned for at least some hours to innocence, sealed by the darkness over their lids.

Tonight she could not attempt to lift up her heart. She could, however, abase herself, and she abased herself for them all. The evil of the moment down in the drawing-room, the moment when she had cried, 'It is never me!' clung like a smell to her, so closely that she had been eager to get her clothes off, and did not like, even now, to put her hands to her face.

Who shall be their judge? Not I.

The blood of the world is poisoned, feels Aunt Fran, with her forehead over the eiderdown. Not a pure drop comes out at any prick – yes, even the heroes shed black blood. The solitary watcher retreats step by step from his post – who shall stem the black tide coming in? There are no more children: the children are born knowing. The shadow rises up the cathedral tower, up the side of the pure hill. There is not even the past: our memories share with us the infected zone; not a memory does not lead up to this. Each moment is everywhere, it holds the war in its crystal; there is no elsewhere, no other place. Not a benediction falls on this apart house of the Major; the enemy is within it, creeping about. Each heart here falls to the enemy.

So this is what goes on . . .

Emma flying away – and not saying why, or where. And to wrap the burning child up did not put out the fire. You cannot look at the sky without seeing the shadow, the men destroying each other. What is the matter tonight – is there a battle? This is a threatened night.

Aunt Fran sags on her elbows; her knees push desperately in the woolly rug. She cannot even repent; she is capable of no act; she is undone. She gets up and eats a biscuit, and looks at the little painting of Mont Blanc on the little easel beside her clock. She still does not hear the Major come up to bed.

★ ★ ★

Queenie understood that the third child, the girl, was dead: she gave back the photograph rather quickly, as though unbearable sadness emanated from it. Justin, however, came down the room and looked at the photograph over Robinson's shoulder — at the rather vulgar, frank, blonde little face. He found it hard to believe that a child of Robinson's should have chosen the part of death. He then went back to the table and picked up, with a jerky effrontery, the photographs of the two little boys. 'Do they never come here?' he said. 'You have plenty of room for them.'

'I dare say they will; I mean to fix up something. Just now they're at Greystones,' Robinson said — he then looked quite openly at the clock.

'With their mother?' Justin said, in a harsh impertinent voice.

'Yes, with my wife.'

'So you keep up the two establishments?'

Even Robinson glanced at Justin with some surprise. 'If you call it that,' he said indifferently. 'I rather landed myself with this place, really — as a matter of fact, when I moved in it looked as though things might work out differently. First I stopped where you are, at the hotel, but I do like to have a place of my own. One feels freer, for one thing.'

'There's a lot in that,' said Justin, with an oblique smile. 'Our local ladies think you keep a Bluebeard's castle up here.'

'What, corpses?' Robinson said, surprised.

'Oh yes, they think you're the devil.'

'Who, me?' replied Robinson, busy replacing photographs on the mantelpiece. 'That's really very funny: I'd no idea. I suppose they may think I've been pretty slack — but I'm no good at tea-fights, as a matter of fact. But I can't see what else can be eating them. What ought I to do, then? Throw a party here? I will if your sister'll come and pour out tea — but I don't think I've really got enough chairs . . . I hope,' he added, looking at Queenie, '*she* doesn't think it's not all above board here?'

'You're forgetting again: she misses the talk, poor girl.'

'She doesn't look very worried.'

'I dare say she's seldom been happier. She's built up quite a romance about this house. She has a world to herself — I could envy her.'

Robinson contrived to give the impression that he did not wish to have Queenie discussed – partly because he owned her, he understood her, partly because he wished to discuss nothing: it really was time for his guests to go. Though he was back again in his armchair, regard for time appeared in his attitude. Justin could not fail to connect this with the telephone and the smile that had not completely died. It became clear, staringly clear, that throughout the evening his host had been no more than marking time. This made Justin say 'Yes' (in a loud, pertinacious voice), 'this evening's been quite an event for us. Your house has more than its legend, Robinson; it has really remarkable character. However, all good things—' Stiff with anger, he stood up.

'Must you?' said Robinson, rising. 'I'm so sorry.'

Lighting-up time, fixed by Nature, had passed. The deaf woman, from her place in the window, had been watching lights of cars bend over the hill. Turning with the main road, that had passed the foot of the mountains, each car now drove a shaft of extreme brilliance through the dark below Robinson's pampas-grass. Slipping, dropping with a rush past the gate, illuminating the dust on the opposite wall, car after car vanished after its light – there was suddenly quite a gust of them, as though the mountain country, before sleeping, had stood up and shaken them from its folds. The release of movement excited Queenie – that and the beat of light's wings on her face. She turned round very reluctantly as Justin approached and began to make signs to her.

'Why, does Mr Robinson want us to go?' she said.

'That's the last thing I want!' shouted Robinson.

('She can't hear you.')

'Christ . . .' said Robinson, rattled. He turned the lights on – the three, each with a different face of despair, looked at each other across the exposed room, across the tea-tray on the circular table and the superb leather backs of the chairs. 'My brother thinks we've kept you too long,' she said – and as a lady she looked a little shaken, for the first time unsure of herself. Robinson would not for worlds have had this happen; he strode over and took and nursed her elbow, which tensed then relaxed gently inside the muslin sleeve. He saw, outdoors, his window cast on the pampas, saw the whole appearance of shattered night.

She looked for reassurance into his face, and he saw the delicate lines in hers.

'And look how late it's got, Mr Robinson!'

'It's not that,' he said in his naturally low voice, 'but—'

A car pulled up at the gate. Alarmed by the lit window it cut its lights off and could be felt to crouch there, attentive, docile, cautious, waiting to turn in. 'Your friend is arriving,' Justin said.

On that last lap of her drive, the eighteen miles of flat road along the base of the mountains, the last tingling phase of darkness had settled down. Grassy sharpness passed from the mountains' outline, the patches of firs, the gleam of watery ditch. The west sky had gradually drunk its yellow and the ridged heights that towered over her right hand became immobile cataracts, sensed not seen. Animals rising out of the ditches turned to Emma's headlamps green lamp-eyes. She felt the shudder of night, the contracting bodies of things. The quick air sang in her ears; she drove very fast. At the crossroads above Robinson's town she pulled round in a wide swerve: she saw the lemon lights of the town strung along under the black trees, the pavements and the pale, humble houses below her in a faint, mysterious glare as she slipped down the funnel of hill to Robinson's gate. (The first white gate on the left, you cannot miss it, he'd said.) From the road she peered up the lawn and saw, between pampas-tufts, three people upright in his lit room. So she pulled up and switched her lights and her engine off and sat crouching in her crouching car in the dark – night began to creep up her bare legs. Now the glass porch sprang into prominence like a lantern – she saw people stiffly saying goodbye. Down the drive came a man and woman almost in flight; not addressing each other, not looking back – putting the back of a fist to her mouth quickly Emma checked the uprush of an uncertain laugh. She marked a lag in the steps – turning their heads quickly the man and woman looked with involuntary straightness into the car, while her eyes were glued to their silhouettes. The two turned down to the town and she turned in at the gate.

Farouche, with her tentative little swagger and childish, pleading air of delinquency, Emma came to a halt in Robinson's living-room. He had pulled down the blind. She kept recoiling and blinking and drawing her fingers over her eyes, till Robinson turned off the top light. 'Is that that?' there was only the reading-lamp.

She rested her shoulder below his and grappled their enlaced fingers closer together as though trying to draw calmness from him. Standing against him, close up under his height, she held her head up and began to look round the room. 'You're whistling something,' she said, after a moment or two.

'I only mean, take your time.'

'Why, am I nervous?' she said.

'Darling, you're like a bat in out of the night. I told you not to come along too fast.'

'I see now, I came too early,' she said. 'Why didn't you tell me you had a party? Who were they? What were they doing here?'

'Oh, they're just people in this place. He's a bit screwy and she's deaf, but I like them, as a matter of fact.'

'They're mackintoshy sort of people,' she said. 'But I always thought you lived all alone . . . Is there anyone else in the house now?'

'Not a mouse,' said Robinson, without change of expression. 'My housekeeper's gone off for the night.'

'I see,' said Emma. 'Will you give me a drink?'

She sat down where Justin had just been sitting, and, bending forward with a tremulous frown, began to brush ash from her arm of the chair. You could feel the whole of her hesitate. Robinson, without hesitation, came and sat easily on the arm of the chair from which she had brushed the ash. 'It's sometimes funny,' he said, 'when people drop in like that. "My God," I thought when I saw them, "what an evening to choose." ' He slipped his hand down between the brown velvet cushion and Emma's spine, then spread the broad of his hand against the small of her back. Looking kindly down at her closed eyelids he went on: 'However, it all went off all right. Oh, and there's one thing I'd like to tell you – that chap called me a genius.'

'How would he know?' said Emma, opening her eyes.

'We never got that clear. I was rather out of my depth. His sister was deaf . . .' here Robinson paused, bent down and passed his lips absently over Emma's forehead. 'Or did I tell you that?'

'Yes, you told me that . . . Is it true that this house is blue?'

'You'll see tomorrow.'

'There'll hardly be time, darling; I shall hardly see this house in the daylight. I must go on to – where I'm supposed to be.'

'At any rate, I'm glad that was all O.K. They're not on the telephone, where you're going?'

'No, it's all right; they're not on the telephone . . . *You'll* have to think of something that went wrong with my car.'

'That will keep,' said Robinson. 'Here you are.'

'Yes, here I am.' She added: 'The night was lovely,' speaking more sadly than she knew. Yes, here she was, being settled down to as calmly as he might settle down to a meal. Her naïvety as a lover . . . She could not have said, for instance, how much the authoritative male room – the electric clock, the sideboard, the unlit grate, the cold of the leather chairs – put, at every moment when he did not touch her, a gulf between her and him. She turned her head to the window. 'I smell flowers.'

'Yes, I've got three flower beds.'

'Darling, for a minute could we go out?'

She moved from his touch and picked up Queenie's tea-tray and asked if she could put it somewhere else. Holding the tray (and given countenance by it) she halted in front of the photographs. 'Oh . . .' she said. 'Yes. Why?' 'I wish in a way you hadn't got any children.' 'I don't see why I shouldn't have: you have.'

'Yes, I . . . But Vivie and Di are not so much *like* children—'

'If they're like you,' he said, 'those two will be having a high old time, with the cat away—'

'Oh darling, I'm not the cat.'

In the kitchen (to put the tray down) she looked round: it shone with tiling and chromium and there seemed to be switches in every place. 'What a whole lot of gadgets you have,' she said. 'Look at all those electric . . .' 'Yes I like them.' 'They must cost a lot of money. My kitchen's all over blacklead and smoke and hooks. My cook would hate a kitchen like this.'

'I always forget that you have a cook.' He picked up an electric torch and they went out. Going along the side of the house, Robinson played a mouse of light on the wall. 'Look, really blue.' But she only looked absently. 'Yes – But have I been wrong to come?' He led her off the gravel on to the lawn, till they reached the edge of a bed of stocks. Then he firmly said: 'That's for you to say, my dear girl.'

'I know it's hardly a question – I hardly know you, do I?'

'We'll be getting to know each other,' said Robinson.

After a minute she let go of his hand and knelt down abruptly beside the flowers: she made movements like scooping the scent up and laving her face in it – he, meanwhile, lighted a cigarette and stood looking down. 'I'm glad you like my garden,' he said. 'You feel like getting fond of the place?'

'You say you forget that I have a cook.'

'Look, sweet, if you can't get that off your mind you'd better get in your car and go straight home . . . But you will.'

'Aunt Fran's so old, too old; it's not nice. And the Major keeps thinking about the war. And the children don't think I am good; I regret that.'

'You have got a nerve,' he said, 'but I love that. You're with me. Aren't you with me? – Come out of that flower bed.'

They walked to the brow of the lawn; the soft feather-plumes of the pampas rose up a little over her head as she stood by him overlooking the road. She shivered. 'What are all those trees?' 'The demesne – I know they burnt down the castle years ago. The demesne's great for couples.' 'What's in there?' 'Nothing, I don't think; just the ruin, a lake . . .'

'I wish—'

'Now, what?'

'I wish we had more time.'

'Yes: we don't want to stay out all night.'

So taught, she smothered the last of her little wishes for consolation. Her shyness of further words between them became extreme; she was becoming frightened of Robinson's stern, experienced delicacy on the subject of love. Her adventure became the quiet practice with him. The adventure (even, the pilgrimage) died at its root, in the childish part of her mind. When he had headed her off the cytherean terrain – the leaf-drowned castle ruin, the lake – she thought for a minute he had broken her heart, and she knew now he had broken her fairy tale. He seemed content – having lit a new cigarette – to wait about in his garden for a few minutes longer: not poetry but a sort of tactile wisdom came from the

firmness, lawn, under their feet. The white gateposts, the boles of
beeches above the dust-whitened wall were just seen in reflected
light from the town. There was no moon, but dry, tense, translucent
darkness: no dew fell.

Justin went with his sister to her door in the square. Quickly,
and in their necessary silence, they crossed the grass under the
limes. Here a dark window reflected one of the few lamps, there
a shadow crossed a lit blind, and voices of people moving under
the trees made a reverberation in the box of the square. Queenie
let herself in; Justin heard the heavy front door drag shut
slowly across the mat. She had not expected him to come in,
and he did not know if she shared his feeling of dissonance, or
if she recoiled from shock, or if she were shocked at all. Quitting
the square at once, he took the direct way to his hotel in the
main street. He went in at the side door, past the bar in which
he so often encountered Robinson.

   In his small, harsh room he looked first at his bed. He looked,
as though out of a pit of sickness, at his stack of books on the
mantelpiece. He writhed his head round sharply, threw off his coat
and begun to unknot his tie. Meanwhile he beat round, in the hot
light, for some crack of outlet from his constriction. It was at his
dressing-table, for he had no other, that he began and ended
his letter to Robinson: the mirror screwed to the dressing-table
constituted a witness to this task – whenever his look charged up
it met his own reared head, the flush heightening on the bridge
of the nose and forehead, the neck from which as though for an
execution, the collar had been taken away.

   My dear Robinson: Our departure from your house (Bellevue,
   I think?) tonight was so awkwardly late, and at the last so hurried,
   that I had inadequate time in which to thank you for your
   hospitality to my sister and to myself. That we exacted this
   hospitality does not make its merit, on your part, less. Given the
   inconvenience we so clearly caused you, your forbearance with
   us was past praise. So much so that (as you may be glad to hear)
   my sister does not appear to realize how very greatly we were
   de trop. In my own case – which is just – the same cannot be

said. I am conscious that, in spite of her disability, she did at least prove a less wearisome guest than I.

My speculations and queries must, to your mind, equally seem absurd. This evening's fiasco has been definitive: I think it better our acquaintance should close. You will find it in line with my usual awkwardness that I should choose to state this decision of mine at all. Your indifference to the matter I cannot doubt. My own lack of indifference must make its last weak exhibition in this letter — in which, if you have fine enough nostrils (which I doubt) every sentence will almost certainly stink. In attempting to know you I have attempted to enter, and to comport myself in, what might be called an area under your jurisdiction. If my inefficacies appeared to you ludicrous, my curiosities (as in one special instance tonight) appeared more — revolting. I could gauge (even before the postscript outside your gate) how profoundly I had offended you. Had we either of us been gentlemen, the incident might have passed off with less harm.

My attempts to know you I have disposed of already. My wish that you should know me has been, from the first, ill found. You showed yourself party to it in no sense, and the trick I played on myself I need not discuss. I acted and spoke (with regard to you) upon assumptions you were not prepared to warrant. You cannot fail to misunderstand what I mean when I say that a year ago this might not have happened to me. But — the assumptions on which I acted, Robinson, are becoming more general in a driven world than you yet (or may ever) know. The extremity to which we are each driven must be the warrant for what we do and say.

My extraordinary divagation towards you might be said to be, I suppose, an accident of this summer. But there are no accidents. I have the fine (yes) fine mind's love of the fine plume, and I meet no fine plumes down my own narrow street. Also, in this place (birthplace) you interposed your solidity between me and what might have been the full effects of an exacerbating return. In fact, you had come to constitute for me a very genuine holiday. As things are, my five remaining days here will have to be seen out. I shall hope not to meet you, but must fear much of the trap-like size of this town. (You need not, as I mean to, avoid the hotel bar.) Should I, however, fail to avoid you, I shall again, I suppose, have to owe much, owe any face I keep, to your never-failing imperviousness. Understand that it will be against my wish that I re-open this one-sided account.

I wish you good night. Delicacy does not deter me from adding that I feel my good wish to be superfluous. I imagine that, incapable of being haunted, you are incapable of being added to. Tomorrow (I understand) you will feel fine, but you will not know any more about love. If the being outside your gate came with a question, it is possible that she should have come to me. If I had even seen her she might not go on rending my heart. As it is, as you are, I perhaps denounce you as much on her behalf as my own. Not trying to understand, you at least cannot misunderstand the mood and hour in which I write. As regards my sister, please do not discontinue what has been your even kindness to her: she might be perplexed. She has nothing to fear, I think.

Accept, my dear Robinson (without irony) my kind regards,

J.C.

Justin, trembling, smote a stamp on this letter. Going down as he was, in the hall he unhooked his mackintosh and put it over his shirt. It was well past midnight; the street, empty, lay in dusty reaches under the few lamps. Between the shutters his step raised an echo; the cold of the mountains had come down; two cats in his path unclinched and shot off into the dark. On his way to the letterbox he was walking towards Bellevue; on his way back he still heard the drunken woman sobbing against the telegraph pole. The box would not be cleared till tomorrow noon.

Queenie forgot Justin till next day. The house in which her rooms were was so familiar that she went upstairs without a pause in the dark. Crossing her sitting-room she smelled oil from the cooker behind the screen: she went through an arch to the cubicle where she slept. She was happy. Inside her sphere of silence that not a word clouded, the spectacle of the evening at Bellevue reigned. Contemplative, wishless, almost without an 'I', she unhooked her muslin dress at the wrists and waist, stepped from the dress and began to take down her hair. Still in the dark, with a dreaming sureness of habit, she dropped hairpins into the heart-shaped tray.

This was the night she knew she would find again. It had stayed living under a film of time. On just such a summer night, once only, she had walked with a lover in the demesne. His hand, like Robinson's, had been on her elbow, but she had guided him, not he her, because she had better eyes in the dark. They had gone down walks already deadened with moss, under the weight of July trees; they had felt the then fresh aghast ruin totter above them; there was a moonless sky. Beside the lake they sat down, and while her hand brushed the ferns in the cracks of the stone seat emanations of kindness passed from him to her. The subtle deaf girl had made the transposition of this nothing or everything into an everything – the delicate deaf girl that the man could not speak to and was afraid to touch. She who, then so deeply contented, kept in her senses each frond and breath of that night, never saw him again and had soon forgotten his face. That had been twenty years ago, till tonight when it was now. Tonight it was Robinson who, guided by Queenie down leaf tunnels, took the place on the stone seat by the lake.

The rusted gates of the castle were at the end of the square. Queenie, in her bed facing the window, lay with her face turned sideways, smiling, one hand lightly against her cheek.

Ivy Gripped the Steps

Ivy gripped and sucked at the flight of steps, down which with such a deceptive wildness it seemed to be flowing like a cascade. Ivy matted the door at the top and amassed in bushes above and below the porch. More, it had covered, or one might feel consumed, one entire half of the high, double-fronted house, from the basement up to a spiked gable: it had attained about halfway up to the girth and more than the density of a tree, and was sagging outward under its own weight. One was left to guess at the size and the number of windows hidden by looking at those in the other side. But these, though in sight, had been made effectively sightless: sheets of some dark composition that looked like metal were sealed closely into their frames. The house, not old, was of dull red brick with stone trimmings.

To crown all, the ivy was now in fruit, clustered over with fleshy pale green berries. There was something brutal about its fecundity. It was hard to credit that such a harvest could have been nourished only on brick and stone. Had not reason insisted that the lost windows must, like their fellows, have been made fast, so that the suckers for all their seeking voracity could not enter, one could have convinced oneself that the ivy must be feeding on something inside the house.

The process of strangulation could be felt: one wondered how many more years of war would be necessary for this to complete itself. And, the conventionality of the house, the remains, at least, of order in its surroundings made what was happening more and more an anomaly. Mrs Nicholson's house had always enjoyed distinction – that of being detached, while its neighbours, though equally 'good', had been erected in couples or even in blocks of four; that of being the last in the avenue; that of having on one hand as neighbour the theatre, to whose façade its front was at right angles. The theatre, set back behind shallow semi-circular gardens, at once crowned and terminated the avenue, which ran from it to the Promenade overhanging the sea. And the house, apart from the prestige of standing just where it stood, had had the air of reserving something quite of its own. It was thus perhaps just, or not unfitting, that it should have been singled out for this gothic fate.

This was, or had been, one of the best residential avenues in Southstone, into which private hotels intruded only with the most breathless, costly discretion: if it was not that now it was nothing else, for there was nothing else for it to be. Lines of chestnut trees had been planted along the pavements, along the railed strip of lawn that divided the avenue down the middle – now, the railings were, with all other ironwork, gone; and where the lawn was very long rusty grass grew up into the tangles of rusty barbed wire. On to this, as on to the concrete pyramids – which, in the course of four years of waiting to be pushed out to obstruct the invader, had sunk some inches into the soil – the chestnuts were now dropping their leaves.

The decline dated from the exodus of the summer of 1940, when Southstone had been declared in the front line. The houses at the sea end of the avenue had, like those on the Promenade, been requisitioned; but some of those at the theatre end stayed empty. Here and there, portions of porches or balustrades had fallen into front gardens, crushing their overgrowth; but there were no complete ruins; no bomb or shell had arrived immediately here, and effects of blast, though common to all of Southstone, were less evident than desuetude and decay. It was now the September of 1944; and, for some reason, the turn of the tide of war, the accumulation of the Invasion victories, gave Southstone its final air of defeat. The withdrawal of most of the soldiers, during the summer, had drained off adventitious vitality. The A.A. batteries, this month, were on the move to another part of the coast. And, within the very last few days, the silencing of the guns across the Channel had ended the tentative love affair with death: Southstone's life, no longer kept to at least a pitch by shelling warnings, now had nothing but an etiolated slowness. In the shuttered shopping streets along the Promenade, in the intersecting avenues, squares and crescents, vacuum mounted up. The lifting of the ban on the area had, so far, brought few visitors in.

This afternoon, for minutes together, not a soul, not even a soldier, crossed the avenue: Gavin Doddington stood to regard the ivy in which was, virtually, solitude. The sky being clouded, though not dark, a timeless flat light fell on to everything. Outside the theatre a very few soldiers stood grouped about; some moodily, some in no more than apathy. The theatre gardens had been cemented over to make a lorry park; and the engine of one of the lorries was being run.

Mrs Nicholson could not be blamed for the ivy: *her* absence from Southstone was of long standing, for she had died in 1912 – two years before the outbreak of what Gavin still thought of as Admiral Concannon's war. After her death, the house had been put up for auction by her executors: since then, it might well have changed hands two or three times. Probably few of the residents dislodged in 1940 had so much as heard Mrs Nicholson's name. In its condition, today, the house was a paradox: having been closed and sealed up with extreme care, it had been abandoned in a manner no less extreme. It had been nobody's business to check the ivy. Nor, apparently, had there been anybody to authorize a patriotic sacrifice of the railings – Gavin Doddington, prodding between the strands of ivy, confirmed his impression that that iron lacework still topped the parapet of the front garden. He could pursue with his finger, though not see, the pattern that with other details of the house, outside and in, had long ago been branded into his memory. Looking up at the windows in the exposed half he saw, still in position along the sills, miniature reproductions of this pattern, for the support of window boxes. Those, which were gone, had been flowery in her day.

The assumption was that, as lately as 1940, Mrs Nicholson's house *had* belonged to someone, but that it belonged to nobody now. The late owner's death in some other part of England must have given effect to a will not brought up to date, by which the property pased to an heir who could not be found – to somebody not heard of since Singapore fell or not yet reported anything more than 'missing' after a raid on London or a battle abroad. Legal hold-ups dotted the world-wide mess . . . So reasoning, Gavin Doddington gave rein to what had been his infant and was now his infantile passion for explanation. But also he attached himself to the story as to something nothing to do with him; and did so with the intensity of a person who must think lest he should begin to feel.

His passion for explanation had been, when he knew Mrs Nicholson, raised by her power of silently baulking it into the principal reason for suffering. It had been among the stigmata of his extreme youth – he had been eight when he met her, ten when she died. He had not been back to Southstone since his last stay with her.

Now, the lifting of the official ban on the area had had the effect of bringing him straight back – why? When what one has refused is put out of reach, when what one has avoided becomes forbidden, some lessening of the inhibition may well occur. The ban had so acted on his reluctance that, when the one was removed, the other came away with it – as a scab, adhering, comes off with a wad of lint. The transmutation, due to the fall of France, of his '*I* cannot go back to Southstone' into '*One* cannot go there' must have been salutary, or, at least, exteriorizing. It so happened that when the ban came off he had been due for a few days' leave from the Ministry. He had at once booked a room at one of the few hotels that remained at the visitor's disposition.

Arriving at Southstone yesterday evening, he had confined his stroll in the hazy marine dusk to the cracked, vacant and wire-looped Promenade – from which he returned with little more than the wish that he had, after all, brought somebody down here with him. Amorist since his 'teens, he had not often set off on a holiday uncompanioned. The idea of this as a pilgrimage revolted him: he remained in the bar till the bar closed. This morning he had no more than stalked the house, approaching it in wavering closing circles through the vaguer Southstone areas of association. He had fixed for the actual confrontation that hour, deadline for feeling, immediately after lunch.

The story originated in a friendship between two young girls in their Dresden finishing year. Edith and Lilian had kept in touch throughout later lives that ran very widely apart – their letters, regularly exchanged, were perhaps more confidential than their infrequent meetings. Edith had married a country gentleman, Lilian a business man. Jimmie Nicholson had bought the Southstone house for his wife in 1907, not long before his death, which had been the result of a stroke. He had been senior by about fifteen years: their one child, a daughter, had died at birth.

Edith Doddington, who had never been quite at ease on the subject of Lilian's marriage, came to stay more often now her friend was a widow, but still could not come as often as both would have liked. Edith's own married life was one of contrivance and of anxiety. After money, the most pressing of Edith's worries centred round the health of her second son: Gavin had been from birth a delicate little boy. The damp of his native county, inland and low-lying, did not suit him: there was the constant question of change of air – till his health stabilized, he could not go away to school. It was natural that Lilian, upon discovering this, should write inviting Gavin to stay at Southstone – ideally, of course, let his mother bring him; but if Edith could not be free, let him come alone. Mrs Nicholson hoped he and she, who had not yet met, would not, or would not for long, be shy of each other. Her maid Rockham was, at any rate, good with children.

Gavin had heard of Southstone as the scene of his mother's only exotic pleasures. The maid Rockham was sent to London to meet him: the two concluded their journey with the absurdly short drive, in an open victoria, from the station to Mrs Nicholson's house. It was early in what was a blazing June: the awnings over the windows rippled, the marguerites in the window-boxes undulated, in a hot breeze coming down the avenue from the sea. From the awnings the rooms inside took a tense bright dusk. In the sea-blue drawing-room, up whose walls reared mirrors framed in ivory brackets, Gavin was left to await Mrs Nicholson. He had time to marvel at the variety of the bric-à-brac crowding brackets and tables, the manyness of the cut-crystal vases, the earliness of the purple and white sweet pea – at the Doddingtons', sweet pea did not flower before July. Mrs Nicholson then entered: to his surprise she did not kiss him.

Instead, she stood looking down at him – she was tall – with a glittering, charming uncertainty. Her head bent a little lower, during consideration not so much of Gavin as of the moment. Her *coiffure* was like spun sugar: that its crisp upward waves should seem to have been splashed with silvery powder added, only, marquise-like glowing youth to her face.

The summery light-like fullness of her dress was accentuated by the taut belt with coral-inlaid clasp: from that small start the skirts flowed down to dissipate and spread where they touched the floor. Tentatively she extended her right hand, which he, without again raising his eyes, shook. 'Well . . . Gavin,' she said. 'I hope you had a good journey? I am so very glad you could come.'

He said: 'And my mother sends you her love.'

'Does she?' Sitting down, sinking an elbow into the sofa cushions, she added: 'How *is* Edith — how is your mother?'

'Oh, she is very well.'

She vaguely glanced round her drawing-room, as though seeing it from his angle, and, therefore, herself seeing it for the first time. The alternatives it offered could be distracting: she soon asked him her first intimate question — 'Where do you think you would like to sit?'

Not that afternoon, nor indeed, until some way on into this first visit did Gavin distinguish at all sharply between Mrs Nicholson and her life. Not till the knife of love gained sufficient edge could he cut out her figure from its surroundings. Southstone was, for the poor landowner's son, the first glimpse of the enchanted existence of the *rentier*. Everything was effortless; and, to him, consequently, seemed stamped with style. This society gained by smallness: it could be comprehended. People here, the company that she kept, commanded everything they desired, were charged with nothing they did not. The expenditure of their incomes — expenditure calculated so long ago and so nicely that it could now seem artless — occupied them. What there was to show for it showed at every turn; though at no turn too much, for it was not too much. Such light, lofty, smooth-running houses were to be found, quite likely, in no capital city. A word to the livery stables brought an imposing carriage to any door: in the afternoons one drove, in a little party, to reflect on a Roman ruin or to admire a village church. In the Promenade's glare, at the end of the shaded avenue, parasols passed and repassed in a rhythm of leisure. Just inland were the attentive shops. There were meetings for good causes in cool drawing-rooms, afternoon concerts in the hotel ballrooms; and there was always the theatre, where applause

continued long after Gavin had gone to bed. Best of all, there were
no poor to be seen.

The plan of this part of Southstone (a plateau backed by the
downs and overhanging the sea) was masterful. Its architecture was
ostentatious, fiddling, bulky and mixed. Gavin was happy enough
to be at an age to admire the one, to be unaware of the other –
he was elated, rather than not, by this exhibition of gimcrack size;
and bows, bays, balustrades, glazed-in balconies and French-type
mansardes not slowly took up their parts in the fairy tale. As strongly
was he impressed by the strong raying out, from such points as
station and theatre, of avenues; each of which crossed, obliquely,
just less wide residential roads. Lavishness appeared in the public
flowers, the municipal seats with their sofa-like curving backs, the
flagpoles, cliff grottoes, perspectives of lawn. There was a climate
here that change from season to season, the roughest Channel gale
blowing, could not disturb. This town without function fascinated
him – outside it, down to the port or into the fishing quarter, 'old
Southstone', he did not attempt to stray. Such tameness might have
been found odd in a little boy: Mrs Nicholson never thought of
it twice.

Gavin's estimation of Southstone – as he understood much later
– coincided with that of a dead man. When Jimmie Nicholson
bought the house for his wife here, Southstone was the high dream
of his particular world. It was as Lilian's husband he made the
choice: alone, he might not have felt capable of this polished leisure.
His death left it uncertain whether, even *as* Lilian's husband, he
could have made the grade. The golf course had been his object:
failing that he was not, perhaps, so badly placed in the cemetery,
which was also outside the town. For, for Southstone dividends
kept their mystic origin: they were as punctual as Divine grace, as
unmentioned as children still in wombs. Thickset Jimmie, with his
pursuant reek of the City, could have been a distasteful reminder
of money's source.

Gavin, like his dead host, beheld Southstone with all the ardour
of an outsider. His own family had a touch of the brutishness that
comes from any dependence upon land. Mr and Mrs Doddington
were constantly in wet clothes, constantly fatigued, constantly
depressed. Nothing new appeared in the squire's home; and what

was old had acquired a sort of fog from being ignored. An austere, religious idea of their own standing not so much inspired as preyed upon Gavin's parents. Caps touched to them in the village could not console them for the letters they got from their bank. Money for them was like a spring in a marsh, feebly thrusting its way up to be absorbed again: any profit forced from the home farm, any rents received for outlying lands went back again into upkeep, rates, gates, hedging, draining, repairs to cottages and renewal of stock. There was nothing, no nothing ever, to show. In the society round them they played no part to which their position did not compel them: they were poor gentry, in fact, at a period when poverty could not be laughed away. Their lot was less enviable than that of any of their employees or tenants, whose faces, naked in their dejection, and voices pitched to complaints they could at least utter, had disconcerted Gavin, since babyhood, at the Hall door. Had the Doddingtons been told that their kind would die out, they would have expressed little more than surprise that such complicated troubles could end so simply.

Always towards the end of a stay at Southstone Gavin's senses began to be haunted by the anticipation of going back. So much so that to tread the heat-softened asphalt was to feel once more the suck of a sticky lane. *Here*, day and night he breathed with ease that was still a subconscious joy: the thought of the Midlands made his lungs contract and deaden – such was the old cold air, sequestered by musty baize doors, of the corridors all the way to his room at home.

His room *here* was on the second floor, in front, looking on to the avenue. It had a frieze of violets knotted along a ribbon: as dusk deepened, these turned gradually black. Later, a lamp from the avenue cast a tree's shifting shadow on to the ceiling above his bed; and the same light pierced the Swiss skirts of the dressing-table. Mrs Nicholson, on the first occasion when she came as far as his door to say good night, deprecated the 'silliness' of this little room. Rockham, it seemed, had thought it suitable for his age – she, Rockham, had her quarters on the same floor – Mrs Nicholson, though she did not say so, seemed to feel it to be unsuitable for his sex. 'Because I don't suppose,' she said, 'that you really ever *are* lonely in the night?'

Propped upright against his pillows, gripping his glass of milk, he replied: 'I am never frightened.'

'But, lonely – what makes you lonely, then?'

'I don't know. I suppose, thoughts.'

'Oh, but why,' she said, 'don't you like them?'

'When I am here the night seems a sort of waste, and I don't like to think what a waste it is.'

Mrs Nicholson, who was on her way out to dinner, paused in the act of looping a gauze scarf over her hair and once again round her throat. 'Only tell me,' she said, 'that you're not more lonely, Gavin, because I am going out? Up here, you don't know if I am in the house or not.'

'I do know.'

'Perhaps,' she suggested humbly, 'you'll go to sleep? They all say it is right for you, going to bed so early, but I wish it did not make days so short. – I must go.'

'The carriage hasn't come round yet.'

'No, it won't: it hasn't been ordered. It is so lovely this evening, I thought I would like to walk.' She spoke, though, as though the project were spoiled for her: she could not help seeing, as much as he did, the unkindness of leaving him with this picture. She came even further into the room to adjust her scarf at his mirror, for it was not yet dark. 'Just once, one evening perhaps, you could stay up late. Do you think it would matter? I'll ask Rockham.'

Rockham remained the arbiter: it was she who was left to exercise anything so nearly harsh as authority. In even the affairs of her own house Mrs Nicholson was not heard giving an order: what could not be thought to be conjured into existence must be part of the clockwork wound up at the start by Jimmie and showing no sign of beginning to run down yet. The dishes that came to table seemed to surprise her as much, and as pleasingly, as they did Gavin. Yet the effect she gave was not of idleness but of pre-occupation: what she did with her days Gavin did not ask himself – when he did ask himself, later, it was too late. They continued to take her colour – those days she did nothing with.

It was Rockham who worked out the daily programme, devised to keep the little boy out of Madam's way. 'Because Madam,' she said, 'is not accustomed to children.' It was by Rockham that, every

morning, he was taken down to play by the sea: the beach, undulations of orange shingle, was fine-combed with breakwaters, against
one of which sat Rockham, reading a magazine. Now and then
she would look up, now and then she would call. These relegations
to Rockham sent Gavin to angry extremes of infantilism: he tried
to drape seaweed streamers around her hat; he plagued to have
pebbles taken out of his shoe. There was a literal feeling of degrad-
ation about this descent from the plateau to the cliff's foot. From
close up, the sea, with its heaving mackerel vacancy, bored him –
most of the time he stood with his back to it, shading his eyes
and staring up at the heights. From right down here, though
Southstone could not be seen – any more than objects set back
on a high shelf can be seen by somebody standing immediately
underneath it – its illusion, its magical artificiality, was to be savoured
as from nowhere else. Tiny, the flags of the Promenade's edge, the
figures leaning along the railings, stood out against a dazzle of sky.
And he never looked up at these looking down without an inter-
rupted heartbeat – might she not be among them?

The rule was that they, Rockham and Gavin, walked zigzag
down by the cliff path, but travelled up in the lift. But one day
fate made Rockham forget her purse. They had therefore to under-
take the ascent. The path's artful gradients, hand-railed, were broken
by flights of steps and by niched seats, upon every one of which
Rockham plumped herself down to regain breath. The heat of
midday, the glare from the flowered cliff beat up Gavin into a sort
of fever. As though a dropped plummet had struck him between
the eyes he looked up, to see Mrs Nicholson's face above him
against the blue. The face, its colour rendered transparent by the
transparent silk of a parasol, was inclined forward: he had the
experience of seeing straight up into eyes that did not see him.
Her look was pitched into space: she was not only not seeing him,
she was seeing nothing. She was listening, but not attending, while
someone talked.

Gavin, gripping the handrail, bracing his spine against it, leaned
out backwards over the handrail into the void, in the hopes of
intercepting her line of view. But in vain. He tore off clumps of
sea pinks and cast the too-light flowers outwards into the air, but
her pupils never once flickered down. Despair, the idea that his

doom must be never, never to reach her, not only now but ever, gripped him and gripped his limbs as he took the rest of the path – the two more bends and few more steps to the top. He clawed his way up the rail, which shook in its socket.

The path, when it landed Gavin on to the Promenade, did so some yards from where Mrs Nicholson and her companion stood. Her companion was Admiral Concannon. 'Hello, hello!' said the Admiral, stepping back to see clear of the parasol. 'Where have *you* sprung from?'

'Oh, but Gavin,' exclaimed Mrs Nicholson, also turning, 'why not come up in the lift? I thought you liked it.'

'Lift?' said the Admiral. 'Lift, at his age? What, has the boy got a dicky heart?'

'No indeed!' she said, and looked at Gavin so proudly that he became the image of health and strength.

'In that case,' said the Admiral, 'do him good.' There was something, in the main, not unflattering about this co-equal masculine brusqueness. Mrs Nicholson, looking over the railings, perceived the labouring top of her maid's hat. 'It's poor Rockham,' she said, 'that I am thinking about; she hasn't got a heart but she has attacks. – How hazy it is!' she said, indicating the horizon with a gloved hand. 'It seems to be days since we saw France. I don't believe Gavin believes it is really there.'

'It is there all right,' said the Admiral, frowning slightly.

'Why, Rockham,' she interposed, 'you look hot. Whatever made you walk up on a day like this?'

'Well, I cannot fly, can I, madam; and I overlooked my purse.'

'Admiral Concannon says we may all be flying. – What are you waiting for?'

'I was waiting for Master Gavin to come along.'

'I don't see why he should, really – which would you rather, Gavin?'

Admiral Concannon's expression did not easily change, and did not change now. His features were severely clear cut; his figure was nervy and spare; and he had an air of eating himself – due, possibly, to his retirement. His manners of walking, talking and standing, though all to be recognized at a distance, were vehemently impersonal. When in anything that could be called repose he usually kept his hands in his pockets – the abrupt extraction of one hand, for the purpose of clicking thumb and finger together, was the nearest thing to a gesture he ever made. His voice and step had become familiar, among the few nocturnal sounds of the avenue, some time before Gavin had seen his face; for he escorted Mrs Nicholson home from parties to which she had been wilful enough to walk. Looking out one night, after the hall door shut, Gavin had seen the head of a cigarette, immobile, pulsating sharply under the dark trees. The Concannons had settled at Southstone for Mrs Concannon's health's sake: their two daughters attended one of the schools.

Liberated into this blue height, Gavin could afford to look down in triumph at the sea by whose edge he had lately stood. But the Admiral said: 'Another short turn, perhaps?' – since they were to *be* three, they had better be three in motion. Mrs Nicholson raised her parasol, and the three moved off down the Promenade with the dignified aimlessness of swans. Ahead, the distance dissolved, the asphalt quivered in heat; and she, by walking between her two companions, produced a democracy of masculine trouble into which age did not enter at all. As they passed the bandstand she said to Gavin: 'Admiral Concannon has just been saying that there is going to be a war.'

Gavin glanced across at the Admiral, who remained in profile. Unassisted and puzzled, he said: 'Why?'

'Why indeed?' she agreed. – 'There!' she said to the Admiral. 'It's no good trying to tease me, because I never believe you.' She glanced around her and added: 'After all, we live in the present day! History is quite far back; it is said, of course, but it does seem silly. I never even cared for history at school; I was glad when we came to the end of it.'

'And when, my dear, did you come to the end of history?'

'The year I put up my hair. It had begun to be not so bad from the time we started catching up with the present; and I was glad I had stayed at school long enough to be sure that it had all ended happily. But oh, those unfortunate people in the past! It seems unkind to say so, but can it have been their faults? They can have been no more like us than cats and dogs. I suppose there *is* one reason for learning history – one sees how long it has taken to make the world nice. Who on earth could want to upset things now? – No one could want to,' she said to the Admiral. 'You forget the way we behave now, and there's no other way. Civilized countries are polite to each other, just as you and I are to the people we know, and uncivilized countries are put down – but, if one thinks, there are beautifully few of those. Even savages really prefer wearing hats and coats. Once people wear hats and coats and can turn on electric light, they would no more want to be silly than you or I do. – Or *do* you want to be silly?' she said to the Admiral.

He said: 'I did not mean to upset you.'

'You don't,' she said. 'I should not dream of suspecting *any* civilized country!'

'Which civilized country?' said Gavin. 'France?'

'For your information,' said the Admiral coldly, 'it is Germany we should be preparing to fight, for the reason that she is preparing to fight us.'

'I have never been happier anywhere,' said Mrs Nicholson, more nearly definitely than usual. 'Why,' she added, turning to Gavin, 'if it were not for Germany, now I come to think of it, you would not be here!'

The Admiral, meanwhile, had become intent on spearing on the tip of his cane a straying fragment of paper, two inches torn off a letter, that was defiling the Promenade. Lips compressed, he crossed to a little basket (which had till then stood empty, there being no litter) and knocked the fragment into it off his cane. He burst out: 'I should like to know what this place is coming to – we shall have trippers next!'

This concern his beautiful friend *could* share – and did so share that harmony was restored. Gavin, left to stare out to sea, reflected on one point in the conversation: he could never forget that the Admiral had called Mrs Nicholson, 'My dear'.

Also, under what provocation had the Admiral threatened Mrs Nicholson with war? . . . Back at Gavin's home again, once more with his parents, nothing was, after all, so impossible: this was outside the zone of electric light. As late summer wore slowly over the Midlands, the elms in the Doddingtons' park casting lifeless slate-coloured shadows over sorrel, dung, thistles and tufted grass, it was born in on Gavin that this existence belonged, by its nature, to *any* century. It was unprogressive. It had stayed as it was while, elsewhere, history jerked itself painfully off the spool; it could hardly be more depressed by the fateful passage of armies than by the flooding of tillage or the failure of crops: it was hardly capable, really, of being depressed further. It was an existence mortgaged to necessity; it was an inheritance of uneasiness, tension and suspicion. One could preassume the enmity of weather, prices, mankind, cattle. It was this dead weight of existence that had supplied to history not so much the violence or the futility that had been, as she said, apparent to Mrs Nicholson, but its repetitive harshness and its power to scar. This existence had no volition, but could not stop; and its never stopping, because it could not, made history's ever stopping the less likely. No signs of even an agreeable pause were to be seen round Doddington Hall. Nor could one, at such a distance from Southstone, agree that time had laboured to make the world nice.

Gavin now saw his mother as Mrs Nicholson's friend. Indeed, the best of the gowns in which Edith went out to dinner, when forced to go out to dinner, had been Lilian's once, and once or twice worn by her. Worn by Edith, they still had the exoticism of gifts, and dispelled from their folds not only the giver's sachets, but the easy pitiful lovingness of the giver's mood. In them, Gavin's mother's thin figure assumed a grace whose pathos was lost to him at the time. While the brown-yellow upward light of the table oil-lamp unkindly sharpened the hollows in Mrs Doddington's face and throat, Gavin, thrown sideways out of his bed, fingered the mousseline or caressed the satin of the skirts with an adoring absorption that made his mother uneasy – for fetishism is still to be apprehended by these for whom it has never had any name. She would venture: 'You like, then, to see me in pretty clothes?' . . . It was, too, in the first of these intermissions between his visits to Southstone that he, for the first time, took stock of himself, of his assets – the evident pleasingness of his manner; his looks – he could take in better and better part his elder brother's jibes at his pretty-prettiness – his quickness of mind, which at times made even his father smile; and his masculinity, which, now he tried it out, gave him unexpected command of small situations. At home, nights were not a waste: he attached himself to his thoughts, which took him, by seven-league strides, onward to his next visit. He rehearsed, using his mother, all sorts of little gratuities of behaviour, till she exclaimed: 'Why, Lilian has made quite a little page of you!' At her heels round the garden or damp extensive offices of the Hall, at her elbow as she peered through her letters or resignedly settled to her accounts, he reiterated: 'Tell me about Germany.'

'Why Germany?'

'I mean, the year you were there.'

A gale tore the slates from the Hall stables, brought one tree down on to a fence and another to block the drive, the night before Gavin left for Southstone. This time he travelled alone. At Southstone, dull shingly roaring thumps from the beach travelled as far inland as the railway station; from the Promenade – on which, someone said, it was all but impossible to stand upright – there came a whistling strain down the avenues. It was early January. Rockham was kept to the house by a nasty cold; so it was Mrs Nicholson who, with brilliantly heightened colour, holding her muff to the cheek on which the wind blew, was on the station platform to meet Gavin. A porter, tucking the two of them into the waiting carriage, replaced the foot-warmer under the fur rug. She said: 'How different this is from when you were with me last. Or do you like winter?'

'I like anything, really.'

'I remember one thing you don't like: you said you didn't like thoughts.' As they drove past a lighted house from which music came to be torn about by the wind, she remembered: 'You've been invited to several parties.'

He was wary: 'Shall you be going to them?'

'Why, yes; I'm sure I *could* go,' she said.

Her house was hermetic against the storm: in the drawing-room, heat drew out the smell of violets. She dropped her muff on the sofa, and Gavin stroked it – 'It's like a cat,' he said quickly, as she turned round. 'Shall I have a cat?' she said. 'Would you like me to have a cat?' All the other rooms, as they went upstairs, were tawny with fires that did not smoke.

Next morning, the wind had dropped; the sky reflected on everything its mild brightness; trees, houses and pavements glistened like washed glass. Rockham, puffy and with a glazed upper lip, said: 'Baster Gavid, you've brought us better weather.' Having blown her nose with what she seemed to hope was exhaustive thorough-ness, she concealed her handkerchief in her bosom as guiltily as though it had been a dagger. 'Badam,' she said, 'doesn't like be to have a cold. – Poor Bisses Codcaddod,' she added, 'has been laid up agaid.'

Mrs Concannon's recovery must be timed for the little dinner party that they were giving. Her friends agreed that she ought to reserve her strength. On the morning of what was to be the day, it was, therefore, the Admiral whom one met out shopping: Gavin and Mrs Nicholson came on him moodily selecting flowers and fruit. Delayed late autumn and forced early spring flowers blazed, under artificial light, against the milder daylight outside the florist's plate glass. 'For tonight, for the party?' exclaimed Mrs Nicholson. 'Oh, let us have carnations, scarlet carnations!'

The Admiral hesitated. 'I think Constance spoke of chrysanthe-mums, white chrysanthemums.'

'Oh, but these are so washy, so like funerals. They will do poor Constance no good, if she still feels ill.'

Gavin, who had examined the prices closely, in parenthesis said: 'Carnations are more expensive.'

'No, wait!' cried Mrs Nicholson, gathering from their buckets all the scarlet carnations that were in reach, and gaily shaking the water from their stems, 'you must let me send these to Constance, because I am so much looking forward to tonight. It will be delightful.'

'I hope so,' the Admiral said. 'But I'm sorry to say we shall be an uneven number: we have just heard that poor Massingham has dropped out. Influenza.'

'Bachelors shouldn't have influenza, should they. – But then, why not ask somebody else?'

'So very much at the last moment, that might seem a bit – informal.'

'Dear me,' she teased, 'have you really *no* old friend?'

'Constance does not feel . . .'

Mrs Nicholson's eyebrows rose: she looked at the Admiral over the carnations. This was one of the moments when the Admiral could be heard to click his finger and thumb. 'What a pity,' she said. 'I don't care for lopsided parties. *I* have one friend who is not touchy – invite Gavin!'

To a suggestion so completely outrageous, who was to think of any reply? It was a *coup*. She completed, swiftly: 'Tonight, then? We shall be with you at about eight.'

Gavin's squiring Mrs Nicholson to the Concannons' party symptomized this phase of their intimacy; without being, necessarily, its highest point. Rockham's cold had imperilled Rockham's prestige: as intervener or arbiter she could be counted out. There being no more talk of these odious drops to the beach, Gavin exercised over Mrs Nicholson's mornings what seemed a conqueror's rights to a terrain; while with regard to her afternoons she showed a flattering indecision as to what might not please him or what he could not share. At her tea-table, his position was made subtly manifest to her guests. His bedtime was becoming later and later; in vain did Rockham stand and cough in the hall; more than once or twice he had dined downstairs. When the curtains were drawn, it was he who lit the piano candles, then stood beside her as she played – ostensibly to turn over the music, but forgetting the score to watch her hands. At the same time, he envisaged their two figures as they would appear to someone – his other self – standing out there in the cold dark of the avenue, looking between the curtains into the glowing room. One evening, she sang 'Two Eyes of Grey that used to be so Bright.'

At the end, he said: 'But that's supposed to be a song sung by a man to a woman.'

Turning on the stool, she said: 'Then you must learn it.'

He objected: 'But your eyes are not grey.'

Indeed they were never neutral eyes. Their sapphire darkness, with that of the sapphire pendant she was wearing, was struck into by the Concannons' electric light. That round fitment on pulleys, with a red silk frill, had been so adjusted above the dinner table as to cast down a vivid circle, in which the guests sat. The stare and sheen of the cloth directly under the light appeared supernatural. The centrepiece was a silver or plated pheasant, around whose base the carnations – slightly but strikingly 'off' the red of the shade, but pre-eminently flattering in their contrast to Mrs Nicholson's orchid *glacé* gown – were bunched in four silver cornets.

This was a party of eight: if the Concannons had insisted on stressing its 'littleness', it was, still, the largest that they could hope to give. The evident choiceness of the guests, the glitter and the mathematical placing of the silver and glass, the prompt, meticulous service of the dishes by maids whose suspended breath could be heard – all, all bespoke art and care. Gavin and Mrs Nicholson were so placed as to face one another across the table: her glance contained him, from time to time, in its leisurely, not quite attentive play. He wondered whether she felt, and supposed she must, how great had been the effrontery of their entrance.

For this dinner-party lost all point if it were not *de rigueur*. The Concannon daughters, even (big girls, but with hair still down their backs) had, as not qualified for it, been sent out for the evening. It, the party, had been balanced up and up on itself like a house of cards: built, it remained as precarious. Now the structure trembled, down to its base, from one contemptuous flip at its top storey – Mrs Nicholson's caprice of bringing a little boy. Gavin perceived that night what he was not to forget: the helplessness, in the last resort, of society – which he was never, later, to be able to think of as a force. The pianola-like play of the conversation did not drown the nervousness round the table.

At the head of the table the Admiral leaned just forward, as though pedalling the pianola. At the far end, an irrepressible cough from time to time shook Mrs Concannon's décolletage and the crystal pince-nez which, balanced high on her face, gave her a sensitive blankness. She had the *dévote* air of some sailors' wives; and was heroic in pale blue without a wrap – arguably, nothing could make her iller. The Admiral's pride in his wife's courage passed like a current over the silver pheasant. For Mrs Concannon, joy in sustaining all this for his sake, and confidence in him, provided a light armour: she possibly did not feel what was felt for her. To Gavin she could not have been kinder; to Mrs Nicholson she had only and mildly said: 'He will not be shy, I hope, if he does not sit beside you?'

Rearrangement of the table at the last moment could not but have disappointed one or other of the two gentlemen who had expected to sit, and were now sitting, at Mrs Nicholson's right and left hand. More and more, as course followed course, these two

showed how highly they rated their good fortune – indeed, the
censure around the rest of the table only acted for them, like heat
drawing out scent, to heighten the headiness of her immediate
aura. Like the quick stuff of her dress her delinquency, even, gave
out a sort of shimmer: while she, neither arch nor indolent, turned
from one to the other her look – if you like, melting; for it dissolved
her pupils, which had never been so dilated, dark, as tonight. In
this look, as dinner proceeded, the two flies, ceasing to struggle,
drowned.

The reckoning would be on the way home. Silent between the
flies' wives, hypnotized by the rise and fall of Mrs Nicholson's
pendant, Gavin ate on and on. The ladies' move to the drawing-
room sucked him along with it in the wake of the last skirt . . .
It was without a word that, at the end of the evening, the Admiral
saw Mrs Nicholson to her carriage – Gavin, like an afterthought
or a monkey, nipping in under his host's arm extended to hold
open the carriage door. Light from the porch, as they drove off,
fell for a moment longer on that erect form and implacable hatchet
face. Mrs Nicholson seemed to be occupied in gathering up her
skirts to make room for Gavin. She then leaned back in her corner,
and he in his: not a word broke the tension of the short dark drive
home. Not till she had dropped her cloak in front of her drawing-
room fire did she remark: 'The Admiral's angry with me.'

'Because of me?'

'Oh dear no; because of her. If I did not think to be angry was
very silly, I'd almost be a little angry with him.'

'But you meant to make him angry, didn't you?' Gavin said.

'Only because he's silly,' said Mrs Nicholson. 'If he were not so
silly, that poor unfortunate creature would stop coughing: she would
either get better or die.' Still standing before her mantelpiece, she
studied some freesias in a vase – dispassionately, she pinched off
one fading bloom, rolled it into a wax pill between her thumb
and finger, then flicked it away to sizzle in the heart of the fire.
'If people,' she said, 'give a party for no other reason but to show
off their marriage, what kind of evening can one expect? – However,
I quite enjoyed myself. I hope you did?'

Gavin said: 'Mrs Concannon's quite old. But then, so's the
Admiral.'

'He quite soon will be, at this rate,' said Mrs Nicholson. 'That's why he's so anxious to have that war. One would have thought a man could just be a man. – What's the matter, Gavin; what are you staring at?'

'That is your most beautiful dress.'

'Yes; that's why I put it on.' Mrs Nicholson sat down on a low blue velvet chair and drew the chair to the fire: she shivered slightly. 'You say such sweet things, Gavin: what fun we have!' Then, as though, within the seconds of silence ticked off over her head by the little Dresden clock, her own words had taken effect with her, she turned and, with an impulsive movement, invited him closer to her side. Her arm stayed round him; her short puffed sleeve, disturbed by the movement, resulted down into silence. In the fire a coal fell apart, releasing a seam of gas from which spurted a pale tense quivering flame. 'Aren't you glad we are back?' she said, 'that we are only you and me? – Oh, why endure such people when all the time there is the whole world! Why do I stay on and on here; what am I doing? Why don't we go right away somewhere, Gavin; you and I? To Germany, or into the sun? Would that make you happy?'

'That – that flame's so funny,' he said, not shifting his eyes from it.

She dropped her arm and cried, in despair: 'After all, what a child you are!'

'I am not.'

'Anyhow, it's late; you must go to bed.'

She transmuted the rise of another shiver into a slight yawn.

Overcharged and trembling, he gripped his way, flight by flight, up the polished banister rail, on which his palms left patches of mist; pulling himself away from her up the staircase as he had pulled himself towards her up the face of the cliff.

After that midwinter visit there were two changes: Mrs Nicholson went abroad, Gavin went to school. He overheard his mother say to his father that Lilian found Southstone this winter really too cold to stay in. 'Or, has made it too hot to stay in?' said Mr Doddington, from whose disapproval the story of Gavin and the Concannons' party had not been able to be kept. Edith Doddington coloured, loyal, and said no more. During his first term Gavin

received at school one bright picture postcard of Mentone. The
carefully chosen small preparatory school confronted him, after all,
with fewer trials than his parents had feared and his brother hoped.
His protective adaptability worked quickly; he took enough colour,
or colourlessness, from where he was to pass among the others,
and along with them – a civil and indifferent little boy. His improved
but never quite certain health got him out of some things and
secured others – rests from time to time in the sick-room, teas by
the matron's fire. This spectacled woman was not quite unlike
Rockham; also, she was the most approachable edge of the grown-
up ambience that connected him, however remotely, with Mrs
Nicholson. At school, his assets of feeling remained, one would
now say, frozen.

His Easter holidays had to be spent at home; his summer holidays
exhausted their greater part in the same concession to a supposed
attachment. Not until September was he dispatched to Southstone,
for a week, to be set up before his return to school.

That September was an extension of summer. An admirable
company continued its season of light opera at the theatre, in whose
gardens salvias blazed. The lawns, shorn to the roots after weeks
of mowing, were faintly blond after weeks of heat. Visitors were
still many; and residents, after the fastidious retreat of August, were
returning – along the Promenade, all day long, parasols, boater hats
and light dresses flickered against the dense blue gauze backdrop
that seldom let France be seen. In the evenings the head of the
pier was a lighted musical box above the not yet cooling sea. Rare
was the blade of chill, the too crystal morning or breathlike blur
on the distance that announced autumn. Down the avenues the
dark green trees hardened but did not change: if a leaf did fall, it
was brushed away before anyone woke.

If Rockham remarked that Gavin was now quite a little man, her
mistress made no reference to his schoolboy state. She did once ask
whether the Norfolk jacket that had succeeded his sailor blouse were
not, in this weather, a little hot; but that he might be expected to
be more gruff, mum, standoffish or awkward than formerly did not
appear to strike her. The change, if any, was in her. He failed to
connect – why should he? – her new languor, her more marked
contrarieties and her odd little periods of askance musing with the

illness that was to be her death. She only said, the summer had been too long. Until the evenings she and Gavin were less alone, for she rose late; and, on their afternoon drives through the country, inland from the coast or towards the downs, they were as often as not accompanied by, of all persons, Mrs Concannon. On occasions when Mrs Concannon returned to Mrs Nicholson's house for tea, the Admiral made it his practice to call for her. The Concannons were very much occupied with preparations for another social event: a Southstone branch of the Awaken Britannia League was to be inaugurated by a drawing-room meeting at their house. The daughters were busy folding and posting leaflets. Mrs Nicholson, so far, could be pinned down to nothing more than a promise to send cakes from her own, or rather her cook's, kitchen.

'But at least,' pleaded Mrs Concannon, at tea one afternoon, 'you should come if only to hear what it is about.'

By five o'clock, in September, Mrs Nicholson's house cast its shadow across the avenue on to the houses opposite, which should otherwise have received the descending sun. In revenge, they cast shadow back through her bow window: everything in the drawing-room seemed to exist in copper-mauve glass, or as though reflected into a tarnished mirror. At this hour, Gavin saw the pale walls, the silver lamp stems, the transparent frills of the cushions with a prophetic feeling of their impermanence. At her friend's words, Mrs Nicholson's hand, extended, paused for a moment over the cream jug. Turning her head she said: 'But I know what it is about; and I don't approve.'

With so little reference to the Admiral were these words spoken that he might not have been there. There, however, he was, standing drawn up above the low tea table, cup and saucer in hand. For a moment, not speaking, he weighed his cup with a frown that seemed to ponder its exact weight. He then said: 'Then, logically, you should not be sending cakes.'

'Lilian,' said Constance Concannon fondly, 'is never logical with regard to her friends.'

'Aren't I?' said Mrs Nicholson. – 'But cake, don't you think, makes everything so much nicer? You can't offer people nothing but disagreeable ideas.'

'You are too naughty, Lilian. All the League wants is that we should be alert and thoughtful. – Perhaps Gavin would like to come?'

Mrs Nicholson turned on Gavin a considering look from which complicity seemed to be quite absent; she appeared, if anything, to be trying to envisage him as alert and thoughtful. And the Admiral, at the same moment, fixed the candidate with a measuring eye. 'What may come,' he said, 'is bound, before it is done, to be his affair.' Gavin made no reply to the proposition – and it was found, a minute or two later, that the day fixed for the drawing-room meeting was the day fixed for his return home. School began again after that. 'Well, what a pity,' Mrs Concannon said.

The day approached. The evenings were wholly theirs, for Mrs Nicholson dined out less. Always, from after tea, when any guests had gone, he began to reign. The apartnesses and frustrations of the preceding hours, and, most of all, the occasional dissonances that those could but produce between him and her, sent him pitching towards the twilight in a fever that rose as the week went on. This fever, every time, was confounded by the sweet pointlessness of the actual hour when it came. The warmth that lingered in the exhausted daylight made it possible for Mrs Nicholson to extend herself on the *chaise longue* in the bow window. Seated on a stool at the foot of the *chaise longue*, leaning back against the frame of the window, Gavin could see, through the side pane of the glass projection in which they sat, the salvias smouldering in the theatre gardens. As it was towards these that her chair faced, in looking at them he was looking away from her. On the other hand, they were looking at the same thing. So they were on the evening that was his last. At the end of a minute or two of silence she exclaimed: 'No, I don't care, really, for scarlet flowers. – You do?'

'Except carnations?'

'I don't care for public flowers. And you look and look at them till I feel quite lonely.'

'I was only thinking, *they* will be here tomorrow.'

'Have you been happy this time, Gavin? I haven't sometimes thought you've been quite so happy. Has it been my fault?'

He turned, but only to finger the fringe of the Kashmir shawl that had been spread by Rockham across her feet. Not looking up, he said: 'I have not seen you so much.'

'There are times,' she said, 'when one seems to be at the other side of glass. One sees what is going on, but one cannot help it. It may be what one does not like, but one cannot feel.'

'Here, I always feel.'

'Always feel what?' she remotely and idly asked.

'I just mean, here, I feel. I don't feel, anywhere else.'

'And what is "here"?' she said, with tender mocking obtuseness. 'Southstone? What do you mean by "here"?'

'Near you.'

Mrs Nicholson's attitude, her repose, had not been come at carelessly. Apparently relaxed, but not supine, she was supported by six or seven cushions – behind her head, at the nape of her neck, between her shoulders, under her elbows and in the small of her back. The slipperiness of this architecture of comfort enjoined stillness – her repose depended on each cushion staying just where it was. Up to now, she had lain with her wrists crossed on her dress: a random turn of the wrist, or flexing of fingers, were the nearest things to gestures she permitted herself – and indeed, these had been enough. *Now*, her beginning to say, 'I wonder if they were right . . .' must, though it sounded nothing more than reflect-ive, have been accompanied by an incautious movement, for a cushion fell with a plump to the ground. Gavin went round, recovered the cushion and stood beside her: they eyed one another with communicative amazement, as though a third person had spoken and they were uncertain if they had heard aright. She arched her waist up and Gavin replaced the cushion. He said: 'If who were right?'

'Rockham . . . The Admiral. She's always hinting, he's always saying, that I'm in some way thoughtless and wrong with you.'

'Oh, him.'

'I know,' she said. 'But you'll say goodbye to him nicely?'

He shrugged. 'I shan't see him again – this time.'

She hesitated. She was about to bring out something that, though slight, must be unacceptable. 'He *is* coming in,' she said, 'for a moment, just after dinner, to fetch the cakes.'

'Which cakes?'

'The cakes for tomorrow. I had arranged to send them round in the morning, but that would not do; no, that would not be soon enough. Everything is for the Admiral's meeting to make us ready, so everything must be ready in good time.'

When, at nine o'clock, the Admiral's ring was heard, Mrs Nicholson, indecisively, put down her coffee cup. A wood fire, lit while they were at dinner, was blazing languidly in the already warm air: it was necessary to sit at a distance from it. While the bell still rang, Gavin rose, as though he had forgotten something, and left the drawing-room. Passing the maid on her way to open the front door, he made a bolt upstairs. In his bedroom, Rockham was in possession: his trunk waited, open, bottom layer packed; her mending-basket was on the bureau; she was taking a final look through his things – his departure was to be early tomorrow morning. 'Time flies,' she said. 'You're no sooner come than you're gone.' She continued to count handkerchiefs, to stack up shirts. 'I'd have thought,' she said, 'you'd have wanted to bring your school cap.'

'Why? Anyway, it's a silly beastly old colour.'

'You're too old-fashioned,' she said sharply. 'It was high time somebody went to school. – Now you *have* come up, just run down again, there's a good boy, and ask Madam if there's anything for your mother. If it's books, they ought to go in here among your boots.'

'The Admiral's there.'

'Well, my goodness, you know the Admiral.'

Gavin played for time, on the way down, by looking into the rooms on every floor. Their still only partial familiarity, their fullness with objects that, in the half light coming in from the landing, he could only half perceive and did not yet dare touch, made him feel he was still only at the first chapter of the mystery of the house. He wondered how long it would be before he saw them again. Fear of Rockham's impatience, of her calling down to ask what he was up to, made him tread cautiously on the thickly carpeted stairs; he gained the hall without having made a sound. Here he smelled the fresh-baked cakes, waiting in a hamper on the hall table. The drawing-room door stood ajar, on, for a minute, dead silence. The Admiral must have gone, without the cakes.

But then the Admiral spoke. 'You must see, there is nothing more to be said. I am only sorry I came. I did not expect you to be alone.'

'For once, that is not my fault,' replied Mrs Nicholson, unsteadily. 'I do not even know where the child is.' In a voice that hardly seemed to be hers she cried out softly: 'Then this is to go on always? What more do you ask? What else am I to be or do?'

'There's nothing more you can do. And all you must be is, happy.'

'How easy,' Mrs Nicholson said.

'You have always said that that was easy, for you. For my own part, I never considered happiness. There you misunderstood me, quite from the first.'

'Not quite. Was I wrong in thinking you were a man?'

'I'm a man, yes. But I'm not that sort.'

'That is too subtle for me,' said Mrs Nicholson.

'On the contrary, it is too simple for you. You ignore the greater part of my life. You cannot be blamed, perhaps; you have only known me since I was cursed with too much time on my hands. Your – your looks, charm and gaiety, my dear Lilian, I'd have been a fool not to salute at their full worth. Beyond that, I'm not such a fool as I may have seemed. Fool? – all things considered, I could not have been simply that without being something a good deal viler.'

'I have been nice to Constance,' said Mrs Nicholson.

'Vile in my own eyes.'

'I know, that is all you think of.'

'I see, now, where you are in your element. You know as well as I do what your element is; which is why there's nothing more to be said. Flirtation's always been off my beat – so far off my beat, as a matter of fact, that I didn't know what it was when I first saw it. There, no doubt, I was wrong. If you can't live without it, you cannot, and that is that. If you have to be dangled after, you no doubt will be. But don't, my dear girl, go for that to the wrong shop. It would have been enough, where I am concerned, to watch you making a ninnie of that unfortunate boy.'

'Who, poor little funny Gavin?' said Mrs Nicholson. 'Must I have nothing? – I have no little dog. You would not like it, even, if I had a real little dog. And you expect me to think that you do not care . . .'

The two voices, which intensity more than caution kept pitched low, ceased. Gavin pushed open the drawing-room door.

The room, as can happen, had elongated. Like figures at the end of a telescope the Admiral and Mrs Nicholson were to be seen standing before the fire. Of this, not a glint had room to appear between the figures of the antagonists. Mrs Nicholson, head bent as though to examine the setting of the diamond, was twisting round a ring on her raised left hand – a lace-edged handkerchief, like an abandoned piece of stage property, had been dropped and lay on the hearthrug near the hem of her skirts. She gave the impression of having not moved: if they had not, throughout, been speaking from this distance, the Admiral must have taken a step forward. But this, on his part, must have been, and must be, all – his head was averted from her, his shoulders were braced back, and behind his back he imprisoned one of his own wrists in a handcuff grip that shifted only to tighten. The heat from the fire must have made necessary, probably for the Admiral when he came, the opening of a window behind the curtains; for, as Gavin advanced into the drawing-room, a burst of applause entered from the theatre, and continued, drowning the music which had begun again.

Not a tremor recorded the moment when Mrs Nicholson knew Gavin was in the room. Obliquely and vaguely turning her bowed head she extended to him, in an unchanged look, what might have been no more than an invitation to listen, also, to the music. 'Why, Gavin,' she said at last, 'we were wondering where you were.'

Here he was. From outside the theatre, stink still travelled to him from the lorry whose engine was being run. Nothing had changed in the colourless afternoon. Without knowing, he had plucked a leaf of the ivy which now bred and fed upon her house. A soldier, passing behind him to join the others, must have noticed his immobility all the way down the avenue; for the soldier said, out of the side of his mouth: 'Annie doesn't live here any more.' Gavin Doddington, humiliated, affected to study the ivy leaf, whose veins were like arbitrary vulgar fate-lines. He thought he remembered hearing of metal ivy; he knew he had seen ivy carved round marble monuments to signify fidelity, regret, or the tomb-defying tenaciousness of memory – what you liked. Watched by the soldiers, he did not care to make the gesture involving the throwing of the leaf: instead, he shut his hand on it, as he turned from the house.

Should he go straight to the station, straight back to London? Not while the impression remained so strong. On the other hand, it would be a long time before the bars opened.

Another walk round Southstone, this afternoon, was necessary: there must be a decrescendo. From his tour of annihilation, nothing out of the story was to be missed. He walked as though he were carrying a guide-book.

Once or twice he caught sight of the immune downs, on the ascent to whose contours war had halted the villas. The most open view was, still, from the gates of the cemetery, past which he and she had so often driven without a thought. Through those gates, the extended dulling white marble vista said to him, only, that the multiplicity of the new graves, in thirty years, was enough in itself to make the position of hers indifferent – she might, once more, be lying beside her husband. On the return through the town towards the lip of the plateau overhanging the sea, the voidness and the air of concluded meaning about the plan of Southstone seemed to confirm her theory: history, after this last galvanized movement forward, had come, as she expected, to a full stop. It had only not stopped where or as she foresaw. Crossing the Promenade obliquely, he made, between wire entanglements, for the railings; to become one more of the spaced-out people who leaned along them, willing to see a convoy or gazing with indifference towards liberated France. The path and steps up the cliff face had been destroyed; the handrail hung out rotting into the air.

Back in the shopping centre, he turned a quickening step, past the shuttered, boarded or concave windows, towards the corner florist's where Mrs Nicholson had insisted on the carnations. But this had received a direct hit: the entire corner was gone. When time takes our revenges out of our hands it is, usually, to execute them more slowly: her vindictiveness, more thorough than ours, might satisfy us, if, in the course of her slowness, we did not forget. In this case, however, she had worked in the less than a second of detonation. Gavin Doddington paused where there was no florist – was he not, none the less, entitled to draw a line through this?

Not until after some time back in the bar did it strike him – there had been one omission. He had not yet been to the

Concannons'. He pushed his way out: it was about seven o'clock, twenty minutes or so before the black-out. They had lived in a crescent set just back from a less expensive reach of the Promenade. On his way, he passed houses and former hotels occupied by soldiers or A.T.S. who had not yet gone. These, from top to basement, were in a state of naked, hard, lemon-yellow illumination. Interposing dark hulks gave you the feeling of nothing more than their recent military occupation. The front doors of the Concannons' crescent opened, on the inland side, into a curved street, which, for some military reason now probably out of date, had been blocked at the near end: Gavin had to go round. Along the pavements under the front doorsteps there was so much wire that he was thrust out into the road – opposite only one house was there an inviting gap in the loops. Admiral Concannon, having died in the last war, could not have obtained this as a concession – all the same this *was*, as the number faintly confirmed, his house. Nobody now but Gavin recognized its identity or its importance. Here had dwelled, and here continued to dwell, the genius of the Southstone that now was. Twice over had there been realized the Admiral's alternative to love.

The Concannons' dining-room window, with its high triple sashes, was raised some distance above the street. Gavin, standing opposite it, looked in at an A.T.S. girl seated at a table. She faced the window, the dusk and him. From above her head, a naked electric light bulb, on a flex shortened by being knotted, glared on the stripped, whitish walls of the room and emphasized the fact that she was alone. In her khaki shirt, sleeves rolled up, she sat leaning her bare elbows on the bare table. Her face was abrupt with youth. She turned one wrist, glanced at the watch on it, then resumed her steady stare through the window, downwards at the dusk in which Gavin stood.

It was thus that, for the second time in his life, he saw straight up into the eyes that did not see him. The intervening years had given him words for trouble: a phrase, '*l'horreur de mon néant*', darted across his mind.

At any minute, the girl would have to approach the window to do the black-out – for that, along this coast, was still strictly enforced. It was worth waiting. He lighted a cigarette: she looked at her watch again. When she did rise it was, first, to unhook from a peg beside the dining-room door not only her tunic but her cap. Her being dressed for the street, when she did reach up and, with a succession of movements he liked to watch, begin to twitch the black stuff across the window, made it his object *not* to be seen — just yet. Light staggered, a moment longer, on the desiccated pods of the wall-flowers that, seeded from the front garden, had sprung up between the cracks of the pavement, and on the continuous regular loops or hoops of barbed wire, through all of which, by a sufficiently long leap, one *could* have projected oneself head foremost, unhurt. At last she had stopped the last crack of light. She had now nothing to do but to come out.

Coming smartly down the Concannons' steps, she may just have seen the outline of the civilian waiting, smoking a cigarette. She swerved impassively, if at all. He said: 'A penny for your thoughts.' She might not have heard. He fell into step beside her. Next, appearing to hear what he had not said, she replied: 'No, I'm *not* going your way.'

'Too bad. But there's only one way out — can't get out, you know, at the other end. What have *I* got to do, then — stay here all night?'

'*I* don't know, I'm sure.' Unconcernedly humming, she did not even quicken her light but ringing tramp on the curved street. If he kept abreast with her, it was casually, and at an unpressing distance: this, and the widening sky that announced the open end of the crescent, must have been reassuring. He called across to her: 'That house you came out of, I used to know people who lived there. I was just looking round.'

She turned, for the first time — she could not help it. 'People lived there?' she said. 'Just fancy. I know I'd sooner live in a tomb. And that goes for all this place. Imagine anyone coming here on a holiday!'

'I'm on a holiday.'

'Goodness. What do you do with yourself?'

'Just look around.'

'Well, I wonder how long you stick it out. — Here's where we go different ways. Good night.'

'I've got nobody to talk to,' Gavin said, suddenly standing still in the dark. A leaf flittered past. She was woman enough to halt, to listen, because this had not been said to her. If her 'Oh yes, we girls have heard that before' was automatic, it was, still more, wavering. He cast away the end of one cigarette and started lighting another: the flame of the lighter, cupped inside his hands, jumped for a moment over his features. Her first thought was: yes, he's quite old – that went along with his desperate jauntiness. Civilian, yes: too young for the last war, too old for this. A gentleman – they were the clever ones. But he had, she perceived, forgotten about her thoughts – what she saw, in that moment before he snapped down the lighter, stayed on the darkness, puzzling her somewhere outside the compass of her own youth. She had seen the face of somebody dead who was still there – 'old' because of the presence, under an icy screen, of a whole stopped mechanism for feeling. Those features had been framed, long ago, for hope. The dints above the nostrils, the lines extending the eyes, the lips' grimacing grip on the cigarette – all completed the picture of someone wolfish. A preyer. But who had said, preyers are preyed upon?

His lower lip came out, thrusting the cigarette up at a debonair angle towards his eyes. 'Not a soul,' he added – this time with calculation, and to her.

'Anyway,' she said sharply, 'I've got a date. Anyway, what made you pick on this dead place? Why not pick on some place where you know someone?'

Mysterious Kôr

Full moonlight drenched the city and searched it; there was not a niche left to stand in. The effect was remorseless: London looked like the moon's capital – shallow, cratered, extinct. It was late, but not yet midnight; now the buses had stopped the polished roads and streets in this region sent for minutes together a ghostly unbroken reflection up. The soaring new flats and the crouching old shops and houses looked equally brittle under the moon, which blazed in windows that looked its way. The futility of the black-out became laughable: from the sky, presumably, you could see every slate in the roofs, every whited kerb, every contour of the naked winter flower beds in the park; and the lake, with its shining twists and tree-darkened islands would be a landmark for miles, yes, miles, overhead.

However, the sky, in whose glassiness floated no clouds but only opaque balloons, remained glassy-silent. The Germans no longer came by the full moon. Something more immaterial seemed to threaten, and to be keeping people at home. This day between days, this extra tax, was perhaps more than senses and nerves could bear. People stayed indoors with a fervour that could be felt: the buildings strained with battened-down human life, but not a beam, not a voice, not a note from a radio escaped. Now and then under streets and buildings the earth rumbled: the Underground sounded loudest at this time.

Outside the now gateless gates of the park, the road coming downhill from the north-west turned south and became a street, down whose perspective the traffic lights went through their unmeaning performance of changing colour. From the promontory of pavement outside the gates you saw at once up the road and down the street: from behind where you stood, between the gate-posts, appeared the lesser strangeness of grass and water and trees. At this point, at this moment, three French soldiers, directed to a hostel they could not find, stopped singing to listen derisively to the waterbirds wakened up by the moon. Next, two wardens coming off duty emerged from their post and crossed the road diagonally, each with an elbow cupped inside a slung-on tin hat. The wardens turned their faces, mauve in the moonlight, towards the Frenchmen with no expression at all. The two sets of steps died in opposite directions, and, the birds subsiding, nothing was heard or seen until, a little way down the street, a trickle of people came out of the Underground, around the anti-panic brick wall. These all disappeared quickly, in an abashed way, or as though dissolved in the street by some white acid, but for a girl and a soldier who, by their way of walking, seemed to have no destination but each other and to be not quite certain even of that. Blotted into one shadow, he tall, she little, these two proceeded towards the park. They looked in, but did not go in; they stood there debating without speaking. Then, as though a command from the street behind them had been received by their synchronized bodies, they faced round to look back the way they had come.

His look up the height of a building made his head drop back, and she saw his eyeballs glitter. She slid her hand from his sleeve, stepped to the edge of the pavement and said: 'Mysterious Kôr.'

'What is?' he said, not quite collecting himself.

'This is –

> "*Mysterious Kôr thy walls forsaken stand,*
> *Thy lonely towers beneath a lonely moon –*"

                                                              – this is Kôr.'

'Why,' he said, 'it's years since I've thought of that.'

She said: 'I think of it all the time –

> "*Not in the waste beyond the swamps and sand,*
> *The fever-haunted forest and lagoon,*
> *Mysterious Kôr thy walls—*"

– a completely forsaken city, as high as cliffs and as white as bones, with no history—'

'But something must once have happened: why had it been forsaken?'

'How could anyone tell you when there's nobody there?'

'Nobody there since how long?'

'Thousands of years.'

'In that case, it would have fallen down.'

'No, not Kôr,' she said with immediate authority. 'Kôr's altogether different; it's very strong; there is not a crack in it anywhere for a weed to grow in; the corners of stones and the monuments might have been cut yesterday, and the stairs and arches are built to support themselves.'

'You know all about it,' he said, looking at her.

'I know, I know all about it.'

'What, since you read that book?'

'Oh, I didn't get much from that; I just got the name. I knew that must be the right name; it's like a cry.'

'Most like the cry of a crow to me.' He reflected, then said: 'But the poem begins with "Not" – "*Not in the waste beyond the swamps and sand* –" And it goes on, as I remember, to prove Kôr's not really anywhere. When even a poem says there's no such place—'

'What it tries to say doesn't matter: I see what it makes me see. Anyhow, that was written some time ago, at that time when they thought they had got everything taped, because the whole world had been explored, even the middle of Africa. Every thing and place had been found and marked on some map; so what wasn't marked on any map couldn't be there at all. So *they* thought: that was why he wrote the poem. "*The world is disenchanted*," it goes on. That was what set me off hating civilization.'

'Well, cheer up,' he said; 'there isn't much of it left.'

'Oh, yes, I cheered up some time ago. This war shows we've by no means come to the end. If you can blow whole places out of existence, you can blow whole places into it. I don't see why not. They say we can't say what's come out since the bombing started. By the time we've come to the end, Kôr may be the one city left: the abiding city. I should laugh.'

'No, you wouldn't,' he said sharply. '*You* wouldn't – at least, I hope not. I hope you don't know what you're saying – does the moon make you funny?'

'Don't be cross about Kôr; please don't, Arthur,' she said.

'I thought girls thought about people.'

'What, these days?' she said. 'Think about people? How can anyone think about people if they've got any heart? I don't know how other girls manage: I always think about Kôr.'

'Not about me?' he said. When she did not at once answer, he turned her hand over, in anguish, inside his grasp. 'Because I'm not there when you want me – is that my fault?'

'But to think about Kôr *is* to think about you and me.'

'In that dead place?'

'No, ours – we'd be alone here.'

Tightening his thumb on her palm while he thought this over, he looked behind them, around them, above them – even up at the sky. He said finally: 'But we're alone here.'

'That was why I said "Mysterious Kôr".'

'What, you mean we're there now, that here's there, that now's then? . . . *I* don't mind,' he added, letting out as a laugh the sigh he had been holding in for some time. 'You ought to know the place, and for all I could tell you we might be anywhere: I often do have it, this funny feeling, the first minute or two when I've come up out of the Underground. Well, well: join the Army and see the world.' He nodded towards the perspective of traffic lights and said, a shade craftily: 'What are those, then?'

Having caught the quickest possible breath, she replied: 'Inexhaustible gases; they bored through to them and lit them as they came up; by changing colour they show the changing of minutes; in Kôr there is no sort of other time.'

'You've got the moon, though: that can't help making months.'

'Oh, and the sun, of course; but those two could do what they liked; we should not have to calculate when they'd come or go.'

'We might not have to,' he said, 'but I bet I should.'

'I should not mind what you did, so long as you never said, "What next?"'

'I don't know about "next", but I do know what we'd do first.'

'What, Arthur?'

'Populate Kôr.'

She said: 'I suppose it would be all right if our children were to marry each other?'

But her voice faded out; she had been reminded that they were homeless on this his first night of leave. They were, that was to say, in London without any hope of any place of their own. Pepita shared a two-roomed flatlet with a girl friend, in a by-street off the Regent's Park Road, and towards this they must make their half-hearted way. Arthur was to have the sitting-room divan, usually occupied by Pepita, while she herself had half of her girl friend's bed. There was really no room for a third, and least of all for a man, in those small rooms packed with furniture and the two girls' belongings: Pepita tried to be grateful for her friend Callie's forbearance – but how could she be, when it had not occurred to Callie that she would do better to be away tonight? She was more slow-witted than narrow-minded – but Pepita felt she owed a kind of ruin to her. Callie, not yet known to be home later than ten, would be now waiting up, in her housecoat, to welcome Arthur. That would mean three-sided chat, drinking cocoa, then turning in: that would be that, and that would be all. That was London, this war – they were lucky to have a roof – London, full enough before the Americans came. Not a place: they would even grudge you sharing a grave – that was what even married couples complained. Whereas in Kôr . . .

In Kôr . . . Like glass, the illusion shattered: a car hummed like a hornet towards them, veered, showed its scarlet tail-light, streaked away up the road. A woman edged round a front door and along the area railings timidly called her cat; meanwhile a clock near, then another set further back in the dazzling distance, set about striking midnight. Pepita, feeling Arthur release her arm with an abruptness that was the inverse of passion, shivered; whereat he asked brusquely: 'Cold? Well, Which way? – we'd better be getting on.'

Callie was no longer waiting up. Hours ago she had set out the three cups and saucers, the tins of cocoa and household milk and, on the gas-ring, brought the kettle to just short of the boil. She had turned open Arthur's bed, the living-room divan, in the neat inviting way she had learnt at home – then, with a modest impulse, replaced the cover. She had, as Pepita foresaw, been wearing her cretonne housecoat, the nearest thing to a hostess gown that she had; she had already brushed her hair for the night, rebraided it, bound the braids in a coronet round her head. Both lights and the wireless had been on, to make the room both look and sound gay: all alone, she had come to that peak moment at which company should arrive – but so seldom does. From then on she felt welcome beginning to wither in her, a flower of the heart that had bloomed too early. There she had sat like an image, facing the three cold cups, on the edge of the bed to be occupied by an unknown man.

Callie's innocence and her still unsought-out state had brought her to take a proprietary pride in Arthur; this was all the stronger, perhaps, because they had not yet met. Sharing the flat with Pepita, this last year, she had been content with reflecting the heat of love. It was not, surprisingly, that Pepita seemed very happy – there were times when she was palpably on the rack, and this was not what Callie could understand. 'Surely you owe it to Arthur,' she would then say, 'to keep cheerful? So long as you love each other—' Callie's calm brow glowed – one might say that it glowed in place of her friend's; she became the guardian of that ideality which for Pepita was constantly lost to view. It was true, with the sudden prospect of Arthur's leave, things had come nearer to earth: he became a proposition, and she would have been as glad if he could have slept somewhere else. Physically shy, a brotherless virgin, Callie shrank from sharing this flat with a young man. In this flat you could hear everything: what was once a three-windowed Victorian drawing-room had been partitioned, by very thin walls, into kitchenette, living-room, Callie's bedroom. The living-room was in the centre; the two others open off it. What was once the conservatory, half a flight down, was now converted into a draughty bathroom, shared with somebody else on the girl's floor. The flat, for these days, was cheap – even so, it was Callie, earning more than Pepita, who paid the greater part of the rent: it thus became up to her, more or less, to express good will as to Arthur's making a third. 'Why, it will be lovely to have him here,' Callie said. Pepita accepted the good will without much grace – but then, had she ever much grace to spare? – she was as restlessly secretive, as self-centred, as a little half-grown black cat. Next came a puzzling moment: Pepita seemed to be hinting that Callie should fix herself up somewhere else. 'But where would I go?' Callie marvelled when this was at last borne in on her. 'You know what London's like now. And, anyway' – here she laughed, but hers was a forehead that coloured as easily as it glowed – 'it wouldn't be proper, would it, me going off and leaving just you and Arthur; I don't know what your mother would say to me.

No, we may be a little squashed, but we'll make things ever so homey. I shall not mind playing gooseberry, really, dear.'

But the hominess by now was evaporating, as Pepita and Arthur still and still did not come. At half-past ten, in obedience to the rule of the house, Callie was obliged to turn off the wireless, whereupon silence out of the stepless street began seeping into the slighted room. Callie recollected the fuel target and turned off her dear little table lamp, gaily painted with spots to make it look like a toadstool, thereby leaving only the hanging light. She laid her hand on the kettle, to find it gone cold again and sigh for the wasted gas if not for her wasted thought. Where are they? Cold crept up her out of the kettle; she went to bed.

Callie's bed lay along the wall under the window: she did not like sleeping so close up under glass, but the clearance that must be left for the opening of door and cupboards made this the only possible place. Now she got in and lay rigidly on the bed's inner side, under the hanging hems of the window curtains, training her limbs not to stray to what would be Pepita's half. This sharing of her bed with another body would not be the least of her sacrifice to the lovers' love; tonight would be the first night – or at least, since she was an infant – that Callie had slept with anyone. Child of a sheltered middle-class household, she had kept physical distances all her life. Already repugnance and shyness ran through her limbs; she was preyed upon by some more obscure trouble than the expectation that she might not sleep. As to *that*, Pepita was restless; her tossings on the divan, her broken-off exclamations and blurred pleas had been to be heard, most nights, through the dividing wall.

Callie knew, as though from a vision, that Arthur would sleep soundly, with assurance and majesty. Did they not all say, too, that a soldier sleeps like a log? With awe she pictured, asleep, the face that she had not yet, awake, seen – Arthur's man's eyelids, cheekbones and set mouth turned up to the darkened ceiling. Wanting to savour darkness herself, Callie reached out and put off her bedside lamp.

At once she knew that something was happening – outdoors, in the street, the whole of London, the world. An advance, an extraordinary movement was silently taking place; blue-white beams overflowed from it, silting, dropping round the edges of the muffling black-out curtains. When, starting up, she knocked a fold of the curtain, a beam like a mouse ran across her bed. A searchlight, the most powerful of all time, might have been turned full and steady upon her defended window; finding flaws in the blackout stuff, it made veins and stars. Once gained by this idea of pressure she could not lie down again; she sat tautly, drawn-up knees touching her breasts, and asked herself if there were anything she should do. She parted the curtains, opened them slowly wider, looked out – and was face to face with the moon.

Below the moon, the houses opposite her window blazed back in transparent shadow; and something – was it a coin or a ring? – glittered halfway across the chalk-white street. Light marched in past her face, and she turned to see where it went: out stood the curves and garlands of the great white marble Victorian mantelpiece of that lost drawing-room; out stood, in the photographs turned her way, the thoughts with which her parents had faced the camera, and the humble puzzlement of her two dogs at home. Of silver brocade, just faintly purpled with roses, became her housecoat hanging over the chair. And the moon did more: it exonerated and beautified the lateness of the lovers' return. No wonder, she said herself, no wonder – if this was the world they walked in, if this was whom they were with. Having drunk in the white explanation, Callie lay down again. Her half of the bed was in shadow, but she allowed one hand to lie, blanched, in what would be Pepita's place. She lay and looked at the hand until it was no longer her own.

Callie woke to the sound of Pepita's key in the latch. But no voices? What had happened? Then she heard Arthur's step. She heard his unslung equipment dropped with a weary, dull sound, and the plonk of his tin hat on a wooden chair. 'Sssh–sssh!' Pepita exclaimed, 'she *might* be asleep!'

Then at last Arthur's voice: 'But I thought you said—'

'I'm not asleep; I'm just coming!' Callie called out with rapture, leaping out from her form in shadow into the moonlight, zipping on her enchanted housecoat over her nightdress, kicking her shoes on, and pinning in place, with a trembling firmness, her plaits in their coronet round her head. Between these movements of hers she heard not another sound. Had she only dreamed they were there? Her heart beat: she stepped through the living-room, shutting her door behind her.

Pepita and Arthur stood the other side of the table; they gave the impression of being lined up. Their faces, at different levels – for Pepita's rough, dark head came only an inch above Arthur's khaki shoulder – were alike in abstention from any kind of expression; as though, spiritually, they both still refused to be here. Their features looked faint, weathered – was this the work of the moon? Pepita said at once: 'I suppose we are very late?'

'I don't wonder,' Callie said, 'on this lovely night.'

Arthur had not raised his eyes; he was looking at the three cups. Pepita now suddenly jogged his elbow, saying, 'Arthur, wake up; say something; this is Callie – well, Callie, this is Arthur, of course.'

'Why, yes of course this is Arthur,' returned Callie, whose candid eyes since she entered had not left Arthur's face. Perceiving that Arthur did not know what to do, she advanced round the table to shake hands with him. He looked up, she looked down, for the first time: she rather beheld than felt his red-brown grip on what still seemed her glove of moonlight. 'Welcome, Arthur,' she said. 'I'm so glad to meet you at last. I hope you will be comfortable in the flat.'

'It's been kind of you,' he said after consideration.

'Please do not feel that,' said Callie. 'This is Pepita's home, too, and we both hope – don't we, Pepita? – that you'll regard it as yours. Please feel free to do just as you like. I am sorry it is so small.'

'Oh, I don't know,' Arthur said, as though hypnotized; 'it seems a nice little place.'

Pepita, meanwhile, glowered and turned away.

Arthur continued to wonder, though he had once been told, how these two unalike girls had come to set up together – Pepita so small, except for her too-big head, compact of childish brusqueness and of unchildish passion, and Callie, so sedate, waxy and tall – an unlit candle. Yes, she was like one of those candles on sale outside a church; there could be something votive even in her demeanour. She was unconscious that her good manners, those of an old-fashioned country doctor's daughter, were putting the other two at a disadvantage. He found himself touched by the grave good faith with which Callie was wearing that tartish housecoat, above which her face kept the glaze of sleep; and, as she knelt to relight the gas-ring under the kettle, he marked the strong, delicate arch of one bare foot, disappearing into the arty green shoe. Pepita was now too near him ever again to be seen as he now saw Callie – in a sense, he never *had* seen Pepita for the first time: she had not been, and still sometimes was not, his type. No, he had not thought of her twice; he had not remembered her until he began to remember her with passion. You might say he had not seen Pepita coming: their love had been a collision in the dark.

Callie, determined to get this over, knelt back and said: 'Would Arthur like to wash his hands?' When they had heard him stumble down the half-flight of stairs, she said to Pepita: 'Yes, I was so glad you had the moon.'

'Why?' said Pepita. She added: 'There was too much of it.'

'You're tired. Arthur looks tired, too.'

'How would you know? He's used to marching about. But it's all this having no place to go.'

'But, Pepita, you—'

But at this point Arthur came back: from the door he noticed the wireless, and went direct to it. 'Nothing much on now, I suppose?' he doubtfully said.

'No; you see it's past midnight; we're off the air. And, anyway, in this house they don't like the wireless late. By the same token,' went on Callie, friendly smiling, 'I'm afraid I must ask you, Arthur, to take your boots off, unless, of course, you mean to stay sitting down. The people below us—'

Pepita flung off, saying something under her breath, but Arthur, remarking, 'No, I don't mind,' both sat down and began to take off his boots. Pausing, glancing to left and right at the divan's fresh cotton spread, he said: 'It's all right is it, for me to sit on this?'

'That's my bed,' said Pepita. 'You are to sleep in it.'

Callie then made the cocoa, after which they turned in. Preliminary trips to the bathroom having been worked out, Callie was first to retire, shutting the door behind her so that Pepita and Arthur might kiss each other good night. When Pepita joined her, it was without knocking: Pepita stood still in the moon and began to tug off her clothes. Glancing with hate at the bed, she asked: 'Which side?'

'I expected you'd like the outside.'

'What are you standing about for?'

'I don't really know: as I'm inside I'd better get in first.'

'Then why not get in?'

When they had settled rigidly, side by side, Callie asked: 'Do you think Arthur's got all he wants?'

Pepita jerked her head up. 'We can't sleep in all this moon.'

'Why, you don't believe the moon does things, actually?'

'Well, it couldn't hope to make some of us *much* more screwy.'

Callie closed the curtains, then said: 'What do you mean? And – didn't you hear? – I asked if Arthur's got all he wants.'

'That's what I meant – have you got a screw loose, really?'

'Pepita, I won't stay here if you're going to be like this.'

'In that case, you had better go in with Arthur.'

'What about me?' Arthur loudly said through the wall. 'I can hear practically all you girls are saying.'

They were both startled – rather that than abashed. Arthur, alone in there, had thrown off the ligatures of his social manner: his voice held the whole authority of his sex – he was impatient, sleepy, and he belonged to no one.

'Sorry,' the girls said in unison. Then Pepita laughed soundlessly, making their bed shake, till to stop herself she bit the back of her hand, and this movement made her elbow strike Callie's cheek. 'Sorry,' she had to whisper. No answer: Pepita fingered her elbow and found, yes, it was quite true, it was wet. 'Look, shut up crying, Callie: what have I done?'

Callie rolled right round, in order to press her forehead closely under the window, into the curtains, against the wall. Her weeping continued to be soundless: now and then, unable to reach her handkerchief, she staunched her eyes with a curtain, disturbing slivers of moon. Pepita gave up marvelling, and soon slept: at least there is something in being dog-tired.

A clock struck four as Callie woke up again – but something else had made her open her swollen eyelids. Arthur, stumbling about on his padded feet, could be heard next door attempting to make no noise. Inevitably, he bumped the edge of the table. Callie sat up: by her side Pepita lay like a mummy rolled half over, in forbidding, tenacious sleep. Arthur groaned. Callie caught a breath, climbed lightly over Pepita, felt for her torch on the mantelpiece, stopped to listen again. Arthur groaned again: Callie, with movements soundless as they were certain, opened the door and slipped through to the living-room. 'What's the matter?' she whispered. 'Are you ill?'

'No; I just got a cigarette. Did I wake you up?'

'But you groaned.'

'I'm sorry; I'd no idea.'

'But do you often?'

'I've no idea, really, I tell you,' Arthur repeated. The air of the room was dense with his presence, overhung by tobacco. He must be sitting on the edge of his bed, wrapped up in his overcoat – she could smell the coat, and each time he pulled on the cigarette his features appeared down there, in the fleeting, dull reddish glow. 'Where are you?' he said. 'Show a light.'

Her nervous touch on her torch, like a reflex to what he said, made it flicker up for a second. 'I am just by the door; Pepita's asleep; I'd better go back to bed.'

'Listen. Do you two get on each other's nerves?'

'Not till tonight,' said Callie, watching the uncertain swoops of the cigarette as he reached across to the ashtray on the edge of the table. Shifting her bare feet patiently, she added: 'You don't see us as we usually are.'

'She's a girl who shows things in funny ways – I expect she feels bad at our putting you out like this – I know I do. But then we'd got no choice, had we?'

'It is really I who am putting you out,' said Callie.

'Well, that can't be helped either, can it? You had the right to stay in your own place. If there'd been more time, we might have gone to the country, though I still don't see where we'd have gone there. It's one harder when you're not married, unless you've got the money. Smoke?'

'No, thank you. Well, if you're all right, I'll go back to bed.'

'I'm glad she's asleep – funny the way she sleeps, isn't it? You can't help wondering where she is. You haven't got a boy, have you, just at present?'

'No. I've never had one.'

'I'm not sure in one way that you're not better off. I can see there's not so much in it for a girl these days. It makes me feel cruel the way I unsettle her: I don't know how much it's me myself or how much it's something the matter that I can't help. How are any of us to know how things could have been? They forget war's not just only war; it's years out of people's lives that they've never had before and won't have again. Do you think she's fanciful?'

'Who, Pepita?'

'It's enough to make her — tonight was the pay-off. We couldn't get near any movie or any place for sitting; you had to fight into the bars, and she hates the staring in bars, and with all that milling about, every street we went, they kept on knocking her even off my arm. So then we took the tube to that park down there, but the place was as bad as daylight, let alone it was cold. We hadn't the nerve — well, that's nothing to do with you.'

'I don't mind.'

'Or else you don't understand. So we began to play — we were off in Kôr.'

'Core of what?'

'Mysterious Kôr — ghost city.'

'Where?'

'You may ask. But I could have sworn she saw it, and from the way she saw it I saw it, too. A game's a game, but what's a hallu-cination? You begin by laughing, then it gets in you and you can't laugh it off. I tell you, I woke up just now not knowing where I'd been; and I had to get up and feel round this table before I even knew where I was. It wasn't till then that I thought of a cigarette. Now I see why she sleeps like that, if that's where she goes.'

'But she is just as often restless; I often hear her.'

'Then she doesn't always make it. Perhaps it takes me, in some way— Well, I can't see any harm: when two people have got no place, why not want Kôr, as a start? There are no restrictions or wanting, at any rate.'

'But, oh, Arthur, can't wanting want what's human?'

He yawned. 'To be human's to be at a dead loss.' Stopping yawning, he ground out his cigarette: the china tray skidded at the edge of the table. 'Bring that light here a moment — that is, will you? I think I've messed ash all over these sheets of hers.'

Callie advanced with the torch alight, but at arm's length: now and then her thumb made the beam wobble. She watched the lit-up inside of Arthur's hand as he brushed the sheet; and once he looked up to see her white-nightgowned figure curving above and away from him, behind the arc of light. 'What's that swinging?'

'One of my plaits of hair. Shall I open the window wider?'

'What, to let the smoke out? Go on. And how's your moon?'

'Mine?' Marvelling over this, as the first sign that Arthur remembered that she was Callie, she uncovered the window, pushed up the sash, then after a minute said: 'Not so strong.'

Indeed, the moon's power over London and the imagination had now declined. The siege of light had relaxed; the search was over; the street had a look of survival and no more. Whatever had glittered there, coin or ring, was now invisible or had gone. To Callie it seemed likely that there would never be such a moon again; and on the whole she felt this was for the best. Feeling air reach in like a tired arm round her body, she dropped the curtains against it and returned to her own room.

Back by her bed, she listened: Pepita's breathing still had the regular sound of sleep. At the other side of the wall the divan creaked as Arthur stretched himself out again. Having felt ahead of her lightly, to make sure her half was empty, Callie climbed over Pepita and got in. A certain amount of warmth had travelled between the sheets from Pepita's flank, and in this Callie extended her sword-cold body: she tried to compose her limbs; even they quivered after Arthur's words in the dark, words *to* the dark. The loss of her own mysterious expectation, of her love for love, was a small thing beside the war's total of unlived lives. Suddenly Pepita flung out one hand: its back knocked Callie lightly across the face.

Pepita had now turned over and lay with her face up. The hand that had struck Callie must have lain over the other, which grasped the pyjama collar. Her eyes, in the dark, might have been either shut or open, but nothing made her frown more or less steadily: it became certain, after another moment, that Pepita's act of justice had been unconscious. She still lay, as she had lain, in an avid dream, of which Arthur had been the source, of which Arthur was not the end. With him she looked this way, that way, down the wide, void, pure streets, between statues, pillars and shadows, through archways and colonnades. With him she went up the stairs down which nothing but moon came; with him trod the ermine dust of the endless halls, stood on terraces, mounted the extreme tower, looked down on the statued squares, the wide, void, pure streets. He was the password, but not the answer: it was to Kôr's finality that she turned.

The Demon Lover

Towards the end of her day in London Mrs Drover went round to her shut-up house to look for several things she wanted to take away. Some belonged to herself, some to her family, who were by now used to their country life. It was late August; it had been a steamy, showery day: at the moment the trees down the pavement glittered in an escape of humid yellow afternoon sun. Against the next batch of clouds, already piling up ink-dark, broken chimneys and parapets stood out. In her once familiar street, as in any unused channel, an unfamiliar queerness had silted up; a cat wove itself in and out of railings, but no human eye watched Mrs Drover's return. Shifting some parcels under her arm, she slowly forced round her latchkey in an unwilling lock, then gave the door, which had warped, a push with her knee. Dead air came out to meet her as she went in.

The staircase window having been boarded up, no light came down into the hall. But one door, she could just see, stood ajar, so she went quickly through into the room and unshuttered the big window in there. Now the prosaic woman, looking about her, was more perplexed than she knew by everything that she saw, by traces of her long former habit of life – the yellow smoke-stain up the white marble mantelpiece, the ring left by a vase on the top of the escritoire; the bruise in the wallpaper where, on the door being thrown open widely, the china handle had always hit the wall. The piano, having gone away to be stored, had left what looked like claw-marks on its part of the parquet. Though not much dust had seeped in, each object wore a film of another kind; and, the only ventilation being the chimney, the whole drawing-room smelled of the cold hearth. Mrs Drover put down her parcels on the escritoire and left the room to proceed upstairs; the things she wanted were in a bedroom chest.

She had been anxious to see how the house was – the part-time caretaker she shared with some neighbours was away this week on his holiday, known to be not yet back. At the best of times he did not look in often, and she was never sure that she trusted him. There were some cracks in the structure, left by the last bombing, on which she was anxious to keep an eye. Not that one could do anything –

A shaft of refracted daylight now lay across the hall. She stopped dead and stared at the hall table – on this lay a letter addressed to her.

She thought first – then the caretaker *must* be back. All the same, who, seeing the house shuttered, would have dropped a letter in at the box? It was not a circular, it was not a bill. And the post office redirected, to the address in the country, everything for her that came through the post. The caretaker (even if he *were* back) did not know she was due in London today – her call here had been planned to be a surprise – so his negligence in the manner of this letter, leaving it to wait in the dusk and the dust, annoyed her. Annoyed, she picked up the letter, which bore no stamp. But it cannot be important, or they would know . . . She took the letter rapidly upstairs with her, without a stop to look at the writing till she reached what had been her bedroom, where she let in light. The room looked over the garden and other gardens: the sun had gone in; as the clouds sharpened and lowered, the trees and rank lawns seemed already to smoke with dark. Her reluctance to look again at the letter came from the fact that she felt intruded upon – and by someone contemptuous of her ways. However, in the tenseness preceding the fall of rain she read it: it was a few lines.

Dear Kathleen: You will not have forgotten that today is our anniversary, and the day we said. The years have gone by at once slowly and fast. In view of the fact that nothing has changed, I shall rely upon you to keep your promise. I was sorry to see you leave London, but was satisfied that you would be back in time. You may expect me, therefore, at the hour arranged. Until then . . .   K.

Mrs Drover looked for the date: it was today's. She dropped the letter on to the bed-springs, then picked it up to see the writing again – her lips, beneath the remains of lipstick, beginning to go white. She felt so much the change in her own face that she went to the mirror, polished a clear patch in it and looked at once urgently and stealthily in. She was confronted by a woman of forty-four, with eyes starting out under a hat-brim that had been rather carelessly pulled down. She had not put on any more powder since she left the shop where she ate her solitary tea. The pearls her husband had given her on their marriage hung loose round her now rather thinner throat, slipping in the V of the pink wool jumper her sister knitted last autumn as they sat round the fire. Mrs Drover's most normal expression was one of controlled worry, but of assent. Since the birth of the third of her little boys, attended by a quite serious illness, she had had an intermittent muscular flicker to the left of her mouth, but in spite of this she could always sustain a manner that was at once energetic and calm.

Turning from her own face as precipitately as she had gone to meet it, she went to the chest where the things were, unlocked it, threw up the lid and knelt to search. But as rain began to come crashing down she could not keep from looking over her shoulder at the stripped bed on which the letter lay. Behind the blanket of rain the clock of the church that still stood struck six – with rapidly heightening apprehension she counted each of the slow strokes. 'The hour arranged . . . My God,' she said, '*what* hour? How should I . . .? After twenty-five years . . .'

The young girl talking to the soldier in the garden had not ever completely seen his face. It was dark; they were saying goodbye under a tree. Now and then – for it felt, from not seeing him at this intense moment, as though she had never seen him at all – she verified his presence for these few moments longer by putting out a hand, which he each time pressed, without very much kindness, and painfully, on to one of the breast buttons of his uniform. That cut of the button on the palm of her hand was, principally what she was to carry away. This was so near the end of a leave from France that she could only wish him already gone. It was August 1916. Being not kissed, being drawn away from and looked at intimidated Kathleen till she imagined spectral glitters in the place of his eyes. Turning away and looking back up the lawn she saw, through branches of trees, the drawing-room window alight: she caught a breath for the moment when she could go running back there into the safe arms of her mother and sister, and cry: 'What shall I do, what shall I do? He has gone.'

Hearing her catch her breath, her fiancé said, without feeling: 'Cold?'

'You're going away such a long way.'

'Not so far as you think.'

'I don't understand?'

'You don't have to,' he said. 'You will. You know what we said.'

'But that was – suppose you – I mean, suppose.'

'I shall be with you,' he said, 'sooner or later. You won't forget that. You need do nothing but wait.'

Only a little more than a minute later she was free to run up the silent lawn. Looking in through the window at her mother and sister, who did not for the moment perceive her, she already felt that unnatural promise drive down between her and the rest of all human kind. No other way of having given herself could have made her feel so apart, lost and foresworn. She could not have plighted a more sinister troth.

Kathleen behaved well when, some months later, her fiancé was reported missing, presumed killed. Her family not only supported her but were able to praise her courage without stint because they could not regret, as a husband for her, the man they knew almost nothing about. They hoped she would, in a year or two, console herself – and had it been only a question of consolation things might have gone much straighter ahead. But her trouble, behind just a little grief, was a complete dislocation from everything. She did not reject other lovers, for these failed to appear: for years she failed to attract men – and with the approach of her 'thirties she became natural enough to share her family's anxiousness on this score. She began to put herself out, to wonder; and at thirty-two she was very greatly relieved to find herself being courted by William Drover. She married him, and the two of them settled down in this quiet, arboreal part of Kensington: in this house the years piled up, her children were born and they all lived till they were driven out by the bombs of the next war. Her movements as Mrs Drover were circumscribed, and she dismissed any idea that they were still watched.

As things were – dead or living the letter-writer sent her only a threat. Unable, for some minutes, to go on kneeling with her back exposed to the empty room, Mrs Drover rose from the chest to sit on an upright chair whose back was firmly against the wall. The desuetude of her former bedroom, her married London home's whole air of being a cracked cup from which memory, with its reassuring power, had either evaporated or leaked away, made a crisis – and at just this crisis the letter-writer had, knowledgeably, struck. The hollowness of the house this evening cancelled years on years of voices, habits and steps. Through the shut windows she only heard rain fall on the roofs around. To rally herself, she said she was in a mood – and for two or three seconds shutting her eyes, told herself that she had imagined the letter. But she opened them – there it lay on the bed.

On the supernatural side of the letter's entrance she was not permitting her mind to dwell. Who, in London, knew she meant to call at the house today? Evidently, however, this had been known. The caretaker, *had* he come back, had had no cause to expect her: he would have taken the letter in his pocket, to forward it, at his own time, through the post. There was no other sign that the caretaker had been in – but, if not? Letters dropped in at doors of deserted houses do not fly or walk to tables in halls. They do not sit on the dust of empty tables with the air of certainty that they will be found. There is needed some human hand – but nobody but the caretaker had a key. Under circumstances she did not care to consider, a house can be entered without a key. It was possible that she was not alone now. She might be being waited for, downstairs. Waited for – until when? Until 'the hour arranged'. At least that was not six o'clock: six has struck.

She rose from the chair and went over and locked the door.

The thing was, to get out. To fly? No, not that: she had to catch her train. As a woman whose utter dependability was the keystone of her family life she was not willing to return to the country, to her husband, her little boys and her sister, without the objects she had come up to fetch. Resuming work at the chest she set about making up a number of parcels in a rapid, fumbling-decisive way. These, with her shopping parcels, would be too much to carry; these meant a taxi – at the thought of the taxi her heart went up and her normal breathing resumed. I will ring up the taxi now; the taxi cannot come too soon: I shall hear the taxi out there running its engine, till I walk calmly down to it through the hall. I'll ring up – But no: the telephone is cut off . . . She tugged at a knot she had tied wrong.

The idea of flight . . . He was never kind to me, not really. I don't remember him kind at all. Mother said he never considered me. He was set on me, that was what it was – not love. Not love, not meaning a person well. What did he do, to make me promise like that? I can't remember – But she found that she could.

She remembered with such dreadful acuteness that the twenty-five years since then dissolved like smoke and she instinctively looked for the weal left by the button on the palm of her hand. She remembered not only all that he said and did but the complete suspension of *her* existence during that August week. I was not myself – they all told me so at the time. She remembered – but with one white burning blank as where acid has dropped on a photograph: *under no conditions* could she remember his face.

So, wherever he may be waiting, I shall not know him. You have no time to run from a face you do not expect.

The thing was to get to the taxi before any clock struck what could be the hour. She would slip down the street and round the side of the square to where the square gave on the main road. She would return in the taxi, safe, to her own door, and bring the solid driver into the house with her to pick up the parcels from room to room. The idea of the taxi driver made her decisive, bold: she unlocked her door, went to the top of the staircase and listened down.

She heard nothing – but while she was hearing nothing the *passé* air of the staircase was disturbed by a draught that travelled up to her face. It emanated from the basement: down there a door or window was being opened by someone who chose this moment to leave the house.

The rain had stopped; the pavements steamily shone as Mrs Drover let herself out by inches from her own front door into the empty street. The unoccupied houses opposite continued to meet her look with their damaged stare. Making towards the thoroughfare and the taxi, she tried not to keep looking behind. Indeed, the silence was so intense — one of those creeks of London silence exaggerated this summer by the damage of war — that no tread could have gained on hers unheard. Where her street debouched on the square where people went on living, she grew conscious of, and checked, her unnatural pace. Across the open end of the square two buses impassively passed each other: women, a perambulator, cyclists, a man wheeling a barrow signalized, once again, the ordinary flow of life. At the square's most populous corner should be — and was — the short taxi rank. This evening, only one taxi — but this, although it presented its blank rump, appeared already to be alertly waiting for her. Indeed, without looking round the driver started his engine as she panted up from behind and put her hand on the door. As she did so, the clock struck seven. The taxi faced the main road: to make the trip back to her house it would have to turn — she had settled back on the seat and the taxi *had* turned before she, surprised by its knowing movement, recollected that she had not 'said where'. She leaned forward to scratch at the glass panel that divided the driver's head from her own.

The driver braked to what was almost a stop, turned round and slid the glass panel back: the jolt of this flung Mrs Drover forward till her face was almost into the glass. Through the aperture driver and passenger, not six inches between them, remained for an eternity eye to eye. Mrs Drover's mouth hung open for some seconds before she could issue her first scream. After that she continued to scream freely and to beat with her gloved hands on the glass all round as the taxi, accelerating without mercy, made off with her into the hinterland of deserted streets.

A Day in the Dark

Coming into Moher over the bridge, you may see a terrace of houses by the river. They are to the left of the bridge, below it. Their narrow height and faded air of importance make them seem to mark the approach to some larger town. The six dwellings unite into one frontage, colour-washed apricot years ago. They face north. Their lower sash windows, front steps and fanlit front doors are screened by lime trees, making for privacy. There are area railings. Between them and the water runs a road with a parapet, which comes to its end opposite the last house.

On the other side of the bridge picturesquely rises a ruined castle – more likely to catch the tourist's eye. Woods, from which the river emerges, go back deeply behind the ruin: on clear days there is a backdrop of Irish-blue mountains. Otherwise Moher has little to show. The little place prospers – a market town with a square, on a main road. The hotel is ample, cheerful, and does business. Moreover Moher is, and has been for ages, a milling town. Obsolete stone buildings follow you some way along the river valley as, having passed through Moher, you pursue your road. The flour-white modern mills, elsewhere, hum.

Round the square, shops and pubs are of many colours – in the main Moher looks like a chalk drawing. Not so the valley with its elusive lights.

You *could*, I can see, overlook my terrace of houses – because of the castle, indifference or haste. I only do not because I am looking out for them. For in No. 4 lived Miss Banderry.

She was the last of a former milling family – last, that is, but for the widowed niece, her pensioner. She owned the terrace, drew rents also from property in another part of the town, and had acquired, some miles out of Moher, a profitable farm which she'd put to management. Had control of the family mills been hers, they would not have been parted with – as it was, she had had to contend with a hopeless brother: he it was who had ended by selling out. Her demand for her share of the money left him unable to meet personal debts: he was found hanged from one of the old mill crossbeams. Miss Banderry lived in retirement, the more thought of for being seldom seen – now and then she would summon a Ford hackney and drive to her farm in it, without warning. My uncle, whose land adjoined on hers, had dealings with her, in the main friendly – which was how they first fell into talk. She, a formidable reader, took to sending him serious magazines, reviews, pamphlets and so on, with marked passages on which she would be dying to hear his views. This was her way of harrying him. For my uncle, a winning, versatile and when necessary inventive talker, fundamentally hated to tax his brain. He took to evading meetings with her as far as possible.

So much I knew when I rang her doorbell.

It was July, a sunless warm afternoon, dead still. The terrace was heavy with limes in flower. Above, through the branches, appeared the bridge with idlers who leaned on the balustrade spying down upon me, or so I thought. I felt marked by visiting this place – I was fifteen, and my every sensation was acute in a way I recall, yet cannot recall. All six houses were locked in childless silence. From under the parapet came languidly the mesmeric sound of the weir, and, from a window over my head, the wiry hopping of a bird in a cage. From the shabby other doors of the terrace, No. 4's stood out, handsomely though sombrely painted red. It opened.

I came to return a copy of *Blackwoods*. Also I carried a bunch of ungainly roses from my uncle's garden, and a request that he might borrow the thistle cutter from Miss Banderry's farm for use on his land. One rose moulted petals on to her doorstep, then on to the linoleum in the hall. 'Goodness!' complained the niece, who had let me in. 'Those didn't travel well. Overblown, aren't they!' (I thought that applied to her.) 'And I'll bet,' she said, '*he* never sent those!' She was not in her aunt's confidence, being treated more or less like a slave. Timed (they said) when she went errands into the town – she dare not stay talking, dare not so much as look into the hotel bar while the fun was on. For a woman said to be forty, this sounded mortifying. Widowed Nan, ready to be handsome, wore a cheated ravenous look. It was understood she would come into the money when the aunt died: she must contain herself till then. As for me – how dared she speak of my uncle with her bad breath?

Naturally he *had* never thought of the roses. He had commissioned me to be gallant for him any way I chose, and I would not do too badly with these, I'd thought, as I unstrangled them from the convolvulus in the flower bed. They would need not only to flatter but to propitiate, for this copy of *Blackwoods* I brought back had buttery thumbmarks on its margins and on its cover a blistered circle where my uncle must have stood down his glass. 'She'll be mad,' he prophesied. 'Better say it was you.' So I sacrificed a hair ribbon to tie the roses. It rejoiced me to stand between him and trouble.

'Auntie's resting,' the niece warned me, and put me to wait. The narrow parlour looked out through thick lace on to the terrace, which was reflected in a looking-glass at the far end. Ugly though I could see honourable furniture, mahogany, had been crowded in. In the middle, a circular table wore a chenille cloth. This room felt respected though seldom entered – however, it was peopled in one way: generations of oil-painted portraits hung round the walls, photographs overflowed from bracket and ledge even on to the centre table. I was faced, wherever I turned, by one or another member of the family which could only be the vanished Banderrys. There was a marble clock, but it had stopped.

Footsteps halted heavily over the ceiling, but that was all for I don't know how long. I began to wonder what those Banderrys saw – lodging the magazine and roses on the table, I went to inspect myself in the glass. A tall girl in a sketchy cotton dress. Arms thin, no sign yet of a figure. Hair forward over the shoulders in two plaits, like, said my uncle, a Red Indian maiden's. Barbie was my name.

In memory, the moment before often outlives the awaited moment. I recollect waiting for Miss Banderry – then, nothing till she was with me in the room. I got over our handshake without feeling. On to the massiveness of her bust was pinned a diamond-studded enamelled watch, depending from an enamelled bow: there was a tiny glitter as she drew breath. – 'So he sent *you*, did he?' She sat down, the better to look at me. Her apart knees stretched the skirt of her dress. Her choleric colouring and eyeballs made her appear angry, as against which she favoured me with a racy indulgent smile, to counteract the impression she knew she gave.

'I hear wonders of you,' said she, dealing the lie to me like a card. She sat in reach of the table. 'My bouquet, eh?' She grasped the bundle of roses, thorns and all, and took a long voluptuous sniff at them, as though deceiving herself as to their origin – showing me she knew how to play the game, if I didn't – then shoved back the roses among the photographs and turned her eyes on the magazine, sharply. 'I'm sorry, I –' I began. In vain. All she gave was a rumbling chuckle – she held up to me the copy of *Blackwoods* open at the page with the most thumbmarks. 'I'd know *those* anywhere!' She scrutinized the print for a line or two. 'Did he make head or tail of it?'

'He told me to tell you, he enjoyed it.' (I saw my uncle dallying, stuffing himself with buttered toast.) 'With his best thanks.'

'You're a little echo,' she said, not discontentedly.

I stared her out.

'Never mind,' she said. 'He's a handsome fellow.'

I shifted my feet. She gave me a look.

She observed: 'It's a pity to read at table.'

'He hasn't much other time, Miss Banderry.'

'Still, it's a poor compliment to you!'

She stung me into remarking: 'He doesn't often.'

'Oh, I'm sure you're a great companion for him!'

It was as though she saw me casting myself down by my uncle's chair when he'd left the room, or watching the lassitude of his hand hanging caressing a dog's ear. With him I felt the tender bond of sex. Seven, eight weeks with him under his roof, among the copper beeches from spring to summer turning from pink to purple, and I was in love with him. Such things happen, I suppose. He was my mother's brother, but I had not known him when I was a child. Of his manhood I had had no warning. Naturally growing into love I was, like the grass growing into hay on his uncut lawns. There was not a danger till she spoke.

'He's glad of company now and then,' I said as stupidly as I could.

She plucked a petal from her black serge skirt.

'Well,' she said, 'thank him for the thanks. And you for the nice little pleasure of this visit. – Then, there's nothing else?'

'My uncle wants –' I began.

'You don't surprise me,' said Miss Banderry. 'Well, come on out with it. What this time?'

'If he could once more borrow the thistle cutter . . .?'

'"Once more"! And what will he be looking to do next year? Get his own mended? I suppose he'd hardly go to that length.'

His own, I knew, had been sold for scrap. He was sometimes looking for ready money. I said nothing.

'Looking to me to keep him out of jail?' (Law forbids one to suffer the growth of thistles.) 'Time after time, it's the same story. It so happens, I haven't mine cut yet!'

'He'd be glad to lend you his jennet back, he says, to draw the cutter for you.'

'*That* brute! There'd be nothing for me to cut if it wasn't for what blows in off his dirty land.' With the flat of her fingers she pressed one eyeball, then the other, back into her head. She confessed, all at once almost plaintively: 'I don't care to have machinery leave my farm.'

'Very well,' I said haughtily, 'I'll tell him.'

She leaned back, rubbed her palms on her thighs. 'No, wait – this you may tell my lord. Tell him I'm not sure, but I'll think it over. There might be a favourable answer, there might not. If my lord would like to know which, let him come himself. – That's a sweet little dress of yours,' she went on, examining me inside it, 'but it's skimpy. He should do better than hide behind *those* skirts!'

'I don't know what you mean, Miss Banderry.'

'He'd know.'

'Today, my uncle *was* busy.'

'I'm sure he was. Busy day after day. In my life, I've known only one other man anything like so busy as your uncle. And shall I tell you who that was? My poor brother.'

After all these years, that terrace focuses dread. I mislike any terrace facing a river. I suppose I would rather look upon it itself (as I must, whenever I cross that bridge) than be reminded of it by harmless others. True, only one house in it was Miss Banderry's, but the rest belong to her by complicity. An indelible stain is on that monotony – the extinct pink frontage, the road leading to nothing but those six doors which the lime trees, flower as they may, exist for nothing but to shelter. The monotony of the weir and the hopping bird. Within that terrace I was in one room only, and only once.

My conversation with Miss Banderry did not end where I leave off recording it. But at that point memory is torn across, as might be an intolerable page. The other half is missing. For that reason my portrait of her would be incomplete if it *were* a portrait. She could be novelist's material, I dare say – indeed novels, particularly the French and Irish (for Ireland in some ways resembles France) are full of prototypes of her: oversized women insulated in little provincial towns. Literature, once one knows it, drains away some of the shockingness out of life. But when I met her I was unread, my susceptibilities were virgin. I refuse to fill in her outline retrospectively: I show you only what I saw at the time. Not what she was, but what she did to me.

Her amorous hostility to my uncle – or was it hostility making use of a farce? – unsheathed itself when she likened him to the brother she drove to death.

When I speak of dread I mean dread, not guilt. That afternoon, I went to Miss Banderry's for my uncle's sake, in his place. It could be said, my gathering of foreboding had to do with my relation with him – yet in that there was no guilt anywhere, I could swear! I swear we did each other no harm. I think he was held that summer, as I was, by the sense that this was a summer like no other and which could never again be. Soon I must grow up, he must grow old. Meanwhile we played house together on the margin of a passion which was impossible. My longing was for him, not for an embrace – as for him, he was glad of companionship, as I'd truly told her. He was a man tired by a lonely house till I joined him – a schoolgirl between schools. All thought well of his hospitality to me. Convention was our safeguard: could one have stronger?

I left No. 4 with ceremony. I was offered raspberry cordial. Nan bore in the tray with the thimble glasses – educated by going visiting with my uncle, I knew refusal would mark a breach. When the glasses were emptied, Nan conducted me out of the presence, to the hall door – she and I stopped aimlessly on the steps. Across the river throve the vast new mills, unabashed, and cars swished across the tree-hidden bridge. The niece showed a reluctance to go in again – I think the bird above must have been hers. She glanced behind her, then, conspiratorially at me. 'So now you'll be going to the hotel?'

'No. Why?'

'"Why?"' she jibed. 'Isn't he waiting for you? Anyway, that's where he is: in there. The car's outside.'

I said: 'But I'm taking the bus home.'

'Now, why ever?'

'I said I would take the bus. I came in that way.'

'You're mad. What, with his car in the square?'

All I could say was: 'When?'

'I slipped out just now,' said the niece, 'since you want to know. To a shop, only. While you were chatting with Auntie.' She laughed, perhaps at her life, and impatiently gave me a push away. 'Get on – wherever you're going to! Anybody would think you'd had bad news!'

Not till I was almost on the bridge did I hear No. 4's door shut.

I leaned on the balustrade, at the castle side. The river, coming towards me out of the distances of woods, washed the bastions and carried a paper boat – this, travelling at uncertain speed on the current, listed as it vanished under the bridge. I had not the heart to wonder how it would fare. Weeks ago, when first I came to my uncle's, here we had lingered, elbow to elbow, looking up-river through the green-hazed spring hush at the far off swan's nest, now deserted. Next I raised my eyes to the splendid battlements, kissed by the sky where they were broken.

From the bridge to the town rises a slow hill – shops and places of business come down to meet you, converting the road into a street. There are lamp posts, signboards, yard gates pasted with layers of bills, and you tread pavement. That day the approach to Moher, even the crimson valerian on stone walls, was filmed by imponder-able white dust as though the flourbags had been shaken. To me, this was the pallor of suspense. An all but empty theatre was the square, which, when I entered it at a corner, paused between afternoon and evening. In the middle were parked cars, looking forgotten – my uncle's was nearest the hotel.

The hotel, glossy with green creeper, accounted for one end of the square. A cream porch, figuring the name in gold, framed the doorway – though I kept my back to that I expected at any moment to hear a shout as I searched for the independence of my bus. But where *that* should have waited, I found nothing. Nothing, at this bus end of the square, but a drip of grease on dust and a torn ticket. 'She's gone out, if that's what you're looking for,' said a bystander. So there it went, carrying passengers I was not among to the scenes of safety, and away from me every hope of solitude. Out of reach was the savingness of a house empty. Out of reach, the windows down to the ground open upon the purple beeches and lazy hay, the dear weather of those rooms in and out of which flew butterflies, my cushions on the floor, my blue striped tea mug. Out of reach, the whole of the lenient meaning of my uncle's house, which most filled it when he was not there . . . I did not want to be bothered with him, I think.

'She went out on time today, more's the pity.'

Down hung my hair in two weighted ropes as I turned away.

Moher square is oblong. Down its length, on the two sides, people started to come to the shop doors in order to look at me in amazement. They knew who I was and where he was: what should *I* be wanting to catch the bus for? They speculated. As though a sandal chafed me I bent down, spent some time loosening the strap. Then, as though I had never had any other thought, I started in the direction of the hotel.

At the same time, my uncle appeared in the porch. He tossed a cigarette away, put the hand in a pocket and stood there under the gold lettering. He was not a lord, only a landowner. Facing Moher, he was all carriage and colouring: he wore his life like he wore his coat – though, now he was finished with the hotel, a light hint of melancholy settled down on him. He was not looking for me until he saw me.

We met at his car. He asked: 'How was she, the old terror?'

'I don't know.'

'She didn't eat you?'

'No,' I said, shaking my head.

'Or send me another magazine?'

'No. Not this time.'

'Thank God.'

He opened the car door and touched my elbow, reminding me to get in.

VINTAGE CLASSICS

Vintage launched in the United Kingdom in 1990, and was originally the paperback home for the Random House Group's literary authors. Now, Vintage is comprised of some of London's oldest and most prestigious literary houses, including Chatto & Windus (1855), Hogarth (1917), Jonathan Cape (1921) and Secker & Warburg (1935), alongside the newer or relaunched hardback and paperback imprints: The Bodley Head, Harvill Secker, Yellow Jersey, Square Peg, Vintage Paperbacks and Vintage Classics.

From Angela Carter, Graham Greene and Aldous Huxley to Toni Morrison, Haruki Murakami and Virginia Woolf, Vintage Classics is renowned for publishing some of the greatest writers and thinkers from around the world and across the ages – all complemented by our beautiful, stylish approach to design. Vintage Classics' authors have won many of the world's most revered literary prizes, including the Nobel, the Man Booker, the Prix Goncourt and the Pulitzer, and through their writing they continue to capture imaginations, inspire new perspectives and incite curiosity.

In 2007 Vintage Classics introduced its distinctive red spine design, and in 2012 Vintage Children's Classics was launched to include the much-loved authors of our childhood. Random House joined forces with the Penguin Group in 2013 to become Penguin Random House, making it the largest trade publisher in the United Kingdom.

@vintagebooks

penguin.co.uk/vintage-classics